MW00805195

Before the Apocalypse

Book One

The Jonah Factor

Linda,
Thank you for your
encouragement

Kepler Nigh *Kepler Nigh*

McDougal Publishing

www.mcdougalpublishing.com

Before the Apocalypse
Book One — *The Jonah Factor*
Copyright © 2008 by Kepler Nigh
All Rights Reserved

Cover photography copyright © 2008 by Kepler Nigh

No portion of this book may be reproduced, stored in a retrieval system, or transmitted in any form or by any means — electronic, mechanical, photocopy,
recording, or any other — except for brief quotations in printed reviews, without
the prior permission of the publisher.

This book is a work of fiction, and although it contains obvious historical references
to public figures and events, all characters and incidents in this novel are the
products of the author's imagination. Opinions expressed by the fictitious characters in this book do not necessarily reflect the views of the author or the publisher.
Any similarities to people living or dead are purely coincidental.

Scripture references are taken from the New International Version of the Bible,
copyright © 1973, 1978, 1984 by International Bible Society, Colorado Springs,
Colorado.

Some Scripture references are taken from the King James Version of the Bible,
copyright in the public domain.

ISBN: 978-1-581581-115-7

Published by:
McDougal Publishing
P.O. Box 3595
Hagerstown, MD 21742-3595
www.mcdougalpublishing.com

Printed in the United States of America
For Worldwide Distribution

Acknowledgments

First of all, I wish to recognize and thank Jerry and Debby Smith, they are true friends! Not only did Jerry give long hours in editing this novel, but Debbie even provided some key content, especially for some of the character descriptions. I can't thank them enough.

Robert Quiring challenged me to show and not tell. Russ Meehan provided "outrageous" advice. Ken Korpi made many valuable suggestions. Others who provided important editorial comment include Peter and Anna Allphin, John Brantley, Patricia Daza, Dr. John Farmer, Thorton "Rusty" Ireland, Joe Irizary, Linda McLaughlin, and Priscilla Morgan.

There have been a number of readers who have made important contributions to this process that has taken me over fourteen years. If I have forgotten anyone, please let me know and I'll mention you in the next book in the series. Special thanks to: Tony and Tammy Adamo, Tim Anderson, Tina Badley, Allen Bare, John Beck, Ken Benson, Kelly Brake, Ben Cleveland, Helen Cobb, Phillip Cobb, Jim Degolier, the Farmers, Dae Ann Fletcher, Brian Flock, the Gurleys, Roger and Donna Hudson, Amy Jones, Charlene Knox, Joe Kozup, Steven Nigh, Linda Smith, Lyna Swanson, Clark Vaughn, Bob Vogal, Jeff Ward, Doug Weber, Judy Whitner, Phil Young, Claude Zimmerman, and Jan Zwart.

Some other friends who have provided particular encouragement are Steve and Sarah Haynes, Terry and Linda King, Ernie and Shirley Smith, Dave and Margaret Swacina, and Don and Sandy Wehr.

Pat Myers provided final proofreading; she is amazing! Thank you!

And a heartfelt word of thanks to Diane McDougal, who has made this book in its completed form possible. How can I thank you enough? Or maybe I shouldn't ask ...

The front cover photo is of Mount Antisana, which I took while flying with Neal Bachman (the pilot) in a Mission Aviation Fellowship airplane in Ecuador. This is the mountain where our fictitious protagonist, James Smith, crashed in his RSB.

I must also remember my big brother Dan and his family. He was not only a reader, and not only provided editorial comment, but simply is the best big brother a little brother could have.

It wouldn't be possible to forget my wonderful wife Blanca and my three children, who have helped make this novel a reality by providing support in ways that they may never know. David listened to me read, even when he might rather have been playing a video game. Keren provided a basis for the cover design and produced the art for The Great Seal. As if that wasn't enough, she also helped me with a final review. Kimberly prayed for many years that "Dad's book would be published," and now her prayers are answered. Thank you!

— KEPLER NIGH
January 2008

In memory of
Jim and Jean
Tarquino and Carmelina

Prologue to the Trilogy

Sometime in the future — Manta, Ecuador, South America

SULTRY AIR and one more sunset — glowing spires of light rose to meet flaming clouds above the dark blue Pacific that stretched to a distant horizon. It might have been gorgeous in the eyes of another, but not now, not in Sandy's.

They've finally won? — she questioned herself, wondering whether it was a question at all. She had nothing to doubt about what her own eyes had witnessed. Her hope had vaporized with the boiling sea, and she realized that even a hyperdimensional DEEP Unit could sink.

She remembered another evening, as if it was a painting. It had been years before, on her wedding day, just a few miles offshore on the deck of Pepe's boat floating on the gentle waves of the Pacific, not far from where she stood. In her memory, she saw her prince — his golden hair agitated by a sea breeze and firm accents in his muscular limbs — lying on his side with his arm for a pillow. Scooting over, she had slowly lifted his head into her lap. He awoke, and she held and softly cushioned him, as she savored his excellence.

She remembered yet another time when they'd been together — on a beach in Mexico. It had been a lovely night — stars glimmered and twinkled — and a moon that was over three-quarters full looked down on them with personality, as if to say, "So lovely the couple." Could it have been Paradise? Faint rhythmic waves with white edges, mildly churning, marked the season of their embrace. She thought it would never end.

But it did. A tear streaked down her face; then another, but she had to be brave — for Christopher and Christine. They stood near her, and two tropical palms — the sort travel brochures always show — arched above them. Softly, the Pacific swelled relentlessly. Life would go on. It had to.

Sandy dried the tears from her face with the back of her hand and then knelt down. She began to speak, and choking, she started to say, "Christopher…. Christine…." She tried to contain her grief, even for a moment, long enough to tell them, "Daddy won't—," but she couldn't — not yet.

They have their daddy's eyes — she thought, and continued to hide her own tears, while looking into their blue eyes. Fair hair capped their heads, and soft features adorned their faces. A puff of sea breeze swept Christine's locks across her tender face, and for a moment Sandy saw herself, as a youth, reflected in Christine's pupils, and she remembered when first they fell in love.

Chapter 1

Jonah — That's a Funny Name

WHEN FIRST we met we did not guess
That Love would prove so hard a master.

— Robert Bridges

May 1976 — London, England

A STATELY BRONZE LION gazed down on James as Nelson's Column cast a long shadow across the square.

Ashley invited, "Let me get a picture," and signaled James, and the others, to move into place. Bright red double-decker buses weren't far from them, and pigeons walked closer than people. As the other cadets fell in around him, he could easily see Ashley, who was about to raise her camera. Her dark blue school uniform, with its sharp-looking blazer and proper skirt falling to her knees, didn't hide her fair features, which he wouldn't have minded photographing himself.

"Okay. Smile!" she ordered with a playful voice.

After Ashley took the picture, Master Teacher, speaking like a tour guide, called the group to gather around, and she began narrating, "We are now in Trafalgar Square ..."

In James's mind, Teacher's voice droned on. It was the fourth day of the field trip, and it would be over soon, but there were no vacations from her incessant lectures — Teacher was always there, even when they were away from Novus Ordo, which wasn't very often. Despite the tedium of her instruction, he always enjoyed getting away, and he never liked the end of a field trip. In particular, he wished that this one would continue, especially because of the experience he had had the evening before, at the banquet, when he had occupied a seat nearly across from Ashley's.

Cosmokrator Sir Geoffrey Higgins had sponsored it, and had given the Alpha Academy cadets — all of whom turned fifteen that day — a birthday party. Higgins had greeted them, with formality, as they passed through the receiving line. When James first saw the elder man's face, perfectly wrinkled, it made him wonder whether the creases hurt.

James had been seated across from Ashley many times before, and really, all things considered, that night hadn't been a better time for him to gaze at her than any other during their years together. He'd seen her almost every day for as long as he could remember, but before that night, she was just another member of the group.

As he looked at her, he really didn't notice that there was little to attract his eye to her more than to any of the other girls. After all, he knew that they were nearly identical — genetically — so there was little difference between her profile, and the profile of the other girls, and all of them were dressed the same, in scarlet ball gowns (just as he himself and his fellow cadets were all dressed in black tuxedos). At some point, however, in the middle of Higgins's address on the coming New Age, and how proud the Committee of the Cosmokrator was of "its fine group of cadets," as James looked across the table towards the podium, his eyes found themselves straying towards Ashley. He could just as easily have looked at any one of the others girls, and for that matter, Nancy was closer — and she looked really good — but he focused on Ashley. All were poised and elegant, and silhouetted by light passing around their ideal figures, but even though the lighting didn't favor Ashley over the other girls, his eyes found that her profile made the most pleasing target.

Ashley ceased to be, in his view, just one of the girls. Cadet Brown was different, especially in the sense of the word *better*, or more pleasing, or, well … but he couldn't quite say. Whatever it was, enveloped him, and he became so absorbed in her — just staring mindlessly— that he didn't hear another word that Cosmokrator Higgins spoke that evening.

That's how the banquet had been, and because of the lighting, and the way she sat, turned away from him, he knew she hadn't noticed his impolite gaze from the evening before. Nevertheless, when the camera came down from her face, after she had snapped their picture and that of the other cadets grouped around Master Teacher, he knew that she had noticed him. Her eyes locked onto his, and he became self-conscious and forced himself to look away from her. He turned to follow the group.

With Ashley's blue eyes still visible in his mind, he wasn't focusing on Master Teacher's discussion of the history of Nelson's victory and, while distracted, caught a glance from a passing tourist. The casually dressed man reached out his hand to him and, as he walked by, extended a small piece of cheap paper that was faded in color, towards James, who received it, figuring he shouldn't have, but vaguely remembering an incident in his childhood when Teacher had reprimanded him for not paying attention, and for not receiving things politely when they were offered. Glancing at the paper, he noted that the title, printed in poorly typeset letters, read, "In the Whale's Belly."

He would have wadded it up and thrown it down, but he had been taught not to litter. Besides, he was curious. The title was bizarre. He thought — I wonder what it says? They never let us read anything they don't give to us. It's surely a joke — in a whale's gut? Imagine! But inspired by the silliness, James, who was standing behind the others, quickly devoured every word, even while his teacher spoke.

When he had finished, he thought — What a ridiculous story! A man named Jonah was swallowed by a whale and spent three days and nights in its belly. Talk about a fish story! And then another man, Jesus, said he would do the same thing. No wonder they prohibit *outer* reading material — he concluded with a silent chuckle. Outers must be naive. Looking at the title again, he decided — It has to be a joke. He took the tract with two fingers, and held it as he twisted his watch.

He recognized the name of Jesus, whom he had been taught was a deluded lunatic and the founder of one of the main outer religions, the most divisive, and the one that caused untold problems and hardship for its deceived adherents. The tract had mentioned that Jonah was a prophet from the Hebrew Bible. Of Jonah, however, he knew nothing. Concerning the Hebrew Bible, his training indicated that in the best of cases it was a collection of myths; and in the worst, part of a Semitic plot to rule the world.

When the group moved on, they passed a litter barrel, and having read every word, James crumpled the tract and tossed it handily away, with a little chuckle, and thought — *Jonah*, what a funny name!

Chapter 2

Infliction

WHILST SHAME keeps its watch, virtue is not wholly extinguished in the heart …
— Edmund Burke

December 1976 — Cordillera Real, Bolivia, South America

IT WAS A PLEASANT DAY for a field trip. A green carpet of tiny resilient plants that looked like a field of recently cut grass crunched under every step as if it was fresh lettuce. They walked together in ranks, three abreast, but not marching; they had already done their drills back in the Dietrich Weller Coliseum.

This is great! — Ashley thought, as she looked to the sky, with its white clouds dispersed across the brilliant blue. On the horizon she saw jagged peaks covered with glistening white snow. The group marched toward a windswept lake that sparkled with crystal waves, teasing the shore's black sand.

All the cadets were in their regular training uniforms: scarlet and purple jumpsuits. After they had walked about fifty meters, Master Teacher, who was visibly content, ordered, "Come, let's gather around for lunch." She instructed them to sit about on the tundra.

As Ashley turned to sit, she caught, in a twinkle, James's blue eyes. He was looking at her again. She bit her lower lip, and felt a blush coming. When she realized that he had managed to get right beside her, she wished she could hide, and she giggled. But she wished she hadn't made a sound. Everyone saw me — she worried to herself. She wanted to tell him, "James Smith, be careful! Teacher will notice if you stay close to me." The thought of what might happen if Teacher found out made her shiver. The cool mountain breeze on her flushed cheeks added to her chill.

Her heart rate increased a few more beats when she felt him gently brush her arm, as if by accident, as they sat. But she knew it hadn't been an accident, and she found herself desiring more than a touch, even if she shouldn't.

Before long, Teacher's assistants were serving them lunches in foam packs.

Ashley deliberately kept her eyes from turning towards James. She tried to converse with Nancy, who was beside her, but she could think of nothing but him. However, other than a few more inadvertent touches (or so they seemed), they had no further communication, until James, pointing towards the sky and glancing at her, excitedly exclaimed, for all to hear, "Look! It's a condor."

Everyone was looking up, except Ashley. After only a wink at the oversized vulture, she fixed her eyes on James, who looked at the soaring bird as if it were a god, or a Skotos. She allowed the instant to expand in her own perception, and studied James's chiseled features as though she was memorizing them for an exam.

After lunch they had meditation, followed by breathing exercises. Then Master Teacher began a lesson. It was only a review, and Ashley's thoughts sometimes slipped away to James's blue eyes. She thought it strange, though. Why his blue eyes? — she asked herself. We've all got blue eyes. Why do I only see his?

Teacher told them, "Today we will have a lesson that reviews much of what we have been learning in our history classes ..."

She began at Babel, when their enemy, Asmina, had ruined the Skotoi's attempt to lead humanity to a higher cosmic consciousness. People were forced to flee in great hardship and suffering. She spoke of what would have been the glory of humanity if the highly evolved Skotoi had been able to continue, without interruption, their Plan. She spoke of the great civilizations, and how, inside of each of them, Aztec, Incan, Roman, Greek, Persian, Egyptian, Chinese, and even before — Atlantean — the Skotoi had carefully, and secretly, established wise groups of men, the Cosmokrator, to guide each generation, and to one day establish Therion, who would save humanity from all the misery Asmina had brought upon them. Then she told the cadets that their heritage, as Alpha Force candidates, was greater than anything outers could ever know, and that the *invested* possessed the knowledge and wisdom, the scientific and technological virtues, of all the ages of humankind. It was an important part of their charge to hide this knowledge from the outer nations, to keep Asmina, their enemy, from disrupting the Plan of the Skotoi. Teacher finished, reminding them that Therion would come back to save humanity, and they, the invested, would reign over the world with Therion as their king.

Ashley had heard the lesson before; she knew it by heart. If she made Alpha Force, her duty would be to help establish the Reign of Therion. But her mind wandered to James's eyes. She caught herself, and told herself NO. If I keep thinking about him, I'll be *divergent*. I've got to concentrate on the lesson. Teacher might say something new, and give a quiz.

It seemed like the lecture wouldn't end, but afterwards, Teacher ordered all the cadets to fall in behind her, and in formation they started marching back towards the saucer-shaped DEEP Unit (Dimensional Electro Ether Propulsion Unit) that had brought them. Its black matte finish seemed to make a hole in the scene, as if the place it occupied was a cutout, for not even a ripple of heat rose from it — this despite the sun's intense bath. They marched towards it, about a hundred meters. It was hovering — floating — just above the ground. Late afternoon's honey-colored light made a stark contrast between the DEEP and the snow-covered *sierras*. The Unit was massive, standing three stories high, and extending more than twice that distance in diameter. Reaching the DEEP, they entered and walked up the ramp, through the bottom hatch.

Soon after the group was inside, the hatches closed automatically. Again Ashley saw James's eyes lock onto hers. She knew it was wrong, and would be considered divergent, but she started trying to think of some way the two of them could meet together — alone. She moved to one side of the large passenger area, wishing he could be with her, but knowing it would draw too much attention. Seating in the Unit's dome was arranged in a concentric pattern. She tried to get a seat where she would be able to see him, but at the last minute, someone sat in front of her and blocked her view. She had a notion to change seats, but by then, all were filled.

On the huge dome monitor that served as a window to the world outside, she watched as they levitated upwards, little by little, above the mountain peaks into the blue canopy. Minutes later they climbed to where there was a bright sun glow, which darkened into a black vault. Brilliant stars lined the hemispheric cupola. When they reached the apogee of their climb, the view changed rapidly, and fire started streaking into an apex over them. An outer would say it looked like a meteor. Only seconds later they stopped abruptly, hovering inches above the surface of the Atlantic Ocean. She knew it, since she was watching, but she didn't feel it when they came to a sudden stop, thanks to the DEEP Unit's inertial dampening.

We're back in the Triangle — she thought. She watched as the waves began breaking against the craft. Air bubbles boiled around the hull, and the DEEP began to dive into the abyss of the North American Basin. It took a few minutes for them to reach the dismal ocean floor, where an immense symmetrical entrance came into view. Its inside wall was outlined with strobe lights, which guided inward. As they floated a few hundred feet away from the entrance, another DEEP Unit exited. Once the path was open, they moved towards the suboceanic entrance. A couple hundred meters to starboard a specially designed submarine that looked like a cigar was moving into another entry, which was also outlined with strobes. Above them, she noted, another DEEP was descending along the invisible glide path in the dark water. They started to move again, and entered the passageway, a gargantuan U-shaped siphon, following arrays of multicolored lights. Coming up, out of the siphon, the dome of their Unit surfaced in a symmetrical lake in the middle of a sweeping underground hangar, which had been carved out of the rock under the seabed.

The dome lights (suspended from the superstructure) hung over a hundred meters above them. Their distant points blurred into swirls as the DEEP spun itself dry, throwing seawater back into the enormous artificial lake. Ashley didn't feel dizzy at all. She felt no motion, and heard no sound. Except for the picture on the dome monitor, she wouldn't even have known they were spinning.

Then, slowly, the Unit hovered and advanced towards the docking bay. A large sign, scarlet and white, marked the position they were about to occupy. It read, "Dimensional Electro Ether Propulsion Unit #14."

Exiting, Ashley looked up and saw the familiar sign: "Welcome to Novus Ordo."

Teacher dismissed them to their quarters, and just before leaving the hangar, she glanced at James. He looked back at her, and she could tell he wanted to keep looking, just as she did, but such activity would be considered divergent.

BEFORE GOING to sleep, Ashley saw his wonderful eyes, and hated herself for having thought about him, but she wanted him to be close to her. Especially, she wanted him to touch her. Every time he had brushed against her, long-forgotten memories came to her — even the times he had touched her when, as children, they had played together.

She longed to feel him near to her. But how could it happen? It had been several weeks since the field trip, when she first noticed he was looking at her, and she realized that she didn't mind — even if their being together wasn't allowed by the *mandates*. As she lay between the covers, she held a small folded note close to her heart. It was written with a pencil on plain white paper. It said: Meet me. Block 12-98G. Utility. 4.72 hours. Come alone. Ashley.

She thrilled to think he might come, but despite her dreams, and his numerous glances and "accidental" brushes, she had no guarantee that he would even respond to her invitation. It would be dangerous. She even considered that he might even turn the note directly over to Master Teacher, but she just knew he wouldn't. He couldn't!

She tried to avoid the thought that her plan was a violation of the mandates. She was invested, and as the top female cadet in her group, she had never disobeyed, at least not so purposefully. So, why now? Why was she trying something so divergent?

Eventually, Ashley slept, and dreamed of James's blue eyes and his wavy golden hair. She saw him looking to the sky, with the condor soaring above.

AFTER A MORNING of hard physical and mental activity — training — the cadets began filing into the mess hall. Ashley came up from behind James, and just before he started into the line she slipped her note into his hand, and quickly stepped by him.

He lifted it, unfolded it, and read the brief message, slipping it into his pocket. He looked at his watch: 4.70. What does she want? Does she want what I want? Could she be trying to trap me? Maybe she doesn't like the way I've been looking at her? But he couldn't resist the temptation to go to the closet, and as inconspicuously as he could, he moved out of the mess hall, thinking of some excuse to give in case he was stopped. Aware of the danger, and concerned that he might be noticed, he moved cautiously, but deliberately, and slipped out into the side hall. It was empty, as he had hoped. He had heard tales from other cadets of how some had managed divergents. But he wasn't one to disobey the mandates, so he had ignored their schemes. He didn't want to disobey, and he knew the consequences, yet he couldn't stop himself. He didn't know why Ashley was calling him to the closet, but he knew why he wanted to go — to be alone with her.

His trek wouldn't be long; even so, the two decimal minutes she had given him to reach the selected place behind the mess area didn't leave him much time. Luckily, it was a secluded area, and not many people ever went there, especially during lunch. When he reached the small door, he turned to look back, and then he looked around the other way. Satisfied that no one was watching, he purposely opened the door and entered the utility closet.

It was dark. It was small. And there she stood, dimly lit by an amber glow from the safety light. Her golden hair made a halo. She held her hand out to him. He needed no further invitation. Of all the words he had thought of saying, he spoke not a single one. Silence was her greeting, and he responded in like manner. Besides, what he dreamed of, and what her extended hand suggested, had little to do with words.

He felt her pulling him closer, and he assented. For a moment, he felt her warmth and breathed her breath. But he didn't try to kiss her; that was for outers. She didn't invite him to do so, either. He couldn't imagine why outers would touch lips; it seemed unclean. He was content to have Ashley near. The thought of how outers kissed was repulsive, but he did touch his cheek to hers. She was soft; so soft that it made him wonder how she could be so soft, and if all girls were the same.

Above them, on the ceiling, a small diamond-shaped point twinkled with a rainbow of colors. It was a SPARQ (Singular Photon Abstraction by Reflected Quanta). Every compartment in Novus Ordo had one. James knew it was impossible to hide from these sensors. Even with a thick black scarf over it, if any light got through to it, any at all, with the

SPARQ they could make a full video from any angle that they chose. With it they could see under the cracks in the door, or even back out into the hall — wherever the light reaching its eye had been reflected. But he also knew that just having the ability to look into every little corner wasn't enough, since it was impossible for them to actually have time to see everything, everywhere. Novus Ordo was a big place — and all the computers in the world wouldn't have been able to make pictures from all the SPARQs in the submerged city. He figured — With so many places to observe, why would they bother looking in this closet? They've got more important things to look for.

But now he didn't want to let go of Ashley. His cares, concerning the SPARQ, and everything else, for that matter, were, during those few minutes, as distant from him as Ashley was close. And, for that matter, he almost didn't care if they got caught. Holding her was worth an *infliction,* if it came to that.

Every second they were away from the group increased the chance of being caught. When she gently pulled away, he was both relieved and disheartened. He released her as she whispered, "I'll go back first."

James accepted, and she was gone, but he still felt as if he held her closely. After an acceptable delay, he opened the door, walked back down the halls, and entered the mess area, but there was silence — and eyes. They looked at them: James and Ashley, who stood just past the entrance. On the large monitor a few seconds of video started — perhaps not even ten — but it seemed like it lasted for hours. It was clear to James that someone had seen them leave and had been suspicious, since they had had enough time to make the video.

All the cadets sat silently and watched the show. It was quite a crime — so divergent. James wondered how many of them had done worse, but hadn't gotten caught. He twisted his watch. Master Teacher pressed a button on the remote and froze the image. She ordered, "Step forward, Smith and Brown."

"It's not his fault," Ashley began, "I did it. I wrote a note and invited him."

Why is she confessing? — James asked himself. Is she trying to protect me? He remembered that he still had the little note she had given him. He reasoned — If Teacher sees it, she'll inflict Ashley. He knew he couldn't let that happen, and rapidly lifted her note from his pocket and stuffed it in his mouth, quickly swallowing the poorly chewed pulp, which made him wonder if he would choke. Everyone stared at him; he knew he was making a show. Teacher yelled, "Smith! Stop! Stop! I'll inflict you!" But he wouldn't be distracted, and hastily finished his "meal."

James could tell by looking at the expression of the tall blond teacher, who was about thirty-five, that he had managed to make her go plasma — she looked hot. He would accept responsibility and hope for leniency, something he wasn't likely to get, but he might be able to save Ashley. With that in mind, he began speaking, after he gulped, and said, "It's my fault ... Master Teacher." He gulped a second time, trying to down the rest of the fibrous material. It felt like it was still in his throat. He continued, "I did it. I invited her to the closet."

"Is that true, Brown?" Teacher questioned.

"No, he's lying," she said, and clutched her hands, as her youthful forehead wrinkled.

James watched as Teacher paused. He knew he would be inflicted; no doubt about it. The insubordinate behavior shown by the video was probably worth ten seconds, he figured, and she would give him twenty more for having eaten the note. He had acted blatantly contrary to the mandates. After thirty seconds of infliction, he figured he'd spend a week in sick bay, if the punishment didn't kill him outright. The only question that remained, in his mind, was if Ashley would be inflicted too.

"Stand forward, Smith," she ordered. Master Teacher was watching him closely. "Are you ready?" she asked, looking straight into his eyes.

James nodded. "Yes, Master Teacher," he answered, holding his hands to his sides, standing at attention with his chin held high. He knew what was expected, and he would do it.

"Such divergent behavior is rare for you, James. I'm only going to give you five seconds. I hope it will be enough to teach you, and everyone else, a lesson."

Then Teacher took a little black box, about the size of a wallet, from an inside pocket of her jumpsuit. He had seen it before. But only twice had it been used on him, and then for only one second each time.

He watched as she pressed the buttons a few more times, programming the control, and he hoped she would get it right — over infliction could kill. Then she extended her hand, and pointed the control squarely at his eyes, sighting across its top. He felt as if his knees might buckle, but he knew he couldn't black out yet, or she would increase his punishment. He tensed. She pressed the button—

He felt himself shake in a violent seizure and cave in upon himself. He felt himself falling to the floor. Time lost its significance; each second could have been a lifetime — maybe like the "eternal damnation" some of the outer religions talk about. Pain that he couldn't describe tore him open — or so it felt. But pain wasn't the worst of it. No. The pain was mild compared to the shame. He felt like something that had been left to rot.

Teacher's infliction control had activated one of his implants, a bioprocessor, which directly controlled his brain's emotional center, producing a feeling of intense shame. The sensation was so refined that it became his only emotion, and yet, intellectually, he still knew he was a proud Alpha Academy cadet. Perhaps that was the worst part of his punishment: being so proud, and so humiliated, all at the same time.

Then it ended. Five seconds? Five days? Five years? Or five millennia? He had no idea, but when it ended, he distinctly felt himself go limp — exhausted. Darkness oozed down upon him like a mudslide — cold and heavy.

ASHLEY WANTED TO SCREAM. She wanted to cry. She wanted to run and grab him as he fell, and hold him near to her. She told herself — Some of my friends have broken the mandates, and they weren't caught. Why did they get us? But she didn't have an answer. Her mind was racing, but she kept her expression hard, staid, like they'd taught her. She wanted to cry, to scream, to swear. Yes, even to curse Therion! But she couldn't.

Having finished with James, Teacher turned to her and asked, "Now, Ashley, do you need an infliction too?"

She felt weak, and began grappling for an answer. Knowing, however, that Teacher wanted a quick response, she spoke, "No, Master Teacher. It wasn't my fault." She knew that she had lied, but after James had taken it upon himself to protect her, she had no reason to say otherwise. Getting herself punished wouldn't help him.

Teacher smiled at her plea. Seeing it, Ashley wasn't sure what the smile meant. Had her plea been accepted?

Then Teacher said, looking around at the group, "Divergent behavior will not be tolerated..."

Ashley, for her part, had learned a lesson: She liked James, but she could see it would be better if she didn't. She wanted to run to him, but she couldn't. She hated leaving him lying on the floor. She felt remorse for him — as if he had died.

Later, during lunch, a classmate asked with bland expression, "Do you have your report for tomorrow?"

It made Ashley want to throw her plate of salad in the girl's face, but she didn't dare. Having narrowly escaped punishment on this occasion, she knew that Teacher wouldn't be lenient the next time.

"I have it ready. It was easy," she answered. And they talked, chatting about school, training, anything at all, but not infliction. Neither did they mention James, even though his limp, unconscious body lay only a few meters away.

Everyone knew the mandates — the inflicted were to be mercilessly ignored. The threat of punishment lay behind everything they did. She wondered — Will I be next? It was a question every cadet lived with. It made clear the words of the mandates: Invested is better than outer; do not be divergent. It made the words of authority as clear as a SPARQ's crystal.

Again, she watched James, in the camera of her mind, as he fell to the floor. She wanted to shriek in disbelief and denial. And she thought — He did it for me! Why did you suffer, James? Why did you lie? Why didn't you protect yourself? Why didn't you tell Teacher it was my fault? Then I would've gotten what I deserve. It was my fault!

But she had learned her lesson: She couldn't let him come near to her. She told herself — I can't let him suffer. I'll have to show him I like him by hating him! The more I hate him, the more I like him. With this train of thought, she concluded — I hate him!

JAMES BEGAN to grope, and slowly he came back around, as his wits and his senses started to function. The reality of his infliction turned into a nightmarish haze, and the haze that had been reality, turned into a cold floor. As he turned over, the sounds of his classmates at lunch greeted him. It took him some time to remember what had happened, and why he was there.

He wondered — Why don't they inflict outers? Aren't we supposed to be invested? Maybe being outer isn't so bad? But it doesn't matter. There's no way out. Alpha Force doesn't give any discharges, and there aren't any deserters. He felt strange comfort in the thought — Maybe I'll get to inflict an outer someday!

James sat up slowly, and got his bearings. Then he remembered it was his duty to walk over to the group.

He remembered one of his classmates, who, just a year before, thinking he could change things, became divergent, and even after heavy infliction, kept speaking outer. He eventually got himself inflicted to death, and became an example for the group. James would do well to go over to the group quickly, but his shame was great.

When he finally did get enough nerve to go back, they ignored him, which was the routine — ordered by the mandates — but his isolation would only last until tomorrow. With the new day, he would be treated, again, as a cadet — just like before.

However, not everything was as it had been: Ashley was distant, unattached, as if she had never invited him to the closet, snubbing him, as though she'd never known him. He wondered — I saved her, and this is how she repays me?

However, he knew why she did it: Teacher would have inflicted him more if she had acted differently, but he would have gladly suffered again, just to see her smile kindly, but now her face was as glacial as the shame he felt.

How he liked her! How he wanted to like her! It wasn't any good, though. If he was going to be a success in the Force, he would do well to despise her.

Chapter 3

Genocide

IRAQ'S USE of chemical weapons in Halabja last March was condemned by the international community. As a result of the attack, Iranian troops have been gravely disparaged, even though most victims were Kurdish rebels, resident in Iraq. Speculation points to an attempt by Iraq's ambitious president, Saddam Hussein, to blame Iran for the aggression and thus gain international sympathy for his war against Iran. Until now, the attack has been kept so secret that reports are only recently coming to light.

— *NewsWorld*, August 1988

"WE'LL LET him gas a few thousand Kurds and blame it on Iran. The world will say, 'Poor Saddam.' Then we'll give him more parts for his pet A-bomb. Unless he acts like an idiot, we can let him have the darling inferno machine he wants."

— Cosmokrator Irving Stonefell

"SPACEPORT Novus Ordo is one of several of our worldwide installations. It is the command center for all DEEP operations. As you can see, it is a marvel of engineering. We have sixty thousand inhabitants in a man-made cavern extending over sixteen hundred acres underneath the ocean floor. It's two hundred years ahead of outside technology. We built it while everyone was busy fighting Hitler. Despite its age, it is in first-rate operational status."

— Cosmokrator Hans Weller, introducing Novus Ordo
to a newly recruited scientist, 1986

March 1988 — Twelve years later — Novus Ordo

CAPTAIN JAMES SMITH had, over the years, had resigned himself to life in the Force, and he had excelled in it. He had recently been promoted from commander to captain, and now stood before a large virtual monitor receiving orders for his next mission.

"Smith," Cosmokrator Hans Weller said, addressing the captain in a commanding voice. "You are to proceed to Iraq." Then Weller, who was sitting at his expansive command hub, paused.

"What's our mission, sir?" James answered, as he watched the near middle-aged, near medium-height Weller on the DEEP Unit's bridge monitor. (The clear picture was coming to him via EWB [Extreme Wide Band] which outers couldn't detect.)

"You are to film the operation in Halabja and ensure that Hussein's people do their job."

It took about an hour for them to get under way, but soon, Smith was surfacing his ominous DEEP, breaking through the gentle waves of the mid-Atlantic, just north of the Tropic of Cancer. It was night, and silent. Outside, according to their meteorologicals, there was only a gentle breeze. The placidly clear sky, with a myriad of stars, was visible on the monitor. James wished he could take a moment to enjoy the warm sea air, but readings from his sensors would have to do for now. With a silent sarcastic chuckle, he thought — It's like life in the Force, only to be experienced with sensors: the long-distance kind.

"Captain," informed First Officer Ashley Brown, "we are ready for ascent."

"Proceed," he ordered.

He watched her "punch" in a command on her virtual console. Her shoulder-length blond hair was neatly pulled back from her oval face in a chignon. She momentarily looked up and caught his eyes, but quickly glanced away. It was the same old story. He remembered how she had treated him with disdain, ever since his last infliction. Officer Brown had ceased to be the fun-loving, youthful girl he had known. He tried to think she acted so aloof because she didn't want him to get in trouble again — and he sort of wished she would have told him as much, but he knew she couldn't. Just the same, her strict formality made him wonder if she hated him. Her refusal to look into his eyes made him feel ashamed — except, he had to be proud, Alpha Force proud. And besides, he admired her — she was the best first officer in the Fleet.

Ashley completed the captain's order, and their DEEP began rising at a leisurely speed of 180 kilometers per hour. "Ascent initiated, Captain," she advised, and continued, "stealth operational."

This maneuver took them climbing slowly into space without breaking the sound barrier, eluding the attention they might have attracted otherwise. DEEP Unit 1 was entirely capable of going halfway around the world in less than two minutes, but instead, Captain Smith chose to rise slowly, playing flying turtle (as he called it) to avoid becoming a UFO sighting. A DEEP could be concealed from outers in several ways, but in this case, the slow climb in the dark of night was a simple and effective option.

Half an hour later they sat, suspended on the edge of Earth's atmosphere. Having received orders from the captain, Ashley called Novus Ordo and solicited, "DEEP Control, requesting permission for hyperdrive activation."

There was a brief delay, and then a reply; "We have you on our screens at 90 kilometers."

"Affirmative," she responded.

"Permission granted. Good luck!"

"Do you have a course locked in for the lake?" Smith asked.

"Yes, Captain," she replied.

"Proceed."

A soft blue glow in the bottom center of the Ether Craft turned into a shimmering violet. With an ample energy supply from the chemical fusion power source, together with the hyperdimensional drive powered by fusion plasma, DEEP 1 rapidly accelerated to a blinding speed. The covert powered dive into Iraqi airspace would be accomplished in moments. Their trace lit up radar screens across Europe, North Africa, and the Middle East. Ground computers, however, eliminated the radar trace, classifying it variously as atmospheric disturbances, falling meteors, or some glitch in the electronics — after all, nothing could move that fast.

"Hull status?" Smith asked.

"Hull stable, supercooling operational and maintaining at forty degrees Celsius."

Through the monitors they could see the flaming trail of their own ship above and behind them, but the temperature inside the Unit was just right. It made quite a show in the area around the Mediterranean Sea, and someone lucky enough to be looking up, would have seen a streak blazing across the sky.

A few seconds later Ashley advised, "We're in Iraqi airspace."

James didn't bother to reply, because he knew she would be giving him their destination status before he could ask. Apparently defying almost every physical law known to man, DEEP 1 decelerated from eighteen thousand miles an hour and hovered just above the lake's surface — but inside the Unit the passengers could hardly tell their speed had changed.

"Submersion sequence initiated," were the words Smith anticipated and heard. "Submersion complete." And then Ashley asked, "Depth, Captain?"

"Five meters, and hold."

At eight miles in diameter, and a couple hundred feet deep, the lake had plenty of room for a DEEP Unit.

"How long until daylight?" Smith inquired.

"Three hours."

"Good. Inform Jackson. When his people are ready, they can proceed."

Soon Jackson called from the upper operational deck, "We're 'go' here."

Smith seemed pleased. The mission was ahead of schedule. He ordered, "Prepare to surface. Ready assault troops."

In response, the first officer "hit" a few buttons on the floating panel. Then she commanded the helm: "Acquire operational depth."

In the thick darkness it would have been impossible to see the black island forming in the middle of Lake Darbandi Khan as DEEP 1 partially surfaced, with only its dome protruding above the waterline. Slowly and silently it became an artificial island, not very big, just forty yards across.

Smith sat in the captain's chair, his own virtual panel stretched in the thin air in front of him. The onboard supercomputer announced, "Operational depth acquired."

Smith ordered, "Open dome."

There was a distant whine, and amazingly — as if seen in a time-lapse sequence of the petals of a sunflower opening — the large black fins of the DEEP's outer shell began to open in the darkness of the moonless night. When the doors had opened, and the dome's motors silenced, a familiar sound began to resonate from out of the DEEP's massive staging area.

"Force 1," Smith ordered, "proceed to destination."

"Roger," came the resolute reply through the COM center.

Through the open dome, one Soviet Mi-24 assault helicopter after another — each one filled with Alpha troops — lifted off the helipad and fixed a northeastern course. They moved swiftly, only a few feet above the lake, and reached the shore quickly. As they moved over land, they barely increased their altitude, remaining as near to the ground as possible.

Alpha Force troops had advantages over outer soldiers. Their training had begun at birth, and they possessed advanced technology as yet undreamed of by outers. One such device was their sophisticated contact lenses, which gave them night vision with digital binocular enhancement. They wore them at all times. Each troop possessed remarkable physical skills. An average of only one minute and ten seconds on a one-mile run surpassed the best that outers could accomplish.

Having deployed the Mi-24s, Smith ordered, "Close the dome and submerge."

"Affirmative," Brown answered, questioning, "Depth, Captain?"

"Dive to thirty meters and deploy antenna."

"Yes, sir."

Three minutes later the swift black helicopters approached their mission's destination.

"Objective acquired," Jackson informed.

"Proceed with operation," Smith ordered.

They landed at four strategic sites around the small town. Jackson ordered, "Alpha Force, suit up and prepare to march."

Dawn's first light was breaking from the east and the muezzin at the mosque began summoning the faithful to prayer. Villagers were on their knees with their heads and hands pointed towards Mecca. Soon afterwards, the town's dusty streets began to fill with people wending their way to daily toil. The markets began to open.

Seeing that Hussein's pilots were late, Smith bristled to himself — Where are the devils, three minutes late? He glanced at his watch and twisted it briefly, looking at it again, as if in doing so he could make time itself obey his orders. Finally he said with a placid tone, "Get Jackson's status."

"He reports all is well, but he isn't sure how much longer they can keep their positions without being detected," Brown answered.

"Tell him to keep us informed."

Smith checked his watch. Come on! Hurry up! — he silently ordered. His facial expression remained calm and even, though he betrayed his edgy disposition by the number of times he checked his watch.

By the time Officer Brown spoke, announcing, "MiGs approaching from the west," Smith had looked at his watch almost as many times as she had patted her hair back.

"Six minutes late," he answered, tightly twisting his head her way, and ordered with an angry glare that he wished Hussein could have seen, "Tell Jackson they're coming."

Inside the helicopters, in response to the news, Alpha troops secured their suits and performed one last inspection to be sure there weren't any leaks. They heard the MiGs' deafening roar, three of them —sweeping over the target—just a hundred fifty feet above the ground, but the small town's residents weren't distressed. Combat's rage had been near-at-hand for years.

The first MiG swept back and dove, firing two small missiles that zoomed directly into the main plaza. Pulling up its nose, and kicking in the afterburners, the war machine accelerated to Mach 2, and a sonic boom shook the village. Then the other carried out its run on another plaza, and finally the third, on a different part of town. Three furious rogues pronounced judgment with thundering voices.

Each of the six gas canisters began hissing. Moments later, a few children started to run towards one of the impact sites. They didn't get very far. Some of them may have sensed a smell of bitter almonds, but the impression would have registered only a split second before a merciful unconsciousness overtook them. Their innocent faces contorted; they went into convulsions. The torment was less for the first victims since they didn't see the horrors of what was happening. But for the living who stood to watch the dying, the torment was far greater, at least until they themselves took a breath and fell into the same writhing death.

"We don't have much time. The show will be over soon. Get moving," Jackson ordered.

Alpha Force troops dispersed on their prearranged courses, and linked images from their on-site cameras to Novus Ordo, and from there to the world's monetary capitals, and to the Skotoi.

Smith watched the scene on the large monitor, a blank expression on his face, but in his mind, he might have asked — Why? What's the point? However, from his perspective, he was only a soldier carrying out orders. He was incapable of any response to the carnage because the ability to react humanely had been inflicted out of him years before.

"Jackson reports unfavorable air current. Western portion of target has not been destroyed," Officer Brown reported. James heard the tightness in her voice, and glanced at her eyes to see what might have been interpreted as shock.

Smith looked away and pulled his hand across his brow. "We're going to have to complete what Hussein's incompetent morons couldn't," he half-exclaimed and half-asked. And then he commanded, "Initiate backup plan." He would have hated himself — if his trainers had allowed it.

"Roger," Jackson replied.

Moments later, two of the helicopters were in the air. They headed far enough to the west that when they dropped their canisters, the winds would be favorable for complete extermination.

* * *

Same time — Virtual reality, somewhere in cyberspace

A DIRE STILLNESS compassed the Skotoi and the Cosmokrator while roaring dark winds swirled outside their perimeter. They seemed to be directly in the vortex of what appeared to be a cyclone, with its turbulence surrounding them.

3-D images, coming to them from Iraq via DEEP 1, began showing the convulsing and contorted Kurds as death visited them. Operation Death Breath was received with visual realism, and the victims' pictures were projected on the gyrating walls of the whirlwind that turbulently encircled the royal chamber of Therion. The screeches and groans coming from the throats of the living portended that they would be lifeless corpses in moments.

In the virtual storm that surrounded the gathering of the Skotoi and the Cosmokrator, the image of a deformed face, drained of life, was visible on the swirling "wall" of the bleak cyclone. Exactly as the little girl's eyelids separated in response to life's absence, behind Therion's throne a bolt of violet lightning forked its way upward along the spiraling wind that reached high above them.

Instantaneously, another bolt fired upwards as another pair of human eyes suddenly opened in a death stare. It began to happen rapidly, and with each death, tempestuous streaks rose forcefully.

As the operation that had been sanctioned by the Cosmokrator reaped its harvest, massive bursts of the strange lightning lit their solemn faces. They understood that with each death in Iraq there was a sudden release of consciousness energy. Violet pulses portraying each death rose violently and surrounded them. When the frequency of the blasts increased enough to create a continuous glow, the critical level required for their transcendental illumination would be achieved. This was the goal, the motive behind the countless acts of genocide they had perpetrated. It was as ancient as human sacrifice, as modern as Hitler's holocaust, as contemporary as fetal abortion, and as common as deliberate African famine or ethnic cleansing.

The effects of the gas were swift, and at the expense of the Kurds, the necessary brilliance was reached. Deaths numbered thousands per second, each one causing its own bolt to race up the sides of the cyclone towards the vortex above Therion's chamber. With the thunder roaring continually, and the violet lightning's electric pulsating into a radiant fluid, they had achieved the requisite sacrifice for illumination.

The Skotoi absorbed the consciousness energy as the Cosmokrator chanted to the roar of the constantly resounding thunder, "Receive our sacrifice, high Skotoi. Be appeased, Therion, with the energy we give you. Allow illumination to flood the being of your servants, the Cosmokrator."

After several prolonged moments of nearly continuous lightning, so full that no single bolt could be distinguished, their frequency began to slow and the thunder lost its power, eventually dissipating into clicking noises, like the sound of a Geiger counter, and then there was silence.

The images coming from the death field of Iraq no longer showed any Kurds standing. Only twisted bodies filled the streets. A voice roared from one of the thrones of the Skotoi, "Well done, Cosmokrator! Your sacrifice has brought us abundant illumination. You shall be rewarded."

Chapter 4

Bought

THE MORE GROSS the fraud, the more glibly will it go down, and the more greedily be swallowed, since folly will always find faith where impostors will find imprudence.

—— Charles Caleb Colton

November 1991 — Three years later — Jet Propulsion Laboratory
Pasadena, California

ENERGETICALLY CREATING a computer virus, Atler moved his fingers smoothly over the keyboard. He added line upon line to the program that would secure his future, and the world's too — at least that's what he'd been told, even if he wasn't sure he believed it, but those who said so had shown themselves capable of paying quite well, and that, personally, was the future he found to be most rewarding.

The fluorescent light provided its bland hue, and it reminded him of the icy cash in his bank account, which made him pleasantly warm. It was tax-free (something he would have wondered about, but there was enough of it —the cash — that worrying didn't seem appropriate). His newly acquired wealth was enough to generate, for the time being, abundant motivation.

It could have seemed to him that there was something immoral about what he was doing, but no, he figured it wasn't so bad. He, according to his own reasoning, was at least as good a person as anyone else. I've even been to church — he reminded himself. And I'll go back — it's the right thing to do. At least — he told himself with a chuckle — just like everyone else, at least three times in a lifetime: when born, when married, and when dead. He chuckled silently.

Besides — he pronounced inwardly and self-assuredly — I need the money: A new car will be great and paying off my creditors will be too. I'll have some security for the future. And what I'm doing is for the public good. I have a right! Who can live on what NASA pays?

The neatest part of it, Atler judged, was that robbing computing cycles from the world's computers was blissfully easy. As easy as doing two jobs at the same time: NASA's and Nova Mundi's. NASA's, for now, was a control routine for a space probe, but Nova Mundi's chore was decidedly more exciting: the creation of a computer virus, a super virus to be sure, to make computers on the Internet work together (without the knowledge of their owners), linking them into one mighty supercomputer. Nova Mundi had told him that his system would be used to predict the weather for months, or even years, in advance. Then it would be possible to know when and where to plant crops, and thus prevent world hunger. Really, it was a noble idea — greed aside.

His foot tapped the carpet with about the same rhythm as that of a puppy wagging its tail at feeding time. But he was smart enough to know that his virus program could be used to do more than predict the weather. He had dubbed it VICE, for Virtual Internet superComputer Emulation. VICE, as an acronym, really gave him a kick — definitely worth a laugh. *"Vice"* would also be good at predicting lottery numbers, the fastest greyhound, the swiftest horse, or anything else that could be predicted. Certainly, *vice* could do more than predict the weather. It was, in his eyes, the maximum expression of what had made him fall in love with computers in the first place: power.

However, he didn't tell the Nova Mundi representative that he had dubbed his masterwork *"vice."* He had simply called it VIS (Virtual Internet Supercomputer), which was the name he'd chosen when he first thought of the concept, and it had been a good idea, too. It had gotten him his PhD, and had now landed him jobs with NASA and Nova Mundi. But it had taken years for VIS to gain any attention. Really, NASA still hadn't taken him seriously, but Nova Mundi had. Well — he told himself as he stopped tapping his foot, losing a beat or two (long enough to scratch his ear) — it's high time I have some income from it. He knew, of course, that without the inside information provided by Nova Mundi, his concept could never become a reality. Ultimately, he needed his friends from "New Money" (as he had dubbed Nova Mundi) as much as they needed him.

He wondered how they had acquired all of the technical details they'd given him — Surely they didn't steal them; surely there hadn't been any industrial espionage — he consoled himself — and it really doesn't matter. But for now, all that did matter was the two hundred thousand in his pocket, the forthcoming two hundred thousand, and the six hundred thousand that would be the icing on the cake, once he finished. With a grand total of $1,000,000 coming his way, he really didn't care what Nova Mundi did with *vice*.

With a few keystrokes, a couple of backspaces, a finalizing touch of the ENTER key, he concluded another line as smoothly as a master playing the piano. Besides having raw power, *vice* was endowed by its creator (a term he liked to use in reference to himself) with one other attribute: No virus protection program would ever find it or stop it. Atler's "New Money" friends from Novus Ordo had given him the secret codes to the new computer operating systems, and *vice* would effortlessly achieve its objective — control the Internet's power and turn it into a virtual supercomputer without alerting anyone, since it became part of the system — a sophisticated root kit.

One thing bothered Atler, and as much as he tried to ignore it, it was getting the best of him. *Vice* was probably worth a lot more than New Money was paying. Sometimes, when that thought bounced into his consciousness, his fingers would stop, and he thought — If only I could find someone else to pay more, millions more, for the power of *vice.*

Sure — he figured — there are bound to be people who would love to run the world's computers simultaneously, and they'd pay millions. But I'll never find them. I can't just advertise: "Computer scientist willing to sell virus to create world's most powerful supercomputer by taking over millions of computers worldwide."

He sensed someone approach him from behind. He was caught off guard. His heart jumped, even though he had nothing to fear. No one could make sense of the code on his monitor's screen.

"Atler, how are you doing on the control routine for the solar panel?" Doug Burnside quizzed. He stood six feet four inches, was fair-haired, and had the trim waist, broad shoulders, and large chest of a body builder. All were characteristics that Atler detested, since they represented everything he wasn't.

"Doug ... Oh, it's you. Caught me off guard."

DOUG THOUGHT — Catching him off guard — that's not a surprise. This guy is a pathetic nerd. Friendless genius! Doug considered that his own intellectual endowment was at least as high above Atler's as Atler's was above a vulture's — a creature which Atler resembled in Doug's eyes. With mostly brown, straight hair, hinting gray and grease, that partially covered his balding head, and a frame that (if it ever attained upright posture) would be a head shorter than his own, Doug could find plenty of reasons to loathe the creep. His physique, he estimated, was barely sufficient for lifting groceries, lugging a garbage bag, or engaging a hand brake. But Doug knew that hidden behind Atler's thick, black-rimmed glasses and green eyes, was a genius, albeit a unique sort of genius, but a genius nevertheless — and it was a genius that he didn't possess. Atler could make a computer sing. But outside of this particular expertise, Atler was a manifest idiot, or so Doug assessed, as he wondered if Atler could even balance his checkbook.

Atler turned around on his swivel chair to face Doug. He asked, "Micro-relay routine?"

"Just checking to see how you're doing. You know the deadline?"

"Sure, Doug. I'll have it done. By the way, what about the rest of the advance?"

That lowlife! — Doug thought. He should know better. "Watch yourself," he whispered. "We don't want this broadcast."

ATLER THOUGHT — Micro relays, sure. And realizing what the real motive was for Doug's visit to his cubicle, he turned around and faced the man. After exchanging pleasantries, it seemed to Atler that Doug was already mad at him. But why? No one's listening, Doug. So why get so upset? Then Doug whispered, "We don't want this broadcast," in a way that sounded far more conspicuous, to his ears, than had his innocent question about the advance. But he had to keep Mr. New Money happy, so he apologetically answered, "I know. But no one's listening. Besides, you're the one who suggested we meet here, that it's safer to talk at work than act like spies."

And after speaking, seeing Doug wince at his word, Atler thought — You're strange, man: you and your New Age stuff — breathing exercises, meditation, and all. But I'm grateful to you, buddy. Thanks for your New Money. Just be cool. Don't get uptight. I'll give you "vice."

"Okay. Enough!" Doug declared in an authoritative way that was also nondescript, a manner of expression that annoyed Atler. "You'll have the rest of your advance as soon as you give me the primary flow charts, and the beta code," Doug declared.

"Fine, Doug. I'm ready. When do you want them? I can e-mail them to you right now."

"Atler, buddy, if you're going to work with us, you'll have to learn to be more discreet. E-mail is too public."

"I've thought of that," Atler said, hoping to impress Doug. "Here's the polynomial."

Atler handed over a little slip of paper with a thirty-two-digit number, mixed with letters. He looks pleased — Atler noted. And then, he whispered, "It would take centuries for anyone to break the encryption, but with this polynomial, you won't have any trouble. I'll send you the goods. Just download them, and when it asks for the key, type in the number." As Atler pointed at the slip of paper, he added, "Just be careful you get it right the first time, or your goods will be erased."

"Okay, if this works, you'll find a new deposit in your Swiss bank account, but our people will check out your work. It'll take some time."

Atler liked the sound of "new deposit" but wasn't thrilled with "some time." That's just the way it had to be, however, he reconciled himself, as he asked in a muted tone, "Two hundred thou' — Right?"

He watched Doug's expression tighten as he answered, "Yeah. It'll all be there. Just think of it as something you've done for God and country," and he lightened as he added, "Remember, you're working for the people who make this country work, and keep it from falling apart. The president depends on them. And this job will secure your future."

Atler already knew the details from previous conversations — It's supposed to be patriotic, Doug had told him. It was for America, and the world too — but the money was all the propaganda that really mattered to him. So what! — he reckoned. Some group of well-meaning philanthropist types who run a foundation that's trying to help America. Sure!

Doug's indoctrination spiel had been good, and flattering. He'd said, "Atler, you're the man. You've got the smarts, and you're in the right place. Why, you're a noble person. You would've done it even if no one paid you, just for the cause of science. So, Atler, don't be bashful; take the money. Don't let opportunity pass you by. This way, you can be a part of making history. Future generations will thank you, Atler. Many lives will be saved when we can predict the weather months in advance. Your program will help us predict droughts — exactly!

And predict hurricanes too, where they'll fall, and on what day too. Think of the lives you'll save! You'll get out of debt and a new car. You can't afford not to take this job — just keep quiet, Atler. Don't say a thing to anyone! But later, when the New Order is guiding America, the president himself will thank you."

With fame and, especially, fortune as enticements, Atler knew he'd never have said no. Their conversation had ended when Doug reminded him, "The people I represent don't want anything to go wrong. If you cross them, they can make life miserable for you, buddy. Understand?"

As Doug walked away, Atler scratched his ear.

Before turning his eyes back to the display, he noted a computer software advertisement from a large Seattle firm. He wondered — What would they pay for some ad*vice?*

Chapter 5

One Small Step

"IF YOU ONLY KNEW what we can really do."

— Quote of an anonymous Air Force scientist speaking
about the capabilities of "Star Wars" technology to *NewsWorld Magazine*

December 4, 1991 — About three weeks later — Mars Base Aquarrian

SEVEN YEARS had gone by since James Smith first set foot on the crimson planet, a long seven years. Across his resilient face a sunbeam burst, causing him to squint. DEEP 1 moved slowly upwards through Mars Base Aquarrian's huge air lock. Reflecting off the frozen red Martian desert, distant sunlight flooded the bridge with a rose tint.

He ordered, "Computer, engage Earth sequence." The intelligent voice recognition system obeyed before his lips had stopped moving. The Ether Craft began its self-check for return to the blue planet.

He easily remembered, as his mind flashed back, the first time he had seen the red countenance of Mars: June 6, 1984, Lunae Planum. His "one small step" had not been heralded, or even noted in the hometown newspaper. The Evening News did not report it, because none of the news syndicates had been informed. Smith knew that even if they had asked, his existence, and the existence of his mission, would have been denied. TerraNova's secrets simply didn't find their way into outer communications.

However, James knew the mysteries of Mars. "For the benefit of all humanity and to the glory of the Skotoi, we come to a New World," were the first words he had pronounced back when his foot first touched the ochre dust. Then he had continued to recite the words the Skotoi had ordered, "To awaken a universal consciousness of Therion and prepare humankind for cosmic citizenship…. Our inward focus…. The majesty within us…."

He had planted the flag — scarlet, purple, and gold — raising it in honor of their conquest. It was magnificently embroidered with the symbol of the All-Seeing Eye and the great pyramid. At the base of the pyramid was the Roman numeral DCLXVI.

Instead of a clear sky blue, the Martian sky was pale pink. Everywhere the expeditionary force stepped that day back in '84, they had made small red clouds of dust. James's vivid memory began to dim, as if he was looking through the reddish powder. His mind returned to the moment, and viewing the red planet, which was now several hundred feet below, he ordered, "Brown, take over launch disposition." He retired from the bridge as the surface of the planet, whose rose hue wasn't graced by a single flower, faded below them.

Smith sat in his quarters, attempting to meditate, but his mind was bombarded by questions — and none of them seemed to have answers. Perhaps the one thought that stood out was: This game is getting old, and I'm a pawn — trapped and blocked.

Later, after wrestling away his troubled reflections, which he had fought with for years, he asked himself — What would it have been like to be an outer? Would I have gotten a job and married a wife? Could she have been Ashley? He loosened his jumpsuit's golden belt, took the lotus position, drew a couple of deep ... full ... breaths and relaxed ... deeply ... comfortably ... imagining himself at the top of a staircase ... and going down, step by step ... into that inner place ...

He saw himself appearing on a stage, standing with a spigot attached to his side. A jester, with a painted face and large ears, jumped from behind and twisted the valve. James could see through the makeup, and the clown looked like his mirror image. He reached down and tried to close the valve to stop the flow that was red, like blood, but deeper and brighter. He reached to shut it off, but the pesky jester kept jumping back. As soon as he twisted it closed, the other-self opened it, laughing all the harder, until James, in frustration, grabbed the spigot and ripped it out of his side. The flow burst loose and he diminished into nothing. All that was left was the spigot he had broken off. The clown leaped back, reached down, grabbed the spigot, and stuck it in his own side. Only, this time, black slime came out, and no one tried to stop it. The clown smiled slyly, and imploded, as if he was a balloon — losing air. Heavy, dark liquid gushed out until the spigot was all that remained.

Some time later, James came out of the trance — feeling drained. He vaguely remembered the absurd vision, and it made him laugh to himself, but even so, he felt as if someone had been playing games with him — as if he had been robbed: like he lacked something he needed.

He arose and left his quarters to return to the bridge. Mars had shrunk in appearance to a size comparable to the moon when viewed from Earth, but it was clearly reddish in hue.

"It seems like we've done this before," he said, and briefly looked into Ashley's eyes, as if he hadn't wanted to do it.

She asked, glancing away from his look, "How many trips will this make?"

Momentarily, Captain Smith paused as her brief smile incited him. Her fair beauty was as vibrant before his eyes as it ever had been. He was attracted, but the threat of infliction spoke louder. He reminded himself — You are invested. Do not be divergent. Finally he responded, "We would have to look in the ship's log to find out."

But the number of trips they had logged didn't interest him, and he knew it didn't interest her.

Though DEEP 1's supercomputer was capable of voice recognition, it was quicker to key in the coordinates of their destination. Smith's fingers bounced nimbly on the pad. He felt a momentary temptation to do something different: to program some new coordinates — and go somewhere and have fun. But what fun? — he questioned himself. A night on the town in New York? A quiet beach in the Caribbean? Skiing in Calgary? Whitewater rafting in West Virginia? A safari in Africa? Dining in Paris? Or even a trip to see the rings of Saturn? But no sooner had the temptation ignited than it was extinguished — the threat of infliction guided his every finger's movement.

More than once James had wondered why he even continued in the Force (as if he had a choice). There were answers: They had *made* him for their ends and he wouldn't make a good outer. Besides, things aren't bad enough for suicide — he supposed, even though, from time to time, some of his companions had exercised that option. It had happened, in one case he remembered, after a particularly shameful infliction. But he didn't want to think about it, and tried to change his thoughts to something more productive.

He asked on an impulse, "Ashley?"

Her blue eyes, feminine blond lashes, and brows looked somewhat surprised as he addressed her by first name. Seldom did he direct himself to his crew by first name, and wasn't sure why he had, just then.

She visibly hesitated before answering, "Yes, sir?"

"Have you ever wanted to visit the rings of Saturn?"

She laughed, and answered, "Don't be divergent, Captain."

The look on her face said it all. "I'm kidding," he replied.

Only a muffled rush of air from a vent was left to be heard. For an instant their eyes locked again. He really wanted to tell her something, even if he didn't know what it was. Stumbling for words, he asked a question that he knew was stupid before his lips stopped moving. It was out of character for him, and it didn't really make sense, but he asked, "Do you wonder what being outer is like?"

"No," she answered frankly. With a smirk, she added, "I'm invested."

From her surprised look he knew there would be no further discussion of the topic. She answered correctly, as programmed. It occurred to him, though, she could be afraid to say what she really thought. After all, she might think that he, as captain, had been testing her. On the other hand, she might be thinking she'd need to fill out a DBR (Divergent Behavior Report, usually pronounced Dee-bar).

He had no idea what she was thinking, but he knew that he had been mistaken to have supposed they could have spoken about something beyond the line of duty, like noting fusion plasma cycles or dimensional transference sets, or dictating and receiving orders. Even conversation during an occasional game of chess amounted to little more than "check" and "checkmate." After years of perpetual shame and silence, he had tried to touch her once more, but she showed no sign of letting down her guard.

He began to worry that she would think he was divergent. He had to say something, quickly, to hide his fumble. And he muttered, "I was only kidding." And with less enthusiasm than he had hoped to voice, he added, "I'm invested."

In answer to his excuse, she nodded, ruefully expressing her acceptance. For a moment he pondered whether she was thinking of opening up to him, or was she masking a fear of being involved, and was really ready to betray him. He had no hint. And since she had been so trained and conditioned, he knew she was entirely capable of filling in a DBR on him. She had surely forgotten the moments they had shared in their youth. If she did remember, her recollection would probably be little more than distant memories. And who would want to remember shameful and divergent behavior?

He wondered why he had even tried to show his true feelings. He had made an error. He hadn't become captain by making foolish mistakes. He wished he had never asked her the question. If she lacked all feeling for him, and filled out a DBR, he would end up in a retreat, or worse, he would be inflicted and stripped of rank — divested. He had seen others suffer more for less.

TWELVE DECIMAL HOURS (which was almost twenty-nine outer hours) after liftoff from Mars, James found himself sitting at a chessboard, squarely across from his opponent, Officer Ashley Brown. He really hadn't wanted to play, but if he had rejected her challenge, it might have given her more reasons to suspect him of divergence.

He generally won, but not always, and not this time. His mind was otherwise occupied; besides being generally disgusted with endless missions, he had been trying to understand Ashley. If her aggressive attack on the checkered board was any indication of how she felt about his personal disclosure, he could only surmise that she had no interest in him.

But he thought about her more than ever. What does life mean? For an outer, it's his woman and his family. Am I any different than an outer? I'm supposed to be. I'm invested — a captain in Alpha Force. But even as he reasoned within himself, it seemed to him that at best, life was a flavorless mush, and at worst, it was what mush became once eaten.

What if she does file a report? — James considered. She could betray me. She might even want my job? And if she files a DBR? They'll send me on a retreat and make me "rest" — he thought, sarcastically.

He glanced at her eyes, and they were glued solidly to the table.

Then he reconsidered — She won't file a report. I'm paranoid. He wondered — Maybe I do need a retreat. A vacation might be good. They'll send me far away to some distant place where there aren't any outers. But even as he sought to reconcile himself to the possibility of a forced repose, he became stuck on "far away" and "distant." Smith questioned — They always say it's to keep the Plan secret, but maybe it's because outers have answers?

He noticed her brush her hair back, and thought — I used to like those retreats. But now — he considered — they're obnoxious. You start the day drinking a gallon of salted water, and then vomit up your morning mucus! "To cleanse your system," they said. It's revolting! — he told himself with a shiver. I probably need the rest. Maybe I should turn in my own request for leave. For a man accustomed to decisive action, he found himself repulsively tepid. He knew he should either get over her, or get out, but he found himself unwilling to do either, which added to his disgust.

"Checkmate," she gloated, as she concluded the trap she started seven moves earlier, and lifted her eyes to meet his, just as he glanced away.

He almost knocked the pieces off the board. Why do I feel like this? — he asked himself. I'm invested. Why can't I get my mind off of her? I'm too old for an infliction.

Standing, he almost left the game room in silence, but he knew he shouldn't act that way. He forced himself to speak to Ashley in the politeness of command. "I must go," he said and left the game room. DEEP 1 wasn't small, but it wasn't big enough for someone who wanted to get away from everything. There were six decks, used mostly for shipping. Automation made a small crew adequate. He would find a corner to himself.

Ashley noted how disgusted James had acted and asked herself — Is he like that because I beat him?

Not long after he left, Chief Nancy Jones, ship's engineer, with cool blue eyes, near shoulder-length blond hair curling slightly around her expressionless oval face, entered the game room. "Ashley, did you win?" she inquired.

Ashley knew she was beaming, feeling satisfied. On the board, the hopelessly mated king gave testimony to the reason for her cheerfulness. "I trapped him! You should've seen it."

"I see you won. Captain's game must be off?"

"Oh," she answered, feeling belittled. "The captain's game wasn't as good as mine," she clarified.

"He's been acting strange, don't you think?"

Ashley nearly agreed, but measured her response, "Maybe a little unusual." She avoided saying "divergent," even if she thought it was the right word. After so many years of denying her own feelings to protect him, she didn't dare say anything to Jones that could harm the object of her adolescent fantasy, and who was now her captain, even if he did seem a little out of touch.

"A little 'unusual,' " Jones answered, rolling her eyes. "You don't think he's being divergent? Shouldn't you fill out a DBR?"

"On who?" and she paused, as she asked, "You?" and then chuckled. Silence fell between them as their eyes met, and Ashley continued, "I'll consider your suggestion."

"I hope so. You know he spends a lot of time in cargo area 6. He sits there, staring ... like ... like he's empty."

Chapter 6

Compromised

DEATH IS A SHADOW that always follows the body.

— English proverb (14th century)

Hours later, the next day — Between Mars and Earth

LEWIS WAS CHECKING the hyperdimensional drive and thinking about routine — his routine. Wonderful routine — he whined to himself, as if it was a curse. What would I do without it?

That particular thought would be his final one.

At 100,000 rpm, the spinning plasma inside the chamber looked absolutely still and harmless, just like Lewis had seen it thousands of times. Nothing but a brilliant white, almost bluish, ball of seemingly harmless light that was suspended in thin air, as it were, or as it was supposed to be.

What would happen during the following microseconds — between the time it took him to finish his silent soliloquy on the subject of routine and the time it would take him to routinely blink — began weeks before in Siberia when a defective polytitanium seal with a microscopic crack mistakenly passed inspection and made its way to one of the single most critical points in DEEP 1's drive unit. However, as often happens, the importance of the seal had been ignored, and it was not reexamined. It hadn't been identified as mission-critical, except in an obscure engineering addendum, lost nearly as soon as it had been published. Such an oversight soon ruined both the cold and high-temperature fusion reactors, not to mention Lewis's routine life and the status quo of the world at large.

A microscopic crack split into a canyon about the width of an insect wing and isotopic fuel leaked — first one drop, then another. No one noticed. It wasn't supposed to be happening on their flawless ship — not then, not ever. But the seal didn't care if contingency planning had been arranged to deal with the eventuality of its failure; it would fail anyway. With Lewis as the only spectator, the time for fireworks arrived. The sudden leak lowered the temperature, reduced the voltage, and caused a violent fluctuation in the field supporting the hyperdimensional plasma mass.

Lewis didn't stand a chance. The plasma crashed through the containment field, spinning faster than sound travels, and faster than he could think. When its outer surface was exposed to the air, it peppered, making a shrill whistle so high-pitched that even a dog's ear couldn't have heard it. However, the explosive, thunderous crash that instantly followed would have been audible, had Lewis lived long enough to hear it, but he was pinned to the floor, lifeless. By the time his eyes opened in a death stare, only milliseconds after the failure, DEEP 1 was doomed.

ALARMS SOUNDED and systems switched to battery power. Chief Nancy Jones rushed to Engineering, where she saw Lewis, charred and crushed. Before cooling to a harmless point, the plasma burnt through the reactor frame and flew apart into thousands of burning pellets, each with torrid destructive power.

Hyperdrive shut down and the supercomputer became useless. Systems shifted to battery power and an automatic Mayday began sending all the remaining mission data — including complete reactor and mission telemetry — back to Earth. It would tell the grim story of their demise: byte by byte. In Novus Ordo they would know what had happened — exactly as it had transpired — albeit several minutes later.

Nothing could be done on the engineering deck. Nancy Jones realized that the craft was crippled. The fusion reactors were ruined and communication was impossible. She began to make her way back to the command deck. Lighting was low. Before she realized it, the two-minute backup for the artificial gravity ran out; there was a violent jolt. She began spinning wildly. Pain shot through her arm as she slammed into the corridor's white metallic wall; and though experiencing no gravitational force, she still had mass, and so did the wall. It took her a moment to collect her wits.

* * *

Novus Ordo

THE TECHNICIAN, dark brown hair, something under six feet tall, with hazel eyes and a bushy mustache, moved about the control room, clipboard in hand, calculating resupply loads for Mars Base Aquarrian. He worked his way around the cramped area, checking to see that everything was in order.

Data from DEEP 1 had been normal, blandly routine, until now: It suddenly stopped. An alarm sounded, and an emergency transmission lit up the status board. On the monitor, this information appeared: MAYDAY, DEEP 1.

The technician's adrenaline rose. He lifted the handset, punched in a five-digit number, and with heart pounding, informed, "We're receiving an automatic Mayday from Unit 1."

"What information are you getting?" spoke a voice from the other end.

"Negative!" he exclaimed.

"Get an analysis, NOW! I'll be right there," the supervisor barked from the other end of the line. He had a near Alpha Force physique, with blue eyes, but they were just a shade too dark to be a perfect example, a flaw that kept him from promotion. He thought to himself — This can't be happening. It must be a technical failure in the console. Nothing can go wrong with a DEEP.

He raced out of his habitation, a fairly comfortable living space, got on the electric vehicle that sat parked on the suboceanic street, and drove away towards DEEP Control as quickly as it would allow.

The design of vehicular passageways in Novus Ordo eliminated the need for stop signs and stoplights. In three minutes he reached Control and ran inside without bothering to park satisfactorily. "Have you gotten anything else?" he yelled, coming through the door.

"The high-temperature fusion reactor failed."

The supervisor began to perspire, as he thought — DEEP 1's the pride of the fleet. "Have we received any messages besides the automatic SOS?" he asked.

"None. Just what we had before it shut down."

Desperately, the supervisor wanted the computer to print out a message with an error, or something that would make sense out of the situation. He asked, "How long since the data stopped?"

"Four minutes."

The supervisor decided he had to inform his superior and picked up the handset. Punching a button, a long series of coded tones followed, and after several rings, he heard a response, "Yes."

"This is DEEP Control. We have a Mayday from Unit 1."

A moment of silence, perhaps indicating stunned disbelief, came from the other end. Finally Cosmokrator Weller asked, "What else do we know?"

"Very little. The high-temperature reactor failed and we've got an automatic Mayday, but nothing else. The Unit might be intact."

A sudden hush made the supervisor wonder if he had lost the connection.

"I want an uplink of everything as it comes in," Weller ordered.

"But sir, it stopped five minutes ago," the supervisor replied with unaccustomed gravity.

"NO DATA! What do you mean? NO DATA? How did you reach the conclusion the reactor failed?"

The supervisor explained, "The reading was part of the last transmission."

"A reactor failure shouldn't shut down emergency data?"

"Affirmative."

Weller shrouded his fright with a commanding tone, "But we're receiving a Mayday?"

"Affirmative."

Severity ripened in his reply, "Uplink what you've got."

"Affirmative." The supervisor could say little else.

* * *

DEEP 1

JAMES SMITH had been on one of the lower decks when the accident happened. Emergency systems considered the cargo area insignificant and cut it off. Attempting to return to Command, he had made some progress, but with difficulty. With the loss of artificial gravity, things floated and spun uncontrollably. Unexpectedly, as he floated in the darkness, he felt his shoulder and back dampen as he collided with a suspended glob of liquid. He continued drifting his way up the staircase, knowing the elevators were inoperable.

ASHLEY MADE IT back to the helm and fastened herself to the seat before the artificial gravity quit. The sophisticated virtual panel had darkened and the keyboards were useless, since there wasn't any main super–computer, although they did have a few portables. She was having trouble with unidentified floating objects inside the cabin, and she was doing everything possible to oversee a situation that was beyond control.

She couldn't believe what was happening. *Our machines are invincible* — or so she had always thought. So much power and tech, but it's all futile. This can't be real! It's got to be a bad dream. It can't be happening. It's just some kind of advanced simulation.

Ashley had good reason to believe that there was a simple remediable mistake, or that there was a simple explanation. During the forty years that Ether Craft had been flying there had only been six disasters with fewer than one hundred deaths, making fatalities per kilometer lower for DEEPs than for any other kind of transportation. Doubts aside, she realized that super-tech could become a super-coffin.

Chief Jones arrived. Seeing her, Ashley questioned, "What happened?"

James also entered through the entrance to the bridge behind Nancy. The door wasn't automatic now, with the loss of power, and she had forcefully opened it. In the dim light, he looked like a bloody mess. Seeing his condition, Nancy pushed herself to his aid, and Ashley unbuckled. He was a horrid sight. The chief helped him pull back his jumpsuit, expecting to find a terrible wound, but the captain was not injured. Ashley examined the mysterious red substance. It wasn't blood.

James, looking startled, said, "It's nothing. Just something I floated into in the dark."

They laughed together, and Ashley wondered if she sounded as nervous to the others as they did to her.

During the next few minutes, other crew members floated in. Jones reported that the engineering technician had died.

"Eleven survivors!" Smith announced with finality, as if that's the way it would be, and nothing more would go wrong. Then he quizzed, "What about our oxygen?"

Ashley replied, "There's no way to know for sure, but we should have enough for the next four hours. By then we'll be close to Earth."

Jones began severely, "There's no time to repair the reactor. It would take weeks of work."

Ashley saw the look on everyone's face as Jones's words took hold. She wondered if her own face looked as distraught as the others. James, however, didn't appear to be shaken. And Nancy's expression was also calm, but everyone else looked as if they'd just been ordered to stand forward for a compound infliction.

"Tell us our options?" Smith investigated.

Jones began slowly, and pronounced "RSBs," saying the "R," then the "S," and finally "Bees," as if they stung. She spoke of Reentry Survival Bubbles. They improved the odds for survival in an accident like the one they had just experienced. An RSB was made of multipolymer-aluminum^3-polyasbestos, and each one was kept in a backpack the size of a large suitcase. Every DEEP carried sufficient RSBs to give passengers and crew one last desperate chance.

Smith turned his eyes to Randy, the computer officer, and asked, "What do we have left?"

"Battery-powered portable systems, but no supercomputer," was his terse reply. Randy had a studious look that befitted his office.

Smith continued, "Do we know where we are? What about our last course correction?"

Ashley saw the answers before Randy even answered — his face said it all. "We've lost everything. Our watches and the stars are all that we have," he responded with a forced solemnity that was betrayed as nervous anxiety by a higher than usual key in his voice.

They all knew that DEEP travel at ten million kilometers per hour demanded precision a watch couldn't give.

Randy continued, "If our last in-flight course correction was made correctly, and the explosion didn't change anything, we should still be headed right towards the belly button."

Randy's demeanor irritated Ashley, and she asked incisively, "What's that mean?"

"The equator," he replied, and then concluded, "RSBs only need forty feet of water, so it looks as though we should have a good chance. Earth is seventy percent water, and most of it's around the equator. We should have about seven chances in ten."

"Of what?"

"Survival."

"So, can you come up with an estimated reentry point and RSB trajectory?" Smith quizzed.

"I'll do my best."

"Get on it, then," Captain Smith ordered, and then he faced the communications officer and asked, "White, do you have any way to get a message back to DEEP Control?"

"Captain," he replied, "everything's dead. Maybe the emergency Mayday is working, but that won't help us now. We're too close, and without communication and some way to steer, at our speed, a rescue would be impossible."

Smith ordered the chief and two others back to Engineering to see if they could ascertain what had caused the disaster. This would be important information back on Earth, if they made it home. Then he ordered Ashley, and some of the crew, to come with him to find the RSBs. Tediously they made their way using emergency lighting. Because of overall DEEP reliability, they hadn't trained much in weightlessness, a fact they now regretted, some of them expressing their regret with a rapid emptying of their stomach's contents and words that epitomized their explicit opinions as related to their current situation. James, however, performed the job of captain perfectly, and made Ashley ashamed of her having even considered writing up a DBR and reporting him.

They advanced to within a few yards of one of the storage areas where a third of the craft's RSBs were stored. Its door was jammed, and there was a sea of floating debris. A survey of the havoc made it clear that it would be a formidable task to get inside, and could prove impossible under the circumstances. To get the RSBs would certainly take more time than they had.

"Shall we try deck 6?" White asked.

"It's too close to Engineering, and damage will be heavy. We'll go back to deck 2," Smith directed.

Initially they had skipped deck 2 because it didn't have an air lock, but with 6 in a ruin, and 4 blocked off, 2 was their best, and only, option.

Gone was the normal low-level hum emanating from Engineering. Ashley knew it had been more of a feeling than a sound, but in the profound silence that followed the disaster, the noise of the crew breathing, with the racket made by their movements, was deafening.

Reaching their goal, Ashley helped crank open the emergency hydraulic door, which seemed as if it had an attitude about opening, sluggishly revealing what it hid. Having worked up a bit of a sweat, when the door was fully opened, Ashley floated back, and Captain Smith passed through first. "There it is," he said as he pointed.

They floated in front of the storage door and again, with renewed vigor, Ashley and a member of the crew continued working on the second entrance until it opened. It was a good way to get her aerobics for the day.

"What a beautiful sight!" she exclaimed, as the door opened enough for her to get a glimpse.

Neatly stowed away were forty RSBs. Each one was complete with a distillery, dried food, a hunting knife, a first-aid kit, and various miniature electronic devices, including a transceiver and a PLOT (Portable LOcator Tablet, which was an advanced mapping Global Positioning Satellite System — better than anything the Pentagon had dreamed of). Each pack had a total Earth weight of 275 kilograms (about 600 pounds).

Everyone took two backpacks each, but James grappled three. Ashley wondered how he did it; she could hardly wrestle her pair. Never had their brilliant scarlet and purple uniform jumpsuits looked so dull in Ashley's eyes. Even the bright reflective gold-colored packs, that under other circumstances would have made her think of a sunrise, brought to her numb mind a picture of goldfish in murky water. Movement was tedious. To return to Command took effort and time.

JAMES HAD MANAGED to juggle the three RSB packs he brought. Despite the difficulty, though, he decided to carry on in hopes that his example would encourage the crew. Seeing Ashley's face concerned him. She looked scared. Probably not as grave as the others, but she was an officer, and needed to be an example. Although, as he thought about it, he had no idea what his own expression was like, he hoped it was sure and confident, worthy of his station.

As soon as he came through the door of the bridge, still pushing the packs that he'd tied together, Randy gave him the news, "Captain, there's a reentry window in the Pacific, but I don't know if we can hit it."

"Keep working on it," Smith instructed. "How much time do we have left?"

"About two hours."

"Do we have anything from Engineering?"

"It seems to be too early; they're probably working on moving things around to find out what happened."

Smith ordered White, with another crew member, to go see what was happening.

After he settled for a moment, James remembered the myth of Jonah in a fish's belly. He wondered, with a muted chuckle, if his plasma had fallen through the core.

Chapter 7

Outrage

EVEN ON the most exalted throne in the world we are only sitting on our own bottom.

— Michel de Montaigne

That same day — Earth

IT WAS PROMINENTLY DISPLAYED on one of the walls of a dimly lit room — a plaque that hung against paneled mahogany. Its dedicatory, which was written in calligraphy upon a gold plate, read, "In Memory of Sir Geoffrey Higgins, Honored Cosmokrator, Distinguished Chairman of TerraNova...." Beneath the plaque there was a plush conference table, and sitting at its head in his penthouse in New York, Irving J. Stonefell — with tight lips and narrow dark brown eyes — occupied the position that had belonged to Higgins. Stonefell had been holding the office for more than twenty years. He wore a tailored black cashmere suit with a maroon silk tie. His multifaceted-diamond-studded tie clasp dazzled, even in the somber light.

Stonefell was participating in a virtual meeting with the other Cosmokrator who comprised the Committee of TerraNova. He could see them as 3-D holographic images and it looked as if he was sitting with them at the same table. Each one was a powerful titan of finance whose personal wealth surpassed that of the richest nations. The other nine portrayals came from London, Paris, Toronto, Rome, Bonn, Brussels, Amsterdam, Tokyo, and Novus Ordo.

One of the ten, Karl Rennedy, sitting at his table in Toronto, said, "Irving, I'm confident I don't have to tell you the danger of our present situation." For a second the animated replica shimmered, as though it was projected on a breeze-swept sheet, and then continued, "DEEP 1 is hurtling towards a crash of monumental proportions somewhere over the equator." Rennedy's voice and partially wrinkled face graphically registered his unease. His wide, partially turned-up nose was the object of caricatures by newspaper cartoonists.

An image of Unit 1's trajectory appeared in all the conference rooms on large video display panels.

Cosmocrator Hans Weller, who was dressed casually, spoke from his office in Novus Ordo: "It looks like we need to get our people in Ecuador moving." He raised his right hand to his temple in a pensive gesture; his blue eyes were sullen and reddened after hours of surveying his computer's liquid ion display.

Hans was the youngest of the ten Cosmokrator and the only Aryan. He was the son of a former German SS officer, Dietrich, who had served at the highest levels under Hitler and had been a Cosmokrator during Novus Ordo's final phase of construction. Before Dietrich was appointed to the Committee, he had been its principal interlocutor with the Third Reich. By war's end, he had disappeared with some of his colleagues and allowed the famous ODESSA files to fall into the hands of the Mosad, whose agents eliminated the remaining SS officers who might have embarrassed TerraNova. Hans was born in the early fifties, when Novus Ordo first began operations.

"Do we have a fix on what caused the disaster?" Stonefell asked, fastidiously raising his brow.

Weller, having completed his own investigation of the data, and proud of himself for having discovered the cause, responded with smug satisfaction, "A polytitanium seal failed and ..."

Stonefell cut in, "Weller, you mean this horrible catastrophe was caused by a piece of synthetic metal no bigger than a button?"

Weller, clearing his throat, continued just as if he hadn't been interrupted, "... the plasma not only destroyed the ship's fusion reactor, but it stopped their communications. The emergency data we received were sent back to us with their automatic Mayday, and that's how we know what happened. But the crew — if any of them are still alive — probably don't know what caused the reactor accident. It looks like they're going to crash in South America, maybe near the city of Quito, Ecuador."

Irving was overcome with disbelief and fury, especially because the pompous blue-eyed brat had snubbed him. "Excuse me," he spoke, while locking his eyes on the kid's laser picture, "you said it was because of a three-millimeter polytitanium seal?" Stonefell enunciated his words with disdainful inflection on "excuse me" and conspicuous belittlement on the word "you." And he thought — I know some words I'd rather use, but we must keep a higher consciousness.

Weller replied with a hushed chuckle, "That's the most reliable information we have." He knew Stonefell was hot under the collar, which gave him some amusement, but he also knew the unwritten rule — no defamation, but rather, a facade of mutual respect.

"What do you know about the seal?" Stonefell inquired with his lips and eyes moving in subtle mockery, while considering — It was a mistake to have made Hans a Cosmokrator. True, Dietrich was intelligent, but perverse (a thought that made Stonefell smile inwardly) — and Hans is a chip off the old block. But maybe he's been given too much authority too soon — he's so young. I despise him, but he's needed. None of us *oldsters* can run the computers as he can. I have to give Dietrich credit; his boy's a technical genius. How could we ever get along without Hans? All of those "cyber-something" words and the technical jargon — we're too old for that. We can recruit computer people, but to have one of our own, right here on the Committee, isn't easy. I'll just have to keep Hans in line.

"The seals were supplied by NHMI's Siberian factory," Weller answered. He spoke of New Horizon Multinational Industries.

"This is deplorable!" Cyril Cyzack steamed. He was in Brussels and the supercomputer provided simultaneous translation of his native Dutch. Stonefell had often been tempted to comment on his porkish physiognomy, but kept it to himself. Cyzack continued, "The seals are easily checked and they have never failed before. There are over two thousand of them on every Unit, aren't there?"

Stonefell roared, "What does all of this mean: Negligence? Sabotage? What are we dealing with?"

From the City of London, Lord Mallory Watkins, who was tall and thin and had the features of a wise old owl, with a full head of distinguished gray hair — a man who carried his office well — began to reason, "Negligence is the only possible explanation. Those who manufacture the seals are far removed from those who know what they are used for, and NHMI has absolutely no idea what they are making," he surmised, with characteristic British inflection, while lowering his golden-framed bifocals to the table.

It was Stonefell, Weller, and Watkins who routinely dominated most Committee meetings. Not that the other participants weren't important, but the three were the members of greatest influence, and had in their charge a substantial portion of the daily operations of TerraNova.

"Are we reaching a consensus that NHMI is responsible for the accident, and has provided defective components?" Irving questioned with thinly veiled hostility.

About the table, there were several nods of agreement.

Watkins, with unusual frustration in his voice, explained, "Quality control on the seal is simple, and every one of them should have been examined. Defective units always show up, but that is dealt with routinely. The rejects are identified by a simple holographic projection, and if there had been any microscopic fissures, the flaw should have been found. Human error is surely to blame." Then, pausing, he added with gravity, "It seems likely they have given us a bad batch. There could be more defective seals ready to fail at any time."

"But in the last forty years we've used hundreds of thousands, and this is the first one we know that's failed before regular maintenance. Perhaps the other seals won't fail," Weller defended.

Watkins emphasized his view, "True, Herr Weller, but a DEEP is an expensive item. You must note, not only does the safety of our DEEPs depend on this particular seal, but imagine replacing Novus Ordo, or Mars Base, or one of our other installations! I dare say, we can't afford to take any chances. What if a reactor fails while a Unit is passing through an entrance siphon? The consequences would be devastating. The power of fusion can't be allowed to escape our control. DEEP 1's incident is tame if measured against what could have happened."

In Tokyo, Heroshi Fujusha — Asiatic, short in stature and round of face, said, "These seals are so important they should undergo double inspection. The ones that are in use should be immediately inspected also." He spoke English well and lived in Tokyo, and owned much of it.

Watkins judiciously insisted on the earlier topic, "Gentlemen, our fleet is going to be inoperable until each one of the seals undergoes inspection. I should say, with upwards of two thousand of the little devils to scrutinize in every Unit, we will be at this for some time. Weller, what does your computer tell you on that one?"

Already anticipating the question, he answered, "I've given orders to begin inspection. Our best estimates show that we'll have the first Unit operational in six days, but it will be forty days before we're back to full strength. It will take at least six days of nonstop work by Engineering to inspect just one." He inwardly thought that it would be a waste to stop all DEEP flights. He reasoned — When one plane crashes, you don't ground all of them. But then again, planes and airports are cheap compared to a DEEP, or worse, a spaceport. An occasional incident — like Roswell — can be beneficial. We're still getting good publicity from that one. But you can't control accidents, and as Watkins says — making a new spaceport would really set us back. So it's best to ground them. Then, being convinced in his own mind, he replied, "It's painful, but I have to agree with Watkins — we'll have to ground the fleet. We have no way of knowing how many defective seals have been placed in service. "

Enraged, Stonefell jumped to his feet and slammed a fist on the mahogany table, the image of his head partially disappearing from view. His sudden outburst startled the rest. After a moment of silence, it seemed that Irving was too angry to speak, so the others broke into a rush of expression and intense conversation. Several paired off and some thrashed it out across the table. Finally, after a minute or so, Irving called for order. As he stood, his fuzzed white hair on his balding head disappeared from view in the holographic projections in the other conference rooms.

Watkins, seeing the "scalped" chairman, thought — He needs to have his viewer adjusted. And then he judged — Perhaps not. The angle does seem to flatter him.

"Six days!" Stonefell exclaimed. "Six days might as well be forever! How can this be happening? In six days we could lose the Soviet Union. That would be a major setback. Gorbachev will be — " but Stonefell's tongue refused to say more. He couldn't get it out — it was too grim.

Chapter 8

In the Whale's Belly

ELECTRONIC NEUTERING of Alpha Force personnel is essential. We cannot have them making babies in space. By short-circuiting selected emotions and reflexes, using our sophisticated bioprocessors, we will obtain the type of control required for this purpose. If we decide to allow them to reproduce in the future, we need only shut down their processors. This should be much more effective than castration, giving us the option of directing their reproductive desires and allowing us control of racial purity.

— Dietrich Weller, in a communiqué to Dr. Himmler

BIOPROCESSORS FUNCTION well in the elimination of erotic impetus, and so long as Alpha Force troops have functioning implants with intelligent nerve pulse blockage, they will be unable to accomplish reproduction. Other complex emotions and their reflexes, such as crying and tears, love, hate, and rebellion cannot be controlled by our implants. We have achieved some control in these areas by conditioning. Using implanted electronic shock, infliction, we can create far more pain for the subject than by using traditional methods of corporal punishment: No ugly bruises are left and the subject responds to discipline quickly. With approximately ten inflictions, a child will be programmed for the rest of his life. Unfortunately it is likely that without our supervision, most Alpha Force troops will experience and react to the entire emotional gamut. I therefore recommend constant observation.

— Dr. Josef Himmler, in a report to Dietrich Weller

"Now the Lord had prepared a great fish to swallow up Jonah. And Jonah was in the belly of the fish three days and three nights."

— The Hebrew Bible

That same day — Between Mars and Earth

Engineering's door had already been cranked open manually, and White, with his companion right behind, came floating through.

Chief Jones hadn't expected them. "What do you boys think you're doing?" she asked with vexation in her voice.

They gazed on the ruins for the first time. With an obscenity, White blurted out, "Look what's happened!"

The other began to explain, "From back there it looked as if you could be in some trouble."

"We do have *some* trouble," Jones replied sarcastically. "But we can't find a sign of what went wrong. I'm guessing the problem started in the low-temperature reactor and caused the high-temperature one to fail, but I can't tell for sure."

White, the communications officer, could see why he hadn't been able to get a message out. An abysmal hole, two feet in diameter, showed where the plasma had penetrated Engineering's floor and boiled the EWB transceiver. "Who'd've believed it!" he exclaimed. "If the transceiver hadn't been there, the plasma would've melted its way into space."

"And I'd be as dead as poor Lewis, floating with him in ice-cold space," Nancy reflected. They looked and saw the badly charred remains drifting in morbid posture. It wasn't a pleasant sight. If he had felt terror, his face never had time to show it. No one had bothered to close his eyes for eternal rest, leaving their fixed gaze to witness the swiftly approaching incineration of DEEP 1. His final cremation, began by the accident and would terminate in the destruction of the Unit, wouldn't even leave any ash. None would mourn him, except there would perhaps be a minute of silence at Aquarrian, if they ever found out.

"Captain Smith sent us to see what was going on, and to see if you need help," White offered.

"No," Jones began, "we might as well get back. There's nothing here. It's too big of a mess."

White noted, "On Earth they probably know more than we do."

"They have the data, but it would've been good to take the blasted thing, whatever it was, back for study," Jones said with a sigh.

"I'm glad this old bird is so well built. That plasma was ten thousand degrees, and could have burnt right out into space." White said, as if he was thinking aloud.

They shook their heads in agreement and drifted, propelling themselves up through the stairwell.

White added, "We still haven't made it out of this mess."

***

RANDY AND ASHLEY, with the others who were back at Command, had started what was rapidly becoming a heated conversation. Randy commented, while staring at the numbers, "It's going to be tricky. I'm not sure we'll survive the initial impact with the upper atmosphere. We could glance off, like a rock skipping across water. If we hit a land mass, nothing can save us; we'll be flattened."

Ashley asked, "Can we do something to slow down?"

Randy looked at her, "What do you think? You know we have decelerators."

She snapped back, "Yeah, a black box, and no one even knows if it works! It's just old-fashioned physics — trying to make a flying blob into some kind of stratocruiser. It doesn't even have hyperdimensional capability. How could it work?"

James heard the incisiveness in her response, and quickly ordered, "Let's calm down."

"Okay. Fine!" Ashley responded harshly, as she looked into Smith's eyes, and then dropped her head.

Indeed — James considered — she should be scared. Decelerators aren't foolproof. He knew they depended on a miniature computer connected to powerful micromotors. By changing the length of the straps, the form of the individual survival unit, which was shaped like a large bubble when inflated, could be controlled; it could be made into a glider for reentry. An RSB didn't look like something you would want to trust with your life.

James was beginning to think that his confrontation with Ashley had calmed things down, but then Randy started, "So, what if we don't make it? We'll be fulfilling our karma, right? We'll be reincarnated?"

Despite his own reservations about survival, he was captain and this was the time to act as such. He touched Randy on his shoulder and ordered, "Calm down! Let's get back to work; we're going to make it."

James surprised himself. He felt conviction in his words, even if he wasn't sure he believed them himself. He had entered hero mode: running on training and programming, and he absolutely couldn't allow his crew the luxury of getting out of control — not as long as they had any chance of survival. So he instructed, "RSBs are designed to brake to terminal velocity. They should withstand a direct atmospheric hit." He spoke with all the conviction he could muster. "If we return at night, we'll look like a small meteor shower," Smith said. He could see that his words were effective, maybe because he momentarily felt that they really did have a chance.

He noticed that Chief Jones had arrived seconds before, and had been listening. He watched her position herself where she could see Randy and Ashley, and then she added to his pep talk, "Soon after we splash down they'll send a DEEP for us."

Ashley began to laugh, "You reminded me of a joke."

"What joke?" Randy asked contemptuously.

"About the airborne recruit."

James began hoping that she wouldn't ruin the calm he had achieved.

"What about him?" another of the crew asked, making the dialogue uneasy.

She laughed, and glanced at James, as she said, "A recruit, back in the old days, when they didn't take IQ tests, found himself preparing to jump for the first time. The lieutenant yelled out instructions: 'Come up, jump, count four, and the parachute will open. If it doesn't, pull the safety cord. Once you're on the ground there'll be trucks waiting to pick you up.' The moment came. Reluctantly, and with a push, he went out, counted four, and nothing happened. He found the safety cord, pulled, and nothing happened. After thinking about it, he said, 'Uh huh, 'dem trucks wouln't be ther' eyeder!' "

James thought it was a sick joke, but seeing that everyone had laughed, he joined in. He was glad she told it, even if the message wasn't inspiring. He would take advantage of the moment of levity to organize their next effort. He began, "I'm glad to see you're back. We have the RSBs. What did you find down in Engineering?"

"Nothing. Back on Earth they probably know more than we do. There's too much damage down there to tell anything," Nancy answered.

Smith directed himself to Randy, "How much time do we have left?"

"Two more hours."

"Good, we can get down to deck 4 and clear a path to the airlock. It shouldn't be too hard," Smith instructed.

A little later they entered deck 4, RSBs on their backs, and quickly cleared the way to the airlock. The floating debris that had been blocking the RSB storage area were still there, but fortunately the way to the airlock itself was mostly clear, which had been his reason for choosing that deck. Once they were in position, he ordered, "Jones, activate emergency battery power."

Nancy approached the small panel beside the airlock and inserted the emergency key. With a quarter turn, it began to whine, but the sound quickly lowered to a murmur, and the entrance light came on. She pressed a button on the panel that activated RSB ejection mode.

"Randy, give me the coding," she requested.

He drifted over and began to read the information from his handheld computer. She keyed it in. If everything worked out perfectly, based on Randy's best calculation, they would splash down safely in the Pacific, between Hawaii and Galapagos, and would be spread out across hundreds of miles of ocean. But they had no way to know for sure. He had taken measurements from the stars, and confirmed they were probably on course, but at ten million kilometers per hour, even the best measurements can have a significant error, and in that error rested their life, or their death.

Chief Jones diligently keyed in the long series of numbers, knowing that one mistake could ruin everything. James could see the tension as all eyes watched her during fifteen unending minutes, until she and Randy finished.

She explained, "If something is wrong, Randy spread us out — to give us our best gamble."

James thought, with a hidden snicker — That really inspires confidence, *Jones*. So he added, "Randy's not going to dump us just anywhere. He's going to be flying one too."

Taking his cue from the captain, Randy advised, "We'll begin ejections in twenty-six minutes. There'll be one every four minutes. That means you'll have to get into your RSB, enter the airlock, and connect to the pressurization valve, quickly. The rest will be automatic. When it reaches the preprogrammed time, the airlock will open and release you."

It was clear they would have to keep moving to make it through on schedule. Seeing that his people were ready, Smith commanded, "Suit up."

Each troop opened his or her pack and removed the RSB — unfolding it and finding the bag's body-sized orifice (the electroseal) — which was a long slit in the material, giving it a "mouth." They would then float inside, opening the material as they went, to make enough space for them to get inside. The large bags looked grossly crumpled, like crushed aluminum foil. In the dim emergency light, their aspect was similar to large floating raisins with pale, wrinkled skins.

"There should be enough battery power for everyone to get out," Nancy said. "We designed it for fifty uses," she added, pulling her clipboard to herself and lifting her head.

Running the airlock was her job, so James didn't intervene. She began ordering each troop into the chamber. One of the technicians would be first, an inconsequential honor. Any of them could live or die; and there was no way to know if changing their order would help. They began ejecting, one after another.

Chief Jones would eject next to last. First Officer Brown would precede her. In the chain of command, Brown was higher, but protocol required the chief to operate the airlock. However, Smith, as captain, could position himself as he desired; he chose to be the last one to abandon the ship.

Through one of the tiny observation ports, Smith watched the ejections. Jones stared through another port as the bubbles, one after the other, inflated from crumpled cocoons into stunning globes.

The crew's escape proceeded quickly, until only the captain, Jones, and Brown (whose turn it now was) were left. As the airlock door sealed behind her, with a lump in his throat, James called behind her, "Ashley, see you on Earth."

Obscured inside the folded RSB, she showed a fleeting smile the instant before she was closed inside and she forcefully called out, "The trucks will be waiting!"

"The trucks will be waiting," James shouted back in affirmation, and after getting a glimpse of Ashley, he glanced at Nancy, who appeared unaware of everything except her control panel.

He continued watching Ashley's progress into the airlock, feeling an increasing sense of doom as she maneuvered farther inside. When she reached the dual pressurization valve, he watched as she deliberately pushed the RSB connector (which she held from inside) onto its mate, while supporting herself against the wall. The large dual connector latched onto the valve. Liquid insulation began to rush into the outer shell of the RSB.

ASHLEY HAD one last glimpse of James through the electroseal before it energized. Her captain waved good-bye. He looked solemn and serene. Just hours before, she had questioned his competence, but when their situation had disintegrated, he had demonstrated his leadership. But she knew that she hadn't kept her composure. She felt crushed. With a lump in her throat, a tear escaped from the corner of her eye just before the electroseal hermetically closed her inside the RSB. Her tear happened so suddenly she wasn't able to keep James from noticing. She saw that his expression, which had conveyed firm assurance, dissolved into turbid anxiety almost as fast as her tear had fallen.

She knew that if their conditioners saw them acting this way, they would send them back for an infliction, or perhaps for an adjustment to their bioprocessors. Had the conditioners been condemned to what could be certain death in an RSB, they would have shed more than a tear, she was sure. She could imagine them trembling and unable to move, but her lone tear hadn't been motivated by fear. Rather, she felt like a failure — empty. And there was one other feeling: loneliness. It filled her as she thought — I'll miss him. This is the end. I'll never see him again. There won't be any trucks: It was a bad joke. I'll burn up. And then his name came to her — James. In that moment, she looked at him and thought — This will be the last face I see. In that moment the tear had slipped from her eye.

Inside the RSB, Ashley reflected — What's wrong with me? She took control of herself for a moment and thought — I'll have to cry later.

Dramatic transformation of her RSB began as the air, rich in oxygen, flowed in through the valve and forced the bubble to inflate. She heard a rushing sound as the cooling liquid gushed into the unit's outer layer. An emergency light mounted on her helmet allowed her to see the suspension straps coming together, crossing above, as though they were making a gigantic series of intersecting webs. In their center they held a harness and a suit. They were completing a system that would allow the decelerator (a "black box," which in this case contained a small but powerful computer) to control her flight. Floating upwards, she slipped into the suit and into the straps that held her, suspended, in the bubble's center. She glanced at her watch; only forty seconds were left.

Having taken one more look to be sure everything was in place, without anything floating, she checked again to confirm that she was securely strapped in the harness. Inside the globe, she began to feel an eerie solitude. Abruptly, there was a metallic sound that snapped as if she was inside a large drum. The decelerator box — using a fusion battery for power — had turned on the electrorigidization field between the outer and inner shells of the RSB. Her watch indicated fifteen more seconds when she turned off her emergency light to conserve power. She began a countdown in her head. Three…. Two…. One….

The large door on the airlock opened to the chill of space. She could only imagine what it must have looked like, since RSBs don't have windows. First, there was a whoosh, followed by silence, and the elegant sphere, twenty-six feet in diameter, moved gracefully and majestically away from the black derelict DEEP 1.

JAMES MOVED away from the viewing port — annoyed. Ashley's tear! He remembered all the tears they had forbidden him. He had been a good boy, overall, and they had only inflicted him a few times, but he remembered his tears of loneliness, and the times he had silently cried himself to sleep. He remembered his many fears and feelings of insecurity. Was he any better off than an outer?

They had always told them that their bioelectromechanical enhancements made Alpha Force invincible. But just then, facing death by cremation in an RSB, he decided — When it comes to death, we're all alike, we and outers too, like moths in a candle's flame. And worse, seeing her tear, he remembered his shame and he was angered by it. But for some reason, he felt especially angry with Ashley. Perhaps it was because her tear caused him to remember. To remember holding her. To remember infliction. To remember pain. To remember ...

Then he realized that Chief Jones was trying to get his attention. When he became aware, he saw her smugly turn and float into the airlock in her RSB. When it recycled, and the display indicated that it was ready, Jones began to connect.

By now, however, James was just barely able to function — overwhelmed by the futility of fighting a losing battle — but he would continue to do his duty. He took his place at the control panel. The chief said nothing as she gave him one last look — her face was empty of emotion. The whole system was automatic and he only had to watch. In moments she was ready, and soon after, she ejected.

Only James remained, alone in the ruins of what had once been one of the Skotoi's glorious DEEPs. He had barely evacuated his crew, but now, the full force of his shame overcame him as he remembered Ashley's tear. Shame churned inside of him and engrossed him, carrying him into profound depression. He asked himself why Ashley's tear bothered him so much, but he didn't have any answer, except that it did.

"Two minutes until ejection ..." the computer advised. It was as if his "plasma" fell through his own "core." "One minute until ejection ..." Maybe I should go down with the ship like the captains of old? "Thirty seconds ..." It was as if his bioprocessor was canceling the wrong reflexes — he just floated there. "Enter airlock now," but James didn't react. He had withdrawn in to himself. His mind raced as he thought — I'll probably die in the RSB, so why don't I just go down with the ship. And he remembered Ashley. Her tear kept tormenting him. I hate her! — he told himself, as he felt her still shunning him, like all the rest. Remembering her cruel joke, he told himself — RSBs are a false hope. She won't make it. They're all lost. What's the use? I'll die here.

The computer gave another warning. For a moment the voice of his mind was silent. He ached. The control panel began to emit a warning. He told himself — It's pointless. There's no reason to eject. I can just die here. Besides, if I live through the RSB ride, they'll probably blame me for the loss of the DEEP. It's better to die here than to go back for an infliction.

"Ejection delayed! Ejection delayed one second ..." spoke the computer's voice.

Self-pity, shame, hate, and now, fear of infliction kept him still. He began to think about Ashley — She's got to make it! Then he thought — But if she makes it and I don't, they'll inflict her. She won't make it, though. She'll die. It's impossible. An RSB is useless. But she's got to make it! I don't want her to die. So why do I want to die? If I want her to live, shouldn't I want to live too? What did her tear mean? Did it mean that she was going to miss me? Or was she just scared? The mortal conflict warring within him was like petal picking while doing a she-loves-me, she-loves-me-not, until reaching the last petal, but when picked, along with an answer, everything would blow up.

"Ejection delayed three seconds," voiced the computer.

Then there was another voice — not the computer's, and there wasn't anyone else. It really wasn't audible, but just seemed that way. It said, "Escape. You're going to live."

Like a slap on the face, the voice brought him back to his senses. He moved desperately towards the airlock, impelling himself with cool fury; his wits were restored. He latched the RSB's connectors onto the supply tubes and the door of the air lock sealed.

"Ejection delayed seven seconds" were the last words he heard from the computer. Air and insulation liquid poured into the outer shell of the bubble, drowning out the alarm.

He knew that his delay had made Randy's calculations useless. Seven seconds could have been eternity. His life, or death, now depended on the whims of chance, or the Skotoi, or the gods, or something: perhaps fate — whatever that was. But he knew — it was the inner *voice* that had started him moving. Maybe it was my imagination — he pondered — but it really doesn't matter: I'm a dead man floatin' in a flying coffin.

The RSB transformed itself into a large bubble. James readied himself, slipping into the suspension unit. But it wasn't fully inflated and he had to wait a while longer — for what seemed like hours.

Tugging gently, the harnesses pulled lightly against him as the bubble was pushed out into space. Darkness was all around him. He remembered one field trip when, as a youth, he had gone caving. He remembered the teacher told them to stand still and turn off their lights so they could see *real* darkness. How deep it was! Now space, in all of its immensity, surrounded his RSB, and inside his lonely sphere he closed his eyes and gloom encompassed him.

He only had thirty-eight decimal minutes left before reaching Earth. James's mind raced. He had heard it said that in the moment of death one's life passed before them. If true — he thought — I'm a dead man! Forget that dumb voice. I won't live.

One of his memories was the silly story of Jonah and the whale. He asked himself — Am I in a whale's belly? He chuckled, and noted that something had made him laugh. The Jonah message was so insane. Why had he bothered to pay attention to it? But now, as he pushed the envelope of death, the tract's common newsprint stood out vividly in his memory.

James didn't have time to remember much more — his RSB slammed into Earth's outer atmosphere. The roar intensified. He felt the suspension suit and the entire RSB react to gravitational and aerodynamic forces. Its shape changed into a glider. It would partially orbit while the decelerator attempted to force it into the lower atmosphere and slow it down without killing its occupant, and without losing control and flying back out into space. However, it had already dropped his speed to a mere one hundred twenty-five miles per second. Not a bad start, but it would have to do a lot better.

Fighting G-forces, James fluttered between consciousness and unconsciousness. If it hadn't been for his implants, which aided his circulation and his heart, he would have been senseless.

Chapter 9

Explosion

December 5, 1991: Quito, Ecuador. At 10:11 PM local time, Quito was privileged to witness a celestial event estimated by scientists to happen once every hundred years, but this incident was of extremely rare intensity and duration. The phenomenon occurred fifty kilometers east of the metropolitan center at an altitude of eighteen thousand meters and consisted of a rare ultrahigh-potential discharge, commonly known as lightning.

— Nova Mundi WireFax

Although the spectacle was explained as lightning, many of Quito's inhabitants were convinced they were witnessing the end of the world. The explosion was so powerful that many supposed it was an atomic bomb.

— *El Diario Quiteño*, December 7, 1991

The same time — Quito, Ecuador, South America

Jon Whitten was dressed for comfort, in khakis and a flannel shirt. Forty-some, with dark brown hair, a respectable six-foot frame, and a soft voice, he was a man with a quietness that belied the strength he had within. He was still working, and it was late. He was preparing his teaching notes for the class he taught at the Great Commission Institute. Looking at his watch, he decided that it was time to shut down.

That particular night Quito was celebrating her anniversary festival, and the streets were full of bands, people dancing, and drunks. A deafening sound, which was mistakenly called music as far as Jon was concerned, saturated the chilly night and it rained steadily. The party continued, even in the miserable weather, and the decadence would last all night, as it did every year.

Jon was backing up his computer file when his home office was filled with light coming from outside, penetrating drawn curtains and making his office lights look dim by comparison. It was as bright as daylight, but bluish — not the brilliant warm radiance of the sun.

He wondered — What could it be? He counted in his head — One thousand one, one thousand two, ... the light continued, ... white, brilliant white, ... one thousand five, and still it radiated. He ran over to the window and pulled back the curtains to look out. It was like noon, and made him think that it could be something apocalyptic, but no angel had appeared yet. The low clouds were hanging on the slopes of the mountains, and were glowing brilliantly. The light came from the east. It couldn't be sunrise — he knew. One thousand eight ...

Again he questioned himself — What could it be? — without an answer. He continued to observe. One thousand eleven, ... and then, after eleven seconds, it was gone and the murky night returned, ignoring the interruption it had suffered. Its darkness was so convincing that Jon wondered if he had actually witnessed the light. It seemed like he had to have been mistaken; it couldn't have happened. But he knew it had, and he quickly reached down and hit the chronometer button on his watch. The rain continued to fall and darkness returned, but the earsplitting music fell silent. He looked at his watch and noted it had been over thirty seconds. He wondered why he hadn't heard any thunder. Shouldn't there have been some sound by now?

"What happened?" Judy asked as she entered Jon's office. She clung to him for comfort. He shook his head, and looked into her eyes. She was an attractive brunette who seemed to him to grow lovelier with each passing year.

They moved back from the window as the reverberating shock wave began to resound louder than any thunder they had ever heard. He looked down at his watch: two minutes thirty-two seconds. Some quick math in his head, and he exclaimed, "That's about thirty miles away!"

As the roar rattled the windows of their house, he reset his stopwatch. There were no other flashes, but visibility was poor. The combination of fog, low clouds, and chilling rain — characteristics of the rainy season in Quito — would make it impossible to detect a distant storm through the amber glow of the city's argon lights.

Tumultuous thunder continued into its thirtieth consecutive second before it began to subside slowly. By the time his watch registered fifty-four seconds the noise had abated and there was silence.

Quito's streets were hushed. The festive celebrants were on their knees. The flash and the thunder were truly awesome. As in most Latin countries, the majority of the people were Catholics. In their minds they attached a religious significance to what they had just witnessed. They were also superstitious, and the event could be an omen. Minute after minute of stillness followed. Whatever it was, it was over. Quito was accustomed to occasional earth tremors, and even earthquakes, but this was different. The windows had shaken, but not the house.

"What could it have been?" Judy asked, for the second time, wonderment in her gentle voice.

Jon looked at her, asking himself the same question, and surmising that more than a million others in the city were probably seeking and inventing answers to the same question.

Judy said, "I'll call the Williamses; maybe Denise and Larry have heard the ham operators talking about something on the radio." She moved over to the desk and picked up the phone. "There isn't any dial tone."

"I suppose the phones are overloaded," Jon said. "Everyone's probably talking about the explosion."

"Was it an explosion?"

"I don't know what else we would call it," Jon concluded.

THE FLIGHT had been pleasant, so far, but the nonstop trip to Miami from Buenos Aires was long. The pilot of the Argentine Airlines 747 was just minutes south of the equator when out of his port window a brilliant high-altitude explosive light appeared. (They were flying at 38,000 feet and the burst was higher, much higher.) The intensity was brighter than the sun.

"Can't see a thing!" the copilot exclaimed desperately.

"I'm almost blind too. Thank God we're on autopilot."

"It's like a flash from an A-bomb. Will it blind us?" the copilot asked.

"I hope not."

When his vision cleared, and the captain was able to see the mushroom cloud through the left-hand window that was eerily lit by the half-moon rising in the east, on the right side of the aircraft, he wondered who would explode an A-bomb over Ecuador.

JAMES HERBERT SMITH was hurtling towards certain death, and he knew it. He figured that seven seconds of delay would take him hundreds of miles from the Pacific, and the only water in the part of the world where he was certain to crash would be in the shallow rivers that feed the Amazon. His chances of a safe landing weren't good. But as to his location, and where he would land (or crash), he was only guessing. He had no way of knowing where he was, and furthermore — in his semiconscious stupor, which was the direct result of the G-forces he was experiencing — he didn't care.

Then there was a sudden jolt that violently shook him. It was turbulent and abrupt, and awakened him at once, with a rush of adrenaline. He switched on his emergency light, and immediately observed that his RSB unit appeared to be functioning, as programmed. He knew this because the spherical bubble in which he had begun his flight had changed its form into that of a small blimp. This new shape indicated that he was flying in Earth's atmosphere and that his Reentry Survival Bubble was gliding under the control of its decelerator, which used the web of connecting straps that ran between the passenger's suspension suit (where James was held) and the inner wall of the unit. Each strap's length could be changed by a micromotor, and the strength of the unit's electrorigidization field modified to alter its shape and its aerodynamics, allowing it to slow down enough to land safely in a large body of water. The decelerator also used thousands of microsensors to "feel" how the unit was flying, and to determine the precise adjustments that it constantly needed to make in the shape of the RSB.

The blimp shape meant that the unit was traveling at Mach speed, and had become a supersonic glider. At this stage in the flight, the decelerator, with feedback from its sensors, was making millions of minute adjustments in the shape of the unit's shell to keep it from falling too quickly, and to slow it sufficiently to keep it from flying back out into space. Even the slightest error would be lethal.

But no matter how well it performed, even if it did manage to slow him down, it was designed to land in water, and not in the jungle, though at this point it would be futile to meditate on the details of the flight that was carrying him to his death.

However, whatever had awakened him was causing his RSB to struggle. The decelerator was making many more adjustments than normal for this part of the flight. The straps were moving too much. If all was well, the straps would be vibrating, but not moving like yo-yos. Clearly, his flight was in trouble, and the turbulence the RSB was encountering had the potential of altering his course even more than his delay in leaving the DEEP had.

He guessed that the reason for the rapid adjustments might have something to do with a shock wave from the self-destruction of DEEP 1, but he could only guess. All in all, his fate would surely be the same —

certain death — and he resented whatever it was that had awakened him. He would have preferred to be asleep at the moment of impact.

Because of his delay, he knew it was likely that he was too close to the DEEP when it self-destructed. That stupid voice! Why did I listen to it? I would rather have died on the DEEP than in this tin can. In the DEEP, I would have been incinerated before I could even feel it; now I'll crash and be splattered like a water balloon.

The straps calmed, and began to make small adjustments only. By the feel, he guessed he was still moving faster than a jet fighter, because he was crushed backwards in his harness. He could feel the G-forces pulling back the flesh on his face. During the minutes that followed, the sound ebbed, and the ride became smoother. Based on this observation, he supposed that the decelerator had managed to slow his unit down to about two hundred kilometers per hour.

Its job was nearly finished; the RSB could land safely. The process of deceleration was a great accomplishment, but unless there was an ocean below, it wouldn't do him any good. Could the shock wave have changed his direction and pushed him back out to the Pacific? It wasn't likely. Could it have propelled him forward to the Atlantic? Probably not. At the most, it may have changed his crash site by a hundred kilometers, but that was far too little to help him.

The idea that death was only moments away was unnerving, but he figured that it wouldn't be as bad as an infliction. Then he remembered the Jonah tract once more, and thought — God of Jonah, if You're as good as the outers say, save me! He nearly chuckled, thinking that he had asked the outer God to do something for him, but he never had time.

There was a deafening sound. It crashed! The moment seemed to pass by in slow motion. James fully expected the collapsing RSB to crush him to oblivion, but it didn't — not yet. He had no idea what was happening; he couldn't even have guessed.

Had he been able to look outside, he would have seen his unit slamming into a snow bridge, where the white powder had drifted to form a massive span between two narrow ridges.

His unit's crash caused an explosion of snow to fly high into the sky. Still glowing hot, the RSB pierced the thin outer crust of the glacier's snow, and the frozen crystals rapidly boiled, making a tail that shot out from behind his oblong glider that was now a sled. It looked like a faint comet in the dark of the night.

Inside the RSB, James tumbled and writhed as he absorbed some of the shock with his arms and legs. The suspension unit was stretching beyond its design tolerance. He had no time to guess what was happening; he could only react. He was tossed around like a tennis shoe inside of a dryer. His right arm buckled under the pressure as he crashed against the interior of the unit. With another tumble, his left leg slammed against the boiling wall. Accelerated reflexes helped him defend himself, and helped him to keep from roasting on the broiling inner wall of the space lifeboat, but his efforts weren't enough.

Though cooling rapidly, the RSB continued to melt soft snow as it skidded against the glacier's firn. His RSB glider became a gigantic snow blower, making its own landing strip as it slid downwards against two thousand five hundred feet of glacier. It was spectacular. It made avalanches and kicked up a cloud of ice, snow, and vapor several hundred feet long. Then it burst off the edge of the glacier, and falling, it crashed two hundred feet and was dented when it hit the black volcanic soil on the lower mountain. But even the crash couldn't stop it, and the unit continued tumbling, pitching over rocks and boulders, and rapidly descending the angled slope.

Barely holding together, the RSB was still doing better than James, who felt he couldn't withstand another slam, having been thrown repeatedly against the hot inner wall of the RSB. The unit had endured beyond all that its designers had imagined, but its ability to absorb the impacts was nearly gone. Its once smooth shell was battered like a well-bruised apple. Its resilience was admirable, but it had suffered more than a boxer's punching bag.

Even so, it continued rolling and pitching down the mountainside, until it reached the thirteen thousand five hundred foot level. James was forced to tumble quicker than a gymnast the whole time, which had only been a couple minutes. With every tilt he took a beating. His attempt to keep himself from smashing against the inner wall of the RSB had emptied him of all his strength. The abuse he was suffering had broken him completely. His mind and his will were blank when the RSB finally stopped, smashing into a boulder. The impact tossed and flattened him one last time. He did nothing to resist. Unconsciousness came to him, as if it had been trying to catch up to him since the shock wave. It enveloped him like fog on a dark night.

JON WHITTEN finished speaking on the telephone. "Pastor Kinderly called to say they'll be down next week as planned," he told Judy with excitement in his voice.

She brightened, "Is he coming with Mercy?"

"Sure enough!"

"They're such a great couple. Did you tell him about the explosion."

Jon laughed, "Yeah. He said someone will probably come up with a UFO story."

"Do you have his schedule ready?"

"Of course, Jack loves to get out and minister. I've lined up a few street meetings. He enjoys them."

"Mercy is a riot," Judy remarked, thinking of her outgoing, happy disposition.

"They both are," Jon affirmed.

Judy called the Williamses to talk to Denise about the explosion, to see if Larry had heard anything about it on the radio.

"Did you see it?" Judy sought, with excitement in her voice.

"Are you kidding? A blind man wouldn't have missed it."

"Yeah," Judy answered with a chuckle. "Has Larry heard anything from the other hams on his radio?"

"No one seems to know anything. It's too overcast. Someone from the Nova Mundi Institute announced it was just lightning."

"Strange 'lightning.' "

The ladies carried on a conversation that lasted ten more minutes, but Jon had already overheard enough to realize that Larry didn't know anything.

* * *

The Pacific Ocean

ASHLEY SNAPPED in the suspension straps from one end of the RSB to the other, as if being tossed by a slingshot. The straps pulled hard against her as the bubble crashed into the placid water of the equatorial Pacific, and water splashed above and behind her bubble, climbing as high as a ten-story building. Her survivable unit suddenly came to a quick stop about forty feet under the surface of the sea, and then began to float back to the surface. It was so loud, and every sound was amplified inside the sphere. She could hear water boiling all around her, as if it was rain on a tin roof, though much louder, and it had a sizzling sound that dissipated as the bubble cooled.

The RSB's insulation liquid began draining, acting as "ballast," while the coolant was released. This allowed her temporary submarine to rise to the surface. There was lots of movement on the straps as the spherical unit started swimming, rotating into an upright position in the water, and leaving the electroseal directly above Ashley. She was still held in the center of the floating globe by the suspension unit, but when ready, it released her and gently dropped her to the concave floor. Lying on her back, she used her emergency light and checked to be sure the door was above her head. Beneath her were the fathomless waters of the Pacific that buoyantly sustained the hemisphere.

Held solidly by internal air pressure and by the electrorigidization of the aluminum^3, the RSB was still hard. Ashley's weight, now on the floor of the RSB, added to the stability of the bubble. Seen from outside, the unit was a floating dome and on its wet surface sparkles of etheric starlight were reflected from the nocturnal sky as calm waves petted its waterline.

Then the electroseal opened above her and the walls folded in upon themselves. Below her, the unit's floor remained rigid as the rest of it changed shape. Finally, the edges started curling back inwards until the once elegant sphere looked like an ordinary lifeboat — about ten feet in diameter.

Ashley and her backpack were left topside. She was now safely floating on the ocean's surface. She dug into her pack for the PLOT and the emergency transceiver. Connecting them together, she switched them on. A moment later a return signal came from Headquarters, confirming contact. Everything was working flawlessly. They knew where she was, exactly 112.536 degrees west and 2.265 degrees north. She had survived reentry, and she knew that help would arrive within minutes.

Chapter 10

New Horizons Multinational Industries (NHMI)

"OUR INDUSTRIAL SUPPLIERS provide sundry pieces of a jigsaw puzzle that's so complex they'll never guess what they're really making. We only deal with them through our benevolent Nova Mundi Foundation."

— Cosmokrator Karl Rennedy, discussing operational security

NO ONE who works in our higher security operations can be allowed to "quit," or find a job elsewhere. They are committed for life and know the consequences of violating the ethics of the society. We treat our people well, and we have the best scientists and technologists. They have a guaranteed future in the New Order. No one else can give them the laboratories or the standard of living that we can. They must consider themselves lucky! Any deviation will be dealt with appropriately and expediently.

— Cosmokrator Irving Stonefell, in a Nova Mundi
directive to Arlien Azard

The next day — Brussels, Belgium

"Yes, Mr. Azard, I understand," Janice responded as their conversation ended and she hung up the desk phone. Looking down at her Swiss watch, she saw that the meeting was only minutes away. Standing, she moved around her expansive desk. Behind her a large bright window looked down on the snow covering the nearby European Parliament building. She stepped into the hall. A secretary came up to her quickly, scurrying to catch up to Janice's rapid pace.

"Ms. Allenburg," she said, sounding a little out of breath, "here are the reports you ordered."

"Thank you," she responded, with full composure, as she came to a stop and partially spun around on the tip of her black, custom-made high-heel shoe.

Her secretary turned back, and Janice entered the conference room. Sitting around an oblong table were eighteen alert, impeccably cosmopolitan young men and women in designer suits and gold jewelry. They hushed as Janice moved to her position at the head of the table.

A little golden plate in front of her place was engraved with the words: "Ms. Janice Allenburg, Chief Operational Officer."

"We'll begin," she announced resolutely.

In an ordered fashion, the different executives began to report on their distinct realms of authority.

At the other head of the table there was an empty seat, and a nameplate that simply read, "Arlien Azard, CEO." Usually Azard attended all the regular daily meetings, but he had been called out, and requested that Janice begin without him.

Perhaps a half hour had gone by when the door suddenly flew open and a medium dark man, fifty-five perhaps, small dark mustache, dark eyes, and a black suit, stormed into the conference room. He stomped around the table and, with an expression that meant he had reached critical mass, grabbed one of the executives by his silk tie's knot and lifted the tall, thin gentleman out of his chair.

The others looked on with blank expressions. The poor soul straightened to a height several inches above Azard's, but it seemed that Arlien was taller. Arlien Azard was in a rage and the veins on his neck stood out. He moved even closer to the subordinate who was the object of his wrath. Glaring up into his eyes, he bellowed, like a marine sergeant at boot camp, "Incompetent! What's going on in Siberia? Can't they make a seal?" Azard expressed his fury with words that Janice didn't appreciate. She had never needed to use such language to express herself adequately.

Again, "Incompetent," and a series of curses poured from the incensed Azard. He continued to humiliate his victim mercilessly.

Janice could see that the other executives around the table were trying to sit in denial. Some of them twitched when a word was particularly irritating and others sat stoically. She figured that all of them would have gladly sought employment most anywhere, but she knew that NHMI didn't provide such options. Theirs was a lifelong commitment. They took care of NHMI, and NHMI took care of them.

As Azard continued, Janice looked down at her papers, as if she was occupied — cool and serene — as if she had been trained to take it, and maybe she had been, for her mind drifted far away to another case of abuse.

* * *

June 1967 — Twenty-four years earlier — Arlington, Virginia
INSIDE the large residential dwelling — located in an exclusive area where most of a football field could have been placed between houses — life was surely ideal.

Janice heard her drunken mother scream a few curses in her face. "Now you get your little butt moving up those stairs. And get out of my hair. Do you understand? Don't be causing trouble for me when your dad comes home."

Janice, with a straight face, took the abuse, and then ran up to her room — as always. She fell on her bed and buried her face in a pillow, crying and sobbing. Tears flowed until there were none, and then she got up, and went over to her desk, as if nothing had happened. Opening up her schoolbooks, she buried herself in homework. Perhaps an hour had gone by when there was a knock at her door.

"Yes," Janice said, with just enough force to be heard.

"Honey," the maid said, "your mama said for you to get ready to go with Uncle Ralph to Aunt Doris's house."

Janice began to shake nervously. For years Uncle Ralph had forced her to play games that she loathed.

She ran down the expansive stairs and found her mom with a cup in her hand. "Please, Mommy, don't make me go with Uncle Ralph," she implored.

"You'll have fun, baby. Aunt Doris is expecting you," Mrs. Darlington said, her tone slowed only a bit by the alcohol.

"But, Mommy," and then Janice came close to her mother, "Uncle Ralph," she started in a whisper, "touches me in funny ways, and ..." but she couldn't finish.

Her mother snapped back, like she didn't care, "Ralph is a good man. Don't you say anything bad about him. You hear me! Now, Jan, you just go ahead. Have a good time."

"But, Mother," Janice tried to whisper, in objection, but she had to raise her voice. Mrs. Darlington didn't seem to be paying attention. He makes me touch him ..."

Just then she felt a heavy hand on her shoulder, pulling her back.

"Ralph, you be good to Jan," Mrs. Darlington ordered, with a smile.

"Don't worry about a thing; she'll have a great time with her aunt," Ralph said.

He forced Janice away and tears began to flood her eyes. Pushing her along, out the front door, he shoved her into his cherry red Mustang.

"Now, young lady, we're going to get one thing perfectly clear. What we like to do and the way we play, that ain't nobody's business. Do you understand me? You don't want anyone to get hurt, do you?"

Then Ralph bent down and smiled in her face, handing her a stick of Juicy Fruit, and asked, "Do you understand?" with a polite manner that his horribly bad breath, right in her nose, negated. "So," he added, stuffing the stick of gum in his own mouth, "you'd best appreciate the fun and care Aunt Doris and I give you. You're so lovely, young lady. You wouldn't want anyone to spoil it. You know how important good looks are, don't ya? "

Janice knew a nod was all the answer he wanted, and complied.

"Now, a fine girl, like you, so pretty and all, in that fancy private school, thanks to your daddy's hard work, you've got to appreciate it, you know ... so, Jan, you don't want that spoiled, do you, hun?

Janice coughed in her cry, she knew it would upset Uncle Ralph even more if she let it out, and answered weakly, "No." She felt things she didn't know how to say, but mostly she felt dirty, like mud.

It was one of the happiest days of her life when her Mom told her, several months later, "Uncle Ralph died of a heart attack," but she acted sad, because people are supposed to be sad when someone dies.

Three months went by and her daddy woke her up one bright morning, saying, "Honey, I've not been here for you too much, but I'm going to try to now, now ... your mom—" and his voice dropped off.

"What's wrong, Daddy?" Janice asked.

He tried to say it again. And coughing, as tears began to stream from his swollen eyes, he managed to say, "Your mom left this note."

Mr. Darlington gave her the tear-stained paper and she read, "Jan, I hope you can understand, but I just couldn't keep living like this. I love you. Mom"

Janice didn't understand, but she seemed to know that it meant Mommy was dead. As the reality of her mom's self-administered drug overdose started to sink in, Janice loathed life more and more.

It didn't seem long to Janice, maybe it was eight months, and Daddy brought home a new mommy, but Janice was already inside a shell that wouldn't easily be cracked. The new mommy never did figure out how to relate to Janice very well, but they got along, and perhaps that helped Janice.

Daddy always provided, but he never did keep his promise. He wasn't there when she needed him. She was twenty-three when he suddenly died of a heart attack. He had sent her to the finest schools — and left her enough wealth that she wouldn't have to work a day in her life, but books and studies were her life.

Since then, she knew, she had lived on an edge. If she fell off, she could go either way. But for now, she had managed to keep things in order, except for a brief experiment with marriage.

She traveled a lot, much of it because of her language, business, and administrative skills, and had fallen in love with a Jewish physicist named Allenburg. Dr. Joseph Allenburg had been good to her. He tried hard to please her. Their experiment lasted six years, until she divorced him due to her own unresolved issues. It really didn't have anything to do with him; it was all her problem. She was miserable, but didn't want him to know. She figured that if she let him go, he would be happier. He could find some other woman who wouldn't be a driven workaholic like she was, and would please him with the marital favors he expected. It was hard for her to give him those favors, because, for her, the memory of Uncle Ralph was still alive.

He told her repeatedly not to go through with the divorce, he loved her no matter what and would never marry another woman, but she knew he would (like a man) and that divorce was the best thing possible for their hopeless relationship.

* * *

December 6, 1991— Brussels, Belgium

AZARD CEASED to scream at the humiliated executive. He then moved to take his seat. There was silence.

After a long pause, he said, "Ms. Allenburg, you may continue."

She was still looking down at her papers, holding them as if she was studying them. She almost didn't take charge. If someone had thought that she hadn't been paying attention, they would have been right. It took her mind a moment to come back.

But finally, she said, "Mr. Earling, would you please continue with your report, where you left off."

Janice looked up and caught Azard's eyes momentarily. By the look he gave her, she knew that his outburst had something to do with their largest account. Everything in Siberia, where the seals came from, was part of an eminently secret operation that New Horizons Multinational Industries (NHMI) maintained for a group that Janice knew only as TerraNova. She also understood that INTEL and IBM would be jealous if they knew what NHMI manufactured, but she had no idea that NHMI's sophisticated microchips and other super-high-tech products had been to Mars and back.

She also knew that it was paramount that NHMI's manufacturing processes be kept secret. It was clear to her that there was more to this seal affair than Azard's outburst and temper, and it wouldn't be long until she was informed.

* * *

Pasadena, California

"MR. REDCLIFT," the business type in a black suit began. The color of his dark tie wasn't distinguishable in the dimly lit restaurant. A gleam from his head shone softly through his tidy, thinning hair. "My company is interested in your code."

"That's great," Atler answered, a smile on his lips, as he scratched his ear. It hadn't been easy, but he had found another benefactor. It was nerve-racking, wondering if Nova Mundi was watching, like Doug always said, but he just couldn't bear the thought that he had sold *vice* to Nova Mundi so cheaply.

"Does anyone else have this program?" the man asked, looking Atler in his eyes.

"Oh …," he began.

Seeing Atler's hesitation, the gentleman from Advanced WorldNet emphasized, "Listen, Mr. Redclift, we don't like being double-crossed."

"Oh, I wouldn't do that," Atler said, and tapped his foot nervously.

"What is the financial arrangement you want us to consider?"

Atler looked the man in his eyes, and then glanced towards another table. He lifted his beverage and took a sip. Then he looked back, having gathered the strength of character (or, he wondered if it wouldn't prove to be stupidity) to go through with it. "I guess I can give you a bargain price."

"Which is …?" the representative asked.

Atler felt as if he might choke, but he got it out, "Five million."

"I suppose you want it tax free?" he asked with a laugh.

Hearing him, Atler began to second-guess his decision of trying to get more money from *vice*. He'd never been much of a salesman, but he figured that now was the time to try. "Listen," he spoke with authority, "I think I'm giving you a bargain. Don't you realize the power my program will give you? Five million is a bargain."

"Well, it's certainly more than I'm authorized to approve, so we'll have to talk again."

"And how much can you approve?" Atler asked with distant hope in his voice, again showing his incompetence at making deals, or better said, his ability to make great deals — for the buyer.

"Well, Mr. Redclift, I think my company can give you two million."

"Tax-free?" Atler asked.

"Do you think we would tell the IRS we're buying stolen industrial secrets?"

"They aren't stolen!"

"Really? Mr. Redclift, perhaps your VIS is original work, but you know as well as I, everything that makes it useful, all of the entry points for the new operating system's code, for instance, all of that, it's stolen."

"I didn't steal it!"

"Of course you didn't, Atler. You're a good man, aren't you? So you didn't steal it. Their owners just walked into your office one day and said, 'Atler, we've got some fabulous secrets we want to give to you. You don't have to sign any nondisclosure statements. Just take our secrets and tell the world!' Sure, Atler, you didn't steal it."

I'm making a fool of myself — Atler thought. The man is right; Nova Mundi gave me the keys that made my *vice* useful. Without the information they supplied, my concept would never be more than an idea. It's the code that Nova Mundi gave me, and now I'm trying to sell it as part of this deal.

"Okay," Atler finally answered. "I don't want to argue. I'm not a thief. If you want to make a deal, let's talk." The man's offer wasn't as much as he had hoped for, but it was twice what Doug was paying! And the IRS would never know. There was just one problem, though; he had already taken Doug's down payment, and he had already given Nova Mundi his code. He could get in a lot of trouble if his patrons found out about each other. But what would they do, sue him?

Chapter 11

Freedom?

By 1994, circumstances will have ripened for the implementation of our Plan and the introduction of Therion. Our recent delay should not be seen as a sign of weakness but, rather, as a virtue. We have consistently moved forward and destiny belongs to us. We shall achieve a New World Order.

— Cosmokrator Irving Stonefell
From a speech and banquet in Novus Ordo, 1985
Given after a failure to catalyze the Plan

"ADOLPH WAS a chosen vessel to play the part of Therion and introduce the New Age, but we had to dump the deranged slob. We could have given him anything he wanted, even the A-bomb. The little tyrant was arrogant enough to think he could do it without us. When he started killing our friends in the Secret Orders, we decided we could no longer struggle with the [deleted by editor], and after '42, seeing the [deleted by editor] manifest his own will over our command, it became clear that the jerk was fatally flawed. We needed to scrap him. It was a disappointment.

"We had to resign ourselves to the delay and let the Allies finish off the megalomaniac. We even placed bets on whether or not he would be able to complete the Final Solution. Had we imagined that the [deleted by editor] Jews would get Israel out of the bargain, I'm sure we would have helped him until he finished the Holocaust.

"In our era, we had to have someone to play the role of Therion. But in the Skotoi's wisdom, the Plan has been delayed. I shall not see its fruition, but I am confident that you will, my son. With your new technology, Therion will not be limited by quirks of personality and will."

— Cosmokrator Dietrich Weller, months before his death,

speaking to his son, Hans

The second day after the explosion — Mount Antisana, Ecuador

JAMES STIRRED, and found himself throbbing in pain. The sun was bright and he wanted to lift his arm to cover his eyes so he could keep sleeping, but his arm didn't want to move. Every thought and every movement was a monumental effort. His mouth was as dry as a forsaken desert. He desperately wanted a drink.

Eventually, he managed to open one eye and then the other, but he didn't see clearly. It took a while. When some notion of his surroundings came to him, and his eyes focused, he saw a condor and the sun. The condor circled gracefully above him. It brought to memory the one he had seen years before — and Ashley. He wondered if she was alive, which made him wonder if he really was. Maybe the bird's circling for me — he wondered. Maybe I'm dinner. Minutes later he drifted out of consciousness.

Hours passed; afternoon had nearly changed to night. He began to awaken and tried again to move his limbs. With difficulty he was able to sit, reclining against a granite bolder that had been sheltering him. The silvery RSB was collapsed around him, and his head was out of the electroseal.

In the last fleeting moments of twilight he saw above him, several hundred meters up the slope, the edge of a glacier that descended from a peak that had a smooth appearance, though in places it looked as though it had been torn haphazardly from a sheet of thick paper. It descended in a steep incline and abruptly met black volcanic sand, forming an elliptical line that was similar to the peak, in that it was both smooth and jagged. Ash, sand, and soil filled below the snow line, and were enhanced in their dark color by the deep shadow that covered most of the mountain. The right-hand slope was brilliantly lit by the setting sun, which made a burning strip, and outlined most of the mountain's lucent ice and snow. Immediately, where he sat, was the bolder, which he had found to be his closest neighbor. Around him the ground was scabrous and sandy and, most of all, damp. Despite the open sky, he felt as if he was in a dungeon, and despite the dampness, he was as thirsty as a lost legionnaire in the Sahara.

I've got to have water, but I'll never find it in this mess — he thought. Every movement was painful. But then he noticed that doing nothing was painful too. He struggled, wanting to raise his arms and hands to open the RSB farther and begin searching for water. But something registered — it was in his hand. In a shaking grasp, he brought the canteen up from inside the deflated survival bubble. While he removed the lid and lifted it to his lips, some of the precious liquid spilled. He couldn't remember when water had ever tasted as good.

A few sips helped revive him. His mind cleared. He began to realize that the immense boulder, against which he now leaned, had been his welcoming committee. It wasn't the minimum of forty feet of water required for a safe landing, this he knew. He looked again at the regal mountain and realized the he was in the Andes, hundreds of miles from the Pacific Ocean.

Above, he saw the condor and vaguely remembered seeing it earlier. His memory continued to clear and he recalled the sweltering sun and the day so many years ago on the high plain and the infliction that had followed. Pain began to torment him as his limbs, and his body generally, began reporting considerable displeasure with the treatment they had received during the crash. But the memory of his infliction made his present pain seem to be little more than a tingling numbness.

The condor soared away. His thoughts drifted and he wondered — Had Master Teacher inflicted the condor until it learned to fly so well? He then sank into a dreamless sleep.

* * *

The Pacific Ocean

"THE TRUCKS aren't waiting after all," Ashley said to herself angrily. She was growing impatient. She hadn't meant for her joke's punch line to be true.

Now I can "celebrate" two days at sea — she reflected sarcastically. There's nothing but pacific blue. Water, water everywhere and plenty to drink, thanks to the distillery, but they should've gotten me by now!

However, she knew the rationale for having a distillery included the fact that things don't always work the way they're supposed to — although the RSB itself had worked perfectly.

She remembered the difficult farewell on DEEP 1 and speculated about the rest of the crew. Were they okay — and especially James?

"I hope so," she mused aloud, before she caught herself. Now I'm talking to myself. It must be too much sun — she reckoned. But with the ocean and the sun being the only things to look at, Ashley didn't find it hard to remember him, and to wonder — Why was it wrong for him to touch me? Could I love him? And what does that mean? She reminded herself — Alpha troops aren't allowed to love anybody. Not only had her *inflictors* prohibited it, but she knew she was forbidden to know the meaning of love.

* * *

The third day after the explosion

GENTLY, THE OCEAN caressed her lifeboat as Chief Nancy Jones waited stoically. The "trucks" from Ashley's worthless joke would be there any moment; otherwise, as she had already calculated, her end was near.

She knew that the designers (for she had been one of them) had only given the transceiver's battery enough energy for three days. They had presumed they could find and rescue anyone forced to use the RSB within hours of receiving the emergency signal. She had even been opposed to giving it a three-day reserve. After all, a DEEP could be anywhere on Earth in minutes. They had finally decided to power it for three days, since there would be little size and weight change if they made it less time.

Laugh or cry? — she couldn't decide. Actually, she had forgotten how to do either, and she did neither, trying to ignore primitive feelings. Her faith in super-tech was absolute. They will find me! — she exclaimed to herself.

Reflecting back on her last hours aboard DEEP 1, she wondered who had been incompetent: the captain, or the first officer. Perhaps both. As chief, she would have taken charge, if she had had time and opportunity. Both Smith and Brown were incompetent. Nancy concluded that she would fill out a DBR on both of them at her earliest opportunity.

* * *

Mount Antisana, Ecuador

IT WAS COLD. James could feel that his face was frigid. The night temperature fell below freezing. Thanks to the RSB's material, he felt pleasantly warm. It made a good blanket.

Sunset had been earlier and night had fallen rapidly. James was again reclining against the boulder. He rested against the massive rock, and in the sky above, the stars were nakedly clear.

With difficulty, he again guided the canteen to his lips and took several gulps. As he did, he began to review his situation and realized that he had been quite lucky. Apparently the dampness from snow and rain had provided enough moisture to make the unit's sensors think it was in water and automatically implode, draining the insulation, and freeing him from its weight, which would have crushed him to death. Also, because of the dynamic collapse, and the breaching of the electroseal, he was given an air supply.

I was lucky, really lucky — he thought. Amazingly, I didn't suffocate. It was almost impossible for the electroseal to open with my head sticking out. He wondered if maybe the boulder and the sloping mountainside had helped the RSB "swim" (rotate) and position itself upright before opening. What if it hadn't been able to right itself? — he questioned himself, knowing that if it hadn't, he would have died inside.

If it had finished its transformation into a lifeboat, it would have trapped him inside. He wondered if maybe it ran out of power while "swimming" against the mountain and the boulder. However it may have been, the RSB hadn't been able to finish. Definitely — he decided — the odds were against me. He thought — I was lucky!

Having noted his own good fortune, he drifted back to sleep.

It was dark, pitch dark, when he awoke in the cold of the night. There were no stars to be seen, and he had no light. His vision enhancements would have permitted him to see in darkness, but a hazy fog had covered everything around him. He lifted his left wrist slightly and said, "Watch, show time." It came to life, and on its glowing screen produced 6.92 UDTC. It wasn't hard for him to recall the last time that he had seen the number: back when he entered the RSB. A moment later he noted another number. It was the date: three days later. A funny coincidence — he thought, and chuckled silently. I've been in the whale three days and three nights. I wonder if Jonah hurt as badly as I do.

He pulled the RSB back up around him and rested, soon sleeping. By the time he awakened, sunrise had bathed creation in a golden glow. The color didn't seem appropriate for the concentrated chill of the mountain air, and its beauty didn't lessen the pain he felt. He considered his situation some more and decided — I should be dead. Then another thought crossed his mind — Maybe I have died. The only reason to think I'm still alive is that my whole body hurts. Besides, they taught us that when you die you'll be reincarnated. Maybe that's what's happened. I've been reincarnated and I'm now an amoeba. The ridiculous thought entertained him.

James watched the sun rise. It was a beautiful, almost heavenly moment, and soon things began to warm dramatically. He managed to squirm his way out of his "blanket," and he sat up. This was my whale's belly — he thought, as he remembered Jonah's fish. The idea made him chuckle again.

Then something else caught his attention — hunger. I have to eat — he told himself. He found a pack of high-energy protein concentrate in his pack and drank it down as his pain permitted.

A while later, starting to feel better, he recovered the transceiver, which was a small black box about as big as a chalkboard eraser. It was battered, and again it made him wonder if he really was alive. Maybe there's more to death than I thought? — he questioned himself. Maybe the dead can feel pain too? Having seen the transceiver's battered condition, he nearly didn't bother to get the PLOT from his backpack. He expected to find it in pieces. It was a slender black plate that was stored in a pocket of the pack's flat inner wall — surrounded by the pack's frame. The extra protection appeared to have preserved it. It appeared to be intact, not even scratched. But the sight of the mangled transceiver didn't inspire hope that it would be functional. James decided to try, however, and plugged it into the edge of the PLOT.

Then he touched the corner of the tablet and spoke, "Map current location." He released his finger and an image began to appear on its surface. The words "Mount Antisana," beside the point in the center, marked his location. In the upper right-hand corner it even indicated his altitude, 4183 meters; along with his latitude, 0.487 degrees south; and his longitude, 78.124 degrees west. The picture soon showed the entire country of Ecuador in topographical relief, and the Pacific too.

He commanded, "Zoom, plus 1000."

A new map began to form, this time with a much closer view. The map showed that he was in rough country. He told it to zoom closer, to the point that he could see only the part of the mountain he occupied. It showed his position on the eastern slope. From the previous projections, he knew that Quito was to his west.

James told it, "Rotate." The image turned 3-D and started to gyrate slowly. Enormous gullies and canyons ran out from the mountain's center towards its skirts. As he contemplated the treacherous terrain, he decided it was time to flip the switch and call the cavalry to come galloping to his rescue — in a DEEP. But he hesitated.

I don't even know what freedom is — he began to reason. Yet right now, I'm free! If I hit that switch, they'll come and get me and put me back in a cage. My whole life's been inside of cages — Novus Ordo, Ether Craft, Mars Base Aquarrian — they've all been cages. This is my chance to be free. But then, in response to conditioning and seemingly against his will, his hand reached, and before he could stop it, he hit the transceiver's switch.

He cursed himself; he hated it. They own me! — he exclaimed to himself. I'm their property and they're going to take me back, like a runaway slave — but the confirmation indicator didn't light. Novus Ordo wasn't getting his signal. Smith looked and stared— ten seconds, but there wasn't any light. Twenty seconds, ten minutes, then twenty minutes, and still the transceiver was dead. He sat in silent wonder and disbelief watching the lifeless screen, unable to do more than stare.

"It's not working!" he finally exclaimed aloud, and after a long pause he began to chuckle. Then he stopped, looking at it some more. Again he laughed. He wanted it to work, and yet he would give anything for it to fail. He didn't know what to think. Like Ashley — he thought — I would give anything to have her with me, and I hate her too. Curse the confusion.

He looked at the transceiver module, wondering how much it was damaged, and yet the PLOT had remained uninjured. He thought — The transceiver was my ticket back — back to prison. It occurred to him — I'd never have to go back to infliction. I have a choice.

A moment later he whispered, "I won't go back." Then he shouted, "I won't go back!" Looking up at the snow, remembering the condor in free flight, he swore, "Infliction upon TerraNova," and he yelled at the top of his lungs, "I won't go back!"

As he looked down at the transceiver, his hand started to tremble. He grabbed the module in rage and disconnected it from the PLOT with a rough snap. With what strength he had, aided by biomechanical enhancements, he slammed it against the boulder — destroying its components.

He suddenly felt new freedom. For the first time in his life he transcended his conditioning and he began to laugh — hysterically, uncontrollably — as if the punch line of a joke had just sunk in. He didn't stop. He openly dared the inflictors to hear his empty-headed, reckless laughter, his sides splitting. He choked and roared at the same time, until he couldn't go on. When he regained his breath, he kept on some more. He laughed so much and so long that he forgot what it was that had been so funny. The laughter itself became its own end — an obsession — and he would laugh until he couldn't, then rest in delirious bliss. This is wonderful, curse the pain — he told himself.

Turning his head he saw the smitten elements of the useless transceiver — its shining components splayed over the dark ground. Somehow it reminded him of Jonah, even though he told himself — I can't see what a busted gadget has to do with Jonah. And this realization only made him laugh more. And even though he ached all over, and inside too, he couldn't stop himself. He eventually calmed, and could only manage a muffled cackling sound, and an outrageous smile.

* * *

The Pacific Ocean

AS HER RSB lifeboat rocked gently in the waves, Ashley looked down at the transceiver and noticed the confirmation light had gone off. She stared at it for some time, but it still didn't come back on, and she thought — That black box was my only hope of being rescued! If the battery's power is gone, and they don't rescue me immediately, I'll be at the mercy of the currents and the winds.

As she contemplated — Where are the trucks? — she realized that the once amusing joke had become a prophecy of doom. What's wrong? One moment I'm in complete control, and the next, I'm helpless. Where are the almighty Cosmokrator and the Skotoi? Yeah! Curse them all! There's no one around to inflict me. So I can say what I want!

She picked up the dead transceiver and began to shake it angrily, but its circuits were dead. In her rage, she boiled, thinking — It's all flawed. DEEP 1 was a death trap. This transceiver is useless. Everything is useless! She took the worthless device, and with an oath, she cast it into the restless blue Pacific.

When her anger passed, and despair beset her, she remembered James. Her heart broke. She would gladly submit to infliction, if she could feel his arms about her once more.

A spark of hope ignited when she reasoned — They have picked up my last coordinates. When they lose the signal, they'll make an all-out effort to rescue me before I drift too far for them to find me. Then more desperate thoughts rushed into her weakened mind — Perhaps they'll presume I'm dead? Maybe the transceiver never really worked? Maybe they sabotaged our DEEP? Maybe they want to replace us?

* * *

Elsewhere in the Pacific Ocean

BEHIND HER BACK, not more than thirty feet away, a sub surfaced. It was startling, after three days at sea. Nancy had been expecting a DEEP to rescue her, not an old supply sub.

It didn't take long before they had her on board. There were moments of greeting as the other survivors of DEEP 1 gathered about her. Later the captain of the sub greeted her and informed, "As the highest-ranking of the survivors, Chief Jones, I must inform you that at the time we rescued you, we lost the other distress signal," spoke the captain of the submarine politely and to the point.

"What is the distance to the last transmission?" Jones asked, showing her authority by her immediate command.

"One hundred twenty kilometers," the captain tersely replied.

"Can't Novus Ordo dispatch a DEEP?" Jones asked, with superiority, "It will take this 'tub' at least four hours to cover that distance, and by then the source will have drifted away."

"I'm afraid your *fine* DEEPs are on vacation, and I know you Alpha people may feel humbled, having to be rescued by Beta Force, but you would do well to observe protocol and show respect while you're on my ship. After all, without this 'tub,' as you say, you'd still be floating above."

"I beg your pardon, Captain. Excuse me, your ship, not 'tub,' but what can be done? Why are the DEEPs "on vacation," as you say?" Jones asked with an expression that was intended to drive home her point.

"All DEEPs have been grounded. There is a problem with the polytitanium seals, and until they are replaced, no DEEPs are being dispatched. If you desire, I'll link you directly to your superiors so you may get more information, but I'm afraid they have sent us because they have no other solution," replied the captain crisply, knowing he had best make the arrogant blond happy; she outranked him.

* * *

The next day — Worldwide

THREE DAYS had gone by since DEEP 1 had exploded and the Committee had lost its mighty Ether Craft. Irving Stonefell steamed, "We're losing everything! Gorbachev is being fed to the dogs and we can't do a thing to stop it. Yeltsin and his thugs are gaining control. Years of work are being lost."

The members of the Committee of the Cosmokrator sat in disarray. The Skotoi had been informed, but for reasons known only to them, they said nothing. Like capricious Greek gods they remained silent. Had they decided to allow events to run their own course?

"Our last intelligence indicates that Yeltsin and his hoods may well wrestle Gorbachev out of power and form some kind of new commonwealth," Karl Rennedy mused with frustration in his voice, while pensively touching his chin.

Hans Weller, at Novus Ordo, with unaccustomed humility in his expression, interjected, "There are delays."

"Delays?" Stonefell exclaimed.

"Seal inspection and replacement isn't going well," Weller spoke with severity.

"Can we deploy the craft? Rennedy asked, knowing it would be impossible.

"My dearest Rennedy," came the voice of Lord Watkins, "DEEP Units do not grow on trees." He spoke in a paternalistic tone that made Karl vehement. "Alpha Force personnel are expensive and it isn't easy to replace them. We can't take a chance of losing them just because it might delay the Plan a few more years. Such slapdash could set us back even further. Survival of the Plan is paramount."

Rennedy said nothing, but he seethed inside. He was as mad at himself for asking as he was at Watkins for the lecture his question inspired.

More than one of the ten considered whether the seal problem might cause another great failure, like 1942's.

After further fruitless discussion and argument, they briefly turned their attention to another matter. Weller informed, "We've recovered nine Alpha Force survivors. One died on DEEP 1 as a result of the accident. We still haven't rescued First Officer Ashley Brown and Captain James Smith. We were receiving a transmission from one of them, but it died."

Chapter 12

Mars Base Aquarrian

OUR INVESTIGATION found no fault in our information control system. The scientists acted independently and went directly to the press, ignoring administrative channels. It was impossible to know that they would announce the discovery of cold fusion, much less stop them.

— Excerpt from a report to Irving Stonefell

"THIS WHOLE FIASCO has cost us dearly. Will we ever make the public forget? We must have tighter controls on information."

— Irving Stonefell's admonition to the Committee

after the cold fusion incident

That same day — Mars Base Aquarrian

WARMLY TUCKED one hundred fifty feet under the Martian permafrost, Mars Base Aquarrian began to receive uplinks from Novus Ordo.

Charles Roguel, auburn hair, about fifty-five, obviously a recipient of age-defying cosmetics and surgery, which gave him an impeccable TV face, was preparing the evening news report they broadcast daily to the populace of thirty thousand.

James Herbert Smith was one of Aquarrian's best-known citizens. Charles had never met him personally, but had seen him at several newsworthy functions. One such incident had been a state dinner given in honor of the visit of Cosmokrator Irving J. Stonefell. Smith had been present, and Charles didn't remember what the incident had been, but he remembered Smith — a perfect specimen of humanity.

Charles recalled his sculptured features and how, at six feet six inches, he towered above everyone else. Smith's blond hair and blue eyes projected an image of a man much younger than his years, and besides, he was just plain handsome.

Charlie had his memories, but he would never see Smith again.

It was ten minutes until airtime. Their programming was extensive, but exactly what TerraNova ordered.

"Charlie, get on the set," commanded the floor producer.

He was running behind. He grabbed the latest uplinks. Brusquely he entered the studio and found his seat at a modern desk. The whole set was white: white desk, white chair, white walls, white ceiling, and an off-white floor. He also dressed mostly in white. The prevalence of white may have been more befitting a hospital or high-tech manufacturing area, and hearing a description of the Aquarrian studio may have led one to conclude that someone wanted the place to look clean. They really knew how to work with white.

Charlie slid into his white seat and punched the RWFloptical into the TelePrompTer. Pointing to information on the flat screen and issuing some voice commands, he finished editing. He didn't exercise any true editorial power. His duty was to present the news just as it came to him from Novus Ordo.

"Okay, countdown coming up," advised the floor producer.

Charlie fastened his eyes on the TelePrompTer. It was Mars Report

Anchor, Charles Roguel, but the lead-in told the audience again, for good measure. Three.... Two.... One....

"Good evening. Today's broadcast is going to be difficult, but first the good news."

"Nine survivors have been recovered ..." During the next hour they would hash and rehash, which, Charles knew, was the job of all good journalists reporting breaking news. "... Captain James Smith and First Officer Ashley Brown are missing and must be presumed dead."

His voice trailed off as he read the last few dark words, and a thought flashed in the back of his mind: Could it be, with all of our technology and all of our power, a piece of rubberized metal, smaller than a dime, could be our downfall?

"From information made available to us through Novus Ordo's Office of Official Information, DEEP flights will be terminated until all seals have been inspected."

There was a groan throughout the Aquarrian superstructure. Most of the thirty thousand inhabitants had been watching. They knew the news anchor's words meant they would be cut off from Earth for at least a week. It would be a grand inconvenience. They had enough supplies to last for months and they would still be able to contact Earth. But there was something unbearable about the thought of being abandoned, on Mars, with no way back to Earth.

Charlie continued, "With us right now is our chancellor, Suveste Besarian. Chancellor...."

The chancellor, with white hair and dressed in a Nehru-style suit, addressed the audience with a sullen expression and sufficient wrinkles on his face to look his years. "My fellow Aquarrians, the news we have just received weighs heavily upon us. Isolation in the depths of space on an unfriendly planet is something that none of us desires. The fate of DEEP 1 has stirred us all, and we cannot know the karma of Alpha Force members now reported missing.

"We too, closed off from Earth because of these events, must strengthen ourselves in the force of our will to survive, and not only to survive, but to conquer."

Charlie thought — The old man sure doesn't sound too convinced. He might as well have let me read the prepared statement. He's only saying what TerraNova sent. At least I could act like I believe it.

"We are prepared to face this challenge," he continued. "We have the training. We have the technology. We are the best. Within nine days, normal flights will resume and, working together as a team, we will overcome those obstacles that are before us. Thank you."

Charlie came back on the screen. "We will go to Patricia Jiménez, who has prepared a report for us from Mars Base Engineering. Patricia ..."

SHE WAS PETITE, and Latin, dressed in a tailored suit, with long, wavy black hair that teased out from her TV journalist's serious, but attractive face. She reported, "The task of inspecting two thousand seals on each craft in the entire fleet is formidable. All of us here at Aquarrian know the complexity of our hyperdimensional devices, and we presently have sixteen of them stationed here. We also have a large supply of new polytitanium seals. Aquarrian engineers will inspect each seal, both new and old. The chief of engineering, Ron Hunter, informed me that the process of examination has already begun, and engineering teams are working around the clock. He estimated that one craft would be ready for travel within six days. He believes the crews on Earth will take at least as long to perform their inspections and make test flights. This means we can expect the first supply flights from Earth in approximately nine days. Charlie...."

"Thank you, Patricia...."

The news kept on until the hour had finished.

That evening Charlie went to bed feeling as though Earth was much farther away. He felt a draft in his habitation. It was as warm as ever, but his thoughts slipped to the frozen surface above. So beautiful — mountains and valleys many times greater than anything comparable on Earth — but it was so desolate and so cold. All that stood between Aquarrian and the frigid surface was a reactor, with all of its seals, just like the one that exploded on DEEP 1.

Chapter 13

Siberia

THE NHMI Siberian plant is a low-level, low-grade secret Russian manufacturing plant, and incapable of producing anything technologically advanced.
— Excerpt from CIA's dossier on NHMI's Siberian operation

"BUMS, THE KGB is our easiest victim. Their technology has yet to surpass the Stone Age. We can tell them anything we want, and they believe it. We play the CIA like a player piano. They have no idea that they're the world's largest collectors of lies. Their listening posts hear only the electronic gobbledygook and digital hogwash we give them. We dupe their spy satellites all the time, and it's getting easier. The new ones are the easiest to fool since they're all electronic. We can start a war anytime we like."
— Hans Weller, explaining to the new Cosmokrator, Cyril Cyzack,
Committee operations

"COMRADE, there is something dubious about this NHMI thing in Siberia, but I don't know what it is. I know it may sound like the babbling of a tired old man, and my words are baseless; one shouldn't look a gift horse in the mouth, but I cannot imagine this Arlien Azard being so generous and selling sophisticated technology to us at unreasonably low prices without some motive."

— Andre Cherninko, member of the Politburo,

commenting to another member in confidence

The next day — Brussels, Belgium

"Janice, you're the only one I trust. You must travel to Siberia," Arlien Azard pleaded. Janice could hear the concern in his voice. He continued, "It won't be easy; with everything that's happening in Russia you'll have to be careful, but I don't have anyone else I can trust. We must not lose the TerraNova account; it would ruin us."

It pleased Janice to know that Arlien had enough confidence to send her in his place. "I'll be on my way tomorrow."

"I understand this is hard, but could you leave now?" Arlien asked with uncommon understanding.

"I'll leave immediately."

"Thank you." Momentarily taking her hand, he looked into her eyes, and then gently kissed it.

Janice paused briefly and then turned to leave. She passed by her penthouse office and packed her notebook computer with a satellite phone connection, along with her documents. Making her way to the elevator, she told the secretary, who scurried after her, to arrange her passage to the airport.

Within hours she left Brussels and was soon in German airspace traveling in one of NHMI's private jets. They would have no trouble with border crossing or flight clearance thanks to the power and influence of TerraNova and their other front organizations, like Nova Mundi. Janice had delivered secret flight orders directly to the pilot the moment she boarded. He had registered a flight plan, but it wasn't uncommon for NHMI's jets to deviate from their "official" intention.

She had several conversations, one of which was to have her secretary inform Siberia that she was on her way. During her long trip, she enveloped herself in work. It was her escape. Reality was, for her, frightening. She preferred to be in control and not dependent on relationships.

Janice knew she was desperately lonely, dying for companionship, but unable to find it. She had compared herself to a dog she had known in childhood. In the house where the pet lived there was a screen door, and the animal would jump and throw itself against the wire mesh in seemingly desperate attempts to attack any visitor. Barking, and yapping furiously, she acted so viciously that whoever got near was scared away. As tiny as she was, the mutt acted like a savage beast, but once Janice had entered the house, she could see that the creature was eager for companionship, no longer barking, but anxious to be petted.

After seven hours in the air they reached the Siberian city of Yakutsk, slightly farther north in latitude than Helsinki. It was still dark, and snow was abundant on the ground, but it wasn't falling, and the runway was open. NHMI's special shuttle helicopter was ready. Janice walked forty yards in the bitter cold, escorted by a couple of Russian Army officers in what looked to be an honor guard. She didn't need to check into Immigration, but went directly to the helicopter. Momentarily the shuttle was in the air and, with advanced jets, it quickly reached two hundred fifty miles an hour.

The helicopter flew through the winter darkness in its high-speed stealth mode. With night-vision helmets the pilots could see in the Arctic night. They reached NHMI's top-secret facility within the hour.

Surrounded by jagged snow-covered peaks, the entrance appeared below them as huge white-camouflaged horizontal doors slowly opened to reveal its hidden interior. Dropping gracefully onto the heliport that had been revealed, the pilot touched down skillfully and the jets died as the rotors slowed.

When Janice exited, the titanium entrance portal twenty yards above her shut, silently and slowly.

This was her first visit to NHMI's secret world. Though both the CIA and the KGB knew of the NHMI factory, neither realized how big it was nor did they know what was done there. It was imperative that it be kept top secret, this Janice knew. To this end, TerraNova skillfully manipulated governments and their politicians, but it wasn't so easy to control an open press. Generally speaking, though, they were successful.

The plant manager, Ghorki Chenski, whom Janice immediately equated with a barrel, at about five feet six, stood several inches shorter than she did. He had a bureaucrat's belly that was neatly covered inside of his well-made business suit. As he stepped forward to receive her, she saw his mild waddle, which accompanied his every step. Reaching her, he pushed himself up onto tiptoes and he gently kissed her cheek in obedience to protocol. He then arched himself back, trying to compensate for poor posture, and stepping back, he forced a smile through his black eyes. His curly black hair made Janice wonder if he was using a hair coloring, since it looked suspiciously young for the fiftyish folds in his cheeks and brow.

CHENSKI NEARLY TREMBLED: The woman cut an imposing figure, attired in an elegant designer suit that was hemmed somewhere above the knees. Her curricula vitae — economist, linguist, systems analyst, Stanford Business School graduate, etc. — were impressive. However, she had no credentials for inspecting his plant. She had no engineering or scientific degrees; nonetheless he had to accept the fact that, in deference to her skills, Azard himself had sent her. Her position in NHMI gave her authority, which overrode her lack of scientific expertise. However, he couldn't help but ask himself — Why send a person without scientific qualification on such an important mission?

At least Chenski had had time to assemble an honor guard of two score security personnel. They stood at attention in their splendid white dress uniforms.

Ghorki invited Janice to follow him. They exchanged a minimum of small talk, mostly silence, since, frankly, he had no idea what he could say. It was obviously her responsibility to initiate any dialogue they would have. Departing the heliport, they entered a turbolift elevator, which smoothly carried them to a depth of fifty meters.

As soon as the doors opened, he invited her to exit first, which she did. He stepped right behind her, and placed himself at her side. It was but a few steps to his office, which he opened, and Janice entered. He followed, while security guards took positions to the sides.

"Please have a seat," he indicated as he stepped around her.

"Thank you, but I've been sitting all day."

His good English was a common language in which they would communicate. "Would you like to rest from your long trip?" he offered.

"Not yet," Janice answered. "Mr. Chenski, I'm sure you are aware of the reason for my visit."

"Headquarters informed us that you are going to implement some new management procedures."

"Yes. But were you aware that there has been a failure of a product made at this factory. It has caused irreparable damage to our principal account, TerraNova."

"What do you mean? Failure?" he asked, and really, he had no idea. "What failed?"

Janice answered with a voice that gave Ghorki a cold chill. "Mr. Chenski, I am speaking of a three-millimeter polytitanium seal."

He nearly allowed a chuckle to escape, but rapidly caught himself. She was dead serious, but absurd — One of their least complex products being blamed for … for what? He didn't even know the details. Whatever it was, though, it had been important enough to send Ms. Allenburg halfway around the world.

"How can we be of assistance?" Chenski asked, struggling to appear concerned and hiding his cynicism.

As she answered, her hazel eyes conveyed urgency and concern, "I want us to look at the division that makes the polytitanium seals."

The woman knows what she wants! — Chenski decided.

Chapter 14

Silence

SILENCE is the ultimate weapon of power.

— Charles de Gaulle

That same day — Worldwide

YELTSIN is a loose gun. There is little we can do to influence him," Cosmokrator Cyril Cyzack in Brussels retorted to the inference of Karl Rennedy that, possibly, the Committee could eventually control the "careless heavy drinker."

"It took everything we could muster to keep Gorby afloat through the August coup," commented a plainly bald Jacque Savee in Paris. He was tall and athletic, was dressed in a tweed designer suit, and had an imposing authority in his style.

Rennedy, in Toronto, replied, "We know we can manipulate Gorbachev. We've done it repeatedly since '85."

"We did it at the end of last year when we were able to get our Nobel Prize winner to elevate Communist Party loyalists to prominent posts," Watkins interjected.

Irving summarized, "If Gorby loses power, we'll have to deal with Yeltsin. But no one knows what direction he will take."

Watkins answered, "He will do exactly what we wish. We never give his kind anything more than an ultimatum. He will work with us, or we will make his life very difficult, if we even let him live." Hearing the wisdom of Watkins's summary, several chuckled, and all were smugly pleased.

"Gentlemen," Weller interrupted, and he cleared his throat; "let's focus our attention on the real problems that have developed. After all, it doesn't matter whether or not we have Gorby, or Yeltsin; the point is, the present situation is out of our control." He had their attention.

"Our DEEPs can't fly. Without them we'll be forced to sit back and see where all the cards fall. For eight more days we can't do anything. It will take at least that long to finish checking them. Father told us that we're too dependent on Ether Craft. We need other technology, not just DEEPs, and we need more people on the ground. Imagine what might have occurred if some glitch had forced us to ground our DEEPs during the Cuban missile crisis. The fools might have blown up the world with their toy bombs. And just look what happened when we didn't use them, and that blockhead Hussein got his missiles all the way to Tel Aviv. We have worked so hard, trying to get all of the Jews to go to their *precious* homeland so we can implement the Final Solution. Now it will take us who knows how long to get them out of all those prosperous and safe countries they're in now. Enticing them to go to a country where they could easily be gassed or bombed won't be easy. This seal fiasco just makes the whole situation worse. With the demise of Gorby, and the rise of Yeltsin, and who knows what else could happen, perhaps even the fall of the USSR, the level of instability in the world will increase and the rich western Jews will just stay wherever they are. It will take a generation, or more, to repair all of the damage that inflicted seal will have caused."

"Perhaps, Weller," Watkins spoke, "but we needn't be too concerned. Therion himself will draw the Jews back from the Diaspora, according to the ancient prophecies of the Secret Doctrine. He will bring peace and prosperity to those slime, and then, when they think that everything is wonderful, and they have peace and prosperity as never before, he will sacrifice them for greater illumination, and rid himself of their kind, and of their infantile, miserable belief in Asmina."

Weller shook his head in agreement, and said, "You're right, as usual, Watkins. But this seal problem isn't going to go away, and it's going to cost more than a DEEP. You're right, though. Therion, when he comes, will gather the Jews and then exterminate them. Whatever happens now won't ruin us. It's just politics. In a few years we'll have undone the damage, and the Plan will be back on track. We'll win!"

Stonefell thought — The brat's right, as usual, and he invoked his father's ghost in his speech, curse him.

By their silence, it was easy to see that all of the members of the Committee were reflecting on what had just been said. They knew their situation was desperate. They, the all-powerful Committee of TerraNova, had to sit and watch years of hard work go tumbling down. Stonefell, as much as he was loathed to admit it, realized that Weller was right: In the end, it would be little more than politics. So what if the Committee had Gorby, or if they had Yeltsin? Whoever took over command would be theirs!

Without secret DEEP operations, TerraNova wouldn't be able to keep Yeltsin and his hounds at bay. Gorbachev would surely be devoured. Though it probably would have happened anyway, Stonefell figured, and he reasoned — The seal's failure will only bring it about sooner. If we had our DEEPs, we could move agents and equipment and gather information, so we can see what's really happening. True, we have people on the ground, but there are too few of them to find out everything we need to know. And even if we had enough SAOs [He spoke of Special Affairs Operatives, pronounced SAY-Ohs, and sometimes SOWs by those unfortunate enough to be victims of their activity] to put one everywhere, they still couldn't do a DEEP's job. One DEEP in the sky is worth hundreds, or even thousands, of ground agents. A lone DEEP can intercept, decipher, and analyze nearly every communication on a continent. When we know what's happening, we can use our DEEPs to move agents to critical areas. With a DEEP, we can tell who is working against us, or in this case, against Gorby. Then we can DEEP in our SAOs, or fly in a few PARASITES [micromechanical robots] to monitor conversations or assassinate some poor devil by lethal injection. We can give the victim a heart attack, or whatever works best. With a DEEP we can abduct someone, or turn a perfectly sane man into an imbecile. We can manipulate the press and even stuff ballot boxes, alter radio and TV programs to our advantage, and well — Stonefell knew — the list of possibilities was endless.

True, Stonefell knew all of this, but he reviewed it in his mind, trying to think of some way to change the inevitable, that without DEEP flights the world would become a different place. Instability would reign. The USSR could die, and then the world wouldn't be as safe as it had been before TerraNova lost control. Of course, it wouldn't last. The Committee would regain everything it might lose, and achieve greater power in the long run. And also, as Watkins had pointed out, the Cosmokrator really didn't need to be concerned with the present situation. Ultimately, Yeltsin would see things their way, or not see at all!

Already, four days had gone by without Ether Craft — Stonefell observed. Weller is telling us that it will take eight more days before we can deploy the fleet again — twelve days in all. That's a long time! We'll have to be "patient," and wait until the DEEPs are ready to fly. Stonefell knew that patience was something he despised, and something he never practiced.

But there was one thing that concerned him even more than DEEPs and politics. It was that even after numerous petitions, their overlords, the Skotoi, remained silent. It was easy for him, the chairman of the Committee of the Cosmokrator, to feel frustrated.

* * *

That same day — Beneath the Verkhoyansk Mountains, Eastern Siberia

GASKETS AND SEALS of all sizes and shapes abundantly flowed from the machinery. Some were ring-shaped; still others had exotic forms. The metallic plastic from which they were made was an exclusive material of TerraNova's, and outer industry hadn't discovered any process that could produce the substance from which they were made — polytitanium.

"So many seals!" Janice exclaimed.

"There's really quite a variety," Chenski commented, "though no one here knows what TerraNova does with them. We insure that everything we make conforms to manufacturing tolerances, but sometimes the workers complain. They say they would do a better job if they knew what they're making. We tell them that they are parts for Yankee vending machines."

"Do they believe you?"

"Probably not."

"What do they believe?"

"That they get paid well, and that they live well. That's what they believe. And you, Ms. Allenburg, do you know what these products are for?"

"Do you think I would tell you if I knew? TerraNova requires absolute secrecy. We give them what they want, and as you pointed out, they give us what we want — we live well." Then she paused, having caught his eye momentarily. She finished her comment, "I think we've said enough. This subject isn't open for discussion."

Even so, she couldn't help wondering what it was they were really making. In this area of the plant they made polytitanium seals, but what did TerraNova do with them? And what of everything else they made in Siberia? How did they use the sophisticated electronics? Where did they use them? For outside of this Siberian plant, she had never seen them in use, not even at their headquarters in Brussels. It was clear to her that they made many pieces of something, but what could it be?

Obviously there was much more to the puzzle. What she did know was that TerraNova paid well, but it didn't tolerate any errors. She also knew that once the products left the plant through the underground tunnel to the sea, and were loaded onto TerraNova's special submarines at the underwater dock, the workers were paid, and rarely were there any complaints, but when a complaint came forward, Azard took it very seriously. She also knew that everyone who worked for NHMI signed on for life.

However, for now it would be useless for her to continue meditating on questions she couldn't answer, so she devoted her attention to the process, watching with fascination as the shiny black objects moved about the maze of conveyor belts. Chenski drove the electric cart that carried them about the manufacturing area that was larger than a dozen football fields. The last place they visited that day, of the many sites that were found in the enormous underground complex, was the area where seals were manufactured.

Production of polytitanium seals required fewer steps than any of the other operations in the plant, but it still involved ultra-high-tech equipment. Janice had only a superficial understanding of the scientific process employed in making the seals, but for her purpose an exact knowledge wasn't necessary. She knew that the problem was not in the science, or in the technology. The problem was human error; of this she was certain. Why did she have this intuition? In part, from past experiences, and also, from the well-documented fact that humans make mistakes. Janice was convinced that the problem would be found at the point where human fingers were most involved, and having studied a flow chart of the process, she had pinpointed the weakest link — the inspection station — so she asked Chenski to take her there.

When they arrived, there was a technician watching a monitor. Chenski introduced him, a Mr. Lepkov, who was of medium height and had dark hair. Janice asked him, "Could you please explain what you are doing?"

"Certainly," he began. "When the seals come through the quality control checkpoint here, a holographic projection is made onto a screen that allows a three-dimensional view, and a computer analyzes it. If there are defects, the computer sounds an alarm, and it's rejected."

Janice, noticing his casual attitude, interrogated him, "Rejections? How often do you have them?"

"About twenty percent are defective." He then bluntly told her, in a voice that caught her off guard, "Put these on." He passed her a pair of safety glasses, or so they appeared. He added, "With these you'll see the defects." Janice noticed that his movements seemed awkward.

What Janice saw through the glasses was gorgeous. How could a lowly seal be so elegant? When viewed with the special lenses, it no longer looked like a seal, nor did it glisten or appear black, but rather, it looked like a shimmering kaleidoscope. It was truly dazzling and superb in its symmetry; it was astounding.

"The seal you're looking at has been analyzed and approved by our computer. It will now move on for packaging and shipping."

Another seal displayed on the screen, and again it made her feel the same. The image was breathtaking, resplendent with pastel hues. "This beauty is astonishing!"

"The holographic projection and the computer imaging process make it appear in that way," Chenski commented.

Janice examined several more seals, each as beautiful as the preceding. She momentarily lifted the special glasses to see what the screen looked like without them. It was bland. The glasses gave the seal life.

Then another seal moved into her view, and there was a warbling alarm sound. Janice looked, and could see a defect. Through the glasses it looked as deep as the Grand Canyon. The crack was portrayed by stark colors boldly outlining it from the pastel hues that were used by the computer to portray the rest of the seal. Again she checked the monitor without her glasses; the crack wasn't visible.

"That alarm means that the computer is going to reject this seal. I'm sure you can see why," the technician said.

"Yes, with these glasses it's easy to see the defect."

"Yes," the technician confirmed.

"What happens to it now?" Janice asked as she turned and looked into the technician's blue eyes.

He answered, "Unless I override, it will be routed back for reprocessing."

She suddenly caught an odor in his breath — a smell. She knew it! It was alcohol. "Why would you override, if the computer rejected it?"

"Sometimes the computer makes mistakes."

"It does?" Janice asked.

"Yeah, it can."

"How's that?"

"There can be dirt on the lenses and we don't want to stop the line to clean them because we might not reach our quota. A circuit could fail; there can be power supply fluctuations sometimes. Sometimes raw materials get contaminated. Really, there's a lot that can go wrong."

"And then you personally make the decision when the alarm sounds?"

"Yes, ma'am."

"The computer analysis is not foolproof," Janice said, "and you never make a mistake." She smiled briefly, indicating that her words weren't to be taken seriously.

"Anyone can see how clearly the flaws appear."

The arrogance of this ignoramus — Janice thought. Thinks he is unable to make any mistakes! She glanced around, trying to see where he might have hidden his alcohol. The room was empty and uniformly painted silver gray. There was a cabinet under the monitor. Knowing that her sense of smell wasn't fooling her, she reached down and attempted to open the swinging door. She saw how startled Lepkov looked. The cabinet was locked.

"That's where I keep my lunch and some books given to us by Novus Ordo," Lepkov said.

"Really?"

There was a pause, and silence. Lepkov looked down briefly, and then to the side, before looking back at Janice. "Of course. What else would be there?" he said with a smile that he tacked on as if it was a last-minute Post-it note.

"Fine, Mr. Lepkov. Then you shouldn't mind opening it."

Lepkov slowly reached for a chain around his neck, from which hung a small electronic key (a computer chip). He bent down, blocking her view, and opened the cabinet. Standing back awkwardly, he announced, "See. My lunch box, as I said."

Looking on, Chenski smiled, as if to say, "Okay, woman, enough."

Janice hadn't finished, and she said, "Mr. Lepkov, I'm not easily fooled. I can smell the alcohol on your breath. You have a bottle of vodka behind your back. Hand it over!"

The technician shrugged his shoulders, and started to speak in his defense, "So what's a little vodka? It helps me pay attention."

Janice remembered an old proverb: A fish is caught by its own mouth.

Upon hearing Lepkov's words, Chenski turned pale and sweat broke out on his forehead. He looked like a man who had seen a ghost. Janice knew he was afraid he would be held responsible for failing to supervise his workers.

Chenski blurted out, "Lepkov, fool! Don't you understand that you need to have good reflexes to operate this inspection? I'm sure you know that drinking while on duty is a sanctionable offense." He added, "I will see to it that you are censured."

Lepkov laughed with disrespect and said, "If you're going to censure me, you should also check the rest of your technicians. There's nothing for a man to do in this underground prison. I'm lucid compared to the rest of your people, and you know it! You simply ignore us as long as we meet your quotas."

"Lepkov, you're in serious trouble! You would do well to be silent," Chenski demanded.

"What are you saying, Mr. Chenski?" Janice asked. "Are you afraid that Mr. Lepkov might say something to embarrass you further?"

Chenski swallowed, and Janice noticed. He answered, "Ms. Allenburg, I'm sorry, but I have nothing to fear from this drunkard. I'm simply letting him know that he won't escape sanctions. And yes, so long as quotas are met, why would I concern myself — searching for hidden bottles of vodka? I believe this is the first time that we have a reason that justifies such a search, and with Lepkov's revelation, I will order an immediate search of all personnel in the plant."

Lepkov looked at Chenski and made a muffled noise that sounded like a hiss mixed with a snarl. Then he turned to Janice and said, "You're too beautiful of a woman to be in this forsaken pit twenty stories beneath the frozen tundra. I regret that you find my vodka offensive; I would have enjoyed sharing a cup with you. And what are these cursed seals used for? Why are they so important?"

"Mr. Lepkov," Janice spoke, addressing him directly and with formality, "you are a fool. You might as well finish your bottle. You are no longer an employee of our company. You'll be fortunate if you don't find yourself in your own forsaken pit. I hope you find some consolation in your intoxication." She handed the bottle back to him. He took the half-empty bottle from her and held it, as he stood silently.

Janice noticed his reddened nose and wondered how much his liver, as well as his mind, had been affected.

* * *

The Pacific Ocean

"Chief, we're at the last known coordinates. There's no signal," the Beta Force captain advised.

"Can't you do an ionic-meson scan?" Jones demanded.

"Yes, sir. We've done that," answered the captain, "but as you know, without a DEEP's hyperdimensional enhancements, we only have a two-square-kilometer range from our last reading. Against the current and winds, and the drifting craft, our chances of finding it are infinitesimally small. Besides, Chief, at this point it's more likely we'll find the RSB on the bottom of the ocean, and not floating at all."

"Well, then," Jones ordered, "I suggest you find it, wherever the odious thing may be." She looked at the captain in a way that made him wonder if the blond could scare away sharks.

Chapter 15

Survival

THE THINNER the ice, the more anxious is everyone to see whether it will bear.

— Josh Billings

That same day — Mount Antisana, Ecuador

JAMES still spent most of his time sleeping. For his few waking hours, he had some painkillers in the first-aid bag, and they helped, but not nearly enough.

Designers of the RSB had made the assumption that it would be used solely for survival at sea, and so they had included a portable personal distillery — which amounted to little more than plastics bags held up by a folding mechanism and a cup that collected the water that evaporated and condensed on the plastic. It worked best in bright sunlight. It could keep a small supply of fresh water available indefinitely and had been intended for use with salt water, but James realized that he could put the muddy slosh that was all around him, created by constant runoff from the glacier, into the distillery. It worked, and gave him a source of fresh water.

However, he was quickly running out of rations. The RSB carried basic survival gear: a line, a net, and other items for fishing, but there were few protein bars and he would run out soon.

He couldn't remain there much longer without more provisions. The PLOT showed him that down the slopes and towards the west he would find civilization within thirty kilometers (more than a day's walk in his present condition), making it seem farther away than Mars.

With the afternoon sun beating down upon him, his thoughts slowly scrambled into a compulsive sleep, a sleep that was aided by the calm mountain air. Snowcapped mountains usually have a climate that is unstable and violent, and there had been few times in history that the weather on the slopes of Antisana had been as merciful, but for now, the climate was kind.

* * *

The Pacific Ocean

How much longer can I keep this up? — Ashley could barely question herself. She wanted to sleep, but couldn't. Drenching rain poured; the sea tossed and churned, and she could do nothing but bail fresh rainwater hour after agonizing hour using an empty container from her emergency rations. It was all she could do to keep up with the storm and stay afloat. She was exhausted and it was twenty-eight hours since she last slept.

It's probably some tropical depression and it's going to drown me if it can — she thought. I can't even see — she complained to herself. Her emergency light had run out of power, and her vision enhancements were nearly useless in the driving rain.

At least this is better than treading water with the sharks — she decided. I've got to keep going. This much rain isn't normal. It's got to stop soon. If only I could rig up a roof. But this thing will sink if I try to get to the material below. Why didn't the tech wizards field-test it? Maybe they never thought of rain? They must have been on Mars. Was it so much trouble just to think of rain? Wasn't Nancy a part of the group that designed this stuff? If I ever see her again … I'll drown her; I'll be *inflicted* if I don't. They're so invested! So Alpha! Ha! A night in a mid-ocean storm would cause them more terror than an infliction!

* * *

The next day — Mount Antisana, Ecuador

IT LOOKS like the climate's going to change — James thought. I'll dig out a place to collect some water. I can line it with RSB material. By morning I'll have enough rainwater collected for a day or two — he hoped, since the distillery wasn't able to produce much water from the slush, and because there hadn't been much sunlight.

James understood that the mountain's peak — a massive glacier — was an excellent snow and rain generation system. The mountain had treated him well, but he knew it couldn't last much longer, and it didn't. Hurricane-force wind ripped through the area and ruined his small rain-collection furrow. Powerful gusts would have taken his RSB, with him in it, but his friend, the boulder, blocked the wind sufficiently to save him.

It was biting, and it roared and howled as hammering cold rain hit him like icy needles. The wind was bitterly cold. Antisana wasn't hospitable, and it began to appear that it might be able to finish the job of killing him that DEEP 1 had failed to accomplish.

Drifting in and out of restless sleep, he had nightmares — falling and crashing. Then he would wake up. His nightmares were intense — and real. One was so vivid, he woke up altogether disoriented to the howl of the night's wind and feverishly fought to get out of the RSB, but unable to get free, he finally awakened to the sting of rain pellets.

Once aroused, he remembered words he had read in the forgotten tract: "In the Whale's Belly." They were words that he never planned to remember, but he did. He even said them aloud, "In my distress I called to the LORD, and He answered me." He thought — That's stupid. How can you call on God? — With a telephone? Does He have a satellite connection? Or does He use direct molecular stimulation? Does He exist in cyberspace, like the Skotoi? With so many outers calling Him all the time, how can He handle them all? And, would He even bother to listen to me? I'm not an outer. God is part of outer culture, like rock, hot dogs, and politics.

He chuckled to himself — Maybe the voice that told me I would live was that outer God speaking to me on the "phone," and He got me out of the DEEP just to murder me on this forsaken mountain. He laughed to himself. Sounds like an outer joke. Maybe that's what I've become: an outers' joke — a genetically engineered bioelectronic freak who crashed into a boulder. At this point, I'd be better off dead, but the outers' God has kept me alive to inflict me. The idea seemed humorous and somber. It made him want to laugh and cry — all at once.

Ashamed of his sarcasm, he realized he was glad to be alive, and it seemed that the outer God had, in some way, helped him. Besides, the pain of a storm isn't as bad as that of an infliction — even if it kills me — he mused. There was something within him that really wanted to believe in the existence of a Supreme Being: a being who was more than some "highly evolved entity."

Finally, the torment of the storm became so great he mumbled aloud, "God, if You're real, save me."

He drifted back to sleep, despite the storm, and when he awoke, the sun shone clear in a cloudless sky. The night's events had faded from his memory, and he had forgotten them — like a dream. Their memory was burned away with the daylight.

Later, in the morning, with blustery gusts of wind blowing against him, and looking towards the glacier above him, he saw abundant clouds beginning to form. From the view, he reckoned that more of last night's weather would be coming. He thought — Down the mountain a few thousand feet it will be much better.

The day brought renewed strength to his body, and his leg didn't hurt as much as it did before. It was a good opportunity to change his campsite, but the RSB was too large and too heavy to carry, so he took his hunting knife and cut a considerable piece of material from its internal wall. It would be useful as a blanket. Cutting the exterior was impossible.

Desperately, he tried to find something to use as a splint, but even with his enhancements he couldn't break the pack's special titanium frame. Inside of the RSB he found nothing, just the wide straps that formed the suspension unit and controlled its shape during reentry. He cut a long piece and used it to wrap his ankle, giving him some support.

There would be a few hours of good weather — he thought. Then something occurred to him — What if they're looking for me? The RSB will catch their attention. And it might catch an outer's eye too. With that possibility in mind, he recovered his backpack and loaded it with those things he might need, stowing the piece of RSB he had cut, and taking particular care to return the PLOT to its special pocket. After crumpling the RSB, he began to kick black volcanic sand over its shiny surface and buried it near the base of the boulder — concealing it as much as possible.

It made him think — as he kicked dirt over it with his good foot — I'm lucky! My body should have been in that bag and this rock should have been my headstone. It's sort of like I'm burying myself. And he considered — I am, sort of, burying Alpha Force's James Smith.

He felt strange: Acting free; like he really didn't want to, but despite the contradiction, he loved it, and he wondered — Could I be free? Really free?

With steps of burning pain, James began making his way down the slope. It would be a steep descent — he could tell from the PLOT — and he would have to climb in and out of canyons and gullies.

Brilliant morning sunlight penetrated the thin air and warmed him as he made his way slowly around the boulder, towards the west. It wasn't easy. His bioenhancements seemed to be functioning normally, but his body wasn't. Pain came with every movement. He couldn't allow himself to think about it, or it would sap his strength.

If his trek thus far hadn't been easy — only around the boulder about twenty yards — it soon became extremely laborious. Standing by the edge, he looked a hundred feet, or more, down into the gully. The descent would be difficult. If he reached the bottom, without falling, he would have to climb out. He sat down and removed the PLOT from his pack, and began searching for a better route. Carefully studying the map, he decided that there wasn't a better way. He would ignore the horror of it, though not because of any fear of heights — he had none — but because of his physical debility. He began the descent; he had no choice.

Treading meticulously like a cat on the soft material, straining to find the hardest rock to support his weight, it took James far more time to descend than he had anticipated. He knew, if he could have taken the pain, his nerve pulse accelerators would have helped him move much faster, but his body was demonstrating its frailty.

Having made it to the bottom, he contemplated the ascent, thinking it might be easier than the descent. But he soon discovered that he was mistaken. The soil and rock were sandy. Each step forward became three backwards, and in his condition each step was agonizing. He crossed the immense gully, its walls so steep, and he wondered more than once — How will I make it out of here?

There wasn't any good way around the mountain; the PLOT made that fact entirely clear. Not only was it impossible to find a good route, but the weathered rock broke apart quickly. Mountain climbers would say it was "rotten."

As the day wore on, he only managed to cross two smaller gullies; each one was over a hundred feet deep. He desperately needed something to use as a crutch, and indeed, there were places where he used his pack — as best he could — for that job. At times its titanium frame served as a walking stick, and at times it helped — to a small degree — as a support, allowing him to push himself up the bank backwards.

Trying to ascend out of the third gully, he became weak and careless. Seeing his proximity to the edge, near the top of the wall, he forced himself harder, working up a good sweat — clawing his way up and kicking with his good foot. At one point, perspiration on his brow fell into his eyes and blurred his vision. Perhaps because he couldn't see well, or because he had become increasingly careless, he missed the right hold, and to complicate his mistake, he clutched the rock so hard that it suddenly broke loose.

He tumbled backwards, falling, his feet following his head; even with enhanced inner ear processors and accelerated nerve-pulse injectors, he couldn't get his balance — he was too weak. Normally he would have been like a cat, landing on his feet, but he kept falling. He tumbled several times, bruising and scraping himself against the cutting rock, but he didn't have time to feel any new pains. He strove, using his enhancements and muscles, to latch onto something — anything at all. As he pitched backwards, his backpack ripped from his shoulders just before he came to a precarious rest on a narrow ledge. The pack kept falling. He watched it. His heart fell with it. Tumbling, it kept on moving, downwards into the chasm. It plunged so fast and so freely that it looked to him like it might have been enhanced. It kept on, and its sound — muffled blows mixed with jingling and ringing — laughed back at him, as if it was scoffing at him, echoing with each tumble, thrashing loose, scabrous rock, and falling deep into the gully — at least thirty yards below.

"Inflict it!" he swore aloud. Now he would have to climb down after the runaway backpack, and he hoped the PLOT had survived the fall.

However, he hadn't yet determined if his own body would move any farther, and lying there on the ledge, the damp rock under him and the chilling air around him, his body soaked in sweat, he knew that he had to have the piece of RSB material that he had cut for a blanket and that was still in the fallen backpack, lest hypothermia finish what the crash had started: ridiculing him in his newly found freedom.

Thick clouds had descended into the canyon. A dismal gray mist surrounded him, and visibility wasn't much more than an arm's length. Soon it would be night.

* * *

The Verkhoyansk Mountains, Eastern Siberia

JANICE RETIRED to her quarters far below the snows of Siberia. The local time, 10:25 AM, wasn't important — her body-time (circadian rhythm) was set at an exhausting 2:25 AM. She felt no rest. The time for relaxing had come and had gone.

Question upon question kept coming to her mind: What is TerraNova? Is NHMI really just a part of Terra Nova? Does Azard know more about the TerraNova account than I? How can you manufacture pieces if you don't know where they fit, and can't try them out as a functioning unit? Mine is not to reason why; mine is but to do or die — she mused. But Tennyson had something more concrete in mind: soldiers facing guns and death. This is a different proposition. Or is it? Azard said that death is the only way to leave NHMI. So maybe, in that sense, I'm in my own charge of the light brigade.

What a long day. Tossing to one side, and then turning to the other, she waited for restful sleep to come upon her, but its repose eluded her.

After some time, she got out of bed to meditate. Sitting on the carpet in the lotus position, she tried to focus on thoughts of peace, but it was useless. Taking a few deep breaths, she invited her body and soul to relax, but they didn't like the idea. Inviting each part of her body to slacken, she sought a place of peace. It took some time, but eventually she met her inner adviser as she had done on other occasions — but something was wrong. It didn't greet her. It didn't look at her, but rather, after only moments, it turned around and walked away. She wanted to run after it, but couldn't. She was helpless. Then she felt someone was touching her from behind — fingers, chilling fingers — daintily creeping over her flesh. She couldn't turn. The touch was Uncle Ralph's. Her dignity melted. Her feet rushed, running as hard as they could, escaping, but the fingers continued, slithering over her flesh — many fingers — vile, creeping fingers. She was powerless to escape the repulsive touch. The fingers warmed. And warmed. They caressed her, and they felt good. But they warmed, hotter and hotter, until they burned streaks in her skin

—penetrating deeper. She screamed! And then snapped out of her trance. Her heart pounded, as if she was running a marathon.

She felt herself a wreck, and shaking all over, she went to get some mineral water from the bar, feeling as if a herd of buffalo had trampled her. Beads of perspiration had popped out all over her, but now the burning hot fingers became flames — shooting up and burning her flesh. The heat was intense. Am I still sane? — she asked herself. She didn't understand, couldn't understand, but somehow — she knew — she was seeing her future.

As the intensity grew, she began to shake uncontrollably, and she dropped the glass of mineral water and it shattered into pieces. The shock of the crystal breaking brought her back to herself. Walking over to the lounge chair, she sat down with a look of emptiness. Sobbing like a child, she cried and cried. Her tears flowed, and the torment continued, but now it was the torment of her own shame.

Janice felt raped! It vexed her, for the memory of Uncle Ralph, and his abuse, had been awakened. But she would keep up her show, concealing her shame and the secrets of her childhood. She wept herself into a tormented sleep.

* * *

Mount Antisana, Ecuador

SCRAPED AND BLOODIED, there was hardly an area on his body that the fall hadn't injured, but James was fortunate: He had no broken bones.

This ledge isn't wide enough. I've got to position myself better — he thought. I'm getting weaker and the only rations I have are in the backpack. He looked up and saw dark clouds — now blackening, and he concluded — All I need is to get caught in a storm. Already, he could feel that the temperature had dropped about twenty degrees since he had descended into the gully.

The blood on his half dozen, or so, larger lacerations had barely dried. I've got to go back down there after the pack. I've got to keep my focus — he told himself. I have to recover my backpack. With calculated precision, he righted himself, found a foothold, and began to descend the treacherous incline. He wondered, as he had from the beginning — Will I slip and fall into the canyon?

* * *

The Pacific Ocean

INHALED SALT WATER made her cough and choke, and awakened her rudely. Ashley suddenly struggled and kicked. She splashed water in desperation, and then began to tread water again. It had all happened so abruptly.

In the dark and heavy rain she was still able to catch a dismal flicker of the lifeboat with vision enhancements. She told herself — I have to get it. She began to swim towards the glimmer, but the dark and the waves were against her. As she swam with her electromechanical strength against the waves, the pounding rain and the darkness fought against her, and the boat was getting farther away.

Coughing, she paused, and began treading water again. She thought — I must've gone to sleep and was thrown into the ocean. She caught one more glimpse of the boat and began swimming with all her strength.

But her every stroke was challenged by the large swells that tossed her about and, disoriented, she lost sight of the RSB boat. By the time she saw it again, it was even farther away. Again, she began to swim as hard as she could. It was a question of life or death.

Even as she fought with powerful strokes, she began to doubt that she could make it to the RSB; but she told herself — I've got to make it! And so she swam on with resolve.

* * *

Mount Antisana, Ecuador

ALTHOUGH JAMES sometimes stumbled on the treacherous jagged rock, he had managed to keep from falling again. Since his vision enhancements were working, he was able to see in the dark gloom, and was able to continue his descent to the bottom of the canyon, the place where his backpack had fallen. He finally recovered it. Fortunately, when the pack had fallen into the canyon, when it had been rent from his back, its contents hadn't been thrown out.

He might have checked the PLOT first thing to see if it was still in working order, but drops of freezing rain and hail stung his face. And though he needed to rest more than anything else, he couldn't rest there. Flooding in the gully was likely, he could tell by the erosion. He would have to climb up the canyon wall a few yards and find a spot where the coming deluge of runoff water wouldn't reach him.

Having seen the erosion, feeling the hard rain and hail, he grabbed the RSB material from his pack, wrapped his head and shoulders, and began to find his way back up the slope. It wouldn't be long until a torrent of water would sweep down the mountain and fill the gully.

Hail rapidly began to build up, finding places to rest among the rocks and gravel, even after having bounced a few times. But the cliff of the canyon wall was so steep that James wondered how the hail could stick at all. The icy pellets added misery to his effort.

He reached a ledge that was just big enough for him to sit. Will this rotten rock hold me? — he questioned, and he slowly sat down on it, leaning against the gully's wall. He was drenched and cold. He removed the piece of RSB material he had cut to use for a blanket from his backpack and wrapped it around his head and shoulders and cloaked his body.

There wasn't any reason to worry about water. He had left the distillery behind, figuring that the water in his canteen would last long enough for him to find some, and indeed, he'd found plenty!

He listened to the clamor of the hail hitting the metallic blanket about his head, but his hearing enhancements removed much of the roar and he only heard a soft murmur, like a brook. This, combined with the warmth he was beginning to feel in spite of his soggy garments, relaxed him, and soon he felt sleepy.

Here, he would bivouac. It would be a long night — cold and wet.

* * *

The next day — The Pacific Ocean

ASHLEY DIDN'T know how much longer she would be able to stay awake. Dawn's early rose-colored light revealed that fact, and the storm had passed, but her RSB lifeboat couldn't be seen anywhere. She had jumped as high as she could in the water, kicking and pushing herself up with strong strokes, trying to see a little farther out, but the storm had done its damage and carried the RSB lifeboat beyond her view. While still in the dark and treading water, when she had first fallen out of the lifeboat, and after she had given up trying to recover it, she had tied knots in the legs of her jumpsuit so she could use it to help keep herself afloat. She pulled it through the air to inflate it, which would give her two or three minutes of buoyancy before the air leaked through the material. Then repeating the same process, she would fill the jumpsuit again — just as she had learned in survival classes.

She figured that she must have gone to sleep and the storm had thrown her from the lifeboat. Exhaustion and exposure were serious enemies, and soon the sun would be beating down and scorching her. Without sunscreen, and with her jumpsuit being used as a flotation device, she had precious little to protect her from the intense sun.

Her only goal was to stay alive, a moment at a time. Exhausted, and frightened by her present circumstances, she had only one thought — I'm going to die. She wondered — Is there a God who can save me?

Certainly the only gods she knew would rather see her dead. Obviously, the Skotoi had done nothing for her.

She told herself in a feeble voice — I'm so thirsty. I'm going to dehydrate, and the day hasn't even begun. I'm going to die out here. But then she took courage, though not sure why, and thought — I can't give up yet. She silently chuckled, as she remembered her sick joke — the trucks weren't waiting. Inflict them.

* * *

Mount Antisana, Ecuador

IT WAS COLD! Even with his vision enhancements, James could only see about three yards through the fog. He couldn't climb while he was inside of the blanket, but he didn't like the idea of having to face the terrible cold. However, he knew he had to get down the mountain soon, but before he would be able to descend, he would need to climb out of the gully. The PLOT indicated that if he followed this gully down, it would take him into the jungle, and that the walls would only become higher and steeper. He had to climb from where he was.

He was starving, but he had water — plenty of water — he told himself with a laugh. After taking several gulps he began to climb, trying not to shiver. He needed to be as steady as possible. His jumpsuit was still damp, though, and with the near freezing air, he found himself unable to stop trembling. He took the blanket and with his hunting knife he cut a couple of holes for his arms and another for his head, and then pulled the "coat" over himself. It worked too well, and soon he was drenched with sweat.

He pushed himself upwards, thinking about every step. He couldn't go too fast, though, for fear of breaking more rock and falling again. As the morning progressed, the heavy fog began to lift. It had been a struggle to climb, but he reached the ledge of the canyon and pulled himself to the top. Without enhancements he wouldn't have been able to have made the climb. He would have died below.

It was turning into a brilliant morning, and warming air pushed the fog away. A panorama opened before him. There were valleys with clouds hanging on the surrounding ridges and another snowcap — not so far away. Of more than passing beauty, there was a lake that had formed when billowing folds of lava blocked the course of a stream. It seemed to be right at his feet. He checked its location on the PLOT and found that its name was "La Mica" and it was about twelve kilometers away. That meant, in his present condition, that it would be a three- or four-hour walk, if all went well.

He could see a small town that was about twenty kilometers away. It looked as if there was a country path leading from the lake to the community. Taking a moment to compare his observation with the PLOT, he determined that the village was Talontag. He saw that there would be two more gullies, but they weren't as deep as the one he had just passed.

He continued down the treacherous slope. Why did I survive? — he asked himself. Reasoning with the circumstantial evidence he had, he came up with a likely scenario, and told himself — Yes, seven seconds of delay brought me over the Andes. Yes, the explosion deflected me. Yes, deep snow made up for the lack of water and cushioned my fall — but I should have died! I was lucky — really lucky.

It was midday as he came out of the second gully, and when he looked up, he saw the lake was much nearer. He still had a long way to go, but it had been an easy trip and time had gone by quickly.

As he walked, now on easier terrain, he remembered the night he had called out to God. But now, looking back, he wasn't sure he had actually prayed at all. It must have been nothing more than a terrible dream — he decided. The storm was probably only a nightmare — he rationalized. God was Jonah's answer, not mine. Though he wondered, as his black ankle-high general-issue boots slipped on the ash and sand, if the outer God made everything — the condor and the sun — like they said. Then he asked himself — Why am I having such ridiculous thoughts? I've got to get my mind on something else. And he started thinking about Ashley. Oh, Ashley… Ashley…

Later, before reaching the lake, now walking in tall grass, he met another obstacle that had been hidden behind a rise. It was a rushing torrent in a shallow channel. There was some white water. It looked as though it would be difficult to cross at that point, so he decided to follow the course.

After a quarter of an hour walking downstream he found a rope stretched over a log that extended over the stream. It wasn't the Golden Gate, but it would do. Balancing himself on the log, and holding to the rope, he reached the other side without difficulty and, getting his bearings, walked towards the lake. In short order, he reached another torrent that was swifter than the first one.

Again, he decided to look farther downstream, hoping to find another crossing like the first. Tall, stiff grass that was growing in clumps made his track difficult. After walking another quarter of an hour, a primitive bridge came into view and he crossed the second stream. James thought, in response to his stomach — It can't be far to the lake. I'll go fishing when I get there.

Twenty minutes later he arrived at La Mica. The lake was large enough that, even with enhancements, he wouldn't be able to throw a stone across it. Beside the lake was a pine forest. All of the trees were in perfect rows, as if they had been purposefully cultivated. Then James realized that there wasn't any other forest around, only tall, stiff grass. Because of the uniformity, it was apparent to him that human hands had cultivated this forest. Indeed, back on the mountain there hadn't been any trees, and for that matter, there hadn't been any plants at all. Seeing vegetation was refreshing.

It was overcast and rain was again imminent, so James decided to start a fire before nightfall and, perhaps, before the rain. With his hunting knife he prepared the wood and, using waterproof matches from the survival kit, he soon had a fire.

Motivated by the thought of fresh fish, and looking towards the lake from his chosen campsite, he removed his hook and line from the survival kit and attached them to the rod. Digging near the lake with his knife, he found some earthworms; using them for bait, James caught several trout.

That night, after he cooked a hot meal on the open fire and warmed himself, he retired into his blanket. Despite the pain in his left leg, he was feeling better, and though it was a miserable night, he didn't have any trouble sleeping. He didn't even notice the gentle rain and the cold night air. It wasn't Novus Ordo, but the material he had cut from the RSB made a good blanket and was a great insulator. It was also waterproof. He was able to stretch out, which was better than sitting up all night as he had on the ledge.

Chapter 16

Scrambled

"PEOPLE ARE NAIVE; they don't believe we exist, or that governments can keep secrets."

> — Cosmokrator Karl Rennedy, commenting on people's rejection
> of conspiracy hypotheses

EVEN WITH THE DISADVANTAGES of extreme secrecy, it works. No one knew about the A-bomb until the day it fell on Hiroshima. Even with workers numbering in the tens of thousands, the whole scheme was kept secret and those working in the various stages of manufacturing didn't know what they were making until they saw the headlines. The Manhattan Project was kept secret by a government that had not been good at keeping secrets.

> — *NewsWorld*, "Fifty Years after the Holocaust, at Ground Zero," 1995

DURING THE LAST forty years nuclear experiments on human beings have been carried out without consent and in absolute secrecy — despite hundreds of deaths.

> — *Our Times Newspaper*, "Concealed Radiation," from an article about unknowing victims of
> nuclear experimentation, 1994

The next day — The Verkhoyansk Mountains, Eastern Siberia

MR. CHENSKI, I will have this operation placed under new management immediately if there are any more negative incidents," Janice advised, solemnly.

Chenski responded, "We will make corrections, as you have ordered. We will also make security inspections for alcohol, and random blood tests." He felt himself twitch involuntarily, and with the high key of his voice, he knew his efforts to hide his nerves had been wasted.

Chenski knew it was really his failure to enforce rules that had led to the careless and slipshod quality control. He had known that there was a problem with alcohol, but he had chosen to ignore it. He hadn't imagined that Ms. Allenburg would be so astute. She had seen the problem immediately.

In her briefing, she set a date for the procedural corrections to be made, and scheduled a return inspection. Chenski felt like a mouse, and the cat, Ms. Allenburg, was ready to pounce.

During the past several days that she had been going around the installation, she had found seventy-eight separate deficiencies, each of which would require countless hours to correct, not to mention implementing security inspections of the workers. This would not help his popularity in the plant. He had been popping antacids like candy, and wondered if he wouldn't end up with an ulcer. He was relieved it was her last day, and especially relieved when he heard the words, "I will be leaving in an hour."

He watched her stride confidently out of his office. The instant she exited, his nerves on edge and shaking like a junkie, he tried to remove a tablet from his desk drawer. It slipped from his fingers and dropped silently into the plush cream carpet, where it nearly vanished, but he recovered the pill that he desperately needed to calm his torrid stomach and downed it, along with a fiber or so of carpet pile. She's gone — he thought with relief.

JANICE WAS EAGER to get back to Brussels. The first night's bad dream had left her psyche in a shambles and she would never forget the vision of Uncle Ralph's slithering hands, and the torturing flames. In minutes she would leave the underground technological palace for fresh air. Her visit had been unpleasant from the beginning, but it had pleased Arlien. Hearing the report of his company's incompetence had made him furious. Heads would roll; he would see to that!

In their last conversation, a passing statement from Arlien to Janice warned her to be careful because the Soviet Union was changing so quickly, and it seemed as if "someone" had lost control. He expressed distaste for "this new Yeltsin guy. You don't know what the power-hungry heel will do next," was one of his milder sentiments.

Saving her last memorandum on the hard disk and shutting off her notebook computer, Janice gathered her things and packed hurriedly. An hour had gone by quickly. Chenski called at the door as she finished. "May I help you?" he asked as she emerged from the guest quarters.

"I have everything — thank you."

Soon they were in the elevator accelerating towards the heliport. Chenski commented, "I hope you enjoyed your stay, Ms. Allenburg."

Janice turned her head slightly, "Mr. Chenski, thank you. The accommodations and the food were excellent." She believed in giving credit where due, and could see that her positive remark surprised him.

When the elevator doors opened to cooler air, it made her remember that she was in Siberia, and she wished she had worn a longer coat. She turned and started walking towards the helicopter. Her footsteps echoed in the stadium-sized subterranean structure and mixed with a rumble, as the massive upper horizontal doors rolled back.

Walking to the helicopter, her heels clicked across the hardened epoxy surface. Suddenly, and without warning, deafening blasts replaced the silence. Flames erupted! It was a firefight!

Elite Russian troops rappelled on nylon gold-line ropes and glided down into the heliport. The heliport's large horizontal gates continued to open. The battle rapidly escalated, and tracers from fired ordnance filled the air. The operator in the control cabin started to reverse the gates, to close them, but the doors had barely reversed direction when a projectile pierced his cabin and exploded, eliminating him and most of his controls. As a result, the gates stopped dead, leaving the heliport open to the frigid Arctic air and to the view of the dull white slopes that surrounded the heliport entrance.

As the battle quickly intensified, Janice panicked, and didn't know where to hide. She thought — I'll escape in the helicopter — and she clutched her bag and started running towards the flying machine that had started its rotors gyrating, but she was still a long way off.

Then, suddenly, a fireball bloomed and replaced the helicopter with a flaming heap of ruin. The shock wave threw Janice back, and flying pieces of shrapnel from the exploding helicopter hit her. Her body withered under her. Flames licked out from the explosion and ignited her choice black coat. Darkness closed in upon her as tormenting flames shot up around her. It was her vision all over, but now vivid and ardently real. Overwhelming pain enveloped her frail body that was fallen on the cold floor.

CHENSKI MANAGED to retreat to the depths and inform Brussels. He also dispatched security forces through the service elevator; but the process was slow. At least another minute would pass before they would be able to reinforce their fallen comrades.

One brave NHMI guard, who had been in the heliport when the fight began, reached Janice moments after the explosion and rolled her on the high-impact floor, out of the fray, and extinguished her flaming clothing. He ripped her coat — what was left of it — from her, leaving her suit exposed, but he decided not to tear what remained of it — carbonized slush — for fear of pulling away flesh. There was a fire hose nearby and, cracking the glass open, he pulled it out and dowsed her, using a minimum of pressure from the valve. He then pulled her, by her outstretched arms — stomach down, as gently as possible — across the smooth floor into a service room. The explosion had badly burned her entire back, along with the backs of her legs and arms, and even the back of her head. At least she had managed to turn around before the full force of the fire burst had hit her, and fortunately, even though she had a few wounds from shrapnel, they had been small pieces. She wasn't bleeding excessively. However, she was losing large amounts of body fluids and electrolytes through the oozing burns. The guard assessed that she would soon be in shock, and he wondered if she could live, even if she received immediate help.

NHMI's security forces were well trained, but not really prepared for combat. Because of the scope of the Siberian operation there was a large contingency stationed in the plant for internal security purposes (like dealing with Lepkov's bottle), but they had never expected to fight an organized army. The invaders badly outnumbered and outgunned them. Besides, Russia was their host, and should offer them protection — not attack them. By themselves, it was unlikely they would be able to repel their attackers. Their number, at most, was two hundred. The Russians had far more personnel.

Chenski wondered what had happened. Why hadn't he been informed? Why were the Russians attacking? Did it have something to do with the new president, Yeltsin? Had Yeltsin thought that since NHMI was a foreign operation, he would take command? Chenski knew that they could evacuate to the sea through the underground shipping tunnel in a high-speed levitated grotto train, if they had to, but allowing the aggressors to have the plant would represent an incalculable tactical and financial loss for NHMI — and he would be held responsible. Curse them! — he thought — What did I have to do with this mess?

Fighting continued as NHMI's troops defended the heliport. They had managed to keep the Russians from easily taking the plant. Already a dozen Russians had rappelled into the heliport, but one of the NHMI guards, who had been able get his rifle, had shot many of them while they were still on the ropes. But the attacking Russians also had sharpshooters, and had reduced the number of NHMI guards left in the heliport to a half dozen.

A contingency of fifty NHMI personnel stood poised and ready to storm out of the service elevator, but a Russian soldier, who was capped and dressed in white camouflage, as were the rest, wasn't asleep, and wasted about fifteen unfortunate souls with his rocket-propelled grenade launcher the instant the doors opened. The rest charged into battle and escaped the blast, moving into defensible positions with fresh firepower. Flames created the appearance of an infernal spectacle, scorching and dancing in the heliport's open pit, like a volcano's crater in the frozen twilight. An orange-red glow reflected on the snowy slopes, and billows of acrid smoke slowly ascended into the frozen, dull Arctic sky, as the Russians continued their attack.

* * *

Brussels, Belgium

It was 4:00 AM, and a loud ring awakened Arlien.

Chenski was panicking. "They're attacking! Russian soldiers are attacking! They've hit Ms. Allenburg. The heliport is a ruin, and the service elevator is out. We can't send more reinforcements."

Arlien was having trouble believing his ears. It can't be — he told himself. Why didn't we see it coming? TerraNova always keeps me informed. What happened to our intelligence operatives?

Arlien kept Chenski on one line and went to another phone that was reserved for emergencies. On the touch pad, he hit a button that played a nonmelodious eighteen-digit tune. He worried — How bad is Janice?

On the other end of the line, a person unknown and unidentified to him answered, "Yes."

"We're under siege!" Arlien exclaimed in a rage.

"Where?"

"Don't you know?" Arlien blasted back, adding a swearword, "NHMI Siberia! My people are being wiped out. Do something. My right-hand woman is down."

Arlien ordered Chenski to hold out until help arrived. He hung up in a rage and exclaimed aloud, "This can't be happening!" Picking up another phone, he pressed a button.

* * *

Novus Ordo

IN SIBERIA the fighting continued. A defender has a certain advantage, at least temporarily, owing to the difficulty of penetrating a well-fortified position, but an aggressor has another advantage: Eventually a defender will run out of supplies.

What the Russians hadn't imagined was the awesome power available to NHMI.

Cosmokrator Hans Weller, sequestered in Novus Ordo's Command Center, recognized the risky situation. They didn't have another supplier to replace the massive Siberian complex. He reasoned — We can't allow Yeltsin, who's probably responsible, to get away with it. Losing Gorby and the USSR was bad enough, but if we lose the Siberian plant, it will set us back years. There's no time to call a meeting. I'll make a command decision and give direct orders.

Weller decided that even if all of their Ether Craft had been grounded, he would have to launch one. He had no other choice and probability was on their side; they would have to take their chances with the seals. After all, a DEEP, or two, would be cheaper than building another NHMI.

* * *

Novus Somnorum

THEY COULD hardly believe their ears. Under the Indian Ocean's floor, two hundred fifty miles south of Chagos Archipelago, DEEP 23's crew went into action.

Alpha Force personnel in Novus Somnorum, which had a population of forty thousand, surged into action — they were being scrambled. It wasn't a drill! In the intensity of the moment, with alarms sounding, they moved with heightened awareness. Their reflexes were keyed — there wasn't time to be thinking — they didn't even notice that they were going to fly an uninspected Unit.

Few people had seen the spectacle that began to unfold. Sixteen jet-black DEEPs sat in a row inside a brilliantly lit hall taller than a large football stadium and several times longer than one, while men and women, looking the size of ants, hurriedly pursued their duties. Eighteen Alpha Force crew, ready for action, rushed to their battle positions inside the craft. Immediately, it levitated with moderate ascent from the docking base and deliberately moved into an access lane that ran the length of the grotto. Leisurely advancing, at thirty feet a second, the saucer came out of the hangar area towards the ocean access conduit, whose mouth opened in the middle of the mammoth structure. Taxiing and surfacing would take more time than reaching the battle. DEEP 23 pulled smoothly to rest. It momentarily floated inches above the surface of the watercourse that formed a small lake that was half a football field in diameter. A moment later it submerged with the grace of a mermaid.

Four minutes after the alert, DEEP 23 catapulted from the sea and bolted into space, accelerating rapidly. The surface of the Indian Ocean exploded. Water, carried by the Unit, shot several hundred feet into the air, causing a mid-ocean fountain. There would be a mild tsunami as a result. In sixteen seconds it reached space.

Human eyes would never have seen the DEEP itself — it was going too fast. It could have gone faster, but that would have put the Ether Craft in Siberia before the crew had finished combat checklists. They were well trained for action, but it would seem to be over before it had started.

DEEP 23's thirty-six seconds in the four-thousand-mile sprint to Siberia would never be registered in the record books. Glowing brilliantly from superheating, the craft arrived five minutes after Arlien made his plea for help. It was obvious that the firefight on the ground was intense. Russian helicopters were buzzing around like hornets. From above, Commander Chester Huvard could see that this was a significant Russian operation.

A sonic boom arrived momentarily after the DEEP and troops on the ground began to look up at the massive Unit as it cooled and darkened. Obviously, this slowly spinning saucer wasn't an illusion.

The Russian who had the laser-guided rocket-propelled grenade launcher decided that whatever the "thing" was — it was a menace. Inspired by fear, he raised his weapon, locked-on, and fired a projectile that traversed the three hundred meters to the Unit in an instant. But the explosion on the highly solidified argon-titanium-aluminum^3 superstructure was no more annoying to the Ether Craft than a mosquito would have been to the Russian.

Seeing no apparent damage to the saucer, he prepared to fire again, but his central nervous system never even felt the intense heat from the DEEP's invisible particle beam. He and his rocket-propelled grenade launcher turned into so much spurious energy.

An instant later, one of the Russian helicopters disintegrated in midair, then another. Two courses of action were open to the Russians: firing with everything they had, which had been ineffectual; the other, the wiser, was to escape — if possible. Men and helicopters vanished into flaming balls, and the DEEP's beam consumed the very flame itself — making a clean kill. Because the beam was invisible, they didn't know what was happening.

Huvard noted that the enemy was fleeing and ordered a cease-fire. Russian casualties exceeded a hundred.

No one would believe the story — a flying saucer with a particle beam? It was nonsense. They would all be put in an asylum. Back home, they would reason that NHMI's people had some sort of gas that causes illusions. An avalanche would be the explanation given for those who were missing in action.

Yeltsin, nevertheless, would receive an important message from TerraNova: Don't play with us!

On the ground they could hardly believe their eyes as they watched the mammoth black object lower itself. The Arctic twilight at 3:00 PM made it look mysteriously surreal, but the Ether Craft had proven itself all too authentic. It was too big to enter the heliport.

There wasn't any wind, any howl, and there was only a barely perceptible moan coming from the Unit. Silence returned with the defeat of the Russians. The battle site darkened as the Unit blocked the iced twilight. Some fires were still billowing thick, black clouds that hung solemnly in the demolished haven, while intense bluish light from the DEEP created the appearance of a sunburst.

From the outer edge of the craft, a large bay door dropped and a stretcher cage was lowered. Chenski, with orders from Brussels, immediately made himself present in the decimated heliport. Guards brought out Allenburg's nearly dead body. The smoke was asphyxiating, but they managed to put Janice in the stretcher cage, which was then raised by the Unit.

Seconds later, the Ether Craft levitated upward and slowly reached six hundred meters of altitude before shooting away and disappearing. A sonic boom shook the installation.

One of the guards, a *Star Trek* fan, commented under his breath, "Why didn't they just beam her up?"

* * *

On the edge of space

JANICE MOMENTARILY regained consciousness with a vacant stare — it could have been Heaven. Everything was white and foggy, yet brilliant.

I must be imagining things — she thought. Her pain was intense and her grip on reality wasn't strong enough for her to realize that it wasn't a fantasy. In a moment, unconsciousness welcomed her back, providing an escape from her agonizing pain, but not before an abysmal hopelessness descended about her, and she uttered in a whisper, "I'm dying."

"We need to get her back to Novus Somnorum, now. Her physical condition is critical; she needs medical care, if she is to have a chance to survive. It looks like over fifty percent of her body is affected by the burns," the chief medical officer spoke with urgency, his Aryan features filled with alarm.

Huvard watching her life slip away with grave blue eyes responded in a businesslike voice, "We'll do our best, but we've already caused

enough UFO stories for now. It'll be at least twenty-five minutes before
we can get her to the trauma center."

"Commander Huvard," came a female voice over DEEP 23's pag-
ing system, "Irving Stonefell is on visual."

Huvard took several steps to the loading bay's monitor and
switched it on. "Yes, sir," Huvard answered.

"Commander," Stonefell began, "were you able to rescue Ms.
Allenburg?"

"Yes, sir," Huvard answered again.

"What is her condition?"

"Critical, sir. She may not live."

"Huvard, get her back to the trauma center, NOW!" Stonefell commanded.

"Yes, sir!"

Huvard switched the intercom and called the bridge. "Yes sir," responded his first officer.

"Lock us in for an immediate dive and submersion sequence, Novus
Iridium, stat!"

"Yes, sir."

"Tell them to have medical personnel on standby at the docking
base. Our ETA," Huvard paused for an instant to think, and ordered,
"four minutes."

"Yes, sir."

Huvard wondered — Will we make it? They haven't even inspected
this bird.

Chapter 17

Mr. Rabbit and Mr. Smith

HE WHO can no longer pause to wonder and stand rapt in awe is as good as dead; his eyes are closed.

— Albert Einstein

BEFORE THE GOSPEL, our men spent everything they had on drinks and women, living in bondage to alcohol and evil spirits. Now there is prosperity, and we have abundant food. For years, the government gave us handouts, and it sent to us teachers and doctors, but we grew worse off daily, until Jesus changed our lives.

— Juan José Bautista, Quechua pastor
(Native South American)

That same day — Lake La Mica, Ecuador

AT THREE in the morning the rain stopped. James had managed to wrap himself in his piece of RSB sufficiently to make it through the night, though damp. Everything looked moist in the early morning light, and the rain had extinguished the fire. Low-lying clouds covered the mountains, and the sun rising toward the horizon illuminated the sky with an icy pastel blue.

As the sun continued its climb, its intense beam slid over the scintillating waters of La Mica, making a brilliant path that seemed to lead to the sky, from James's viewpoint. Turning his head slightly, he saw the mountain, Antisana, where he had been. It looked very cold — a giant snowcap that towered royally over the lake and high plain. Clouds moved swiftly across its face as air currents stirred, driven by the sun's rapid heating of the glacier. The biting winds he had endured on the mountain were visible by the clouds that quickly stirred around the peak. From below, where he was, it looked harmless, like a hurricane viewed from space.

At the campsite the air was calm, though it was damp and rainy, and the lake was peaceful in the early light. James was still in the shadow of the great snowcapped mountain, and it would be another hour before the sun would warm the surrounding air. It felt like it was about forty-five degrees Fahrenheit, perhaps lower with the wind.

The mountain's pink hues changing to golden on its snow-covered glacier were unforgettable, and James realized that no artist could capture the drama of light, color, and shadow now unfolding. Cameras, film, not even holographic images could reproduce this awesome perfection, and in minutes, only vague memories would remain.

Then a thought came to him — Could it be there really is a God? And he reasoned — They've worked so diligently telling me I don't need God, telling me the universe is an accident and there is no God. Why? If a person doesn't exist, you don't have to debate the question. Those who believe have to convince others that their unseen God exists. So why does TerraNova make such an effort to explain God away?

For years, thoughts about the fallacies of TerraNova and the New Age had often passed through his mind, but he kept these reflections to himself. He watched the light show on the mountain and asked himself — Could this be the signature of the One called the Almighty? Is the Almighty more than an outer deception? He helped Jonah; could He help me?

Then his reason battled back — Absurd! This is divergent! I can't allow myself to entertain such concepts.

Hearing enhancements brought keen perception to James. The devices, through artificial intelligence, eliminated most noise. About four yards behind, and to the right, his sound processor picked up a faint sound. It would be impossible for him to tell what the source was without turning.

It was a whisper. If it had been one of the languages he understood, he might have deciphered it, for it was a human voice; of this he was sure. This could be good news, or bad, but it was necessary for James to take action; if those who were following him sought his harm, in his weakened condition he would have to act quickly to gain the advantage.

The whisper that his enhancements were tracking was stationary. Why hadn't he picked it up earlier? Perhaps his thoughts were occupying him. Apparently — he reasoned — whoever it is doesn't wish me harm, or they would already have made their move. Still, James decided not to take any chances.

In one dramatic movement he rolled out of his blanket and jumped into a standing position, but he was surprised at who he saw. Indeed, they were children. Their full round faces, with chubby red cheeks, deep brown eyes, and pudgy noses, showed fright. His quick movement had scared them. The bewildered children turned away, and ran.

He nearly ignored them for a moment, and let them run their way, but after an instant of thought, he wondered if they could help him find civilization. He wondered if they spoke Spanish, some of which he knew.

"*Amigos,*" he called, trying to use one of the few words he knew, and then again, "*Amigos,*" he repeated in a louder voice.

He heard them giggling. Maybe they'll turn around and look back, he thought. I don't feel like running after them. I'll watch where they go. Maybe it'll give me a clue which direction to head.

Then the children stopped, about fifty feet away, and turned. James thought — I'll wave; it's the universal sign of friendly intentions. Not that he felt friendly, but is seemed expedient. He raised his hand and waved, remembering to smile, and called again, *"Amigos,"* making a sweeping motion towards himself, hoping they would return.

They just stood still, so he decided to slowly walk towards them.

Off to his right he saw a rabbit in the tall grass. He imagined it might help him make friends, and pointed to it, making a sign with his finger and lips for them to be silent. James dove, lunging forward with his good foot, as a cougar leaps upon its prey. He used as much enhanced power as he could manage. In a snatch he seized the dark-gray animal, a native of the Andes.

James held the animal out towards the children. They frolicked in his direction, and he bent down as far as he could to receive them, holding the animal so they could pet it. Scared to death, the rabbit's heart raced wildly.

Stooping beside them, he could see his own reflection in their eyes. Both children, natives of the Andes, wore black felt derby hats.

He found himself smiling at the children. It felt good. It struck him that he hadn't smiled in a long time, and if he had, it was for some wicked humor, or some remark of ambiguous sarcasm.

"Conejo," the little girl squealed lightheartedly, and the little boy began to laugh too. They pointed at the gentle creature, and petted it.

After the children had petted, and fed the rabbit some tall grass, James felt sure his new friends wouldn't run away. James released the animal, and it jumped to freedom.

He quickly gathered his backpack as the children watched.

The air was still chilly, even though the sun was now visible, and their breath rose in puffs of vapor.

Stooping down again, he said two words he hoped they would understand. While pointing to himself, lifting his eyes and pointing away, he said, *"Mamá. Papá."* He doubted they had understood him, because they laughed. So he started to walk, inviting them with his hand and signaling them to follow, hoping they would lead him to their parents. Soon they were dancing circles around him — making a show, and for a moment he forgot his pain and found himself smiling again.

Following the western edge of the lake for a couple hundred yards, the three came to a steep slope. There were several fields of potatoes that were growing under the neatly tilled volcanic earth. He saw two adults working the furrows, tending to their field that rested on a steep incline. The noisy youngsters should have drawn their attention, but their heads remained bent forward and they continued occupied in their work. James continued to approach and the little ones pulled him along by his right hand. In his left, he grasped a stick to steady his gait.

When they were thirty feet away, a native Ecuadorian lady, dressed in a deep-blue combed-wool poncho, looked up with sparkling black eyes at the oncoming spectacle. James towered into the clouds, or so it may have looked from her viewpoint of four feet eight inches tall. Concentrated mountain sunlight had cut furrows into her deep brown skin. She said something to her husband, who then looked up. The couple beckoned their offspring to come. Giggling and laughing, the youngsters ran to their parents.

James advanced with prudence. He could not understand what they were saying, but they didn't seem anxious, so he decided to try a few more Spanish words, and said, *"Buenos días."*

In response, the man answered, *"Buenos días."*

It was James's turn to say something, but he wasn't sure what, except to ask, *"¿A Quito?* — To Quito?"

The small man with a long woolen poncho pointed behind him and indicated a path.

James said, *"Gracias,"* and began to step away. He could tell that the children were telling their parents about the rabbit.

He had forgotten his pain momentarily when he was with the children, but now, as he turned away, his ankle began to throb. He had planned to splint it earlier, and decided that now was the time, before he went farther. Still a short distance from the children and their parents, he stopped by a tree to select a branch.

JUAN JOSÉ BAUTISTA watched the *gringo* as he reached into a eucalyptus tree and broke off a small branch. The *gringo* was covered with dirt and dried blood. As Juan José watched the stranger sit down and make a splint for his ankle, he began to remember a time years before in his hometown of Talontag:

PAIN SLAMMED his shoulder as a stone tore his shirt. Another hit his leg. The infuriated mob yelled in their native Quechua dialect, "Death to the heretic!"

Juan José ran from the horde of enraged villagers. Their priest had incited them. Juan tried to run ahead of them and hide, and tricked the crowd by plunging between two huts. Then he crawled back into a small ditch — covering himself with a burlap bag he had been carrying to market.

He remembered when he was a child, about eleven years old; he had been a member of an angry throng that was pursuing a tall blond missionary they had driven out of the village. They had gotten rid of the "preacher," a degrading term of contempt. On a few other occasions, when missionaries had also come to the village, the people would give them the same reception. Every meddling *gringo* who came was turned back.

Will I live though this? — Juan José asked himself, his thoughts slipping back to another tall blond stranger he had met a year earlier. He had been walking the streets of Quito, trying to get back to the bus stop, when a street preacher caught his ear. He listened and, moved by the Gospel story, decided that the message was very important.

Every time he returned to Quito for Friday shopping he found the preacher in the same spot, and listened. Eventually he introduced himself. The missionary invited him to a meeting, and as the months went by, the humble Quechua man began to take the Christian faith more seriously, and decided to model his life after Jesus. Finally, Juan José decided he was going to tell his own people, just as the *gringo* had told him.

Many listened to him with curiosity and interest as he spoke in the village market. Two of those who had listened even prayed with him when he invited them at the end of his message. But when the village priest found out, he pronounced, "The evangelists must be removed!"

Juan José wondered if he would see Jesus that day. His missionary friend had taught him about the thousands of martyrs who had already gone to heaven and how the apostles had given their lives for their beliefs.

Yelling obscenities and shouting curses against the heretic, the crowd rushed past his hiding place. When he thought they had all gone, he lifted his head out of the ditch. He shivered. Cold water completely soaked his body. He looked around, and his eyes caught an enraged woman's stare.

She screamed, "Here's the heretic," and made a show of it, pointing, jumping, shouting, screaming — she was acting as if she was being attacked. She appeared to believe that she had found the devil himself. Though a small woman, shrouded in many layers of dark wool, she easily showed herself to be as scandalous as a siren, raising a ruckus.

Juan José never imagined she had it in her, having known her since he was little, but he didn't have time to worry, and stood out of the ditch, sopped in dripping, muddy water, and ran back past her. Trying to escape the mob — but it didn't help. Soon he was exhausted and turned to confront those who were rushing after him. Looking into their eyes as they approached, he remembered the story of Stephen and said, "I forgive you." Then he looked skyward and said, "Father, I forgive them." He fell to his knees as a stone hit his stomach. As he bent forward, another struck his head. He collapsed.

Two days later he awoke — in his own bed. His wife had dragged him home after the mob left him for dead. After the incident, it didn't seem to matter to the village people whether he lived or not. Perhaps they thought they had taught him a lesson. His stoning had served two purposes: First, when the people had taken time to reflect on what they had done and his reaction to it, they began to think that he might have something to say. Second, it gave Juan José a certain aura of invincibility and of being a man of truth and love. Eventually, a small group of converts began to meet together privately with a pastor from Quito.

Within a year, and another attempted stoning, when the people ran after Juan José and the pastor who was visiting (fortunately they escaped), the church began to grow to hundreds. Within two years, nearly every family in the village had been affected and was softened to the message.

JUAN JOSÉ'S THOUGHTS returned to the present, and with dark black eyes that understood suffering, saw the poor *gringo* sitting under the tree covered with scrapes and bruises as he wrapped the splints to his ankle. This tall man must be cold and he must also have suffered much — Juan José decided. Seeing that the *gringo* was finishing his task, Juan José approached him, and with a furrowed hand, invited, *"Venga con nosotros* — Come with us."

JAMES HADN'T expected the offer, but he was glad to follow along. Juan José and his family gathered up their tools and started walking.

The ascending sun had risen sufficiently to have warming power. The thin air in the high elevation didn't hold heat, and his back, the side where the sun was hitting, was pleasantly warm; but in the shadow, his chest was ready to shiver.

His ankle throbbed with pain, but fortunately, with his homemade walking stick, he was able to take much of his weight off the joint.

They passed several houses as James observed that some of the huts didn't have chimneys and smoke poured up through their tile roofs. Some of the huts had dirt floors and adobe walls. He could tell when he saw one that had an open door. Reaching a particular home, Juan José, a little man only a few inches taller than his wife and dressed in a black poncho, invited James to enter. The door was much lower than his stature and he had to bow to comply. It was a respectable dwelling with a tin roof, block walls, and a concrete floor.

Numerous mats, all woven from dried reeds, were spread on the floor, especially in the sleeping area. The kitchen had a chimney, a truly important item for their woodstove. A homemade table with benches made from crudely cut and partially finished pine sat in the middle of the dimly lit room. Juan José pointed to a seat; and James, taking care not to break it, sat down cautiously. Compared to where he had been during the past several days, the home was luxurious.

He smelled a hot meal cooking. Not long afterwards, Juan José's wife and children began to bring food to serve the two men. First, a big bowl of boiled potatoes in a simple wooden bowl obviously hewn by hand, seasoned with green leaves that were sprinkled sparsely over them. Then another plate — with something disturbingly similar to a dead rat without a tail cooked on a skewer and well charred — was followed by boiled rice and a half dozen hard-boiled eggs. In the center of the table, beside the candle, was a white substance that looked like salt. Beside it was a dish of red liquid, and finally a plate heaped with large, dark beans.

James had sufficient appetite to eat, even with the eyes of the creature, apparently an indigenous rodent, looking straight up from the plate. Seeing the thing was disturbing. Is it a rat? — he questioned himself. James turned the plate slowly. Juan José, thinking that the contents of the plate could be a curiosity for his visitor, pointed and said, "*Cui.*"

James looked briefly at his host. Pointing at the plate, he too said, "*Cui,*" without understanding the meaning.

"*Sí,*" was the response of the little man, who smiled and said, "*Oremos...*"

Feeling a bit strange with the *cui* eyes looking up at him, James waited to see what his host would do. Juan José closed his eyes, and inclining his head, spoke words, but he said them too quickly for James to understand. Having finished, Juan José looked up, gestured, moving his hand to his mouth, and invited his visitor to eat.

Cui, as it turned out, wasn't so bad, just greasy.

As he was eating, he noticed a sound that he had heard earlier, but he had ignored. It was a piggish squeal, and restless scampering. It was distant, but coming from the kitchen area. As he concentrated on the sound more, he realized that it was from some animal, and there were at least several of them. As he thought about it more, he remembered that he had heard it in Novus Ordo, in the laboratories — guinea pigs. Looking at the partially devoured meat, with numerous small bones that were difficult to negotiate, he realized what it was he was eating, and felt reconciled in that it wasn't a rat.

Flavoring the insipid food with salt and red sauce did wonders to make it tasty and pleasing. His hunger was quickly satisfied, but there was so much food heaped up on his plate, and they seemed to expect him to eat all of it, that some of the enjoyment of having a warm meal was taken away from him. He was able to eat everything, though, aided by sheer hunger, and the piquant sauce.

Lastly, they brought him a big cup of boiling hot milk in a large tin mug. It had the familiar smell of coffee.

"*Café con leche,*" Juan José commented while pointing to the mug.

James noted that they were sipping the *café con leche* using large spoons.

Juan José had been looking at James, and he wondered why. It wasn't long after that he invited James to rest on a woven mat, and gave him a dark and rough woolen blanket. It was large, and James enveloped himself within it. Soon thereafter he drifted into restful sleep.

* * *

The Pacific Ocean

QUARTERS ARE SO TIGHT! How do they live in this inflicted tub? — Chief Nancy Jones was furious. I don't care if the captain likes me calling his craft a tub or not. Two days of searching, and nothing! Enough of this tin can! But I can't give up, not if there's a chance of finding Smith or Brown. They wouldn't give up their search if I was missing.

How absurd, to ground the whole fleet over a seal. But it makes sense. I guess I would have done the same thing. It just seems like a waste to have all that power sitting still and let the world go its own way without TerraNova's guidance. I'll never install a seal again without doing a laser projection first. I've learned my lesson.

Jones maneuvered back to the bridge of the tub to see if there was any news. She laughed to herself, seeing the "sophisticated" control room where multiple colored lights on panels were blinking and a reddish hue bathed the Beta Force personnel in a psychedelic aura. There wasn't even one virtual holographic panel. She wondered how they could concentrate with all of the blinking lights. No wonder they can't find anything. But she knew her thoughts were expressed through a haze of frustration.

Approaching the screen where the operator of the ionic-meson scan sat, she looked down on its faint amber glow.

ENSIGN CHARLIE TENSED as he heard Chief Jones order, "At ease."

"Yes, Chief," he answered, relaxing his body so that it would look as though he was obeying.

"Anything?" She asked, curtly.

"No, Chief," he answered, wondering why she made him so nervous and feeling a drop of perspiration fall from under his arm and coolly strike his side, beneath his uniform. It almost made him shiver, even though the cabin's temperature was comfortable. He then added, "Permission to speak freely, Chief?"

"What is it?" she asked with impatience. Her tone told Charlie that it would have been better if he had kept his mouth shut, but he had to speak now.

"Well, Chief, that tropical storm probably finished off whoever we're looking for." And he swallowed.

"That's all the more reason we have to find them soon."

Charlie was surprised that she didn't lash out at him, but he could tell that if he said anything more, he would probably bring on her wrath.

NANCY JONES realized that she needed a way to improve the scan. Schemes to improve it systematically raced through her head and she saw them as diagrams and flow charts. She would find a way to improve the tub's scanner.

"Where's your shop?" she asked.

"Yes, Chief," the Ensign answered, and told her where to find it.

Jones marched away, shortening her stride in the confined area.

* * *

Pasadena, California

SO WHAT if it was Friday the thirteenth, Atler wasn't superstitious, and he didn't believe in bad luck — not that things were going so badly. Really, with his new income, everything was wonderful, until flashing blue lights appeared in his rearview mirror. The officer was a gentleman, but the ticket, for doing eighty-five in his new Viper in a fifty-five-mile-an-hour zone, wasn't what Atler would have chosen to begin his day with, but he was glad he could afford it.

He wondered whether this was an omen, a ticket on the thirteenth. Despite all his efforts to rationalize his new wealth, it still didn't feel right. He kept expecting something to go wrong, feeling that sooner or later his benefactors would catch on to his crooked ways.

With a million from Nova Mundi in his Swiss bank account and two million more from Advanced WorldNet in several other Swiss accounts, he felt like a child who had a tremendous inheritance but couldn't touch it until eighteen. He had nightmares about what would happen when all of his employers found out about each other. NASA would feel it had some right, Nova Mundi would consider itself the owner, and Advanced WorldNet would feel as though they had exclusive rights. Which brought up the question: If TerraNova had taken expedient steps to avoid the IRS, and Advanced WorldNet also, then maybe, if they found out what he had done, would they not find expedient ways of dealing with him? It was a dilemma and he fully realized that he had developed a disease called "nerviosis," a close cousin of psychosis, induced, in his case, by his own greed.

It worried him to no end. Why was I so greedy? But I have a right! I deserve every penny I've gotten, and more! How can those scoundrels pretend to have exclusive rights to something that clearly belongs to humanity? Atler, however, knew his reasoning was hypocritical; the good of humanity was as stimulating to him as the ticket the officer was handing him through his window.

"Please drive safely, Mr. Redclift," the officer told him with a professional smile.

"Yeah," Atler answered with painful reluctance. "I'm sorry, sir."

"Pretty car, nice red," the officer noted with reserved admiration.

"I like it," Atler answered, smiling.

The officer began walking back to his patrol vehicle.

Cars hurtled by, creating their own miniature hurricanes as they passed. Atler accelerated and pulled back into traffic. He was still wrapped up in his own thoughts, supposing that the worst thing that could happen would be a fierce court battle over the rights to his program — and he figured — I'll lose everything to the lawyers: Curse those vultures! Doug's really a civilized guy and he said his people were philanthropists. They won't do me any harm. And I've got a legitimate right to every penny I've made, and *more!*

About then he heard the siren and saw the flashing lights, again! Twice in the same day? He looked down; this time he was only doing 60, barely above the limit. He thought — This isn't fair. When the officer came up to his window, he reluctantly rolled it down.

"Mr. Redclift, please keep your eyes on your speed, sir," the officer ordered. "I really don't want to give you another ticket today."

"Right," Atler answered. "I'll be careful."

"Yes. Please!" The officer implored, and walked back.

Atler felt himself at least a little lucky — Not bad for Friday the thirteenth — he reasoned to himself. Maybe my clients won't ever find out about each other. I'm a pretty lucky guy, after all.

Chapter 18

The Road to Quito

Quito, Ecuador, is located in the Andes Mountains, and on the slopes of the active volcano Pichincha, which last erupted in 1666. Quito is the oldest of all South American capitals, and the second largest city of Ecuador. It has been severely damaged by earthquakes several times.

— LaBrooke's Modern Encyclopedia
2000 edition

The next day — Near La Mica, Ecuador

It was still dark and James had been asleep since midday of the day before. Juan José and his wife were stirring. Coming out of a heavy sleep, it took a while for him to become oriented, but hunger swiftly confronted him as breakfast's pleasant smell filtered in to where he lay.

Getting up from the mat on the floor, he found his way to the bathroom (cornfield) that circled the hut and took care of primitive necessities in a primitive way. Orion was setting to the west and a distant sign of twilight was visible in the east. I could sure use a good bath — he envisioned — some hot water to relax in, but the cold morning air, which James guessed to be only a few degrees above freezing, didn't allow his illusion to endure more than an instant and motivated him to return to the warm blanket. Chuckling to himself, he thought — How can it be so cold on the equator?

Inside again, the air in the hut was only a little warmer than outside, and he shivered — his teeth ready to chatter.

As he lay bundled up, he began to ask himself some serious questions. Perhaps the outer God had made everything, like outers say. Alpha Academy taught me about a universe that's just a grand accident — they said it evolved. Doesn't that mean that the Skotoi, our highly ascended masters, are accidents too? So they aren't really any better than I am. At least I'm genetically engineered, with enhancements. They're just accidents.

Besides — James continued reasoning — when an accident happens, things usually get worse, not better: DEEP 1 is proof of that. It took intelligence and hard work to make it; and then, bang! — it was all gone. A "big bang" makes lots of dust.

He felt uncomfortable with his present line of reasoning, and began to remember Ashley, and in his memory she was shunning him and he hated her! He remembered how they had parted on DEEP 1, and again he saw the tear fall from her eye. Curse her tear! Yet he knew he cared for her, and he felt confused, but in his hate he respected her, and in that respect he knew he had never stopped longing for her.

Trying to anchor himself to reality, and to clear the confusion from his thoughts, he told himself — Look at real life. Feel the hard floor and the cold. And then, with frustration he concluded — *Inflict* it all! This is the way outers think. I've lost my objectivity. It's useless. If I start thinking like an outer, I'll be as useless as one. But here I am. I'm acting more divergent all the time. But I can still turn it around. If I get to Quito, and make contact with Nova Mundi, then I can forget all of these outer thoughts, and things will be fine.

Daylight's first rays began to slip through the small windows. Juan José came into the room. Still wrapped in a wool blanket, James sat up on the mat and raised his eyes to greet the short man who had been so gracious, which was something that perplexed James. His host was wearing a plain dark blue woolen poncho with a black border. James decided that it must be his native costume, since it was the same thing he had worn yesterday. The poncho itself wasn't like the rain ponchos James was familiar with; obviously it wasn't for rain, but warmth. Juan José brought something with him and placed it on the nearby wooden table, as he inquired, "*¿Cómo está?*— How are you?"

James answered, "*Estoy bien* — I'm fine."

Then Juan José asked, "*¿Tienes frío?* — Are you cold?" and wrapped his arms around himself, trying to help James understand.

"*Sí,*" he answered, shaking himself as if shivering.

Juan José took a folded poncho, which looked identical to the one he was wearing, and presented it to him, saying, "*Es para ti* — It's for you."

Accepting Juan José's gift, James stood up and nodded. He said, "*Gracias,*" with an early morning scratch in his throat. He unfolded the dark blue woolen poncho and, finding the hole for his head, slipped it on. He sensed its warmth and it covered his scrapes, the dried blood, and the ground-in dirt, which was on both his uniform and his flesh.

James's new poncho was the same size as Juan José's, which hung above his knees, but James's covered only his hips. The soft sheep wool brought him warmth, and again, Juan José's kindness complicated what had been his simplistic view of outers.

Juan José and James went back to the table together where breakfast, with eggs, rice, potatoes, and coffee, waited — fortunately there wasn't a guinea pig, James noted. Again, Juan José paused to repeat some words before eating and James heard what seemed to be a reference to the Christian deity; he hadn't thought that isolated Indian folk would espouse such a religion. Weren't their traditional beliefs good enough?

After the abundant breakfast, James asked, *"¿Quito, qué distancia?* — Quito, how far?"

"Como cuarenta y cinco. — About forty-five."

"¿Cuarenta y cinco kilómetros? — Twenty-eight miles?"

"Sí. Por bus. Desde Pintag. — Yes. By bus. From Pintag."

"¿Pintag?" James asked.

"Es un pueblo, — It's a town" Juan José informed.

They didn't converse much more, and James informed his host that he would be leaving, *"Tengo que salir."* He felt awkward, leaving so soon, but he wouldn't stay any longer. Clumsily, he began his exit. He didn't want to leave, but he had no choice. Conditioning impelled him, and he reflected — I've got to make it to Quito. I have no choice.

"Adios," came to James's mind and lips.

Juan José ordered, *"Quedase. No se vaya.* — Stay. Don't go."

James repeated, *"Adiós."* His Spanish vocabulary wasn't large enough to say more, and even if he had known more words, he really didn't feel that he could say more. He knew that the little man wanted him to stay, and he would have enjoyed staying, yet nothing could detain him. He would reach Nova Mundi without delay. He turned and ducked under the door, and began to walk away from the sunrise. James looked back and saw Juan José and his family waving at him. He briefly turned and returned their gesture, and then continued to the nearby path.

If only I could resist my conditioning now; I resisted back on the mountain, but I don't have the strength. Not now. Besides, life was good in Alpha Force. Freedom would bring me too many problems — too many choices. What would I do? Get a job and go to work like an outer? The thought initially made him chuckle to himself, but after a moment, it seemed to him that it might not be such a bad idea.

James couldn't forget his past inflictions. Though few, they weren't events easily erased from his mind. They kept their hold on him. He felt like an animal that had experienced the limits of an electric fence and after a few shocks, wouldn't approach the edge again, even when the biting current had been switched off. James knew he didn't want to be trapped in Alpha Force, but he couldn't see any way to fight it. And he knew he had been playing near the fence for too long. He remembered the shocks, and it was time to back off.

Strengthened by food and rest, he started along the mountain path, limping and depending on his walking stick. He knew he needed to see a physician. But what if they discover me? — he considered. My implants will be a sure giveaway. An x-ray will show an outer forbidden technology. But if I don't receive prompt treatment, my ankle may not heal right. I don't have any money. I don't have any way to be free, even if they'd let me. I've got to report to Nova Mundi. There's no choice.

The path took him through sparse vegetation. Occasionally he passed a clump of tall grass. There were also blue-green plants consisting of wide, sturdy leaves that bunched together at the base and extended upwards, spanning into graceful arches, just over knee-high. At their upper tips, they were sharply pointed and thick, and looked as though they could be dangerous. He thought they might be a type of hemp plant because they looked fibrous, but he wasn't sure. After a time, he came to a place where the vegetation thinned even more, and he began to travel over loose volcanic rock. The arduous path snaked its way up and down and about the lava flow, showing its disregard for his shoes and his injured ankle. The hardened lava was as sharp as a knife and he was unable to move as quickly as he wished. His splints, and the walking stick, helped, but each step was agonizing and slow.

He had plenty of time to think about what life would be on the outside. Juan José and his family had been so generous. He considered — I would have stayed longer, but I've got to get back. Curse it all! I'm like a pawn that's been dropped from the master's fingers. Soon they'll sweep down and grab me, and put me back on the table.

Toying with the thought of being an outer had its appeal, but it wouldn't work — and it couldn't work. I would never fit in; outers wouldn't accept me.

Several hours later he found that the path led him to a narrow cobblestone road, and the terrain had changed considerably. His shadow began to disappear in the intense brightness of the equatorial high noon. Earlier, he had taken off his poncho, as the day warmed, and put it in his pack.

The morning's trek had gone slowly. About two hours later, now in the afternoon, the climate began to change. Brilliant blue sky turned into patches of partly cloudy and was quickly developing into full overcast. It was starting to look dark. It would rain.

His progress, though painful, brought him closer to signs of civilization. The town that Juan José had mentioned was before him. From the distance, the red brick tiles, the prevalent roofing material, looked deep violet in the darkening light. He started to see many natives along the path that now looked more like a small road. They were all clothed in a fashion similar to the way that Juan José and his family had dressed. By the way they looked at him, he was certain that he was a spectacle. Soon he was in the main thoroughfare of the village.

Buzzing with activity, the street was full. It was difficult to walk. People were buying and selling food and wares of every kind. Everywhere he turned, something was for sale. The crowd in the street made movement slow. It was a marketplace on cobblestone. Capitalism was alive and well, but James needed money if he was going to participate. What would it be like to have money? Would that be freedom?

With the establishment of TerraNova's New Order there wouldn't be any need for old-fashioned currencies. James began to reason — We'll replace cash with electronic exchange, and ugly wads of crumpled bills will be eliminated. Then they won't have to worry about losing their money, being robbed, or being charged an unfair price — Therion will be in control.

People were yelling, children screaming, pigs squealing, chickens clucking, dogs barking, and not so far away he heard the deafening blare of a horn — it wasn't the silent hum of DEEP 1. His earlier weather prediction — rain — wouldn't wait much longer. The sun had disappeared and the mountain air cooled quickly. Finding a place to one side hadn't been easy. He took the poncho from his backpack and slipped it on. It was amazing how quickly the temperature had changed, but he felt grateful to Juan José as warmth replaced the sting of chilling air.

There were vegetables — lettuce, radishes, carrots, tomatoes, corn, green beans, beets, lima beans, peas, cucumbers, and other items James didn't recognize. He saw all kinds of fruits and more kinds of bananas than he knew existed. Someone was eating a strange thing, perhaps a fruit that came out of a large "green bean" one meter long. The fruit was visibly moist, but white and fluffy like cotton candy. As it was eaten, it revealed a large black seed an inch long. He never had seen such a variety of foods and articles in one place.

Then James saw a table with many knives, both large and small. He realized that his hunting knife might prove to be his means of obtaining some cash — not enough to be free — but it might help him reach Quito. He took the knife from his backpack and presented it to the short, round-faced man with a trimmed black mustache who was the proprietor of the cutlery table.

"*Vendo* — I sell," James pronounced while pointing at the beautiful instrument and looking the man in his eyes. He had no idea how much it was worth and no idea of the value of the local money, so he wouldn't know if he was getting a good deal, or not.

"*¿Cuánto?* — How much?" questioned the merchant.

James responded, "*¿Cuánto?*" for he had no idea what it was worth.

THE MAN who owned the cutlery stand could tell that the *gringo* was in a desperate situation and needed money. The stranger was dressed oddly and was terribly dirty, but the knife that the European was showing him wasn't like any he had ever seen. It was a quality instrument, too good for his humble table, and he knew that his clients wouldn't pay as much for it as it was worth. Besides, he had a family to feed — so his offer would be limited.

Gringos have plenty of money — he figured. They've always got some in a bank somewhere. He just didn't budget for his trip, and now he's got to sell his used equipment to buy some last-minute souvenir. These *gringos* can always call or wire a bank. He's not poor. I'll offer him half of what it's worth. Then he'll ask me for more and we'll bargain — that's our custom.

After a second look at the tall man, who was obviously in a bad situation — dirty, bloodied, scraped, bruised, unshaven, bloodshot eyes, grossly chapped lips, sunburnt, short wiry blond hair that looked like it could scour a pot (or needed scouring itself), limping, using a walking stick, and besides all of that — strange — the cutlery man concluded, and reflected — *Gringos* have funny styles and peculiar clothing, but this guy is wearing something under that poncho that's scarlet with purple stripes up the legs. It looks like it glows.

He couldn't remember having seen a *gringo* in such a desperate condition, or so strange, so he decided to offer a little more than he had planned, but when the *gringo* accepted his first offer, he puzzled as to why the *gringo* hadn't bartered for a higher price.

It LOOKED TO JAMES to be a large sum of money as the multicolored bills came into his hand, but he guessed that it wasn't, knowing as he did the workings of TerraNova and Nova Mundi in the local economies of smaller countries.

At the end of the street were the buses Juan José had mentioned. As James approached, a young man's voice rose above the clamor, "*A Quito, a Quito en este rato...*" This was the bus he needed.

Darkness and cold mounted, and abruptly a large drop of cold rain hit his head and splattered. Other drops followed quickly. He decided to board the bus as fast as he could. It vaguely resembled the school bus it once was. It looked ancient. So far as use, it could have gone to Mars and back more times than DEEP 1 before its tragic end, but the Ether Craft had had better maintenance. Somehow though, this bus, a monument to mechanical deterioration, had managed to outlive TerraNova's technological perfection.

Bending down as he entered, James discovered that the interior decor was even unsightlier than the outside shell. The metallic roof of the bus amplified the sound of the rain into a thunderous roar. At least his hearing enhancements eliminated the racket. He managed to give his fare to the wiry driver who presided over a dashboard full of saints, having handed him one of the bills he had received for the knife. He hoped it would be sufficient. Seated in a metal frame strung with clothesline, the operator made change from an assortment of dirty, multicolored paper money.

The bus's instrument panel could have been mistaken for junked tin and the ruined seats were crudely upholstered. Derelict metallic surfaces abounded and it was obvious that placing a hand in the wrong place could cause a laceration. In addition, the unsanitary stench made for mild nausea. He wondered what caused the odor — Perhaps it was rotten food? But he didn't know.

A dirty burlap bag, containing chickens, blocked the aisle, limiting movement in the confined area. Because of his height and the lack of space, both standing and sitting were impossible — stooping was his only option — and he would have to do it while holding onto the tarnished bar above the aisle, which was occupying the space he needed for his head.

By now the bus was full — all standing room was gone. Let's get moving — James thought — there's no more room in this thing.

But the people continued to press in on all sides until he began to feel warm. Then, five minutes later, packed like sardines and smelling much worse, the bus jolted and lurched forward on the cobblestones. The motor roared powerfully, but that was mostly because it had a faulty exhaust system.

Suspension, or the lack of it, added to the ride's discomfort, and sharp jarring movements banged him against the handrail and roof. It was similar to riding in the RSB, in that it made James wonder if he would get out alive. Maybe this bus would accomplish what the DEEP, the RSB, and the mountain had failed to do.

There was no place left for anyone else, but the driver stopped and more passengers appeared to be boarding.

The hard rain continued, and it was only when he felt the additional pressure against the back of his head and shoulders, which were pressed to the ceiling, that he realized what was happening — they were climbing aboard the bus's roof!

He couldn't believe it. The cold and bitter rain would be *inflictive*. And he realized that the only thing that was separating him from those who were on the outside was a thin layer of sheet metal!

He couldn't see out, so he began to observe those around him. There was a mother, who was giving breast to her baby. So bundled, the wee thing looked bigger than it was. Its teeny nose pressed up against mother's flesh and it looked so innocent as it suckled. James never had experienced such closeness, even in infancy. They had "grown" him in an environment so aseptic and cold it would have made the passengers on the roof shiver. Smith's mother had been Alpha Academy, and she gave impersonal bottles of formula to her numerous wards. She was a machine and manufactured those that suited her fancy. She found a place only for the best unflawed Aryans.

Mother, however, for the diminutive one just under James's eyes, where he couldn't keep from seeing, even in the embarrassment he felt, was mother. She was close and genuine. Warmth! It was the opposite of everything he was, and had been.

She wouldn't win a pageant. At Novus Ordo, she and her baby would have been incinerated. Their dirty, unattractive clothing was little more than woolen bags. But even though their appearances were unsightly, and the picture they made represented everything outer, for a moment, James could have thought it was beautiful. It's a painting — he thought. But what it shows, I cannot understand.

Then he remembered Ashley. He found it pleasant to think about her, even if he "hated" her, and he laughed at himself, silently, for he knew he really liked her. Where is she? Is she safe? He felt a lump in his throat, and a tear came to his eye when he thought of her name. He felt lonely, and it sank down through him like molasses, slow and sticky.

* * *

The Pacific Ocean

FLAMING IN GOLD, afternoon's hues began to fill the western sky. Ashley watched, resigned to the fact that it would be her last sunset.

So beautiful — she thought. She whipped her jumpsuit over her head again. I'll never make it through the night. Soon I'll go to sleep, never to wake.

"God help me!" she cried out, audibly, with strength in her voice, but only to be ignored by the now gentle waves. Why would He want to save me? Why do I want to be saved? She began to laugh and cry all at once. Saved for what? Saved to murder the innocent and infirm for the glory of the Skotoi?

Again the jumpsuit flew over her head as she swung her arms around and the knotted legs filled with air. She leaned back against it for a couple more minutes.

My biomotors can keep this up for weeks, but I can't fight sleep much longer. It's tropical water, but even so, it's draining me. Soon I'll descend to the depths below. She wondered — Is there a hell, like outers say? And again she cried out, "God! God! If You're real, save me! Please save me!"

Maybe it was another hour, maybe it was two, or maybe it was less. Near darkness surrounded Ashley and calm waves gently buffeted her. Her eyes closed, her limbs relaxed, the jumpsuit slipped from her grip, and a moment later, she capsized, flipping over, facedown in the water, and her knotted hair floated and spread about her head. Then her arms reached limply out into a dead man's float.

Chapter 19

Tears

THE QUESTION is not so much whether there is life on Mars as whether it will continue to be possible to live on Earth.

— Anonymous

That same day — Quito, Ecuador

IT WAS 4:30 PM and the bus was approaching its destination. James would need to find a phone book to look up Nova Mundi. Smoother road and fresh air reduced his nausea. Many of the passengers (those that could) were asleep. One gentleman had managed to sleep while standing, supported by the press.

James's nausea had passed, but he felt sick with something else: himself. He didn't want to go back to TerraNova, even if he knew he couldn't keep himself from it.

They were in city traffic. Sudden stops and rapid accelerations, which made him and everyone else struggle for equilibrium, told him so. There was a decided final stop. The bus's door opened, and people began to find their way out. Their trip had taken over an hour. James limped behind the others, still with his rough staff. I'll be glad to get out of here. I never want to be trapped like this again. He even wondered if he would ever stand up erect again.

Reaching the bus's three steps, he stepped down onto the pavement. He straightened himself as Quito's nippy cool air reminded him of the chill he had felt back on the mountain. Everything was moist from the rain, which had stopped earlier and left the streets and the sidewalks with an icy-looking glaze.

Disorienting sights and sounds forced him to take a moment to get his bearings. People packed the streets, and he thought — It's about as crowded as that bus was. With so many people around about he wasn't able to walk very fast.

Shoeshine boys, black with polish, tried to get his attention. His black Alpha Force shoes needed cleaning, but not the kind the youngsters offered.

Directly in front of him, in the distance, beautiful green slopes towered up to the clouds, and on the inclines were numerous buildings with houses on the higher slopes. Looking around, James came to the conclusion that the city, and therefore a telephone, would be towards the mountain.

His condition hadn't improved with all the walking, and his progress up the wide, sloping street was slow, especially because of the mobs of people around him. More of the city came into his view, and he saw hundreds of buses, both parked and circulating. Christmas decorations and cut pine trees were all around, and someone was selling something everyplace he looked.

As he continued, the view broadened to his right, and located on a prominent rise was a large building. It was definitely an example of religious architecture (a towering and lofty structure). James thought of the Plan, as taught by the Secret Doctrine, and knew that it was only a matter of years, perhaps a few decades at the most, until churches everywhere, and places of worship of all religions, would be turned into sites of meditation where Therion would be worshiped.

Out of the corner of his eye he caught two happy children dancing with glee. An adult, surely their father, was buying a Christmas tree. The sight made James wonder about his own father, whom he had never seen. His conception had been in a test tube and they never revealed to him who had been the mother whose womb he once occupied. In Alpha Force, those who came from his generation, who had actually gestated in a woman's body, were getting old. Now, the infants were bred in tanks, and it wouldn't be many years until they, the new generation of "tankers," were running the show. He asked himself — What would it have been like to have a mother and a father? A family?

After five minutes, still moving up the gentle slope, he began to smell something. It was nearly too good to resist. Written on the sign were the words *"Pollos de Don Pancho."* The looks, and pleasant smell, of dozens of chickens being barbecued in a large machine, each dripping in grease, tempted him to visit the establishment, but memories of inflictions past kept him pushing onward, right past the chickens, continuing his search for a phone.

It seemed that Quito didn't have many public telephones. He had hoped to see one by now, but he'd come six blocks without any luck, so he decided to ask.

"Teléfono," he pronounced, unsure he would be understood.

The gentleman, who had been stationary enough for him to address, answered, *"En la plaza del teatro."* His lips were covered with a black, neatly trimmed mustache.

James wasn't sure, and looked the way the man seemed to indicate, which prompted the gentleman to point in the same direction that he was going.

James understood, and answered, *"Gracias."*

Advancing through the commotion, he slowly made his way. It wasn't long until a plaza opened. He spotted the telephone and rapidly made his way towards it. To his dismay, there wasn't any phone directory, and there weren't any instructions for dialing Information. How am I going to call? he worried.

Frustrated, and nearly ready to take it out on the innocent telephone, James heard some familiar words from behind him, and he turned to hear. It was an amplified voice and it said, "As Jonah was in the whale's belly ..."

It struck him; he understood, without concentrating. It was English! Someone was speaking English! Disoriented and concerned, he immediately wondered if TerraNova or Nova Mundi's people had found him. Such was his paranoia, he thought they must have been reading his mind. After all, how else could they have found out he was thinking about that old piece of paper about Jonah?

His heart raced as he looked to see the source of the voice. There were two men standing above the crowd in the plaza. They weren't natives, and were dressed in a casual American style. Apparently the one was a fan of outer sports, guessing from the patches on his dark blue windbreaker. The pair didn't look like SAOs from TerraNova, so he stepped nearer.

One man spoke in English, and in the next instant the other translated into Spanish. These were the first words he had heard in English in over a week. "So shall the Son of Man be in the belly of the earth," the man recited. James had heard these words before.

The speaker continued, "Jesus died on a cross, was buried, and on the third day He rose from the dead."

With this, James realized it was a religious message, and he thought — They're obviously fanatics — but he wanted to listen.

"Jesus loves you! It doesn't matter what you've done, it doesn't matter who you are, it doesn't matter where you're from; Jesus wants to save you. He wants to take His rightful place in your heart," the voice pounded James as it came from a large loudspeaker. He felt unsettled, but continued to focus on the words, as he thought in response — The man said it didn't matter where you came from. Would he say that if he knew where I'm from? He says Jesus wants to free me. Can Jesus free me from Alpha Force? Can He save me from infliction?

Then he heard the man say, "I repeat, it doesn't matter where you're from; even if you're from Mars," he said with a smile, "Jesus loves you!"

It took James unawares — How does this man know I came from Mars? How does he know what I'm thinking?

Then, several phrases later, the preacher said, "I don't know what you're thinking; the Holy Spirit is dealing with your heart."

Who's the Holy Spirit?

And again, several sentences later, the speaker clarified, "The Holy Spirit is the Spirit of God."

Is he reading my thoughts by telepathy?

"...Jesus, Creator of Heaven and Earth — your Creator — is speaking to your heart."

This was the answer to what James had always wondered about — Who made the condor and the sun? The man just said God did. That's outer, of course. Totally divergent! But it makes more sense than saying that everything is from some big bang.

Then James heard a voice in his mind telling him the things he had been taught. It said, "Christians are despicable. Don't listen to the liar. He is lying. You know he's lying! He's just saying things because he wants power. You know that TerraNova will find you. You can't be free! Don't kid yourself. Someone will see you here, listening to that preacher. Don't waste your time! You hate Christians. Christians hate you! Christians are weak. You are strong. Don't listen! The fanatic will turn you into a worthless outer. There's no God! You're the only god!"

James was nearly ready to turn away.

Then the man on the platform said, "You feel confused. You have doubts. But Jesus is the answer to your confusion. He will give you a sound mind. Doubt is the enemy of faith. Satan wants you to doubt that there's a God. Satan wants to take you to the pit of hell. Don't let the evil one destroy you. Come to Jesus today, before it's too late. God, Himself, through His Spirit, is dealing with you. He wants to fill the void in your heart. He wants to give you a sound mind. He wants to love you."

A tear slipped from James's right eye, and he spoke in thought, as though he was speaking aloud, "God, I'm so empty. I'm so confused. Could You love me? I've done such terrible things. I've even exterminated Your worthless outers. And You're not really as powerful as outers think. They believe You're Almighty, or whatever. Are You, God? Are You really? Or are You like my teachers said, just an ascended master like Therion?"

The preacher kept on, but James started hearing another voice. It was like the one that had gotten him moving back on DEEP 1, and it said, "I *can* love you. I *do* love you."

Initially, it seemed so clear, as if spoken directly in his ear, but when he realized that the outer God was speaking to *him*, he scoffed at the implications. The great God, ASMI, is speaking to me? Sure! I'll be inflicted! I'm hearing God? This is crazy. It's too good to be true. It's just my imagination."

Then he determined to keep moving, and started to turn away for the second time, but he heard the preacher say, "If you'll receive Jesus, you'll be filled, and you won't feel empty."

Looking back over at the useless telephone, he felt utterly disgusted, and hearing the word "empty," he asked himself — How does he know I feel empty? He stopped and looked towards the phone; then he turned and looked at the outer.

"You'll become a friend of God. You'll be freed from the power of sin and death. God will give you eternal life!"

"Sin?" That's divergence! What's the fanatic trying to say? — James asked himself as the voice of his instructors echoed in his mind — You can't become a Christian; the outers will never accept you! They'll laugh at you. You won't be able to go back to TerraNova and they won't want you either. You'll be hopeless and homeless. You'll be destroyed! TerraNova will find you and inflict you. They'll make you wish you were dead. And then they'll kill you to make an example out of you.

James reasoned — The preacher said Satan wants to destroy me. The voice in my mind says I'll be destroyed. If the outer is right, the voice must be Satan's.

"Jesus overcame Satan. If you receive Jesus, He'll free you from the power of Satan."

It sounds good — James thought. The man's offering me eternal life, just like the voice did back on the DEEP, but the other voice in my mind is telling me that it will kill me.

"If you wish to be delivered from the whale's belly, call on Jesus. He's here to listen. He loves you. Jonah called out to God when he was in the belly of the whale. He was near death. He had been there three days and three nights. Imagine, the stench, the burning acid, the rot and the slime — darkness so deep that even the blackest night would be brighter. He was in torment.

"God, in His mercy, heard Jonah and caused the fish to spit him out. God delivered Jonah from the horror he was living. Jesus can deliver you from your torment."

Something began to happen in James. Whatever it was, he didn't understand, but he felt that he wanted what the man was offering.

The preacher began calling people to come towards him for prayer if they wanted to receive Jesus. James didn't understand what that meant, but he watched. Then they "prayed." The people were "inviting" Jesus into their hearts. James found himself wanting to feel Jesus in his heart. He wanted to be part of the group who had "received Jesus," but he couldn't get his feet moving. They seemed to be cemented to the pavement. Even though he couldn't get himself to move to join the group, he repeated the words to himself where he was, as the man spoke, and the group of about twenty repeated them also.

"Lord Jesus, come into my heart," he said to himself, wondering — Why heart? Why not mind? Then he repeated in his mind, nearly speaking aloud, the same words the preacher instructed. "I have sinned. Forgive me, Lord," and another tear came to the corner of his eye. But he questioned himself — Why? Why does repeating these words make me feel this way? Is this how outers inflict people? He knew it wasn't, though. It was simply so foreign to him that he found nothing in his previous experience to compare it to. Then the speaker directed the group to say, "God, have mercy on me." James almost repeated the words, as he had the others, but couldn't, without interrupting himself with a snicker. He thought — I'm invested. I don't need any mercy from an outer God. But after a moment of hesitation, he realized that if God was all that outers believed Him to be, then he would be destroyed by Him, unless He, the ASMI, showed mercy, for he, James, had sinned by fighting against ASMI. So he haltingly repeated the words, aloud — but his voice was muffled, like that of a dying man who was speaking with his last breath.

When he had finished, things seemed different to James. A peaceful quiet replaced the tormenting voices, and he felt fresh air cool his tearful eyes. He had no idea why, but he knew things weren't as they had been. For a moment he remembered smashing the transceiver back on the mountain, and he began chuckling to himself, thinking of how he had been so silly. He might have broken into full audible laughter, except there were so many people around, and he noticed, just then, that the preacher was moving towards him. He had a bright and joyous face, with abundant and respectable gray hair. His physique was athletic.

When the man extended his hand towards him, James responded haltingly, but managed to get his hand out of his poncho and accept the greeting of the man with clear green eyes.

WHEN JACK KINDERLY had finished praying and looked up, he saw a tall man in a poncho standing behind the crowd who was ... well ... he concluded — out of place. He stood out from all of the others. Not only was the man the tallest, the whitest, the dirtiest, and frankly speaking, the strangest, but Jack felt oddly attracted to him. He thanked Jon for the translation, who had begun directing the jobs of counseling the new believers and getting their sound equipment together. Turning, he moved towards the stranger. When he approached, he extended his hand and said, "Hi. I'm Jack Kinderly." He felt certain that the stranger would understand English.

"James Smith," was the reply.

"James, where are you from?" Jack asked, but saw that Smith's expression changed, showing perplexity. It almost looked as if he was going to have a crisis. The stranger's gestures were subtle, but Jack was used to ministering to people and could tell that his question was difficult for the stranger to answer. Jack began to wonder — Maybe he's a German tourist, but he really looks beaten-up.

With this thought — and looking at the man's golden backpack that was reflective (like something from the space program) and didn't look at all like any other Jack had ever seen — he began to wonder who he might be, and examined him closely. Smith's watch was also different, unlike any other he had seen before. Underneath the poncho, which was ridiculously short, it was apparent that the man was wearing some kind of uniform. By now, Jack was wondering if "James Smith" was even the stranger's real name.

Jack saw that his question about Smith's origin had made a dramatic impact, and seeing that his expression was beginning to dull, Jack decided to change the subject and asked another question, passing over the previous one, "How do you like Quito?" Jack found himself wondering if "Smith" was on the run.

Smith answered, "I haven't had time to notice."

"Just arrived?" Jack asked, as he looked up into the man's eyes. He looked so vulnerable, even pitiful.

JON WHITTEN was finishing his duties with the help of several others from the local church. They had taken the names and addresses of twenty-two who made decisions for Christ, and were now stowing the equipment.

With everything under control, Jon was able to walk over to Jack and the European, who looked like he'd had a bad trip to one of the snowcapped mountains. Jon made himself a part of the conversation, and said, "Introduce me to our new friend."

"James Smith, meet Jon Whitten," Pastor Kinderly said.

Jon extended his hand, and James returned the gesture. Jon, without knowing, started to make the same mistake Jack had committed initially, and asked, "Where are you from?"

It was immediately clear to Jon that the question didn't make Smith happy. He could almost see Smith tremble, but after only a momentary pause, he answered, "I'm from Novus Ordo."

"Oh. Where's that?" Jon asked.

"It's southwest of Bermuda — in the Atlantic."

Jon tried to remember where it might be and asked, "Is that an island?"

"No," he answered.

"It's not?"

"No," he replied again, and hesitantly offered, "it's a city under the sea."

Oh, yeah — Jon thought, and evaluated — he's odd. Maybe he's some kind of aquanaut who lives under the sea— something experimental. Sounds interesting: "a city under the sea." But he's such a mess, and there's no place for diving around here.

Then he heard Jack ask, "Under the sea?"

"Yes."

Again, Jon heard vagueness in Smith's voice, even though his answer was a monosyllable. It didn't seem likely that he was being honest — Jon evaluated — so he decided to end the conversation. He considered it unwise to interact with suspicious people. To avoid appearing rude, he offered, "James, please take this card," and he pulled one out of his shirt pocket. "It has our church's address. Maybe you can come by and visit us while you're in town."

Smith accepted the card, and put it in a pocket of his jumpsuit, under his poncho.

Jon began to justify to himself his dismissal of the man, and he thought — What's his trouble? Is he running from the law, or something? He looks like he's been hiding out. I wonder what's happened to him. It seems like he's limping. And he has that rough walking stick. Then Jon had a deeper thought — He probably needs help. I just hope I'm not the one who has to give it to him. Who knows what I'd be getting into? Then he argued back at himself — You should be ashamed. You have an opportunity to help a person in need. But the less noble part of him contemplated — Yeah, but I'd probably get myself into a lot of trouble.

So just let him find his way back to Bermuda, or wherever. He'll never visit the church. He's just a tourist passing through, and his kind never wants to hear the Gospel. I've lost my time with them more than once. He's just passing through, and he looks like he could bring more trouble with him than the thugs at the prison. (Jon was thinking of the group of men he occasionally ministered to, and how a few of them had tried to use him to gain favor with the judges.)

Pastor Kinderly was a little perturbed by Jon, who, he could see, was trying to get rid of James. As for himself, his own curiosity had been aroused; so he emphasized, "Yes, James. It would be important for you to visit the church. Please come by. I'd like to talk more. We could take you to dinner."

"I don't know if I'll be in town very long," James answered.

Jack was about to say something, trying to find out more, but Jon interjected, "Okay. Have a good time here in town. We'll see you when-ever."

Jack ignored Jon, and quickly asked, "What happened to you? You're limping."

He saw Jon shrug in a way that was a mix between a "why-do-you-care?" and a "don't-waste-your-time." And in answer, James turned his eyes to observe Jon's body language. Seeing it, Jack coughed and asked again, "Are you okay?"

Smith began to answer, "Yeah ..." but he stammered.

Jack, trying to give him more opportunity to answer, said, "I bet you've had a hard trip. Looks like—"

But just then someone who was walking past brushed James's poncho, and for an instant his sleeve was exposed. Jack, whose eyes were right at James's shoulder level, caught a glimpse of what looked like a patch on his sleeve. It reminded him of a pilot's or an astronaut's jumpsuit, and he asked, "Is that a uniform you've got on?"

He was slow to answer, but responded, "Yes, it is."

Jack started trying to make sense of the patch he had seen. Surely it had fooled his eyes, but he replayed the glimpse in his mind's eye. It had to be — he decided, and asked, "May I see the insignia?"

James hesitated, but went ahead and reached across, with an attitude, as if he was breaking something. Jack wondered why he was being so dramatic. He pulled the poncho back and exposed an elegantly embroidered patch. The show so surprised Jack that he almost forgot to look, but as he began to see the details in the patch's design, he studied it and couldn't take his eyes off of it. Lavish scarlet, purple, and gold made the emblem vibrant. It wasn't the familiar green he'd seen so often. Notwithstanding James's filthy appearance, the symbol stood out splendidly: the great pyramid and the all-seeing eye. Around the bottom edge was written the Latin phrase *"Novus Ordo Seclorum,"* just like it was on a dollar bill, but this was gorgeous. It looked like it was three-dimensional.

By now, Jon had moved around beside Jack, where he was able to see too. A small group was beginning to gather, and all of them were eyeing the extraordinary emblem. James began to look uneasy, and pulled the poncho down and turned. Jack looked around and saw the curious stares of the onlookers.

Jack usually wasn't one to notice details, but during his brief observation he judged there was at least one thing that set the emblem apart from The Great Seal on the dollar bill, something besides the colors. It was a small thing — perhaps trivial — but the Roman numerals written across the base were fewer than those used on the dollar bill. Perhaps he had noticed it, since, from childhood, the symbol had been one of his curiosities. This led him to a question, which he directed to James, "What was that Roman numeral at the base of the pyramid?"

James's expression was again cloudy, and he didn't reply quickly, but finally answered, "DCLXVI."

Jack asked gravely, "Six hundred sixty-six?"

"Right," James answered.

"Jon," Jack said, "don't you think we can invite our visitor back to your Jeep so we can talk better?"

"Okay."

Jack could tell that Jon was also curious.

* * *

The Pacific Ocean

EARLIER, Pepe had felt an irresistible urge to change his fishing boat's course by several degrees. He was returning home with a great catch. It had been a long and successful day and his detour would take an extra hour, but he knew his crew understood. More than once he had saved their lives by paying attention to his feelings.

Several times Pepe had nearly turned back to the right course, but each time he started to do it, he felt it wasn't yet time. A compulsion moved him to the bow. He looked down into the dark waters that were lit by only a trace of rose twilight, but there was still enough light to see an object — bright scarlet and purple — floating twenty yards to the east.

In his native Spanish, Pepe ordered the diesel motor disengaged. He then enjoined the crew to fish the body-sized cloth out of the sea.

He saw that it was some kind of uniform. He began to think that the owner could be near, but looking in every direction, he saw nothing. He ran and jumped up to the floodlight and began to sweep the gentle waves. Perhaps half a minute had gone by when he saw a floating mop of golden hair about fifty feet to the port side.

They brought the boat around and Pepe kicked off his beat-up running shoes and jumped into the sea. Swimming several powerful strokes, he quickly came to what appeared to be the corpse of a *gringa.* He lifted her head out of the water. Her body was still warm.

Two more, from his crew, began helping him in the water. They aided him by hoisting her onto the deck. One of his crew ran back up to the floodlight and began to search, looking for something else.

Pepe positioned the *gringa* facedown, and tried to force water out of her. She didn't expel much. He reached to see if he could feel a pulse. Was it there? — perhaps, but different: slow, very slow. Every few seconds it seemed as if it made a beat. He rolled her on her side and tried to see if she was breathing at all. He could barely tell — maybe she was; maybe she wasn't.

One of the crew brought out several blankets and they wrapped her sun-crisped body, since she was likely suffering from shock.

Pepe turned her over, onto her back. They huddled around her for what seemed a long time, but it probably hadn't been a minute. Suddenly, she coughed, and he rolled her over onto her side. A few swallows of seawater came out of the corner of her mouth, and she began breathing slowly.

One of the crew stayed with her as Pepe went to take over the search, but they found nothing else. It looked as if the jumpsuit had to have belonged to her, and from the knotted legs, they decided that she had been using it as a life preserver. It also looked like a uniform, but not at all similar to any they had ever seen.

Pepe steered them back on course. In two hours they would reach port. He prayed that she wouldn't die. It would be a hard thing to explain: bringing back a corpse, especially the corpse of a strange *gringa.*

Maybe ten minutes had gone by, when the *gringa* coughed some more, and she began to open her eyes, but closed them before Pepe reached her. He checked her pulse, and it seemed normal. She was sleeping like a baby. Will she live? — he asked himself.

* * *

Elsewhere in the Pacific

JONES KNEW that her idea would work. Making the fine gold mesh in the tub's limited machine shop had been more of a challenge than coming up with the idea. And finding enough gold wire! You'd think it was a precious metal — she thought. We always have plenty, whatever we need! Here, there's almost nothing. They really ration things on these tubs. It had taken every ounce of inventiveness she had. Cannibalizing a few items that she considered of limited use for their present mission — a torpedo included — she was able to put together enough materials and parts to make her idea a reality. It would take her most of the day, but when she finished, the ionic-meson scan would be able to see four times the area.

She was on her back with her legs sticking out from under the panel and her feet cramped against the navigation station when she heard Charlie say, "Sir."

"Yes, Charles," the captain recognized.

"Sir, there's a faint surface blip on conventional radar, east by south-east, ten kilometers, possibly a fishing boat. Perhaps they've seen something. Should we pursue?"

By now, Jones was on her feet.

"Chief Jones?" the captain asked.

Nancy thought — Why waste time? Couldn't be anything. If we start chasing every fishing boat we'll never find anything. She spoke, "This is where the signal last came from; we'll search here." She pointed to a point on the map. It was in the opposite direction, about 60 kilometers. She considered — They don't even have a PLOT. It's a wonder they even had this old scanner I'm working on.

THE CAPTAIN'S INTUITION told him that they should have checked out the fishing boat, but the insolent Alpha Force witch had other ideas. It seemed to the captain that Miss Universe — a term he thought described her well, not because of her refined Aryan savors, but because she apparently thought she owned everything — was committing a grave error by not checking the boat, but she was running the show. So the captain ordered, "Bring us about. West, by northwest ..."

Chapter 20

DCLXVI

THIS CALLS for wisdom. If anyone has insight, let him calculate the number of the beast, for it is man's number. His number is 666.

AND SAYING, Alas, alas, that great city, that was clothed in fine linen, and purple, and scarlet, and decked with gold, and precious stones, and pearls!

— John the Apostle

AFTER THIS I saw in the night visions, and behold a fourth beast, dreadful and terrible, and strong exceedingly; ... and it had ten horns. I considered the horns, and, behold, there came up among them another little horn, ... and, behold, in this horn were eyes like the eyes of man, and a mouth speaking great things.... I beheld, and the same horn made war with the saints, and prevailed against them.

— Daniel the Prophet

That same day — Quito, Ecuador

CAPTAIN SMITH wasn't sure why he had exposed his insignia to the outers. He knew that the inflictors wouldn't like it, but he figured it would be best for him if he never saw them again, even if he had no idea what he would do, or how he would escape them. At least he had momentarily felt the pleasure of showing off in front of the outers, and he felt like he merited some recognition. The symbol was the same one that was on the flag he had planted on the red planet years before. He thought — Armstrong got his parade; I deserve something.

For now, since he hadn't thought of anything better, he was following the gentlemen who had invited him. While walking in the press of pedestrians, they didn't say much. When they reached the Jeep, he was the last one in and was given the front passenger seat after the man who had been speaking in English, who was called Jack, got into the back seat.

"So, James," Jack started, "could I see the insignia again?"

Having committed himself, he decided that he might as well. Besides, they were simply outers, and if they caused any problems, he knew that TerraNova would find them and terminate them, which was also the fate most likely to befall him. He felt stupid for having allowed himself to deteriorate to the point of showing off for outers, but on the other hand, especially after his experience in the plaza, he really didn't care to go back to Alpha Force. Things were different now, even if he couldn't quite say why.

So James reached around and pulled his poncho over his head, exposing his uniform, and said, "Here it is."

SMITH'S JUMPSUIT came into full view and its three brilliant colors — scarlet, purple, and gold — emerged, even through it was covered with numerous ground-in dirt and dried blood smudges. Jack observed that the words "Captain James H. Smith" were written over the left pocket. He thought — It looks like something out of a movie.

The sight of the uniform nearly made Jack forget his questions. On the opposite sleeve there was another insignia. It showed a detailed graphic of what could have been Mars with a large black saucer-shaped object zooming away. Underneath of it were written the Latin words

"Fraternitas Martis Dividere." The Great Seal's beauty fascinated Jack. It had never been like this on a dollar bill, and even in dusk's low light it was stark, nearly fluorescent.

"Do you know why your insignia has the number six hundred sixty-six?" Jack asked, at last finding words.

"Yes," he answered, and that was all he said for a moment. James seemed to be remembering, and he repeated aloud, as if it was a mantra, "It's the number of Therion, the coming messiah."

Jack was speechless. Jon didn't say anything either. James looked as though he was wondering if he'd done something wrong. When Jack began thinking of what James could really mean, and the implications, questions filled his mind, but he wasn't sure if he could, or should, ask even the first one. Jack looked at Jon, who looked irritated, as if he had been waiting in traffic for too long.

James interrupted the hush, and asked, "Why are you silent?"

Jack answered, "Oh … No … it's nothing. We're just thinking. Maybe you could tell us more about yourself; that way we can get to know each other."

"What can I say?" he questioned. And then added, "I'm really grateful for your speech," he said, looking into Jack's eyes. "I feel different now, but I probably should be on my way."

James turned and started to open the door, but Jack answered emotionally, "You don't have to go, James. You're welcome. Please stay." He knew he had to understand this stranger. Then he looked at Jon, desperately, trying to say — Help me!

"Yeah, James, please stay. We would like to have you with us for dinner tonight," Jon said, a touch of reluctance in his voice.

James looked down, hesitating, but he still had a hand on the door.

"What about it? Jon's wife really cooks great," Jack said, winking at Jon, not because Judy wasn't a good cook, but rather because he knew he was presuming there would be enough in the pot for another mouth.

James slowly answered, "Well …" and paused. "I'll accept."

"Good," Jack said.

"Fine," Jon added, though Jack could tell his heart wasn't in it.

Jon started the engine and moved into traffic.

Jack asked, "Maybe, James, you could tell us more about the place you said you came from? What did you call it? Novus ...? What was it?" Actually he had remembered the name, but he was trying to get the conversation going.

"Novus Ordo," James answered.

"And where is that? You said, 'Near Bermuda'?"

"Really, it's about 250 kilometers southwest."

"And you said it's not an island?"

"No," James answered, and then paused. It was apparent that he was thinking, and he was uncertain. When he continued, he said, "You'll have trouble believing me if I tell you. Can we talk about something else?"

"Jon, I think we can believe the man, don't you?" Pastor Kinderly commented, trying to help James.

"Of course," Jon confirmed, with a shade of curiosity in his expression.

"Well," James said, and again hesitated before continuing. "An hour ago I wouldn't have told you, but now things are different." His voice was profoundly sincere. He added, "And I want out."

"Out of what?" Jack asked.

Listening for James's answer, Jack wondered if he'd heard the man groan before he answered, saying, "Where do I start? If I tell you, I might put your lives in danger. The people I worked for will stop at nothing to keep their secrets."

With this revelation, Jon squirmed in his seat and Jack thought — What is he? Some kind of secret agent? They must be after him. Then Jack offered, trying to overcome his own fears, "You don't have to tell us anything if you don't want to, but we promise that whatever you tell, we'll keep in confidence."

In response James revealed, "There are two worlds: yours, and the one I lived in." He continued in a somber voice: "In our world, we call you *outers*."

Jon, now seeming to take interest, interjected, "We know there are two worlds. One belongs to Satan, and the other, to Jesus."

"Maybe the one I lived in was Satan's. I really don't understand what that means, but the world you live in isn't like you think."

Jack began to have some doubts about Smith's credibility, and thought — I'll let him talk it out. He was limping. Maybe he had an accident. Maybe he hit his head. Maybe he's paranoid, running from shadows. And there are so many conspiracy theories around. He's probably involved with some group of misled fanatics. If he talks a while, he'll contradict himself.

But then Jack reconsidered, while looking at his uniform again, and figured that he might be telling the truth, however far-fetched. He listened closely as James explained, "Novus Ordo is a deep-sea spaceport. It's a city under the sea. My Unit was headed there when I was coming back to Earth from Mars and our fusion reactor exploded. We had to abandon ship. I crashed on a mountain east of here."

Hearing the captain's words nearly made Jack repent of his previous decision to give him an ear, and rather, categorize him as a member of a conspiracy cult. Why, he hadn't even gotten through the "city under the sea" story and now he was saying he had been in space, coming from Mars, no less.

Jon questioned, with obvious incredulity in his voice, even if it was clear that he was trying to hide it, "When did it happen?"

"It was nine days ago. It would have been the night of December fifth."

"Jon, didn't you tell me about that tremendous explosion when we talked on the phone?" Jack asked.

"I did. Don't you remember your joke?"

Jack did remember — that someone would make up a UFO story. He couldn't help but wonder if Smith wasn't simply taking advantage, and pretending, but if so, he was good, not only sincere, but in uniform too. However, there wasn't any doubt that it was strange: a man who claimed he came from Mars and lived under the sea.

"Was there an explosion?" James asked.

Jon asked, "You tell me?"

"Well," James began pensively, "there should have been an explosion, but I must have been unconscious. There was a shock wave that hit me during reentry. My Unit was programmed to self-destruct at an altitude of twenty-five kilometers."

Jon was now driving along at increased speed as the streets in the northern part of the city widened.

"What do you mean by two worlds?" Jack questioned.

James's reluctance could be seen as he turned his head momentarily, and then answered, "I'll try to explain. There are ten men who govern the world. They are known as the Committee of the Cosmokrator, and until today I worked for them. They trained me from infancy for Alpha Force, which is their army. They have great power, and they are about to rule the world."

"Why are you so sure?"

"Because outers don't have any way to stop them. The Cosmokrator are only waiting for the right time."

"When's that?"

"They don't know, but the Skotoi will tell them."

"And who are the Sko ... toy?"

"The Skotoi are highly ascended masters. They are in touch with Scotopia."

"Scotopia? Is that some planet?"

James chuckled, and said, "Outers," and he looked slyly. "You don't know anything. Scotopia isn't a place in the sense that we are here and they are there. No, it's like the 'parallel universes' your science fiction writers tell about."

"A what? Universe?" Jack asked, though not really asking. And then he said, "I'm sorry, but it sounds so strange."

"If you wish, we don't have to talk about it."

"No, I'm interested, James. Tell me," Jon said.

"Right," Jack interjected eagerly. "Tell us." He had decided that he would do well to listen to him, in case there was any truth to what he was saying, and he still had a lot of questions he wanted answered. Besides, if it was just a fantasy, it sounded good. And he said, "I'm interested too. You said you worked for ten men. Who are they?"

"As I said, they're the Cosmokrator."

"Is that their name?" Pastor Kinderly asked.

"Right."

"And they do what the Sco-toys tell them?"

"Skotoi is plural," James corrected, and affirmed, "Yes, they carry out the plans of the ascended masters."

They began to drive into a residential area where the houses were made of concrete. Some were painted and others were decorated with stone. Some roofs were made with red baked tiles and others were simply concrete slabs. It wasn't like the colonial dull white of the downtown area. Each house sat behind a wall, and all the walls were joined, forming a continuous structure, though it varied from lot to lot, showing off a certain individuality that would otherwise have been lost. It changed in color, in material, and even in height and in design. There were occasional trees that rose out of the enclosures, and the majority of the houses were at least two stories, also rising above the surrounding barriers. The sidewalks were quite narrow, but blocked from view by the many vehicles that filled both curbs. The space left for driving was little more than it had been downtown, even though the streets were wider. This forced them to move along much slower. But it wasn't long until Jon announced, "We've arrived."

"We'll continue our conversation inside," Jack offered, relieved to be able to leave the vehicle's enclosed space. Smith's uniform wasn't only stained; it was also saturated with unpleasant odors. He didn't look like the type who would have a cleanliness problem, but it was noxiously plain that the captain needed a bath.

Jon pulled in front of a metallic garage door. It was painted flat black. Jon jumped out to open the doors, and soon drove through them.

Inside the small compound there was a grassy area and beside it was a patio and a wooden door. Jon opened it and invited them to enter.

Once inside the house, he invited them to sit down in the living room and continue the conversation, but just when they were ready to do so, Judy entered, along with Mercy. Jon introduced James to the ladies. Then they started to sit down, but Judy spoke, whisking her brunette hair back with involuntary disgust that caught the men off guard, and she said, "Mr. Smith, would you like to shower before supper?"

"I would love to, but I have no other clothing," James answered.

"I'm sure Jon can find you a robe, or something, until we can wash your clothing," Judy said, as she gave Jon a look.

"Excuse me," Jon began, "I didn't realize, or I'd have offered sooner; you don't have anything in your backpack that we can wash for you?" he inquired.

"No. Everything I have, I'm wearing."

"Oh …, well, I'll find you something. Please come with me." And he added, directing himself to Jack, "I'll take him to the outside guest room."

As the two men walked out, Judy informed, "Supper will be soon."

BEHIND THE HOUSE there was a guest room with simple but adequate furnishings: a bed, a lamp, a plain rust-colored rug, curtains embellished with an ivy pattern, and a shower. Jon led the visitor, wondering how wise it had been of Jack to invite him, and if it hadn't been better to let him go. He was also overwhelmed by the implications of the patch on the uniform, and by everything he was already imagining about these Sko-toys, or whoever they were. The visitor had called them "ascended masters" and said they wanted to rule the world. It seemed like it could be something demonic. He also remembered the number 666 on the uniform and tried to fathom what it could all mean. It sounded terribly apocalyptic, or like something that should be feared.

But Jon had always avoided "end-of-the-world alarmism" — as he called it. And all that he was hearing sounded as if it could fall into that category: like an advertisement to stock up on freeze-dried food for the end of the world. But if Smith worked for these people called "Cosmocrats," or whatever, it sounded like they could be dangerous. It also sounded like they would likely be looking for their runaway captain.

Then there was the "Unit" that supposedly exploded, and Jon considered — He said they were coming from Mars, so it must have been some kind of spaceship, and if so, the Cosmo people probably have more of them, which means they're awfully powerful — especially since they seem to be able to keep everything secret.

As far as Jon could tell, it also meant that it might not be long until the Cosmos would be busting down the door of his home, looking for their captain.

As they approached the room's door, Jon told James, "Please make yourself at home." And then reaching to open it, he turned and asked, "Do you have anything at all? Maybe some underwear?"

"Just what I've got on," James responded, showing an awkward expression in the quickly fading twilight.

"I'll do my best to get some clothing together for you. So, go ahead and shower. I'll take your things to wash and dry. You can leave them outside the door."

Having let the visitor in the room, and showing him the bath, Jon waited outside while Smith undressed. When he handed a small pile of clothing back out the door, Jon took it with some degree of anticipation, despite its odor, since he was curious to examine the uniform. As Jon walked the short distance back to the house, he wondered — What kind of nutcase could come up with such a story, and a uniform to match? Then Jon answered his own thought — The captain isn't a nut. He may be a lot of things, but he's too good to be crazy.

Jon found a change of clothes and a sweater and took them back out to the room, leaving them inside the door for Smith. Then he made his way back to the living room. The topic of conversation wasn't the weather, or how many souls had been saved, but rather the captain. Jack was trying to explain everything to the women and they were besieging him with questions, few of which he could answer.

Jon called for Judy, and Jack and Mercy too, to come with him to the laundry room and see the uniform. They stood there looking at the emblem. It has a terrible beauty — Jon thought. Like nothing I've ever seen. As he examined it, he could see that it was the product of quality workmanship, despite the dirt and grime.

Jon began to see other details in James's clothing that reinforced his story. On every piece, except his poncho, was the imprint "TerraNova — Alpha Force."

* * *

Worldwide

"THERE'S NO DOUBT, gentlemen, that the DEEP 1 disaster has forced us to delay," Watkins informed, as he summarized. "With this cruel fact in mind, it is obvious that we have no choice but to move the date for the presentation forward."

"I agree," Weller affirmed, "but until the Skotoi tell us to alter the Plan, we have to continue as ordered."

"But how? We're losing Gorbachev and the Soviet Union too," Savee questioned.

It was about then that Chairman Stonefell, and the others, heard a sound: a moan, or maybe it was a rustling, as if it could have been either, or both — it was their summons.

Finally, they're calling us — Stonefell thought. It's been a long wait. He looked expectantly at the other nine as they all prepared for changeover.

In an instant he felt himself moving into a distant realm at amazing velocity. Soon after, there was a beautiful light at the end of a winding tunnel. Slowing to a walk, he came into the presence of his lords — the Skotoi. He lifted his eyes and witnessed the countenances of the highly ascended Skotoi. He had visited them many times, but their presence was as captivating now as it had been the first time, twenty-four years earlier. So vivid was the experience, it occurred to him that "reality" wasn't as "real" as this.

He stepped into the court of a splendid palace, regal, yet modern. He, and the other Cosmokrator, fell prostrate before the ten Skotoi. Each one sat on his own throne — half were on one side of Therion and half were on the other. Then one, Psudes, who sat at Therion's right hand, addressed, "Our servants, Cosmokrator, the day of our glorious reign nears. Therion shall rule the destiny of humankind."

Ritually, the Cosmokrator answered, "So be it."

Therion was considerably smaller than the towering Skotoi, even smaller than the other Cosmokrators — truly a midget. He looked like a wise old man with a long white beard. But Stonefell knew that Therion and the other Skotoi weren't human at all. They were highly evolved entities.

Each Skotos had a pointed beard and a shaven head — similar to Therion's. They were dressed in silky black oriental gowns and sat in the lotus position with their legs crossed. They looked down upon the Cosmokrators with blind white eyes.

Therion had a full head of long, curling white hair. Unlike the Skotoi, who seemed incapable of sight, his pupils were dark and pierced with intoxicating seduction that was both alluring and spurning. However, though he had sight, he lacked a mouth and he never spoke. Psudes spoke for him. The Secret Doctrine of the Skotoi promised that during the time of Therion's magnificent reign he would be given a mouth, and it would speak marvelous things.

Descending from his throne, the Skotos whose name was Psudes, and who stood tall like a Goliath, began to tread about arrogantly, each of his steps thundering. He moved within the large triangular area enclosed by the Skotoi and the Cosmokrators. Therion sat at the apex, and Stonefell and the others were opposite, prostate in their business suits on the immaculate white tiled floor of the palace. Psudes spoke in a commanding voice, "Our servants! Untold millions of years of evolution have brought us to our present exalted state. We, the Skotoi, have achieved glory that you, as mortals, cannot know. In our benevolence, we labor to guide your humanity to a higher evolution, but the path has been difficult. For thousands of years we have attempted to raise the consciousness of humankind, but you, bumbling morons, always fail!

"On the plain of Shinar we nearly achieved a quantum advance. How marvelous it was, as the tower rose magnificently. However, your miserable species was confused and divided by the powers of Asmina, our common enemy. The sublime evolution we sought for your feeble kind was delayed.

"Our work has been long and taxing. Oftentimes, we have been delayed. Long shall we remember the miserable Golgotha Incident. We shall have our vengeance!

"Such failures are the consequence of the flawed, primitive judgment of an inferior species, but we are now closer to our common objective than in any other moment in history. Asmina shall be defeated!

"We will soon stabilize the harmonic consciousness of the universe. We have learned much, and have attained a greater evolution — especially through our superior technology.

"However, once again, we have been brought face-to-face with the ugly brow of delay — again, because of your ineptitude, wretched creatures! We do not take this lightly. Be warned! We will not always strive with miserable humans. We have achieved our greatest evolution, far beyond a material body. We bow to aid your cause, only to be free of Asmina, but do you expect us to continually tolerate your failures? Could we not simply eliminate your miserable kind? In our benevolence we have chosen to lead and to guide you to a higher consciousness.

"How could you have allowed something as elementary as a seal to postpone our great Plan? Aren't you capable of overseeing even the fundamentals? Miserable creatures, how long shall we endure your stupidity! You are a shame! A disgrace! Do not take this warning lightly. If you fail us again, you will be terminated and we will entrust our kingdom to wiser, more diligent hands.

"Cosmokrator, heed our warning. Devote yourselves to our noble cause. Soon the advancement of the harmonic awareness will be universal and your world will be ready for Therion.

"This present delay, though representing the loss of an empire, is merely political. There is yet time for you to redeem yourselves, Cosmokrator. We have great expectations. If you show greater diligence, we will be able to bring harmonic consciousness to your wretched world. Our common purpose, the universal awareness of humankind, such as we sought on the plain of Shinar, will be achieved.

"Once you have eliminated our enemies, the wretched followers of Asmina, the harmonic rhythm of the universe will be restored and Therion shall reign gloriously. Humanity will then achieve its highest evolution, higher even than the lost civilization of Atlantis. In our benevolence we shall do this for your miserable kind.

"Be warned! Another incident of this magnitude," he said as he looked down with a scoff, "will not be taken lightly."

Psudes then said, abruptly, "Enough!" Halting in step, he returned to his throne. He seemed to fix his gaze on the Cosmokrator, but it was hard to tell, since he didn't have pupils in his eyes. He laughed with depraved inflection, and continued, "Empire, fallen to chaos! Superb your demise: Grievous 'tis."

Each Cosmokrator knew that Psudes bemoaned the loss of the USSR, and the delay it would cause in the Plan.

Then Psudes spoke solemnly, "Cosmokrator, the presentation of Therion must now be delayed until the beginning of the new millennium. Take steps, therefore, to reevaluate and update the Plan."

When the meeting ended, Stonefell and the other Cosmokrator departed virtual reality and found themselves seated in their corresponding positions at their particular conference tables in each of the world's financial capitals — exactly where they had been all along.

As Stonefell reviewed in his mind what Psudes had said, and the exhortations received during the virtual conference, he began to think — I'm glad I had Allenburg rescued from the Russians. She zeroed in on the problem in Siberia. No one else would have caught the slob with his bottle. She's the right person. I need her, to be sure there's never another fiasco like that one with the seals. By the time we're able to try again, I'll be too old to start over — things will have to be perfect. Janice will do the job right. Her doctors say it'll be eighteen months, or so, until she's ready for work. By then, we'll have recovered from this setback and started working towards another attempt. We can't let Operation Therion fail again.

Then he remembered Janice's shapely figure and her ideal features — Yes, she's the right person. And she has a proven track record. I'll have her working close to me. I like that. She can be trusted. We won't even have to do a background check. We know her, and besides, any friend of Azard's is a friend of mine — he told himself, and in his mind he laughed, wondering if his old friend would have any objections to "sharing" his worthy manager, Janice, for the good of a higher cause, thinking of himself, personally, as the cause. Stonefell decided — Arlien won't mind. He needs our business. Without us, there isn't any NHMI.

Chapter 21

Proof

AN IDENTITY is questioned only when it is menaced, as when the mighty begin to fall, or when the wretched begin to rise, or when the stranger enters the gates, never, thereafter, to be a stranger ...

— James Baldwin

December 14 — That same day — Quito, Ecuador

THOUGH STILL LIMPING, James felt much better. Never before had he taken a shower that made him feel as clean. He'd even been able to shave. The clothing that Jon had left for him didn't quite fit. It was short enough to make him look like a kid who was growing too quickly.

For a moment, he remembered how the outer's message, back in the plaza, had made him feel, and he wondered about the source of the message's power, what it really meant. It seemed too simple. It really couldn't be anything more than flawed outer thinking.

However, in contrast, he also considered — Christians aren't the way they taught us. They're kind. But his next thought made him stumble — I'm turning into an outer, now. He had to ruminate on it, like trying to think through a quantum-relativity hyperdimensional problem.

After a pause, feeling as though he should have felt bad for being with outers, he thought — Isn't it funny, though? I have no desire to go back to Alpha Force now.

He left the guest room and returned to the house, making an unspectacular, and perhaps embarrassing, entrance: A tall man wearing pants that were several inches short. But James had such dignity no one would have dared comment, and after everything he had been through, he didn't care. He was glad he had fresh clothing; whether or not everything fit was the least of his concerns. When he limped into the living room, he became the center of attention.

"Are you okay? That limp looks nasty," the one woman, who sat beside the preacher, asked. If he remembered the introduction correctly, she was the Jack's wife, Mercy.

"I'll be okay," James responded.

"Have a seat," Judy invited, motioning towards one of the empty couches.

He felt their stare, as everyone's eyes followed him.

"Captain," Jack addressed, trying to get a conversation started, "please tell us about yourself."

James looked up, having sat down on the soft cushion. It was a temptation to remain silent. He hadn't been so comfortable since leaving his quarters back on DEEP 1, and besides, the answer wasn't going to be simple. Although he was tired and hungry, he knew he needed to answer. He couldn't expect them to receive him otherwise, and since he had determined not to go back to Alpha Force, he would need outers to help him until he could get along by himself. They would have a hard time with him. He reasoned — I'm an outer to them, and they will think of me as something from their science fiction.

When James began to speak, his throat was dry, "I was a member of Alpha Force, which is the army of TerraNova …" Pausing, he coughed.

Hearing him, Judy offered, "Could I get you something to drink?"

"Please," he answered simply.

Having asked everyone what they wanted to drink, Judy slipped into the kitchen.

"Jim … Is that all right? If I call you Jim?" Jack asked.

"That's okay."

"I'm sure you realize that this Alpha Force and TerraNova you're talking about isn't something we're familiar with," Jack commented.

"I can see that it won't be easy for me to explain. Perhaps my watch will help me make my point." He took off his watch and passed it to Jack, who was sitting nearest to him.

Jack examined it carefully. "Why, it's just like the ones they use on *Star Trek*," he said with a smile.

James was familiar with outer science fiction, and though the particular work mentioned wasn't necessarily inspired by TerraNova (even if a lot of popular science fiction was), it had certainly served them well. By making people think that flying saucers, alien beings, and super-tech in general were all futuristic, and that such things would be found in the hands of "superior beings," they would be able to use their own super-tech, at the presentation of Therion, to help convince outers that they, TerraNova, had all of the solutions for Earth's problems. With this in mind, James, for the sake of his own credibility, decided to take advantage of the myth, and said, pointing to the watch, "But this one's not a toy." His words were a jest that he knew would be taken seriously once they had seen the watch in action.

James watched Jack's expression change from a patronizing smile to one of amazement, and the others sounded uneasy chuckles.

It was easy to see that Jack was enthralled. He was obviously realizing that the device, though similar to a watch in appearance, wasn't like any he had ever seen before. James knew its materials and its design were unknown to outers, and taking advantage of his momentum, he suggested, "Tell it, 'Show UDTC.' "

"How do I do that?"

"Just say, 'Show me UDTC.' "

Jack spoke towards the watch, "Please show me UDTC."

James watched as Jon, with a curious look, moved around to see over Jack's shoulder.

"What on Earth!" Jack exclaimed. "It says, 0.237 UDTC."

Realizing that Jack didn't know what UDTC was, James offered, "Ask it what Eastern Standard Time is."

With visible fascination, Jack requested, "Show me Eastern Standard Time."

SEEING THE AMAZING WATCH, with the screen displaying 7:34:27 PM as fast as Jack had asked, Jon thought — We're in trouble. This guy's definitely on the run. That watch of his has to belong to a top-secret operation. Even the bureaucrats who make the secrets probably don't know about it. Every counterintelligence agency in the world is probably searching for this guy. He said he's a captain. I bet he knows plenty. Guys in black suits are probably swarming after him, and they'll be knocking on our door any minute. Or maybe they're already outside, spying on us, waiting for the right moment. Then Jon reprimanded himself. Don't be so paranoid. Don't let a spirit of fear get you. If God sent the captain your way, then He has a purpose."

About then Smith suggested, "Ask the watch to show you the square root of two, or for that matter, of any number you want."

Jack looked back over his shoulder at James and asked, "Is he kidding?" But then, excited like a child with a new toy, he asked, "Watch, show me the square root of one thousand five hundred thirty-one."

As soon as he finished speaking "one," the number 39.12799509303 appeared, brilliantly, printed in white numbers on a blue background. By now the two wives had moved close enough to see, and get in on the fun. They all took turns yelling instructions at the watch, which gave mixed results.

"What is two plus two?" Jon asked.

The watch displayed four.

"Who is the president?" Grace inquired.

The watch went blank.

"What is the price of eggs in China?" Judy yelled with a giggle.

But it was wondrous when the watch's screen asked, "Exchange rate?"

"This is incredible!" Jon exclaimed again.

Jon asked Jack if he could hold it, and then watched, transfixed, as answers appeared on its screen at lightning speed. It was so different from anything he had ever handled, and though extremely light, it felt sturdy, ready for abuse. Engraved on the back plate was the symbol of the great pyramid and the all-seeing eye, just as on James's clothing. But there was also a number: 10000M.

"You mean this thing is waterproof to ten thousand meters?" Jon exclaimed.

"Perhaps more, but they don't test them any deeper," James replied, matter-of-factly.

"Look, James," Jon began hesitantly, "this fancy watch of yours certainly seems to prove that you must have access to top-secret stuff, but a watch out of the movies doesn't prove that you've been to Mars, or that you actually came from this ... shall we say, 'hidden' world."

Judy gave Jon a look as he finished stating his position. He could tell she felt ashamed he doubted the visitor's word so openly, but he felt it was the right thing to do, as he considered — I can't just be expected to swallow a big story about an exploding spaceship. I have a right to know the truth. But he hadn't meant to sound so openly disbelieving, even though it was plain that his words had come across in that tone.

In answer to Jon's interrogation, James swallowed as he looked back at him. Slowly he answered, "I don't have any way to prove I've been to Mars, but I have one more thing. It's all I've got left. Excuse me, I'll get it."

He stood and limped away quickly. Jon felt sorry for the stranger, but he had to know. He had to know the truth. What else is he going to show us? — Jon asked himself. A ray gun?

Everyone continued to be entertained by the watch while James was away. When he returned, he took the same seat, with his audience's eyes following him. He had a jet-black "plate," for lack of a better word. It looked so dark — blacker than ink, as if it sucked light into its interior; it seemed to make a hole in James.

"What's that? — James," Jack questioned.

"A PLOT."

Whatever that is — Jon thought, and nearly asked aloud: A plot to blow up the world? But he knew his thought was cynical and if he had spoken it aloud, it would not have been humorous.

James held the flat rectangular plate out in front of him and asked, "What's the address here?"

"Rodrigo Carrera 423," Jon informed, wondering why the PLOT needed an address.

James spoke, "PLOT, Ecuador, Quito, Rodrigo Carrera 423, zoom 1500."

"What's it doing?" Jon asked, watching incredulously.

James was silent. He had their attention.

This is little more than another top-secret toy — Jon surmised. But he didn't yet voice his appraisal of the object. Despite his skepticism, it was beautiful. He had seen city maps, but not like the one the PLOT was showing. In the center of the map he could see his house.

Then James spoke and said, "Zoom 2000, 3-D, rotate."

Jon watched with fascination as the picture closed in and showed the neighborhood. Then it suddenly seemed to jump into the air. It wasn't ghostly or transparent. It looked solid. As if such a stunt hadn't been fantastic enough, the projection started rotating. Watching it happen made him think — I've always liked science fiction, but it's not supposed to walk into your living room after crashing on a rainy night.

Jon couldn't resist the temptation and reached down to touch, but his hand went right through it, proving itself the phantom it really was.

It stunned Judy. She thought her husband had broken it, and she exclaimed, "Jon!"

"Don't be alarmed," James said. "It's okay."

With that, all of them began to "touch" the projection. Of course, there wasn't anything to feel but air.

Then James asked, "Where are you from, Jack?"

"Orlando, Florida."

In an instant James was showing Orlando on the PLOT. When he zoomed down on Jack's church, everyone watched, dumbfounded.

Then James offered, "I'm going to show you where I'm from."

"Okay," Jon said, starting to realize how extraordinary the PLOT was. "Let's see."

James directed, "PLOT, 3-D, Novus Ordo, zoom negative 4000, progressive."

An instant later, a beautiful globe appeared, floating in air. It was the blue planet. Perfect in every respect, the globe was about eight inches in diameter. It almost looked like it would have if seen from space, but Jon noticed there weren't any clouds. Then the image began to move in, zooming progressively down. The coast of the Sunshine State disappeared off to the side and the view moved right into the ocean. Contour lines of the ocean depths appeared and the image kept moving closer to the bottom, until a large hole became visible, with contour lines running back through it. And then suddenly the map of a city appeared. It was labeled Novus Ordo.

There was a large area labeled "DEEP Hangar." Another area was designated, "Fusion Generator." These and other fascinating names made Jon wonder — What movie did he pull this thing out of?

"Now, I'm going to show you where my spaceship was when we left for Earth, before the explosion," and he spoke: "PLOT, 3-D, Mars Base Aquarrian, zoom negative 2500, progressive."

Like magic, there it was, the red planet — with a clarity that made Jon wonder if astronomers had ever seen it so. Again the image began to move down into a deep valley surrounded by mountains that seemed to tower right up into the living room's ceiling, although they were only about ten inches tall, but the 3-D map was enthralling, enveloping, as if it was sucking the viewer into it. Jon noted something that fascinated him even more. When he moved his head, or walked around, he could see different perspectives, even though James didn't move the device.

Then, as the map progressed closer to the surface, there was a gigantic round circle marked and labeled "Air Lock." Passing inside, deeper, a map appeared, in many ways similar to the one of Novus Ordo, but obviously different and a bit smaller.

"This is our base on Mars," James said, with a hint of pride.

Jon was tempted to say — Yeah, and I'm from Alpha Centaur ... or whatever they call it. But besides having forgotten the name of the star, he was beginning to believe there was a whole lot more to James than was easily imagined. James suddenly became, in his eyes, a superhero — right out of the pages of a comic book. He remembered the old adage truth is stranger than fiction, and thought to himself — But this is stranger than truth, or fiction. However, he felt satisfied, and asked, "Please, tell us about Mars."

"It's beautiful, faraway and lonely — above all, it's cold." With that description, James paused.

Judy took advantage of the moment, "It's starting to get late and we haven't had dinner. Please, come to the dining room. We can talk more there."

"Thank you! I'm so hungry," James said, salivating.

Chapter 22

The Secret Doctrine

He will honor a god of fortresses; a god unknown to his fathers he will honor with gold and silver, with precious stones and costly gifts. He will attack the mightiest fortresses.

— Daniel the Prophet

That same day — Quito, Ecuador

Jack considered that had it not been for James's willingness to eat and Judy's hospitality, they might well have forgotten it was dinnertime. Jack was enthralled. He started to feel that God had some purpose in all of this, and that James hadn't come to them accidentally. Jack felt awe, as if they were making history. There wasn't any good reason for him to feel this way. There wasn't any reason to believe that James would even be with them the next day. Yet Jack knew — simply knew

— that God had sent James, and that in some way the course of world events would be influenced because of it.

Jack had always been good at seeing moments of opportunity, which was one of the reasons he had been so successful in the ministry, and even though he had a personal aversion to end-time prophets of doom, and even though James was describing something that sounded like a "666 book" (as he called them), Alpha Force Captain James Smith was an opportunity. He would tell them about the hidden world that was plotting to rule the world, and from him Jack would learn, and be prepared to warn and aid others.

"Jack, would you lead us in prayer?" Jon solicited

Jack prayed, "Heavenly Father, we thank You for Your provision and the food we share. Bless it to our bodies and bless the hands that have prepared it, as well as those who have provided. Father, bless James, our new friend. Help him to grow in You. In the name of Jesus. Amen."

James, looked satisfied after the prayer, and he said, "Thanks, Jack. I'm glad you called me a 'friend.' "

Soon conversation turned back to TerraNova.

"How could they have kept all of this a secret?" Mercy inquired.

"Please believe me; you too must keep it a secret. TerraNova doesn't allow its secrets to escape, and they have people everywhere. They even have an office here in Quito, called the 'Nova Mundi Foundation.' I don't think it's large, maybe a half dozen people at the most, but they'll kill you if they ever find out you know anything."

"Jesus will help us," Jon responded. "I wasn't too sure about you, James. But after seeing everything, and getting to know you some, with this evil empire you're describing, I'm starting to feel like we need to do something, resist somehow."

"I don't think that would be wise," James answered.

"You don't think there's any way we can resist?" Jack asked.

"I don't see how, but for right now, all I want is to survive."

Jon asked, "But why are you leaving them? It sounds like you had a good position in this Alpha Force. You were a captain?"

"True. And I don't know if I can give you a good answer. At least I don't know if I like the answer myself, but back on the mountain, where I crashed, there was a moment when I had to press a button for them to come get me. I didn't want to do it, but I couldn't keep myself from it. But after I pressed the button, the transceiver didn't work, and when I realized they wouldn't be coming to get me, I felt something I'd never known before. I think it's called freedom. I was free! But then I started towards Quito, and the closer I got, the more certain I became that I would turn myself back in and call Nova Mundi. I looked for a phone, but when I found one in the plaza, there wasn't any phone book, and I couldn't find the number—"

"Your watch didn't have the number?" Jon asked with a chuckle.

"No. It didn't. Ecuador's phone system isn't advanced enough for direct dial. So then I heard you two, and got closer, trying to listen. It was as if you knew what I was thinking. Years ago, someone gave me a little paper about the Jonah you were talking about. I read it and threw it away, thinking it was absurd. But when I crashed, I remembered it. It said that Jonah called on the Lord when he was in distress and that the Lord heard. When I was on the mountain, there was a night when it seemed that the storm was going to blow me away, and then I remembered the words from that paper. I repeated them aloud, and soon the weather calmed. The next morning I remembered, but thought it must have been a dream.

"When I heard you, I felt like my life was rotten, and that I needed, and wanted, the new life you said Jesus would give me. I repeated the words you told the crowd to repeat, and now I feel different. I still don't know what it means, but I don't want to go back. Before, the only thing I could think was how to get back to Nova Mundi, but not now."

"That's quite a testimony, James," Jack said. "What are you going to do now?"

There was a long pause, and he began with a stammer, "I ... I don't know. Can you help me? I don't have any money, or anywhere to stay."

"Yes, James. We'll help," Jack said, looking him in the eyes, and then looking at Jon.

"Right, we will," Jon added.

"I appreciate that," James answered.

Jack didn't want the conversation to lag, and asked, "Jim, you mentioned that the number six-six-six speaks of the coming messiah. You called him a name?"

"Yes. That's what they taught us. His name is Therion."

"I'm not sure. I'll need to look it up, but those words you're using sound like Greek. Therion, … Cosmokrator, … and that other one?"

"Skotoi," James answered, and confirmed, "They are Greek."

"Why Greek?" Jon asked. "Why not English?"

"It is the language of the gods," James began. "They taught us that it's the language of culture and reason. And it's the language of Therion.

"We were taught that Therion, during one of his attempts to establish his kingdom, around 170 BC, invaded Palestine and overcame the chosen ones of Asmina. He victoriously celebrated in the temple of Asmina, his greatest enemy. He sacrificed a sacred boar — an animal loathed by Asmina, but esteemed by Therion. Then Therion took the broth from the sacrifice and poured it out, all over, to desecrate the temple and to break the faith of the people in their weak deity. Finally, Therion erected, upon the very altar of Asmina, an altar to Zeus — who was also one of Therion's manifestations.

"It was a great moment for Therion. He nearly achieved his objective of converting the chosen of Asmina. Most of them accepted his new ways, but a few didn't. In order to complete what he started, he was going to eradicate the remnant of Asmina and ordered that none of Asmina's followers be allowed to keep their holy day. He ordered them to stop their barbaric circumcision of their male infants and commanded them to eat pork. If they didn't obey, he would exterminate them, and then all memory of Asmina would be gone."

By now, Jack was thinking — This is something. I've heard this. But who's As-mine, or whatever he's called? What James is describing — the desecration of the temple — sounds like what Epiphanes did to the Jewish temple. And the date he gave is right about that time. But who's Asmina? Is that what the TerraNova people call Yahweh?

"But something happened," James continued. They had all stopped eating to listen. "One day, a priest of Asmina killed one of Therion's soldiers in the temple. It sparked a revolution, and the war lasted years, until the forces of Therion were defeated. By that time, the opening in the cosmic frame had passed and Therion had to abandon his effort to consolidate his power. It was a terrible incident. Therion had nearly achieved his goal of restoring the harmonic consciousness — but in the end he failed."

Jack wondered what sect James was with. His story certainly had a unique twist.

"Therion was attempting to make Greek the universal language. Today, when there's another opening in the harmonic frame and Therion tries again to establish his kingdom, to rid the Earth of the chosen of Asmina, the language he uses will be English. But he really doesn't care which language is used — so long as everyone speaks the same one. Back in the nineteen forties it looked like it would be German. Through the years there have been different ones, like Babylonian, Persian, Assyrian, Latin — Therion has tried many times.

"His goal is simple. If everyone speaks the same language, then the disruption of the harmonic consciousness caused by Asmina back on the plain of Shinar, when the languages were confused, will be undone, and Therion will be able to unite the world under his rule and restore the cosmic balance."

Jack thought — If I used Yahweh instead of Asmina, and if I were telling history from Satan's viewpoint, I might explain history the way James is explaining it.

"So the reason Therion uses Greek names is that he fondly remembers his success in the desecration of the temple of Asmina. It was one of the few times in history he came so close to restoring the universal consciousness. But he has other names," James concluded.

"What names?" Jack asked.

"Serpent, Jackal, and Scorpion — to name a few. It has a lot to do with the time and the culture. But he's also known by the names of the men he's used during different cosmic frames, like Nimrod, Nebuchadnezzar, Epiphanes — "

"Who did you say?" Jack asked, interrupting.

"Epiphanes. Why?" James asked.

"You mean Antiochus IV Epiphanes?" Jack questioned.

"Correct," James answered, and asked, "Why?"

James thought it curious that Jack knew enough history to know who Epiphanes was, because most outers wouldn't have had an inkling. James continued, "Well, there are many more. Some are more famous than others. Some of them you won't find in your history books, but there have been many."

"Go ahead, James," Jon urged, "tell us some of them."

"There was Herod and some of the Caesars ... and like I say, some you won't find in your history books, and in modern times, one of the most important was Hitler."

"So, what do you mean by 'cosmic frame'?" Jack questioned.

"You see, that's one of Therion's biggest problems. If he could work continually, he would have defeated Asmina long ago, but he has to work in cycles. He's limited by the nature of the ether-time continuum. Because of Asmina's disruption of the harmonic consciousness, and because of the intrinsic nature of Therion, there are times when he loses phase. At other times he's stronger."

"Don't they believe this also affects Asmina?"

"No. That's part of the reason Asmina did what he did at Babel. The Secret Doctrine teaches that the present phasing of the ether-time continuum is favorable to Asmina. However, there will be a time, which is predictable by astral projection, and it's believed to be coming soon, when the phasing will favor Therion. It will be the best opportunity he's ever had to defeat Asmina."

"When will that be?" Jack asked, his attention riveted on James.

"Because of the instability provoked by Asmina, it's impossible to tell with absolute certainty, but the general time should be during the first half of the new millennium, especially the first years. The cosmic frame opens and closes all the time, as in 1942. It was an excellent opportunity, and Therion almost accomplished his goal. With just a little more time he would have managed to eradicate the chosen of Asmina. Then 1984 was a strong possibility, because of the alignment of the planets. Right now, the Cosmokrator has been gearing up for a window in 1994, but it's a small one. However, the cosmic frame that's coming at the beginning of the next millennium will be the longest one in 6000 years. The Secret Doctrine teaches that it will last seven years, and afterwards, Therion will rule a thousand years. During that time humanity will achieve its highest evolution and many will become ascended masters. People will no longer need bodies since they'll become one with the ether-time continuum."

Some of this is hard to figure through — Jack thought. It sounds like some kind of high-tech devil-sect.

"And does Asmina have other names?" Jon asked.

"Certainly," James answered. "He's the One, the outers call Him God—"

"I knew it!" Jack interrupted. And he asked in the same breath, "Is that what your people call us, 'outers'?"

"Right. Excuse me for not explaining. But let me finish what I was saying. They taught us that there isn't any God, at least not an Almighty or omniscient God — not a Creator. They taught us that everything evolved, and that both Asmina and Therion are highly evolved ascended masters."

Jack asked, "So, James. What do you think of everything that you're telling us? Do you still think that way, the way they taught you?"

He didn't answer quickly, but after a palpably long stare into space, he said, "Well, as far as what happened with Antiochus Epiphanes is concerned, it's history. It's true history, not just outer history. But even so, it's simply their interpretation. For years I've seen problems with their idea that there's no Creator. I've studied the laws of physics, and New Order plasma and ether physics too, and the universe must have had a Creator. Things don't evolve into higher states on their own. I've never seen it demonstrated. Things naturally become more disordered. Even Therion's schemes have problems all the time and he has to start over. I always wondered why they tried so hard to tell us there wasn't a Creator God. If He didn't exist, why try so hard to convince us? So I've always had trouble accepting what they taught us.

"After this afternoon, I feel really different. I can't explain it, but I know a Creator exists and things aren't highly evolved accidents. In the moment when I repeated those words with you, for the first time I knew my life had a purpose, and that by His will the Creator had brought me to that moment. Even the crash of my spaceship was part of His plan. Things are different now, and I've decided: I'm not going back to my previous life with TerraNova."

Jack discerned the contrite resolve in his voice. It touched him.

"Will they be searching for you?" Jon asked.

Before James could answer, Judy interjected, "The food's probably cold by now. Does anyone want me to put his plate in the microwave? James, can I help you?"

James looked puzzled and asked, "*Microwave?*"

Judy pointed toward the counter.

James looked, and answered with a smile. "Well, I thought you were talking about a microwave radio. We cook with *eterkilns*. They're faster and they cook better."

After Judy had taken his plate, he answered Jon's question. "They don't know that I'm alive and my position isn't where they'd expect. My ship self-destructed. And if I were to have survived the crash, I should have landed in water. So they won't be looking for me here in these mountains. And I don't think they're looking for me at all, since they would believe I'm dead. But I still need to be careful that I don't do anything that would draw their attention."

"I wouldn't walk around in that fluorescent space suit of yours," Jon commented with a chuckle.

James agreed.

"Do you know about the origin of the word *Asmina*?" Jack asked.

"It's from the Sanskrit. It means, the 'I AM not.' "

"Yahweh calls himself the I AM," Jack began. "Is 'I AM not' a way your group has of belittling God?"

"Well ..." James replied in a pondering tone, "I don't know. We were told that it's because Asmina is disruptive, and is forcing the universal lattice, the ether, to disorganize — what outer scientists call increasing entropy. Ever since humankind began seeking enlightenment, Asmina has stopped supporting the lattice and it is becoming more disorganized. He wants humankind to become dependent on Him. If the lattice was perfect, the world would be a paradise and there wouldn't be any hunger, disease, or death.

"According to the Secret Doctrine, only an absolute being, of the highest evolution, must support and maintain the ether structure upon which everything in the universe depends. This is because such a being reaches infinity, and is omnipresent. A being of inferior evolution can only maintain the ether in a limited area of the universe. But even so, the decay of the universal lattice will eventually force the destruction of the ether structure, even in those areas where lesser beings may have been supporting them. This quality of absolute being is called: I AM that I AM, or ASMI. It can only be achieved by the most highly evolved of ascended masters and there can only be one ASMI. It is impossible for two ASMIs to occupy the totality of the space-time continuum in absolute harmonic resonance. Asmina, however, is allowing the universal ether lattice to weaken. So he has become the I AM not, or the ASMIna."

Jack was uncertain which question he should ask, but he tried, "So this Secret Doctrine contradicts Yahweh's claim in the Bible to be the I AM?"

"Not really. Yahweh was, and is, the I AM, since He sustains the ether order and existence through His own existence. He just isn't doing a good job, they say. It's because man is trying to reach a higher evolution and wants to become like Asmina, so Asmina is allowing this to happen to keep man from being able to evolve any further. That's why Therion is trying to establish himself as the ASMI and to free the universe of Asmina."

"So, you accept that Yahweh is the I AM?"

"Right. That's what the Secret Doctrine teaches, as I was saying."

"And how does Therion think he can take over?" Jon asked with a smirk.

"Simple," James began. "Belief is the substance that makes evidence of absolute ethereal existence possible. If Therion can eliminate all belief in Asmina, then he will be victorious."

"So that's why Therion tried to convert the chosen of Asmina to himself?" Jack asked.

"Or kill them."

"Your people believe that *belief* is a substance?" Jon queried.

"Right, but not substance as we know it. It is not a physical substance that can be measured with standard instrumentation. It belongs to a higher dimension."

"That seems similar to Hebrews eleven-one," Jack noted.

"What's that?" James asked.

Jack informed James, "Hebrews is a book in the New Testament of the Bible. I'm referring to a verse that teaches that faith, which is what is believed, is the substance, or evidence, of things not seen, and maybe that is the higher dimension you're talking about. But it's hard to say without a better understanding of your ideas."

Jon questioned, "Does that mean your people believe that if they keep people from believing in Yahweh He'll cease to exist?"

"Not really, but His power will be broken, and He'll cease to be the ASMI."

"Well," Jon answered with indignation, "we believe that Yahweh is the I AM that I AM, no matter what!"

"Cool it," Jack said under his breath, directing himself to Jon.

"I'm just telling you what they taught us," James answered defensively. "It's what the Secret Doctrine says."

"Tell me about this 'Secret Doctrine.' Is that like Therion's Bible?" Jack asked.

"I guess you could say that."

"You do know what the Bible is?"

"Right. It's the holy book of the Judeo-Christian people. You were talking about it this afternoon."

"Do you know anything else about the Bible's message?"

"Not really; just, it's a book that talks about Jesus and Jonah."

"From what I can tell," Jack began, "what your Secret Doctrine — "

"It's not my Secret Doctrine," James clarified, defensively.

"Oh. Excuse me. What this Secret Doctrine seems to say about ASMI — and you've said that He's Yahweh — seems to contradict the Scriptures, the book that Yahweh, whom we usually call 'the Lord,' gave to tell us about Himself and His plans. However, there are similarities. The Bible also talks about the Lord being the One who sustains everything. However, the Bible teaches that man's search for 'enlightenment' apart from God is actually rebellion against Him. Actually, it teaches that the first man, Adam, wanted to be like God, and that Adam's failing represents the failing of all of mankind. In other words, man wants to be God. And that's exactly what this Therion you've talked about wants. He wants men to evolve and to become God."

James listened attentively as Jack spoke. Jack could almost feel James drawing the words out of him.

"But there's only one true God according to the Bible," Jack continued in solemn intensity. "Neither man, nor any other being, can hold the universe together. Not even this Therion you've told us about can do it, although he thinks he can. If this 'lattice' you've talked about ceased to be, then Therion would also cease to exist, along with you and me and everything else, because this lattice is the very structure of the universe, as you have said. Our Bible also proclaims, in Colossians chapter one and verse seventeen, that He is before all things, and that in Him all things consist, or hold together.

"The reason it's falling apart isn't because God desires for men to be ignorant, but because of sin — specifically rebellion. As long as man wants to take God's place as ASMI, as you say, the universe won't be the way God wants it to be. The God of the Bible is more than some highly ascended master. He is absolute being, and that didn't happen by accident, or because He evolved into it. He is God because He *is*, and always has been, and ever shall be. He didn't start existing. Satan and man came into existence at some moment. They were created and the Lord gave them life. Without the Lord, nobody or nothing can have 'being.'

"As to this Therion being a messiah, like you mentioned back in the Jeep, it would seem, from what you've said, he may be the one the Bible teaches is going to be the false messiah, the same one whom many Christians call the antichrist. On the other hand, the Bible teaches that Jesus is our Messiah.

"Jesus promised that He is going to come back to Earth again, and He taught that He would rule. He also taught that in the last times — before He came back — another one would come. We call him the antichrist, as I said. In a book that Jesus gave through a prophet named John, He identified the one who would come as a man, and said that his number or identification would be six hundred sixty-six. You've said that that's the number of Therion. You have DCLXVI on your uniform, which is also six hundred sixty-six. I'm wondering if another name for Therion will be Antichrist.

"Antichrist is the one the Bible identifies with the number six hundred sixty-six. He will present himself to all the Earth as a man of peace and as the one who can solve all problems. Daniel the prophet taught that he will be a great orator and that people will be captivated by his rhetoric. People will love him and trust him. While he is governing the Earth he will attempt to eliminate all knowledge of the Lord Jesus. He'll do this during a period of time we call the Tribulation. It will be seven years long.

"Daniel also tells us that the Antichrist will have some kind of super military, shall I say, 'technology,' that will allow him to overcome even the greatest fortresses. Could that be the spaceships and the technology these TerraNova people possess?"

"The Bible says all of that?" James asked.

"Yes, Jim. Most of the Bible's prophecies have already been ful-filled. Sometimes the prophets foretold the destruction of cities and kings. Sometimes they talked of famine and natural disasters or of the rise and fall of nations. They wrote in detail about Jesus' coming hun-dreds of years before the event. Most of the things they wrote came to pass as they foretold, but there are portions of their writings that haven't happened yet, and their fulfillment is still to come. We believe that like everything else they said, it will all come to pass the way they wrote it."

"Do you have a Bible? Could I read it?"

"I'll give you one after dinner."

"A question, James," Jon began, "What was that on your watch. UDTC? I've heard of UTC; that's like Greenwich Mean Time, but what's UDTC?"

"Universal Decimal Time Coordinated. It's UTC converted into a decimal system in which each day has ten hours. It makes one standard time for all of TerraNova's operations, including Mars."

"I'm eager to hear more," Jack commented, seeing James take a forkful of mashed potatoes from his plate.

As promised, after dinner, and after much more discussion, Jack got the Bible for James. He was grateful. He explained that he wasn't used to getting gifts — that they didn't have gifts in Alpha Force. Jack told him, "If you read any, let me show you two places you might find interesting. A man named John wrote both of them, but not him," he said with a laugh, motioning towards Jon.

Jack marked the Gospel of John and Revelation. With James's knowledge concerning six-six-six and with his unique view of history, Jack wondered if James might understand more about the dramatic last book in the Bible than he might himself. Jack was now convinced that James could have a valuable mission to the Church. Jack wondered what he could do to devise a way to tell other Christians, especially leaders, about the knowledge that James carried. It wouldn't be easy. It wouldn't be possible to simply publish a book, or get an interview on

TV. He didn't know how he would be able to spread James's story, but he knew he would, and for now, he would concentrate on keeping James near, and if at all possible, away from TerraNova's people. Jack wondered if it would even be possible. It would be like fighting the very powers of evil in the flesh, but he knew that with God, all things are possible. And he was convinced that God had sent James.

Jack wasn't sure how he would get the mission board of his church to approve it, or if perhaps he could find another source for funding, but sharing James's story with Church leaders meant keeping James, which meant providing for James. So Jack knew he would find a way, with God's help, one step at a time.

AFTER MORE CONVERSATION, and exchanging good nights, James went back to the outside guest room. Regardless of being tired, he wanted to read the Bible. He quickly read through the first few verses of John. The Bible was saying that God was the Creator. He felt some temptation to deny it, as he had been taught, but this was exactly what he had already concluded on his own. It would have excited him, except it sounded so outer, which, as he was beginning to see, wasn't necessarily bad.

After a while, he lay back. Feeling the pain from his ankle, he reminded himself to find something to make a splint and wrap it up.

* * *

The next day — The Pacific Ocean

THIS IS taking me too long — Chief Nancy Jones fumed to herself. Instead of improving the scan, it seemed to her that she might have lowered its coverage. Her well-ordered thoughts became a blur of expletives and — what's-wrong-here? — interrogations. She didn't, and wouldn't, let on that she really wished she had some help, and especially that she had some good tools, like a phasing-dicormeter or a pulsed-holographic-spectrometer.

FOR HIS PART, the captain tried to keep his pleasure from showing on his face. It was fun watching Miss Universe. She must be having the time of her life — he considered, mordantly. Her training was too thorough for her to betray herself with words, but the captain could see it — not in her expression, for it was as stoically cold as it had been when they rescued her, and not in her manner, for it was as chilling as it had been when her crew met her. Indeed, it wasn't visible at all, but the captain saw it. She was simmering and could have boiled water in the galley. Even if he was only Beta, he could see right through the Alpha arrogance.

Chapter 23

Luck?

WHEN GOD throws, the dice are loaded.

— Greek proverb

The next day — Manta, Ecuador

AS SHE OPENED her blue eyes, Ashley saw a plump grandmotherly lady in a straight cotton dress. She began to loosen the blankets that were about her. Sunlight burst through the window in the concrete block wall and saturated every corner of the small, neat room. With a generous smile, the older Latin woman, whose round face glowed warmly in the golden light, helped Ashley into a more comfortable position.

"¿Ashley?" inquired the older woman, who was looking down on her with large brown childlike eyes as she lifted her jumpsuit that had been washed and folded, and pointed to the name "Ashley Brown" that was inscribed above the chest pocket.

Ashley realized that the little lady probably spoke Spanish. She had tidy peppered hair that was tied into a bun and helped accentuate her youthfully high forehead, her short turned-up nose, and her double chin. Having observed her, Ashley answered, *"Sí,"* and pausing, she then continued, *"¿Usted...nombre?"*

She knew she wouldn't get any awards for her command of the language of Cervantes, and her accent, with mixed English and French inflection, must have sounded rough in the ears of her host, but she tried to express herself.

Answering, the elder woman pointed to herself and said, *"Ma-rí-a,"* pausing between syllables.

Ashley looked about the small room. The blocks in the wall were not plastered, but were painted a cream color. There was a small desk with a small lamp; the bulb was bare, without a lampshade. The desk had a small wooden chair, painted blue, with stocky structure and a plywood seat.

At this point she was feeling several things, and all of them were personal necessities, but especially thirst! As she was wiggling out of the blankets, her sun-baked and blistered shoulders smarted. She looked, and was appalled by the sight of her crusty skin.

"¿Baño?" María asked, and passed her a pink bathrobe, which was too small, but it covered her.

"¿Agua?" Ashley asked in return.

"Un momento," María replied, and moved with agility towards the door. She hadn't seemed young enough to dart away so quickly.

Ashley was grateful when she returned an instant later with a pitcher of water and a glass. Three glassfuls were like three swallows. Ashley drank the plain water that tasted unrefined as fast as María could pour, but it satisfied more than if it had been bottled water imported from France.

Later, when Ashley had finished bathing, she slipped into her jumpsuit. It was clean, but it looked like it had faded some. She felt ridiculous in bare feet, a problem that María quickly resolved, giving her a pair of pink slippers. Ashley imagined how silly she must have looked, but she had no choice. She didn't want to walk on the concrete in bare feet. She began to smell pleasant aromas coming from María's kitchen. It was especially pleasing after everything she had been through. A hot meal! — the thought filled her with anticipation. She was famished and felt tempted to devour everything in sight, but she forced herself to go back to the little bedroom and wait until her host was ready.

Slowly, she walked around the bed and looked out the small window. There were several palm trees toward the beach, and beyond was the lovely Pacific that had nearly been her graveyard. She felt weak, and soon sat back down on the bed, but when María came to the door after only a few minutes and signaled her to come to eat, Ashley jumped up and followed her to the tiny dining room.

Ashley took the seat that María designated. She reached for the fork, ready to consume the contents of the plate, but María reached over and gently took her hand. She said, *"Vamos a orar."*

Ashley had no idea what that meant — she didn't recognize the verb *"orar,"* but wondered if it had anything to do with speaking. In answer to her bewilderment, María pointed to Heaven, and then cupped her hands. María apparently wanted to do something religious. Ashley felt so hungry that she could hardly bear it. María closed her eyes and inclined her head. Then, an instant later, she opened her eyes and looked at Ashley. She wants me to do the same — Ashley thought. And she inclined her head and closed her eyes. María said only a few words.

María's action made her think of God, and how she had called on Him when she was dying. Was this His answer, or just her good luck?

María pointed to the plate, and made a motion, as if taking food to her mouth. Ashley understood. Fried onions were on top of the fish and beef. The bread was freshly baked. One curiosity was the cup of hot milk. Ashley observed as María poured some dark liquid into it, and then took what might have been sugar, and stirred it into the brew. But if it was sugar, it was much coarser and darker than what she was accustomed to.

After several mouthfuls of beef, which she barely took time to cut, she began to make her own cup of whatever María had. It wasn't long until she found out that the mysterious brew was *café con leche*.

Finished the meal, Ashley felt much better and tried to show her satisfaction by smiling at María.

About then, another lady, who was mature but seemed younger than María, came in through the door. She had lively brown eyes, and her hair, which was mostly gray, was well kept.

María introduced, *"Te presento mí amiga, Sara."*

"Mucho gusto," Ashley answered, trying to pull Spanish words from her memory. She wished she had retained her lessons better.

"Te vamos a medir," Sara said.

Ashley didn't understand. Sara took out a measuring tape and held it up to her. She pulled her fingers down it. Seeing her action, Ashley concluded — She wants to measure me. But why?

"¿Por qué?" Ashley asked.

"Para ropa," María answered.

Ropa? What's that? — Ashley asked herself. Rope? Why do they want to measure rope?

Then María fluffed her dress, and pointing, said, *"Ropa. Vestido. Te vamos a medir para un vestido."*

With this, Ashley realized they wanted to measure her for clothing. I wonder what they want from me? They know I don't have anything.

Ashley lifted her arms, indicating that she was ready. The ladies giggled, looking at each other. Sara then began, taking one measurement after another and writing them down on a small notepad. As soon as she finished, she left, after only a few brief exchanges with María.

Then María left Ashley, insisting that she have a seat, and entered the kitchen, which was almost part of the small living room. Ashley began to contemplate the simple furnishings, and the plain unfinished concrete floors and the painted cement block walls. Everything was clean and in order, but it wasn't like anything she had known. It was small, even cramped, but a lack of space wasn't new. Most of her life she had spent in compact places; but this house impressed her immediately as a home — a pleasant home. It wasn't clear to her why she had so quickly come to that conclusion. Was it the simplicity, with no hums and vibrations, and lots of natural lighting reflecting through the small windows? Was it the small vase with cut pink, yellow, white, and red gladiolus? It surely didn't have anything to do with the sparsely padded furniture or the cool feel of the clean polished concrete floor.

She stood up for a moment and looked out the small bright window. She approached, feeling a light breeze that cooled her in the heat. Looking out and seeing a narrow street, and small houses with little space between them, she thought — Maybe they ran the neighborhood through a compactor. She wasn't trying to be sarcastic. That was how it looked. Some dark-skinned mestizo children were playing nearby. A little boy saw her at the window, and ran over. He yelled, *"Buenos días."*

Ashley understood and returned his greeting. Soon several children were pointing at her and giggling. This made her self-conscious, and she realized that her hair was hopelessly tangled.

Had she known, however, the children weren't looking at her hair. They were tittering because she was a pretty *gringa*.

She stepped back from the window, and went back to the bedroom, where she found a comb and a mirror. Her task seemed unending, but after a long struggle, she managed to comb out her hair.

It was perhaps an hour later when she made her way back to the small living room. She saw something on the bamboo coffee table. It was a black book with red-edged pages. Having nothing better to do, she began trying to make some sense of it. After looking it over, she decided it was a Bible, the "holy" book of the Judeo-Christian ethic, but since it was in Spanish, she didn't get much from it, and was only able to recognize common words. She wanted to despise it. After all, it was just a book of myths, and it had caused much harm to the world's harmonic consciousness. Her teachers said that people who believed in it were narrow-minded bigots. Not only that, but they were backward and uneducated.

But as she thought of how María was treating her, and seeing the Bible so prominent in her home, Ashley began questioning whether her notions of Christians were erroneous, knowing that María was treating her well.

About then, María came and found her with the Bible in her hands, and said, *"Biblia,"* with the kindness of a mother.

Ashley looked back, and captured the sweet smile on María's face, and though dark, it seemed to reflect a radiant light as she repeated the word *"Biblia"* again, while smiling broadly.

IT WAS LATE afternoon when Sara came with a present. She must have worked on it all day — Ashley surmised. She saw it wasn't an exotic fashion, but she appreciated the beauty of simplicity, knowing that the fundamental laws of physics, the same ones that had been taken advantage of to permit DEEP flight, while profound, were also simple.

Ashley felt excited, and pulled it against herself, spinning a bit in a carefree turn. At once she decided that it was attractive — and she saw that the ladies were as joyous as she was pleased. She could tell they wanted her to try it on as much as she wanted to herself, and so she took the flowered blue pastel dress and went back to her room. In a few minutes she came out. She was lovely, and felt that way. Alpha Force uniforms hadn't ever given her the feeling she was savoring. It was the first time she wore something that had been made just for her. And it dawned on her — It's mine! All that she had worn before, even ballgowns, had been uniforms of one kind or another. Having something made especially for her struck her profoundly. Alpha Force had never given her anything she could call her own.

Ashley couldn't contain herself, and felt she had to say something, which she did, *"Gracias,"* though she didn't know how to express what she felt, in any language, much less in Spanish.

Later, when the emotion of the moment had passed, and Sara had left, she sat again in María's living room and thought of James. She thought of him for a long time, wondering what had happened to him.

Did he get trapped in the storm too? Had they left him to die also? Then she thought of God. Remembering how she had called out for His help, and realizing that she had lived, she pondered whether it was God who had saved her. Afterwards, she thought of TerraNova and Alpha Force, deeming that she would have to make contact. And then she asked herself — How and why? — and concluded — I've a notion just to stay here. She wished she could.

Later that evening, when it was dark, Pepe, with his family, came by to visit. They weren't able to communicate very well, but Ashley began to get a picture of how her rescue had taken place. He showed her how he had found her, facedown in the water, in a dead man's float. Then he took his fist and held it near her heart, making slow pumping motions and pointing to her.

Ashley realized that her bioprocessor had saved her life by automatically putting her into biosuspend, a special suspended-animation lifesaving mode. It would only have helped for about twenty minutes, at the most. So again, she realized, she had either been lucky, or the outer God, whom she had asked for help, had answered.

She became a little more convinced it might have something to do with God when Pepe took the Bible and tried to read it to her. She got the idea that he was trying to show her that he believed God had brought him to save her.

"*¿Ashley, quieres una Coca-Cola?*" María asked.

She wasn't sure, but apparently she was being offered a Coke. She responded, "*Sí.*"

María sent one of Pepe's boys, a handsome ten-year-old, and he was gone in a flash, and back as fast, carrying a cold one-liter glass bottle of Coca-Cola. It was sweating in the heat. María received it, and soon brought several glasses of the black liquid on a tray. Ashley accepted hers, but it didn't have any ice. Even though it lacked the frozen blocks of H_2O, she found it to be genuinely refreshing. Somehow, she hadn't expected to be served Coke, but noted it tasted the same, just like it did back on Mars.

She noticed how good-natured they were — how sincere. Not at all like her mentors had portrayed Christians. It was obvious they were poor; but they didn't seem to be bigoted, hateful, or spiteful. Certainly not! But she wondered — Could they be hiding it? Maybe they think they'll get something out of me? But what? I don't have anything, and they don't know anything about me.

She wanted to ask this God whether He had sent Pepe. She questioned why He should even bother with her. Yet, as much as she wanted to know, something inside of her laughed at the whole idea. Something inside of her told her that when she was able to travel, she would have to abandon her fantasies, and go back to Alpha Force. She had no choice.

* * *

The next day — The Pacific Ocean

"QUADRANT is complete, sir — no fix on any RSB aluminum^3," the officer reported. "Should we continue to another?"

"Well?" asked the captain, looking into Jones's cool blue eyes.

"Continue to this quadrant," she demanded, pointing resolutely at the map.

Every failure meant the chances of finding the RSB decreased, and the amount of ocean to be searched increased greatly, since, as they moved out from the center point, the area multiplied rapidly.

The captain thought — When is she going to give up? Her insolence isn't going to find the missing RSB. Even with her improvements to the scan, it's hopeless. She might find it if she had a DEEP. Then she could scan a hundred times more area. But this is just a supply ship. They must be desperate, to send us looking for DEEP survivors.

Chapter 24

An Enigma

AND I STOOD upon the sand of the sea, and saw a beast rise up out of the sea, having seven heads and ten horns, and upon his horns ten crowns, and upon his heads the name of blasphemy.

— John the Apostle

That same day — Quito, Ecuador

JAMES FELT GREAT, even if his ankle was still tormenting him. He wasn't sure why he should feel so good, when after all, he was fundamentally a fugitive. If he didn't call the Nova Mundi office soon, he could consider himself a man without a future. He knew he couldn't avoid them forever, yet nonetheless he felt content living an outer's life. That morning he had awakened early, and began reading the Bible again. He finished the Gospel of John, unable to put it aside.

He could see that Jesus kept telling people what was going to happen, beforehand, so they would believe. In the New Order they always presumed to know the future, and even to plan it, but they were habitually wrong, and had to change the dates for their Plan. Reading the Cosmic Script and calculating Cosmic Frames, wasn't as good as they said it was.

Jon called him for breakfast, and afterwards they left for the church. Arriving, they pulled off the street onto a field where a large tent stood. They started to get out. "The tent is lovely," Mercy commented.

James noticed that they all seemed content. He wasn't sure what to make of the meeting under the large artificial canvas. He couldn't say that the music did much for him, but as for the others in the crowd, of which there was a small multitude, perhaps a thousand, he could see some who were quite emotional. They all had big smiles and were enjoying themselves. Sometimes they clapped their hands, and at times some of them had tears in their eyes. He had no idea why they were acting this way, because he thought that music was for quiet enjoyment. He hadn't thought that people could be so involved with such a loud roar. It was repulsive. However, he did remember studying about cases of fanaticism relating to some types of outer music. Is this something similar?

After an hour, or so, James observed that Jack got up to give a speech. It was from the Bible, and Jon translated it into Spanish. He began:

"Jesus is alive."

"*Jesús vive,*" Jon echoed.

James listened to the words. Remembering what he had been reading, he found Jack's description of a living, active God, who was concerned with the individual, to be captivating. Therion had never been described as being concerned, in any way, with the singular person. His announced goal was that of achieving the overall good of the human species, but the individual was considered expendable. In Therion's view, some people were superior, and others were inferior.

The weak were to be eliminated and the strong were to dominate.

Jack's speech, however, emphasized how the great Creator had individually made Adam a living being, by His own hands, whereas the rest of creation came into existence by the Creator's spoken word.

"This shows," Jack indicated, "that God is concerned with the who, what, when, where, and why of every individual." Jack pointed to other reasons, also based on the "inspiration" of the Scriptures. James wondered why Jack seemed to dogmatically claim that the Bible was the "only true revelation of God's message to man," but it did seem, from what he could tell, to be something worthwhile. He felt that the message was true, despite the bias he had entertained against outer religions.

James found himself struggling with his programmed reasoning that contradicted Jack's words. And yet he found himself absorbed by a superior logic, and by the "Gospel," as Jack called it.

On the way home, conversation on what had become their favorite topics continued. Mars, the Ether Crafts, and DEEP ports under the oceans all sounded like "Hollywood fantasies," as Jon called them. At one point Jon said skeptically, "James, you could probably write a novel about all of this and people wouldn't believe it. It's too fantastic."

James answered, "You're right. Indeed, TerraNova uses science fiction to make outers believe that the technology they have comes from other worlds that are more advanced than Earth. This will help them when they introduce Therion."

When they got home, the conversation continued and they learned some of the details of James's crash landing, as he explained, "I was seven seconds late, and it caused me to crash … To survive, the bubble must fall into at least forty feet of water. I should have been killed. And even if I did hit the snowcapped mountain at the right angle, I should have died."

"God saved your life. He has a reason for it. Besides, seven is a good number," Jack said.

"You mean seven's lucky?"

Jack replied, "No," and chuckled.

Jon clarified, "Seven is a number God uses for things that are complete, and that come from Him. When you read Revelation, you'll see the number seven many times. Maybe Jack was trying to say you were seven seconds late to show that God has a special plan for you."

"Don't worry about it, James. I was forcing the symbolism," Jack confessed.

"I don't know if seven had anything to do with it, but I was a lucky man," James said.

"Maybe what I was trying to say," Jack began, "is that God helped you, somehow, and that He has a reason for keeping you alive."

James wasn't sure he understood what "God helping him" meant, but he knew he had lived through the crash. He also understood that God — according to Jack, and unlike Therion — was concerned about him: James Smith. However, despite Jack's explanations, it was hard to believe.

THAT AFTERNOON, after a lunch like James couldn't remember — mashed potatoes, gravy, meat loaf, German chocolate cake, vanilla ice cream — and much conversation, Jon suggested that they rest before the evening service.

But once back in his room, James found himself unable to rest. He was anxious to read the book of Revelation. They had mentioned it so often, they'd aroused his curiosity. It didn't take him long to reach chapter six. There was something that detained him and kept him questioning himself — Where've I seen this before? He had never read the Bible in his whole life, but this wasn't the first time he had seen it. Pondering for some time, James was just about to go on and read further, but he felt compelled to reread.

However, even after reviewing, and reading it several times, he couldn't figure why it seemed so familiar. He thought about it for some time, but still didn't have an answer.

He lay down to think about it. What are the four horsemen? Why the different colors? Soon, he slipped off into a well-deserved nap.

Chapter 25

Pastor Is a Strange Name

ONE MUST be poor to know the luxury of giving.

— George Eliot

December 21 — Four days later — Manta, Ecuador

WHAT A WONDERFUL DAY! María had been letting Ashley use her slippers, which were too small for her. She needed real shoes, so María had taken her to the cobbler. Her feet were unusually large for a woman, the cobbler thought, and almost couldn't help, since he didn't have a form that big, but he had managed to come up with a pair of low-heeled black shoes. Ashley thought they were beautiful, but wished she hadn't lost her standard-issue Alpha Force shoes.

She had recovered her strength, and occasionally accompanied María to the market, and on other outings.

It was seven o'clock on a Friday night, and they had spent another great day together. María kept saying something about *"iglesia"* to Ashley. Fifteen minutes later, María indicated that she should come along with her, and she put a *Biblia* in her hands.

With a hurried gait, the little lady didn't lose any time. Ashley wondered — Where are we going? With Bibles?

Several blocks later, María led her into a small storefront with a sign that said *"Iglesia ..."* and other words Ashley couldn't distinguish.

Passing through the entrance, which looked like a garage door, the ladies mobbed Ashley. They seemed so friendly, or were they *too* friendly, with all of them shaking hands and exchanging hugs. And *Biblias* — there wasn't any lack of them. Some of the people began to take positions up front, including María and Ashley, on the right side, where they sat down, like mother and daughter, on one of the wooden benches. Ashley bore no family resemblance to María, but she felt a closer kinship to her than to anyone else she had ever met, and they had only known each other for a few days. And she did not know why, because María was only an outer.

Then Pepe caught Ashley's eye. He was up front tuning a guitar. She spotted the other men from the fishing boat, with their families.

Someone took the microphone and, after saying something solemn, which Ashley gathered was the same thing María always did before each meal, the group began to sing with the loud music. It didn't appeal to her. It was boisterous, lacked melody, obviously out of tune, just plain bad, and Pepe needn't be preoccupied with getting awards for his talent. Everybody was clapping their hands to the beat, and singing with their whole heart. Many would look up, some would incline their heads, and others would raise their hands as if they were giving up in surrender. It's *strange* — she thought.

This wasn't like the organized breathing exercises accompanied by hypnotic New Age music she was familiar with. It was gauche.

She would have made her way out, frustrated by the show, but decided to stay out of respect for the people, since they had been kind to her. Sara was there too, and Ashley was genuinely grateful for the small wardrobe that had now grown into three dresses. She would endure the noise for a while. At least they all seemed to be enjoying themselves.

Standing, as the others were doing, whatever it was they were *doing*, Ashley began to notice how sincere they all seemed. The beat changed, and the noise turned melodic.

She looked again. There were some people with tears and some had their hands in the air, with their faces towards the ceiling. Looking up, she didn't see anything but sockets on the ends of wires holding bare light bulbs. There were no fixtures, and the dirty white electric tape on the simple black wires was ugly. Besides, it wasn't finished. Apparently, that couldn't be the object of people's attention.

A dignified little man, past middle age, black eyes, dark skin, topped with still rich black hair, gave some instructions and the people began smiling, shaking hands, and hugging — again. He wore what looked to have been, at one time, a proper tailor-made suit, and though still proper, it didn't look to fit his slightly bulging midsection as well as it had. It was also significantly worn.

Ashley thought the meeting was over and it was finally time to leave. However, the man in the proper suit, who was a little older, but not the oldest, stood behind a wooden podium and began to speak, and kept on. It didn't end. What could he be saying? She fidgeted in her seat, tapping her fingertips silently, for no one made any noise. Looking up from time to time, she stared at the bare wiring, sure that it was a fire hazard. After about ten minutes, she began to think of ways to describe the wooden bench. She felt certain that all of the words that came to her were inappropriate. "Uncomfortable" was the kindest one.

About fifteen minutes into the discourse, she wondered how she could endure any longer. She knew she could not leave. She had to please the people who had saved her life.

Without a watch, she could only guess, but it must have been half an hour. Numbness had taken over the portion of her that was against the bench. Again, she nearly decided to stand up and walk out. Then, the little man, whom María had named *"Pastor,"* appeared to be finishing whatever he was saying. Ashley thought — *"Pastor"* is a strange name.

But he didn't finish.

She tried to find new and innovative ways to cross her legs discreetly. When an hour had gone by, according to her best estimates, she would have decided that this was a method of outer infliction — forcing people to sit on hard benches for extended periods. But, apparently, they were enjoying themselves, save for the babies, whose cries seemed louder than *Pastor's* voice.

I can't take this any longer — she resolutely told herself, and nearly stood, when she heard *Pastor* say her name and make a sign in her direction. Everyone looked towards her, smiling. She presumed it would be good to smile in return, but wasn't sure what was going on, and wondered what they were doing and what they wanted.

María took her gently by the arm, and she realized that she was expected to stand. She wondered if she would stumble if she walked, since her legs were numb. María looked up to her like a proud mother. Two of her rescuers went around passing trays, and people began to pile on grubby bills of the Ecuadorian currency, called *sucres*.

There was another moment of what these people did repeatedly: *oración*, in which they appeared to attempt to make contact with a deity without going into a trance.

The manner in which María took Ashley's arm surprised her. Now standing, she led her forward. *Pastor* presented a heap of *sucres* to her. She didn't have any pockets or a pocketbook to hold them. María took care of it. It would have been easy for the meaning of the moment to escape her, but it didn't, and a tear almost came to her eye. She said one of the few words she knew, *"Gracias."* It stunned her; the outers were giving her money.

Then *Pastor* signaled, and several of her rescuers, and other men, stood around her and began, once more, this thing of *oración*. She understood that whatever it was, they were doing it for her.

Afterwards, *Pastor* made more comments, and dismissed the group. There were plenty of handshakes and hugs, with kisses, from the other ladies. They really liked doing this, and she began to enjoy it herself. *Pastor* came up and shook her hand. He made some comments, but she had no idea what he had said.

Eventually, María led her back home.

The collection dismayed Ashley. She had never had money in Alpha Force, but having experienced, with María, the freedom and joy of shopping, when they had gone to the market together and bought some necessary items for herself, she knew the wads of paper would be useful. Perhaps she could use the cash to find a representative of Nova Mundi, but right at the moment, she was having too much fun. This was better than any field trip.

María disappeared for an instant and then returned to present her with a purse to match her dress and shoes.

As she lay down that night, Ashley pondered why they treated her with so much kindness. They couldn't have a selfish motive. Was it too good to be true? Then, she felt James holding her. The memory was triggered by hugs the outers had given her at church. She tried to stop her fantasy before the infliction began, but the memory of his torture was permanently attached to the shame she had brought to him.

* * *

The next morning — The Pacific Ocean

"WE HAVE IT, sir!" the watch officer exclaimed.

"Advise the captain," the officer ordered.

Waking quickly from a nap, the captain was on the bridge in a moment, and ordered, "Report."

"We have an RSB floating on the surface, 3250 meters northwest."

"Well, gentlemen, and ladies, let's go see," the captain directed.

It didn't take them long. Within fifteen minutes they surfaced beside the RSB.

"It's empty, chief," the captain reported. "Orders?"

Nancy Jones had never imagined the rescue would take so long, and this despite her upgrades to the scanning equipment. She was frustrated, and now, it was over, and a failure. Whoever had been in the RSB, hadn't been able to stay aboard. Why didn't we plan for this outcome? There are so many straps, but not a single one to assist someone during a storm. What poor planning! We believed our design wouldn't fail under any circumstance. And it didn't. But we still lost the life we were to have saved. It was just one of those cursed details. But she didn't tell anyone her thoughts, and hoped they wouldn't realize what had really happened.

"Recover the RSB and return to Novus Somnorum," she ordered sternly, trying to cover any sign of failure in her voice.

CAPTAIN ANDERSON of Beta Force chuckled to himself. He heard the failure in her voice; he enjoyed seeing her fail, for it made him feel less of a failure himself. He always felt he should have been in Alpha Force, and Jones proved that even Alpha's best could be wrong. He answered her, "Yes, Chief."

Disdain settled lightly into his voice, like oil on water — reflecting a rainbow that could only be seen from the right angle. The captain knew that Jones couldn't see what lay upon the undulating surface. Her viewpoint was much too elevated.

Chapter 26

Special Affairs

THE PROBE BLASTED OFF from Cape Canaveral, Florida, riding a Titan 3 rocket. Its originally scheduled mid-September launch had been postponed, owing to the discovery, by NASA, on August 25, 1992, of contamination inside the sealed device. Metal filings, paint chips, and fibers of paper and cotton were found inside the Mars Observer. Because the satellite had spent its entire life inside surgically clean work environments, the origin of these impurities remains a mystery.

— *NewsWorld*, "Observer Delayed," October 1992

The next day — California

TWO SPECIAL AFFAIRS OPERATIVES dressed in gray camouflage, moved swiftly through the corridors, covering one another and rotating the lead. It was night and the building was empty.

For this operation, each SAO used a special hearing enhancement that, unlike the ones they used daily, allowed communication between them. Fitting right in the ear canal, the device picked up the sound of the speaker's voice directly through his or her Eustachian tube, and transmitted it (after processing to keep it from sounding muffled). This gave the SAOs hands-free communication, and allowed them to speak to each other directly, and even to speak across significant distances with only a whisper.

Before entering areas of possible danger, they used a portable SPARQ to see around corners. Its image could be seen directly with enhanced contact lenses, and provided a 3-D heads-up display that was visible only to the operative.

Their mission was simple. They were going to sabotage the Mars Observer space probe. TerraNova didn't need NASA snooping around on Mars. It wasn't convenient for them to allow NASA to have easy access to pictures from Mars, unless they could control the content.

Entry into Morton International Corporation (the company that was making the Mars probe) and its white room, required passage through a decontamination chamber (to keep things clean), but the SAOs had taken the back door, through the offices. They picked up numerous contaminates, especially paper particles and cotton fibers. They carried high-energy weapons, but if all went according to plan, there wouldn't be any need to use them. SAO 2 reached her surveillance station, and quietly spoke, "One, I'm in position; proceed."

"Affirmative," One answered, and reached for a large syringe. He inserted the needle, which was really a small tube, into the Mars Observer's panel lock and injected a micromechanical PARASITE (Programmable Aeronautic Robot And Semi-Intelligent Tactical Explorer). TerraNova manufactured PARASITEs in many sizes and shapes for diverse uses. A PARASITE could be made to look like a flying or walking insect. In this case, the device would open the probe's door from the inside out.

Having achieved entry, it actuated the release on the panel. In seconds, the lock opened. SAO 1 opened the probe's interior, located the clock transistor, and with his drill, unscrewed the heat dissipater. Once the probe was in space, on its way to Mars, the transistor would burn up, and the computer would stop. Observer's mission would be successfully ruined, and no pictures of Mars Base Aquarrian would ever reach Mission Control. The one-billion-dollar probe would be lost in space.

In one more minute the job was finished. SAO 1 returned, and with SAO 2 they began to retrace their entry, covering each other alternately. A guard happened to step into the wrong place at the wrong time. "Identify yourself" were his last words. SAO 1 didn't hesitate to "answer." She fired her weapon, a PHENIX (Portable High ENergy Ion eXterminator). The unfortunate guard was ionized, and disappeared. His poor widow and children would never grieve over his body. A massive manhunt by local police never revealed anything, and the life insurance provider refused to pay, citing the lack of a body or some other concrete evidence of death.

After exterminating the guard, the SAOs continued to move back through the building. Just before entering the fire escape to go back up onto the roof, SAO 2 reached up above the door, and removed the SPARQ image manipulator from the surveillance camera. They had placed it there during entry. Its purpose had been fulfilled and no evidence of their activity was recorded by the surveillance system. During the last five minutes it had provided the security camera with a perfect picture of an empty hall.

* * *

"SOLAR FLARE?" asked the controller, who was staring at his radar screen with tense eyes. At LAX (Los Angeles Airport) his radar went blank momentarily. Down the line, the other air traffic controllers also panicked, but the outage lasted only a few seconds.

"This is the fourth time in ten minutes. At least the interruptions are brief," rejoined the supervisor. "We'll have to launch a full investigation."

Radar operators, military and otherwise, were scratching their heads. Someone who was passing by Morton International on the Interstate swore they'd seen a "black flying saucer," but with the night's darkness, and by the time they blinked their eyes, the phantom had disappeared.

At Morton International the surviving guards felt a sensation similar to a tremor as the building shook, but only for an instant. The guards never did associate it with the pale burn marks on the floor that almost looked like shoeprints, or with the unexplained disappearance of their fellow worker.

* * *

USING STEALTH, SPEED, and ASCANS (Advanced Sound Cancellation Anti-Noise System) to eliminate any sonic boom, DEEP 51 picked up the SAOs from the roof of Morton International. Their rooftop penetration had avoided much of the building's security.

While plunging in from space, supercooling kept the outer shell of the DEEP black. In less than five seconds the SAOs had boarded the Unit, following the choreographed plan they had practiced many times. Ether Crafts can accelerate so quickly, and yet so silently, they cannot be seen or heard. They're faster than the human eye. A Unit is capable of disappearing before its direction of flight can be seen. An instant after the SAOs boarded the DEEP, the craft shot into space, but even with ASCANS operational, there was a mild shock wave. This shock wave was the real explanation for the four tremors the building's surviving guards had felt that evening. There was one when the DEEP had initially deposited the SAOs, and seconds afterwards, another, when the DEEP returned to hide in space. Then there was a third one when the DEEP returned to retrieve the operatives, and the last tremor happened when the Unit returned to space at the end of the mission. Since small natural tremors are commonplace in California, the guards had ignored the minor quakes.

Chapter 27

Christmas Eve

WHILE THEY WERE THERE, the time came for the baby to be born, and she gave birth to her firstborn, a son. She wrapped him in cloths and placed him in a manger, because there was no room for them in the inn.

— Luke the Evangelist

December 24, 1991 — The next day — Quito, Ecuador

IT HAD BEEN a week since the Whittens, along with Jack and Grace Kinderly, had left for the States. James had been staying with the Williamses, another missionary family who worked with the Whittens. He felt as if he'd barely had time to get to know Jon and Judy. And though James had been with Jon and Judy just a few days, it saddened him when they left for the USA. It was now Christmas Eve.

Larry Williams was tall with a stocky build, brown hair, blue eyes, a gentle spirit, and a self-effacing manner that made him a quick friend for James. Denise was petite and lively; her smallish turned-up nose gave her an inquisitive look. She was a joyful person with curled and attractive dark hair.

For the purpose of conversation, *"others"* became a euphemism for Nova Mundi and TerraNova, and anyone else who was related to James's previous life. Right now, the *others* weren't a concern to any of them. The fire in the hearth was beautiful and the Christmas tree was colorfully decorated. Presents were spread at its base. James saw that the children, from the smallest to the largest, were full of anticipation.

Christy was the youngest, five years old, and full of giggles with no shortage of energy. She had long dark-brown hair, large hazel eyes, and a tiny nose. Carla, at eight, was a "full-fledged third grader," she told James. She was a dark brunette, and also had hazel eyes. She tried to display more sophistication than her sister, but lost it when she couldn't avoid the temptation to join in the havoc. Romping about the Christmas tree, the two girls tried to get "Uncle" James's attention. Larry had stepped out to attend to a petition of Denise's, and had left him to the girls. They seemed rather excited, having their new "uncle" to themselves, and the show they were giving him was ongoing.

This wasn't like life had been in the New Order. He could hear the *others* telling him how fortunate he had been, something they never stopped reminding him. "Outers are deprived of technology and power," they would say. But he wondered if they were really deprived at all. It seemed that even if they didn't have the hidden knowledge of TerraNova, they did have warmth and humanity.

His two small "nieces" continued with their show: dancing, laughing, screaming, jumping, and shouting — all at the same time. He couldn't help but enjoy them. Before the evening, he had been having some feelings of self-pity. It wasn't easy to make the transition from captain to outer, and while hand washing his own clothing that afternoon he had reflected on the conveniences he had enjoyed in Alpha Force.

The Williamses' son, David, with dark brown hair parted down the middle, blossoming muscles from weight lifting, came into the room and found a seat. He and James had met already. David had ignored him at first, but James saw his indifference melt when they had been able to shoot a few hoops together.

James's ankle had healed quickly. He wondered if the quick healing had had anything to do with all of the prayers the missionaries made on his behalf. It seemed like they were always praying for something, and he found himself the subject of many of their petitions. However it may have been, it seemed to him that the ankle had mended faster than normal and it felt good to have been on the court. Also, it felt good to be with David, who became, to him, the "kid" brother he'd never had.

Of course, there had been children in Novus Ordo, from other *lots*. But fraternizing between lots was prohibited. Each lot was bred for a special function. James's lot was bred to become Alpha Force officers. Other lots became technicians, or Beta Force personnel, or whatever was needed. They would breed a line of service personnel to cook and wash dishes or to do maintenance, and they created a new lot for every function they required.

DAVID THOUGHT James was "cool." He could really handle the ball, and he never missed a basket. It fascinated David, watching Uncle James. His moves were right. He looked like some player on TV, but maybe better. Nobody's that good — David thought. James didn't miss and no one could keep up with him. And, he acted as if it was nothing, not even breathing heavily in the thin mountain air.

"Where did you learn to play?" David asked him the last time they were on the court.

James had simply responded, "Back home."

Even though David had come to the conclusion that James wasn't ordinary, he figured, if he couldn't beat him on the court, he might get him in a video game, so he interrupted his sisters and invited James, "Let's go play Star Invader."

"What's that?" James asked.

"It's a video game."

"Let's go," he answered.

James followed David, with the girls behind him, up to the TV. David got the game running and gave James the controller. He quickly explained some of the rules and buttons.

It wasn't long until James was zooming through the stars and galaxies faster than a UFO. James engaged all of the hostile aliens. David wasn't sure whether to be excited, or mad. He couldn't help feeling elated as he watched James burst his way through every obstacle. The barrage of enemies that kept attacking didn't intimidate him. David could see that he was no match for James, who had been given the title of Master Star Invader by the game. By now, David knew, anyone else would have been in their third and final game life, but James was still in his first. The score was higher than what David ever imagined, and James was still untouched by the aliens.

"Where did you learn to play like that?" David wondered aloud, as James burst through another alien barrier, catapulting him into a higher skill level.

"I guess you could say I'm a natural."

An instant later, James came to the grand finale, and with imaginary lasers and missiles exploding, the attack was on, but he easily blasted the enemy into oblivion.

Just about then, they were called to dinner.

* * *

Novus Somnorum, Pacific Ocean

STANDING in front of the large wall monitor, Chief Nancy Jones looked into the perplexed and flaming eyes of Cosmokrator Allen Weller, that despite their icy blue, burned passionately, as he berated her, cursing as if he was inspired by a Skotos. After finishing his "stimulating" introduction, he blurted, "Jones, don't you dare infer that there's been any negligence on this end! Do you understand? You were the engineer in charge, and it was your Unit."

"Yes, sir," she responded, standing at attention, hoping this wouldn't escalate into an infliction, and realizing that they were probably looking for someone to blame, and as chief engineer of DEEP 1 — the highest ranking surviving officer — she would do nicely.

"Now, that's better. I don't think we need to let this thing get out of control." Weller's expression changed, becoming more relaxed. "You gave us all of the coordinates, and we found everyone where you indicated, except Smith and Brown. The floating RSB you found was storm swept from its impact coordinates by two hundred kilometers. Smith could have been driven by the same storm, which would have driven him to the coast of Ecuador."

"Yes, sir," she answered, still standing straight and tall. Weller had paused, but she didn't dare speak until asked.

"We don't have enough personnel in Ecuador to do a very serious investigation, and besides, Smith would have looked for our Novus Ordo office in Quito," Weller paused again, as though he wanted Jones to speak.

"May I, sir?" she requested.

"Yes, what is it?" he replied sharply, making her wonder if she had spoken too soon.

"Sir, I believe that if First Officer Brown had survived, there would be no question of her loyalty, and she would immediately seek our personnel. However, sir," and she choked some, as if she wasn't sure if she should say anything more, and continued, "Captain Smith was displaying unusual behavior during the weeks before the crash, especially the last few days."

"What 'unusual behavior'?" Weller snapped back. He knew Smith, and couldn't imagine his faithful captain showing any disloyalty.

Nancy realized what was going on; she'd been around. By challenging the commander's credibility, she was putting her own in further jeopardy. Besides, Weller had no reason to suspect Smith; but with the demise of DEEP 1, they would be looking at her, for liability. How do I get through this one? — she questioned herself, knowing she had to say something. Now that she had managed to get herself into the trap, she would have to see if she could talk her way out. "If it pleases you, sir, I have no doubt as to Captain Smith's loyalty, but sir, First Officer Brown had indicated to me that she would be advising superiors that the captain should be allowed some vacation. She was prepared to fill in a DBR, sir."

Weller thought — Jones doesn't have any reason to lie. She doesn't know it yet, but the crash wasn't her fault. "Well, then, Jones, what do you recommend?"

"Sir, I know that this is a difficult time, our resources are stretched, but if there are agents that can be moved to Ecuador, perhaps from Colombia, I'm sure, if the captain is there, they'll find him. He would look out of place in a fishing village."

"I agree," Weller answered, and his expression lightened. "As for your situation, Jones, I don't believe that anyone has told you yet, but our studies into the causes of DEEP 1's explosion indicate that you, and your crew, aren't responsible." Weller paused, so he could see the effect.

Nancy Jones nearly smiled, and thought of Weller with terms that were at least as inspired as the ones he had used to begin their conversation. She summarized, for herself, saying in her mind — He knew we were *invested* from the beginning. He's been playing with me — it's cat and mouse.

Chapter 28

The Fall of an Empire

DEAR FELLOW COUNTRYMEN, compatriots. Due to the situation ... as a result of the formation of the Commonwealth of Independent States, I hereby discontinue my activities at the post of President of the Union of Soviet Socialist Republics.

— Mikhail Gorbachev, December 25, 1991

The next day— Christmas — Worldwide

"YELTSIN has already proven his ability to cause trouble," Antonin Grivaldi blasted with hatred and vehemence. "He had no business fooling with our Siberian operation."

Antonin's image came from Rome, a place of much importance for the Plan. The empire still lived; it had never died — it just looked that way to the outer world. Grivaldi's intense brown eyes, with glistening black hair, combed back, suited his perfectly trimmed thick black beard.

"Look on the bright side. He's only got Russia, and instead of one vast region, we have new nations springing up like dandelions. Gentlemen, you would do well to buy stock in cartography," Watkins added with a sarcastic smirk.

Savee groaned as he mused, "Delays, delays, delays — Gorbachev is gone, and we're still at only twelve-percent capacity."

About then, in the various conference rooms, the Cosmokrator saw an ordinary television image on each of their screens.

"He's going to go through with it. What a way to spoil Christmas!" Rennedy said, while blurting out several curses and comments, none of which were appropriate for the season of love and universal peace.

"Yeltsin is getting his Christmas present. Too bad the rest of us have to live with it." Stonefell's tone showed his displeasure.

Each of their flat wall monitors began to show an irksome low-quality picture. The voice of Mikhail Gorbachev droned through. An instant later, simultaneous translation to English came over the harsh Russian. "Dear fellow countrymen, compatriots. Due to the situation … I hereby discontinue my activities at the post of President of the Union of Soviet Socialist Republics …"

Each Cosmokrator bristled with grim expression as the remarks of their scrapped protégé came to their ears.

"Addressing you for the last time in the capacity of President of the USSR … This country was suffocating in the shackles of the bureaucratic command system … The old system collapsed before the new one had time to begin working … The consequences may turn out to be hard for everyone."

One distraught Cosmokrator hissed, "Gorby has a gift for understatement!"

"But I am convinced that sooner or later our common efforts will bear fruit; our nations will live in a prosperous and democratic society. I wish everyone all the best." Gorbachev's lips stopped moments before the translation caught up. The image broke into static, and then silence — it wasn't particularly reverential — but it seemed to be in order; after all, it marked the death of an empire.

Stonefell finally spoke, "Let's make plans for our new friend Boris. At least we have our DEEPs back."

Watkins, and perhaps more than one of the others, thought — It's too late to change a thing.

* * *

Quito, Ecuador

PERHAPS GORBACHEV had chosen Christmas Day to make the announcement while people were occupied in the festivities, giving natural cover for the catastrophic fall of the Union, commented some analysts, but at the Williamses, Gorbachev's resignation went unnoticed, as in the rest of the West, where people generally ignored the news in favor of the Christmas holiday.

The Williamses had invited James to be at their house at 9:00 AM; but by then, the children had already waged the siege of the Christmas tree. They had strewn wrappings and Christmas paper high and low. However, there were still other presents waiting, and with James's punctual arrival, Larry and Denise cleared an area in the sea of wrapping paper, which permitted them to open the door and lead him through.

Christy couldn't contain her joy and grabbed his hand to take him to see her gifts. Carla had the same idea, which resulted in a minor tug-of-war. Obviously, two little girls, pulling on a bioengineered man, couldn't overcome him, or could they? Was James off guard? In a flash, he came toppling down. He made quite a crash.

Larry, seeing the tug-of-war, ordered, "That's enough, girls!" But he had been too late to keep James off the floor. Having fallen, he quickly stood up again. Larry then invited him to have a seat. David and the girls gathered around and presented him with brilliantly wrapped gifts.

James questioned in exclamation, "For me?" He had seen gifts under the tree, but never thought to be included, and felt embarrassed, knowing he had nothing to give in return.

Everyone shouted for him to open the gifts. As he realized what they were expecting, he began.

The Williamses, when trying to select gifts for him, had had the difficulty of finding the right thing for the man who didn't have anything. Perhaps it was harder than the proverbial selection of a gift for the man who has everything.

James took his time. He unwrapped his first gift with care. It was fascinating. In Novus Ordo they had never exchanged gifts and whenever they did receive gifts, everyone got the same. Initially, with puzzlement on his face, but moments later, unmistakable joy, James exclaimed, "Thank you!"

Buried in the wrapping and box, James found a homemade gift certificate that indicated he was the recipient of a new tailor-made wardrobe — from Jack Kinderly. It was good towards the purchase of a suit, seven shirts, seven pairs of pants, and other items and had characteristic markings from the Williams children, to whom Denise had given charge of making the certificate in Jack's absence. Tailor-made was the cheapest and best way to get clothing for him — especially for a tall man in a country where most men are much shorter.

To continue with the event, the girls jumped and clapped their hands. David smiled from ear to ear. James took the next gift and began to open it. Larry cautioned the girls to calm down. The box was small, and though not heavy, it was substantial. Soon the wrapping came off, exposing shiny gold leaf between golden pieces of wood. Its spine was made with leather. James didn't quite realize what it was, but studied it with admiration.

"It's a New Testament, bound with covers of olive wood," Larry explained. "Pastor Jack brought it from the Holy Land."

James looked puzzled.

"Holy Land," Larry added. "From Israel, where Jesus lived."

"Israel, you mean where the Jews live now?" James asked.

"Yes," answered Larry, "our Lord Jesus was a Jew, one of God's chosen people."

This gave James something to think about. Jews — they're enemies of Therion! But I've left Therion's world. So I'm an enemy of Therion now! Does that mean that I'm now a friend of the Jew? Jesus was a Jew! Christians were enemies; are they now my friends? Yes. They are. So I must think differently now. That means that I like Jews and Jesus. Why not? If I'm going to be divergent, I might as well be fully divergent!

Having come to this conclusion, James decided he wanted to know more, and asked, "The Jews are God's chosen people?"

"Yes, Jim, that's what the Bible teaches. Today, however, God's chosen people are those who have Jesus in their hearts. People who, like us, have Jesus in their hearts, are called the "Church." It's a big subject, but simply speaking, the Jews were chosen by God to bring His Word and Jesus to the world, and God still loves them, but not all of them love Jesus, which means that they have rejected the only way God has given for people to come to Him."

Larry's answer left James with more questions than he had had before the conversation started, but for now, he decided, it was a festive moment, and it wasn't the right time to decipher outer enigmas. Looking closely at the gift, James saw that the New Testament was a work of art. Its polished olive wood felt extraordinarily smooth; he slowly opened its pages, which initially stuck together.

"James, let me show you a portion to read," Larry said, taking the Testament from James for a moment. He handed it back, pointing, and added, "Will you read it aloud?"

James began, "And the angel said unto them, Fear not: for, behold, I bring you good tidings of great joy, which shall be to all people. For unto you is born this day in the city of David a Savior, which is Christ the Lord. And this shall be a sign unto you; Ye shall find the babe wrapped in swaddling clothes, lying in a manger."

The girls nudged up closer to him.

"That's the Christmas story!" Carla exclaimed.

Soon, they had him opening the third gift. None of the presents had been big, but this one was the smallest, and everyone expectantly looked for him to open it. The gift was a black plastic digital watch. It would be practical. His own watch drew too many curious eyes, so he had been walking around without knowing the time. Even if he wasn't steering a DEEP through space, the correct time was a necessity.

Soon the watch was on his empty wrist. Obviously it was an inferior device, and wouldn't take even 100 meters — let alone 10,000.

"Thank you," he said meekly.

"Don't thank us. Pastor Kinderly provided everything for you. Tomorrow we'll take you to the tailor to be measured. Soon you won't have to run around in clothing that's half your size."

The children began trying to get him to look at their gifts. Diplomatically making the rounds, from the youngest to the oldest, he visited each one to find what new toy they had received for Jesus' Birthday.

David had a new video game and when James sat down to play, he nearly couldn't.

"What happened?" David asked. "You aren't winning!" he exclaimed, distress in his voice. "Are you okay? My sisters knocked you down. Is something wrong?"

James's vision enhancements had gone dead early that morning, and though he didn't need them to play video games, their loss had brought him disorientation.

"You better take advantage and beat me while you've got a chance," James answered. "I'm just having a bad day. I'll get you the next time."

"I don't want you to give me the game."

"I'm not giving you a thing. If you win, it's because you're the better man."

This excited David. He was winning by a comfortable margin.

James was beginning to see that his life would be different without super-tech. Later that afternoon they went to the basketball court. James couldn't do anything right and was stumbling all over himself. David could see something was wrong and asked, "You feel okay?"

"Yeah," James answered slowly. "I'm just learning what it means to be ordinary."

"You aren't ordinary," David said with conviction.

James missed another shot. "You still think I'm not?"

David looked at James, and said with sincerity in his voice, "You'll be okay."

"I hope so," he answered, hoping that the disorientation caused by the loss of his vision enhancements wouldn't last long. They had failed quickly because their battery had to be replaced every few weeks. Even TerraNova hadn't figured a way to make power from nothing, and a contact lens didn't have much space for an opaque battery. At least the rest of his bioelectromechanical endowments would work for many years, perhaps as many as thirty, but no one really knew, since they hadn't been tested over such a long period.

* * *

December 31 — New Year's Eve — Worldwide

"FINE," WELLER ANSWERED. "One more point," he said, speaking hurriedly, trying to get everyone's attention before the special New Year's Eve virtual meeting in the cyberspace of Novus Ordo's quantum computer ended. They were trying to catch up on unfinished business.

"Yes, Weller. Is it urgent? Perhaps we can deal with it tomorrow?" Stonefell asked as he looked directly into the blue eyes shown in the holographic projection and hoped that the brat would take a hint, and back off. After all, New Year's Eve was too special for business.

"I'll only be a moment," and he went ahead, not concerned that Stonefell might try to stop the discussion. "According to our best analysis of DEEP 1's explosion, and the escape and recovery of its crew, it seems highly probable that Captain Smith landed in the Pacific during a heavy storm. It's possible that he is in the country of Ecuador because of the proximity of his expected landing site to that country. We have no idea why he hasn't reported, and why his transceiver didn't activate, unless his entire RSB failed during reentry. However, an exhaustive search for it, or its remains, using ionic-meson scans, hasn't been successful— "

"Please be brief!" Stonefell cut in.

"I am," Weller impatiently responded. "We found Ashley Brown's RSB, but without her in it. Chief Nancy Jones used an ionic-meson scan, which she improved, on the Beta Force sub that retrieved her and the other members of DEEP 1's crew. We were able to confirm that the RSB was Brown's by its serial number. It's safe to assume that the Pacific consumed her. But the most important news is that Brown has provided reason for us to believe that Captain Smith may still be alive, and currently in Ecuador, as I said.

"Based on this new information, I'm going to move two SAOs from Colombia to work with the two we have in Ecuador. I would like to have more, but I can't take any more from Colombia. We can't allow the coke operation to shut down. They will assist the agents in Ecuador and try to find Smith. Chief Jones's description of Smith before the explosion indicates that if he is alive, he may be in need of rest, or infliction, as the case may be. Our doctors will need to determine which, if he's found alive. However, he should have had great difficulty breaking his conditioning and not returning to us, if he's alive. On the other hand, if he did manage to break loose, he may be hiding from us in some fishing village — thinking he's escaped. We must prove him wrong. An Alpha Force captain knows far too much to be permitted any freedom among outers. He's probably dead, but we need to be sure."

"I believe, my good Weller, you have chosen a correct course of action," Watkins commented.

"Thank you," he answered.

"Well then, will just four SAOs be sufficient? Can't we muster any more?" Watkins asked.

"I could probably send in several others, but for this job they'll need native Spanish and Latin appearances. Our other agents in black suits won't do."

"Weller, do as you think. You know your job," Stonefell ordered, hoping that this would be the last item of business.

"Fine. I'll start immediately," Weller answered, while chuckling to himself. He enjoyed getting Stonefell riled.

Chapter 29

Flying Terror

YOU DON'T NEED to pray to God any more when there are storms in the sky, but you do have to be insured.

— Bertolt Brecht

January 17, 1992 — Two weeks later — Pasadena, California

ATLER SPED, something he was occasionally good at, especially when the police weren't around — his investment in a radar detector had been essential. The narrow mountain road unwound under his Pirelli tires. My, how he enjoyed driving his new red Viper! He felt like he was making a TV commercial — and the fine print across the bottom of the screen read, "Professional driver on closed course." His fantasies were coming true, and it even seemed he might get by with the sale of his program. Neither Nova Mundi (Doug's people) nor Advanced WorldNet had approached him with any complaints.

A couple of his "friends" had asked him where his new car came from, and he told them, "An inheritance." They had answered, "Not bad." And he had added, "Yeah. It's my midlife crisis thing." One had replied, "I hope my crisis is resolved soon."

Atler's car was speeding up the twisting mountain road, which had a significant embankment just off to his right. Doug had called him and told him to come back to work to fix an emergency problem with the computer software. It wasn't the first time they had phoned him to come back to work, but Doug had never called before. Doug had told him that it was important to come on the mountain road because a pileup from an accident was blocking the Interstate. Well, it didn't bother Atler. With his Viper's horsepower, the mountain road was more exciting. The Viper was a fine machine.

An exciting curve was coming. Atler wanted to see how fast he could take it. Downshifting and accelerating, he turned the wheel gently and then moved into it with anticipation. The Viper was moving like a dream, but suddenly, everything locked: The steering wheel wouldn't turn. Atler tried to force it, but it didn't budge. He fought, trying to make it unlock. He took his foot off of the accelerator, as the rpm kept increasing, and slammed on the brakes. It was useless! In the fear that gripped him, just as his car flew over the embankment into the gulch below, Atler Redclift screamed in terror.

Atler hurtled into the gulch. Treetops raced by. This was the end. He knew it. He slammed into a few trunks, one of which tore through the car. The airbag clobbered him and the shoulder belt locked onto him in a way that said, "I'll never let go." The high headrest held him delicately.

Part of the motor slammed through the firewall, burning hot, and landed in front of the passenger seat. Newton's laws made their effects plainly evident in the ruin of his sixty-thousand-dollar Viper. He thought, just before impact with the ground, that the insurance would pay. He wondered — Shouldn't my life pass before my eyes? Everything seemed to happen slowly, as if filmed by a high-speed camera, but no life played back.

When the dismembered car slammed, nose first — at about a forty-degree angle — into the ground, piling against the base of the trees, there wasn't any conceivable way that Redclift could have escaped death. It would have been obvious to any casual observer that the driver could not have survived. Or, if he lived, he would survive only a few minutes, maybe until 911 paramedics made it to the scene. But there wasn't anyone around to call in a report, and no one had seen him drive off the road; it was unlikely that the paramedics would arrive soon enough to see him die. He'd be pleasantly dead, or more likely cremated, before they got to him.

Doug's VIEW was fabulous. And it required no small amount of skill, controlling four PARASITEs all at the same time. He guided them, viewing virtual-reality projections through his enhanced contact lenses. Being able to control all of them at the same time was a good test of his nerve-impulse accelerators, but he figured he could handle a couple more, if he had to. But for now, he didn't need any more. He had one for the steering column, a second for the clutch, and a third one for the accelerator. He used the forth one to provide him with a general view of the scene.

Sitting in the back of TerraNova's panel van, a safe distance away, he had been guiding his toys. When he heard Atler scream, Doug thought — That's like a miserable outer!

At that point, Doug flew the PARASITEs out of harm's way, since they had accomplished their mission. They were too expensive to sacrifice unnecessarily, and it was obvious that no mere outer could survive the crash that was unfolding. However, he was a bit disappointed that the Viper didn't burst into flames. Fireworks are always fun. He waited for some time, but nothing. He started contemplating whether he should send a PARASITE back to explode the gas tank. Cremation would be what the double-crossing traitor deserved. But he chose to wait a few minutes, since starting a fire might destroy the PARASITE, and it was still possible the car would explode on its own. He would wait to see what happened, but if the car didn't explode soon, he would fly back and take care of it.

He wished he had been able to let Redclift know why he was being exterminated, but it was against standard operating procedures. No need to give a victim any chance to escape, even if it would be impossible. Tracking down an escapee would take longer and cost more, so a clean assassination was always preferable.

AFTER THE CAR came to a rest, and pieces of bright red Viper had been strewn over a hundred fifty feet, or so, of forest — against all odds Atler sat there: held securely by the car's safety devices. He wondered, while sitting in the dark, if he really hadn't died back when he had plowed through the first tree, and if what he now experienced was the first stage of the afterlife. He wiggled his toes; they wiggled, or so it seemed. He shifted his legs; they moved. He couldn't find anything that was in pain. He tried to imagine he was in pain, and it didn't work, although he had managed to convince himself that since the hot motor had scorched his jacket's right sleeve, his arm was probably burned, but he just hadn't felt the pain yet. He considered that maybe his neck had snapped and he was now a quadriplegic, and that he had only *fancied* moving his toes.

After a moment, or two, of trying to figure out if he was injured or not, he decided he'd better try to get out. It occurred to him, if the crash hadn't gotten him, surely the coming fire and explosion would. I need to get away from this thing. Superheated fluids hissed out of the radiator and steam, pluming upwards, was clearly visible in the moonlight. With the torrid motor sitting beside him as a reminder, it was fair to say there were plenty of heat sources. Fuel had to be around and oxygen wasn't lacking. Fire would soon follow.

He reached for the seat belt and it miraculously snapped loose. He tried to pull himself around to see if the door would open. It didn't. Every window in the car was broken.

Forcing with both hands, he managed to get his seat to recline enough to separate himself from the airbag. He pulled himself upward and headfirst through the window beside him. The smell of gasoline hung in the air. This encouraged him to force himself all the harder and he managed to crawl out and slip over the side; the car teetered in the heavy redwood limbs that sustained it.

By the time he had both feet on the ground he had gotten some gasoline on him, which made him feel certain his escape would be in vain. So far, he had been uncannily lucky. People weren't supposed to be so lucky. He managed to get away, about fifty feet, and then, what was left of the car exploded. The concussion hit him and threw him against a tree, but even then, nothing happened. He started to feel a little immortal, like a cat that still had a few lives.

DOUG MADE HIS WAY into the area. When the explosion ignited, he felt satisfied that his job had been finished, and dialed his cellular phone. In the night darkness, he stood by the edge of the road while studying the crash scene, but the bright flames against the cool of the dark night tended to blind his full view. An answer came back, "Yes."

"Douglas Johnson, operative A1656," Doug said, just about the time a car zoomed by.

A CAR ZOOMED by as Atler stumbled nearer the road. Just then he heard Doug's voice. He almost yelled for him to come and help him, wondering why he was there. But as soon as he heard Doug's name, rank, and serial number, so to speak, he reclined silently against a tree, waiting to hear more. The word "operative" had really gotten Atler's attention. "Operative?" It surely didn't sound like the Doug he knew. Doug was a scientist, wasn't he? A physicist?

Then he heard Doug say, "Redclift was eliminated. The PARASITE assault was successful."

Parasites? They are organisms like tapeworms. They're harmful to your health. Doug said that I was eliminated by parasites. That is really strange. But whatever happened, it seems to have been planned for my destruction. Vipers don't suddenly go wildly out of control. Since he believes I'm dead, I had better not do anything to change his opinion. I must be still and not move since Doug is out to finish me off. I need to hide.

Atler began to think — Doug is a ruthless hit man. And I'm his target! These were frightening thoughts, even for a man who had just been churned in the bowels of death.

"Subject was terminated at eight hours, eighty-seven minutes, UDTC," Doug informed.

Why — thought Atler — didn't he say, nine hours, twenty-seven minutes? What is UDTC? I know what UTC is. It's Universal Time Co-ordinated, like Greenwich mean time. But what's the "D" for? And Atler derided himself — I'm worried about the "D" and he's calling me a "terminated subject."

Then Doug made another call. Atler heard, "Yeah, he was a fool."

Atler agreed. I was a fool! That two-faced liar. Acts like he's doing me a favor and then almost murders me.

"Okay, Sterling. I'll hop on the next assignment."

That's our boss! — Atler thought, hardly able to believe his ears.

Then Doug signed off saying, "See you tomorrow."

Atler heard more tones from the phone. Doug keyed in three digits. Were they 9-1-1?

"Yes, I wish to report an accident, a car seems to have driven off the road ..."

Curse him! — Atler thought, looking at the wreckage of his car.

Doug quickly jumped into a van. Atler barely caught a glimpse as he drove away. What a strange white van — he thought.

Atler made certain that Doug had left before dragging himself up the steep embankment. He started thinking — Doug and Sterling are against me. I can't even tell my boss. Doug talked about the New Age, a new president, and his friends in high places, and they gave me a million. If all of this is true, it's horrible. He must have jimmied my car to drive it off the road. There must be evidence in the wreck. But he wasn't afraid to call 911. He and Sterling, and their "concerned" millionaires have bought off the police, too. If I go to them, they'll turn me over to Doug to finish my assassination. I had better get out of here before the police arrive and finish the job he started.

Atler really wanted to pretend nothing had happened, and that he could press rewind. He said Nova Mundi was benevolent. I don't think so! He told me that if I didn't cooperate, they'd make my life miserable. What did I do to deserve this?

Atler began to feel terribly sorry for himself. He nearly wished he had died in the crash. As bad as being a hunted man made him feel, he felt worse for the Viper, poor thing, than he did for himself. It was such a fine car — he mused.

It had always seemed to him that if someone lived through an accident like he had experienced, it would make them a nobler person. With that thought, he mocked — You're supposed to think about God and country, family and charity: things like that, but I could care less. I just wish I hadn't lost my Viper.

I'm a mess, he noted, looking at himself in the dim light. My clothes are torn. I'm caked in grease and covered with scrapes and scratches. And I'm a hunted man. He reached the highway. It was abandoned. There didn't seem to be any traffic. But that would change with the arrival of the 911 people.

I've got to get out of here! Please, let someone come by — he begged. A minute later someone zoomed passed. He was sure they would stop to help a man in distress, but their rpm didn't even change. Somehow, he expected people to stop to help him, but had he been driving past, he knew he wouldn't have stopped.

Two minutes more and another went by. Atler waved his arms and jumped, yelling, "Help!" But the man with his date sped by.

Nine-one-one will be here soon. I've got to hide, or escape. It looks like blinking lights are coming up the mountain. I think I hear a distant siren.

He looked up the mountain and saw a vehicle winding its way down the road toward him. He stumbled weakly across the pavement to the other side of the road, limping as it were, but he could have walked normally. His limp was entirely psychological. A person couldn't live through what he had just experienced without showing some sign, at least a limp, but his walk hadn't changed. He was the same old Atler.

He heard the sirens advancing quickly.

Atler kept looking back and forth. Who would make it first? He had already decided that if the descending vehicle didn't stop, or didn't take him, or if the police got there first, he would duck back into the woods behind him. His logic told him that the sirens were bringing Doug's people.

His heart raced as he signaled the descending vehicle. It was a dark Toyota Land Cruiser. The driver stopped! As the window came down, Atler said, panic clearly in his voice, "I need a ride!"

"Get in," the lone driver offered.

Atler looked at the "angel" sent to save him. He was a large man with a jolly smile, gray-haired and middle-aged.

They started down the mountain, and before they had much time to introduce themselves, a sheriff's car zoomed past, climbing the mountain road. Atler turned his head, watching it go by, going around the turn, where he figured it would stop.

"I'm Dale," offered the driver in a husky voice.

"Atler," he replied, barely introducing himself.

"You look like you've been through a wreck, or something," Dale observed.

"Yeah," Atler answered, hesitantly.

"What happened?"

"Hard to say," Atler replied. "Seems like something forced me off the road."

"Do you need to report it?"

"Yeah," he answered, with hesitation still in his voice.

"I think there's a phone at the bottom of the hill," Dale offered.

There was a momentary silence until Dale asked, "What's your business?"

Computer scientist? Hunted victim? Atler questioned himself. "I work at JPL," he answered, thinking that perhaps he should phrase it in the past tense.

"With all of the space stuff?"

"I guess you could say that."

"Sounds exciting," Dale offered.

I wish it wasn't as "exciting" as it has been today. I've got to get this conversation turned around. I don't need him digging, "Sometimes," Atler answered, and asked, "What's your business?"

"Oh," Dale began, "I'm just passing through. Let me give you something." He pulled a folded paper out of his Bible. "It's got a message you should read."

There wasn't much light, so Atler folded it and put it in his shirt pocket.

About then, they were reaching the bottom of the hill. It widened, and there was a gasoline station. Atler pointed, and said, "Can you let me out here?"

"Okay, Atler. When you get a chance, read over the paper I gave you."

"I will," he promised.

They came to a stop and Atler got out. Dale pulled away.

As Atler walked, he took the paper out of his pocket, glanced at it, and seeing it was a Gospel tract, he wadded it up and trashed it. He reached the pay phone, but found himself without any change. He went inside, where several pairs of eyes tried to see him without staring. Atler knew he looked more scarecrow than human. After he managed to get a dollar's change, he went back out.

He first thought to call JPL to apologize for not being able to take care of the programming problem, but why? To let Doug and Sterling know he was still alive? They'll know soon enough, when they learn there's no body in the wreck.

So he called home and a feminine voice answered, "Hello."

"Norma, I'm here. Near ..." and he went on to explain his location.

He really wasn't so far away. He made arrangements for her, his wife, to come after him. She would be there in about ten minutes, he guessed.

Atler and Norma's marriage had ceased to be anything more than a certificate years before. "Atler and his computers," Norma would say to herself. "Norma and her flower store," Atler would think.

They lived independently from one another. They shared the same roof, but not even the same bed. Independent checking. Independent existence. Independent friends. They had ceased to complain about each other years before. They were too busy for any relationship, at any level. Each had eliminated their mutual relationship from their lives: Atler had substituted his computers, and Norma, her store. Each blamed the other and each had given up blaming. But there were benefits in sharing the same domicile: like — Atler reflected — she'll come to pick me up. He was right.

Atler visited the rest room, trying to spruce himself up, but there wasn't much he could do. He had always had a dash of scarecrow in his look, and his present image only accentuated the obvious.

In about ten minutes Norma pulled into the station. Atler got in her Lexus. She almost ordered him out. Her look said it all. But after she had gotten over the initial shock, she asked, "Do you need to go to a hospital?"

"No," Atler answered definitively, adding, "no thanks to that beast! Actually, I think he would've been happier sending me to a morgue."

"What do you mean? What happened?" she asked, but not with any hint of sympathy, which Atler didn't expect, or seek. Her questions merely sought information. But he really didn't know the answers. Had Doug's people caught on? Did they know he had double-crossed them? Shouldn't a lawyer have spoken to him? Wouldn't they give him a chance to give the money back?

WHEN ATLER told her, "I really don't know why they're after me?" she nearly hoped they would get him. She remembered the five-hundred-thousand-dollar life insurance policies they had on each other, and figured that collecting on his would give her some great capital. She could expand the business.

But she wouldn't have him murdered, or anything, to get it. She didn't even like to swat a fly. However, if someone else did it, she wasn't sure she'd shed a tear. Five hundred thousand dollars — that would be nice.

Atler told her as they reached the house, "Look Norma, I don't want to get you mixed up in this. I'm going to take a vacation, and it'll be a long one. If anyone comes looking for me, tell 'em the truth; you don't know where I am."

Chapter 30

Papers

ATLANTIS, THE LOST CONTINENT, was a land whose inhabitants lived in perpetual fog. Because of this, Atlantians developed a third eye. Physical sight was useless, but they were empowered by the third eye of psychic vision.

ASTRAL PROJECTION, achieved in an altered state through meditation, takes the initiate traveling through perspectives of time, leaf after leaf falling away as he is accelerated, into visions of the spirit origin of the universe. The destiny of *Homo sapiens* is then unfolded before his eyes, revealing ever-transforming states of life and cycles of progression.

— The Secret Doctrine

FOR THE SECRET POWER of lawlessness is already at work; but the one who now holds it back will continue to do so till he is taken out of the way. And then the lawless one will be revealed, whom the Lord Jesus will overthrow with the breath of his mouth and destroy by the splendor of his coming.

— Paul the Apostle

January 28, 1992 — Ten days later — Worldwide

"**I'M GLAD TO REPORT,**" Karl Rennedy spoke with a deep voice, "our long-term efforts are having success. Fifty-four percent of high school students in the USA have had sexual intercourse. The resulting increase in single-parent homes and the general decline in morality prove that our efforts in Hollywood are working; we will soon have a significant rise in the number of delinquents on the streets. With greater lawlessness, people will be ready for our strong leader, Therion."

"It has taken many years, but this ingenious project has made great progress," Wilhelm Gernik in Bonn, Germany, observed as he adjusted his glasses' brown designer rims. Gernik's thinning gray-brown hair, large square forehead, and twisted smile fit his vernacular. "It has been easier than we thought," he continued. "Few people are as moral as they pretend. They're all hypocrites!"

"How are we doing in Russia?" Arslene Nuvonah, past middle age, tall, with well-groomed sandy-brown hair, asked from his Amsterdam office.

Cyzack answered, "Yeltsin seems to be working in our direction. The turkey doesn't know any better." There were several laughs as Cyzack shrugged his shoulders as if to mimic the beleaguered Yeltsin.

Static came on the flat wall screen; then an image formed. They began to view the State of the Union that was coming from the US Congress.

"George and his New World Order," Watkins remarked sarcastically. "Where did he get that idea from?" Lord Watkins said, provoking snickers from around the table.

"He really doesn't know," Nuvonah guffawed. "And he wouldn't know if we told him! He makes a genuine pawn."

The State of the Union filled the ten conference rooms. Behind Stonefell's seat was a mural of awesome power, whose centerpiece was the familiar symbol of the Great Pyramid and the All-Seeing Eye.

When President Bush declared that the USA was the "sole and prominent world power," they laughed. Then Bush announced the end of the "Cold War," saying the United States had won.

"He thinks he's won!" Stonefell declared, unable to hold back his laughter.

Congress stood cheering and a nation sat convinced, but the Cosmokrator laughed hysterically.

* * *

Quito, Ecuador

STANDING OUTSIDE of Quito International Airport's disembarkation area, Larry and James waited in the cold night air for the arrival of flight 971.

"We missed the State of the Union," Larry remarked.

James looked a bit perplexed, "State of the Union?"

"The President's annual speech to Congress."

"You mean the President of the United States?"

"Yeah…. It takes them forever to get out of customs." Larry said.

The moderate note of disgust in Larry's voice led to a brief pause in the conversation, because James wasn't entirely sure how to respond. There were several hundred people gathered around them, all waiting for passengers to come out of the terminal. James watched as one climbed the fence a few inches trying to get a view inside of the building.

James felt like a perfect outer. His new wardrobe looked great, and he even had a casual black jacket to replace his poncho, which he still liked. Jack sent him the new clothing by Air Express, along with several odds and ends. Such shipping was expensive, but the alternative was surface mail, and anything sent that way evidently went to China (on a slow boat) before coming back to Ecuador. Non-airmail packages usually arrived within six months, but not always.

Watching the people with their passports and visas in hand, Larry commented, "You're going to need some papers."

"Papers?" James asked.

"Passport, visa, birth certificate, driver's license," Larry listed.

James wasn't exactly sure what he meant, and Larry kept on explaining, "You can't go anywhere without them." Then he pointed at the people and said, "Identification, James. To travel you have to have documents that show who you are, what country you're from, and all that."

He was beginning to understand. "You mean I have to be able to prove who I am?"

Larry shook his head, and explained, "That's the deal. If they catch you without papers, they'll put you in jail."

He was familiar with security, but there were no "illegals" where he came from. They couldn't merely slip across a river to get into Mars Base Aquarrian, or Novus Ordo. And he was familiar with the fact that Therion would require invisible laser tattoo identification on the foreheads of everyone, and that the prefix for the universal identification bar code would be DCLXVI, which would be visible only to special scanners provided by Nova Mundi. But he hadn't really paid attention to current outer identification systems. It seemed to him that "papers" would be easy to falsify.

Larry asked, "Have you ever flown on a commercial airline?"

"No, we always had better methods of transportation."

"You were proud of what you did, weren't you?"

"They taught us to be proud. They told us we were the best, and we were, but they tried to make us into machines."

"Speaking of 'getting old,' this wait is too long. It's after 10 PM. Besides, it's cold."

"Yeah," James agreed. "What is it, about eight or nine degrees?"

"I guess," Larry answered. "What's that, about fifty Fahrenheit?"

"I suppose."

Shortly, and to James's relief, Jon and Judy were visible at the final point where they took the baggage checks. They saw him standing out above the rest of the crowd, and waved. He felt excited, but other than shifting his weight from one foot to the other in a slow standing walk, he didn't show it. He looked at his watch, and twisted it on his wrist. It was 10:15. He was meeting his long-lost "kin folk." He watched Jon and Judy make their way through the confusion. As they came through the gate, they were quick to greet the travelers.

Quito International wasn't big, and it was only a short jaunt to the parking lot. Larry had a typical get-you-there Jeep-type vehicle for multipurpose transportation. Piling the luggage into the back, they were soon on their way out of the parking lot.

The airport was practically in the center of the city, and the ride home took only minutes. Denise had seen to it that everything would be the way Judy would have it, and even though the guest room was in back, away from the house, they had planned for James to spend that night at the Williamses'.

"We brought you some gifts, James," Jon advised as they made their way together through the door. "We'll have them ready for you tomorrow."

It was 11:30 PM when James finally made it to bed. There was a lot on his mind, as he thought — Papers! I have no identity.

James wasn't keeping any record of changes that outer life brought to him, but adjustments weren't easy. Looking after himself, losing his vision enhancements, communicating in outerspeak (as though he was learning a new language) — it was staggering — but on top of all this, he had a new problem: papers. He realized that falsifying them might lead to trouble.

Fortunately, all the changes made life as an outer a thrilling new experience. He didn't miss being captain of a DEEP, although he had wondered more than once if he would.

James discerned that papers were the key to slavery. He knew the Committee's plans for the future of humanity. Six-six-six, the mark of Therion, was to be the ultimate "paper," the invisible mark on the forehead that only Nova Mundi's scanners would be able to read. Without it, no one would be able to buy or sell. A memory came to him as he envisioned the vast underwater warehouses of Novus Iridium. There were huge undersea warehouses filled with equipment, all of it ready for the implementation of Operation Therion. It had been sitting there so many years that they had junked much of it and replaced everything with updated programmable equipment. There were hundreds of thousands of microchip-embedding apparatuses, holographic imaging devices, notebook computer drives, and everything else they needed to implement a cashless society. Any need for money and papers, as in identification, would be eliminated since people would have their identification with them everywhere they went (unless someone cut off their hand and their head).

Control — it was all control. The thought made James boil, and he grasped that in TerraNova some are "more equal" than others.

Why are they so racist? In the Alpha Force it didn't matter much. I was one of the most equal. We were the elite, pampered and given the best — TerraNova's crack troops. It was our duty to make Operation Therion happen, but why did they make us Aryans? Noncombative personnel, technologists, scientists, and even janitors came from nearly every ethnic background, but there were no Jews. Every Cosmokrator represented a distinct race. But James knew the answer, even if it sounded strange. It was the Secret Doctrine. And simply, even if he didn't know why, it mandated the restoration of "the original glory of the supermen of Atlantis." He had never fully understood, but the Aryan race was supposed to be the end point of higher evolution. However, even he knew that without his enhancements he wouldn't be able to beat Michael Jordan on the court. (A fact that had made James respect the world-renowned outer, and a contradiction that made him wonder why his mentors had taught him that he was superior to all outers and all other races. Was he truly superior if his superiority depended on gadgets? It was a contradiction that he had thought about many times, but had found more convenient to ignore, until now.) So— James wondered — Am I really as "highly" evolved as they say? Could there be some deeper reason for TerraNova's racism that I don't know about? With that question, an answer came to him: They're racist because they need an excuse for their Final Solution. If race wasn't an issue, they wouldn't have a good reason for exterminating the Jews. To be able to say that someone is inferior, you have to make someone else superior.

Then he wondered on the more practical side, thinking — I bet my tech's getting old. How long would it have been until my *lot* was replaced by *"natural"* selection? By now, they've probably developed better enhancements in the laboratory.

It took him a while to get past his disturbing analysis, but he finally figured he might have a better chance at the future as an outer than as an *other*.

* * *

The next day

COLD AND MISERABLE rain made the day dreary. Quito could feel colder than it was, and today was one such example. It was six in the afternoon when the Williamses, with James, came to call on the Whittens.

Judy had warm drinks and Jon had a fire in the hearth. Fireplaces in Quito were designed more for decoration than for heating purposes, and had little heat-retaining ability, so the fireplace didn't warm much, but it helped.

It had taken two extra suitcases to bring the things for James and the Williamses. The distribution of belated Christmas gifts from family and friends made the visit a festive event. James received two new pairs of shoes: tennis shoes and another pair for dress. Pastor Jack had taken care to get his measurements before leaving; one couldn't buy size-sixteen shoes in Ecuador.

Jack had his reasons for wanting to keep James happy. Several members of his church worked for NASA. Robert Towley, a former director of the institution, was one of the reasons. Robert and Jack had known each other for years, and on a few occasions, Robert had shared some of the strange things he had seen while in space, and other unusual things — like how there seemed to be more to the Challenger disaster than just an O-ring failure. So Jack knew, as soon as he understood what James might represent, that his old friend would be very interested in contacting James. With that in mind, Jack took James's measurements back to the USA. He wanted James to remain with his friends. He'd never have said it aloud, but he wanted to keep James happy. He couldn't have said why, but he was convinced that God had an important task for James. He knew it because he felt it in his heart, and though he didn't have any better reason, he knew he must act to aid the strange man who said he had been to Mars.

After receiving his gifts, with a content smile, James looked up from the couch as Jon remarked to him, "Pastor Kinderly told me to tell you that his church is going to help you have money to live on, and rent a small apartment. He wants you to feel at home. If you accept, he feels — with what you know — you'll have a lot to tell people. He understands you can't just run around telling everyone. It could be dangerous. But he thinks there's a way it could be done secretly. He feels like the time is coming when you could help a lot of people with what you know.

"He wants you to think it over. If you don't like the idea, you're welcome to stay until you figure out what you're going to do next. But if you want, we'll be glad to have you stay until we figure out a way to get you to the States."

"Why the States?" James asked.

Jon thought — Why not the States! Don't make this hard. Don't look a gift horse in the mouth, but he answered, speaking calmly, "Well, James, if you don't want to, none of us will force you into doing anything, but I think Jack feels you could be effective there, in the States, telling a few important people, and pastors, about the world you came from, its history, and its plans. But you don't have to decide right this second. Take your time."

JAMES WAS ALREADY thinking about it. It seemed controlling, being "kept" by the outers. Control was something he could easily identify, having been under domination most of his life. Yet it really wasn't the same. They were offering him total freedom. He had the ability to do as he wanted, and they were willing to help him. It was easy for him to see that if they hadn't taken him in, he would be back in TerraNova's "prison." They weren't demanding anything from him, so he thought he would take advantage of the offer, and answered, "It seems fair. And I like the idea of leaving Ecuador and going somewhere. I'm so out of place here. People can't miss me — I'm so different. In the States

— as long as I don't get listed in the computers — I'd be able to live like a normal person." He almost said, "like an outer" instead of "person," but he was learning.

However, his hosts were learning *other* talk, and Judy proposed, "You'll make a good outer, James. You're about normal."

Larry laughed and said, "Good observation, Judy." And then he asked, "Can you cook?"

James began to answer, haltingly, as he realized that Larry's question was about more than cooking. He thought — In Alpha Force we never had to worry about the next meal, but as an outer, I'll have to learn to do things for myself. He responded, "No, but I learn quickly."

They all laughed. He didn't see why the *outers* thought his answer was funny, but figured that the *normal* thing would be to smile, which he did.

"Do it! Do it! Zap 'em! Go! Go! Go! You did it!" David was on the edge of his seat and couldn't contain himself. James whizzed through galaxies, nebulas, and supernovas right up to the end. The enemy couldn't touch him. He was back to *normal.*

During the past several weeks, since Christmas, James had been learning to live without vision enhancements. His nerve-impulse accelerator would last at least ten more years — probably more. It worked by secreting a microscopic quantity of a stored drug that improved the conductivity of his nervous system. Long-term side effects were unknown, but no one in Alpha Force had lived long enough to know if they were serious.

The next devices that would likely fail him would be his sound processors. They had about two years of battery power left. They were like hearing aids, but made from a clear substance, and were hidden in each ear's channel. James began to leave them out occasionally to accustom himself to life without them.

The kids formed a thunderous cheering section when the game named James a Master Star Invader.

Chapter 31

The Hunt Begins

THERE IS A PASSION *for hunting something* deeply implanted in the human breast.
— Charles Dickens,
British novelist

That same day — Grand Central Hotel, Guayaquil, Ecuador

SAO HENRY LÓPEZ anxiously entered his suite, a few steps from the elevator. He was running a minute late. Dressed casually, in white Bermudas and a dark T-shirt, he was content that this wasn't a black-suit assignment. Barely through the door himself, he heard a knock. Two longs and a short, and while it didn't prove anything, it was likely to be the people for whom he was waiting. Looking though the peephole, he recognized two of his coworkers. He opened the door. They shook hands. Henry began, "Did anyone see Felix?"

"He's here," Alicia answered.

And, as if in response to a cue, there was another knock, again two long and one short.

"Felix, my friend," Henry greeted, having confirmed it was Felix before opening the door.

There wasn't much small talk and soon they were sitting around the table.

"Shall we ask for room service?" Henry offered.

"It's too early," Alicia said. "We just had breakfast."

"Then let's get down to business," Henry started, resolutely. "Our mission is to find Captain James Smith, if he's alive. We have reason to believe he may be here in Ecuador. Chances are, he's dead, but they didn't find his RSB Earth-reentry device, so we need to locate him, or some fisherman who may have fished a strange shiny bag out of the sea. Or maybe we'll find someone who reported it washing ashore."

"So, we're looking for Smith, or his RSB." Felix summarized.

"Yes," Henry answered and then continued, "It's going to be tough, and there are just a few of us, but I understand more SAOs are on the way. In the larger cities we can probably take advantage of our friends in the cartel. But if people start thinking they can get rich by telling us a *gringo* story about how they had seen a tall blond foreigner, we will be flooded with reports. *Gringos* all look the same. We must be discreet. We accomplish our mission without looking suspicious ourselves. You have your training. We will implement our plans carefully.

"This directive comes from Herr Weller, himself. Unless we stumble upon Smith or his RSB, this assignment is going to take some time. We should have DEEPs soon, but while we are starting, we must make do with what we have. As soon as we have DEEP support, we'll request an enhanced ionic-meson scan of the entire Ecuadorian coast. That should take us right to the RSB. Any questions?"

"Why don't we just wait for DEEP support?" Felix asked.

"The boss wants us working," Henry said with a smirk, and then clarified, "I have no idea, but I guess it's important. Anyhow, we'll split the coast between us, and go looking for Smith."

AFTER ALL THE OTHERS had left for their rooms and for their assignments, López opened his notebook computer and typed in his password. Every key press formed an asterisk. The computer looked like any other that was commercially available, but it wasn't. It had abilities that wouldn't be commercially available for at least thirty more years.

His thumb hit the mouse button, but he didn't need to move it, since the computer locked onto, and followed, the pupils of his eyes — it was a look-and-click interface, which added security, since no two people have the same irises.

In seconds he had linked his computer directly to TelSat (without need of any phone line or antenna dish) and after entering another code word and password, he was connected to the supercomputer. (His laptop would have been considered a supercomputer by outer standards.) A full graphics screen downloaded in an instant. It was colorful, and read, "Welcome to the Nova Mundi Foundation." He looked, and clicked on a virtual communications "button." A screen for typing in a message came up, but he looked and clicked on another part of the screen, which appeared to have no button, but it was there. His iris was scanned. Blood flow in his retina was measured to insure that he was alive and to avoid the possibility that someone might try to kill him and use his iris to circumvent security. He was authenticated.

At that point, the image appeared directly in 3-D, right in López's enhanced contact lenses. He heard Weller speaking directly in his ears in surround-stereo, "What do we have, López?" Weller's voice came to him through his enhanced sound processors in his ear canals. The computer monitored his every movement and the movement of the pupils of his eyes. It also added a virtual-reality image to the one coming from Novus Ordo, making López feel that he was sitting there, with Weller, right at his boss's desk. If he turned his head to his right, he could look through one of the picture windows in the spacious office. There were banks of computer terminals and technicians. In front of him, and behind Weller, was a pictorial of the Great Seal. And to his left was another picture window, which gave a view downwards into the gargantuan DEEP hangar.

He answered, "Sir, no luck yet. There's no trace of Smith, or his RSB."

"I don't like that, López. What about our contacts in the cartel?'

"They don't have much influence here, especially in Manta, and no tip they've given us has led us any closer to Smith. It's difficult, sir — finding a *gringo* isn't as easy now as it used to be. The country is full of them. The inflicted missionaries, the oil people, and the tourists, too, not to mention businessmen and oceanographers ... as far as the natives are concerned, they all look alike."

"Well, López, curse it! Just keep looking, understand?"

"Yes, sir."

Weller terminated the communication, and López found himself sitting in the hotel room exactly as he had been. He hadn't even left.

WELLER TURNED his attention to the report from the ionic scan. They were still looking for Smith's RSB, but there hadn't been any progress. The equipment only worked from a maximum of sixty thousand feet, which was low enough to be seen by the naked eye. The DEEPs couldn't use holographic cloaking while scanning, so they had to work at night, reducing the number of hours they could collect data. Even so, they had managed to scan the entire coast of Ecuador, but they hadn't found a trace of the RSB.

They had gone to the point of performing a chaos track of the storm that blew Brown's RSB, and had found that Smith should have splashed down, according to Chief Jones's calculations, near Machala, Ecuador, but there wasn't any inflicted RSB there! — Weller blurted to himself.

Maybe Smith's corpse is floating in space, frozen inside his RSB. All the others were found quickly. Our calculations for their reentry were correct. So Smith should have landed on Earth too. Weller decided to try a long shot. His hunch would be about as good as everything else they had attempted. Super-tech hadn't eliminated the communication delay with Mars, so Weller began an e-mail bound for Mars. He addressed it to Chief Engineer Nancy Jones, Mars Base Aquarrian:

"Jones, I have noted that you frequently conceptualize breakthrough engineering designs. You have a command of advanced theory that few of our other scientists have. I know that you are aware of the capabilities of hyperdimensionally enhanced ionic-meson scanners. Using a DEEP, at an altitude of 20,000 meters, we have the ability to scan up to ten square kilometers every six hours. Could you examine our present system and see if there is a way to heighten our definition, so that we can locate Captain Smith's RSB? I would like our DEEPs to operate at higher altitudes and perform daytime scanning also. Scanning can't be performed while the DEEP is in motion and neither can holographic camouflage be used. Therefore, for daytime scanning, we must increase altitude. I'm certain that your efforts will be rewarded if successful. Thank you."

Several hours later, Weller found the following note in his e-mail.

"Cosmokrator Weller, I accept the ionic-meson assignment with pleasure. I will have better access to the resources I require at Novus Ordo. Therefore, I will return to Earth ASAP. Thank you."

Chapter 32

Family Reunion

LIVING NEAR THE CITY of Santo Domingo de los Colorados, located at the base of the western edge of the Andes Mountains, the Colorados are a peculiar tribal people. Their males dress in bright, multiple-colored garments, have painted faces, and use a Moe-style haircut capped in bright red clay. The females wear a short "miniskirt," with wide horizontal bands of intense fluorescent color, draping their torsos with similar cloth, or using an undergarment for covering when in the city, to abide by local ordinances. The men use similar, but distinct, skirts that copy the brightly colored tropical birds that live in the treetops of the local rain forests. Exhibiting themselves for the benefit of tourists has become one of their principal industries.

— *Brown's Guide to Touring in Ecuador*

Four days later — Santo Domingo de los Colorados, Ecuador

WHAT A CHANGE! The hot sun beat down on them. A few hours ago they had been in the cool, refreshing air of the Andes, but now they were suffocating and perspiring in the tropical heat — shedding all the excess clothing they could. Larry and Jon had left Quito that morning. They had invited James, who was glad to get out and see the countryside. Along the side of the road there were many sheer drop-offs into chasms hundreds of feet deep.

James was trying to ignore them, but thoughts of returning to TerraNova were bothering him. He knew that if he returned, they would kill him; but first they would inflict him until he told them the name of every outer he had told about TerraNova. So, he couldn't go back and betray his new friends. But it wasn't easy to give up the life he'd known from birth, even if it had left him feeling drained and lifeless.

There were overturned trucks along the road, and numerous white roadside crosses, barely visible in the thick fog. Apparently, they were there to remind travelers that the road wasn't safe. Landslides were common, and the traffic was heavy. Larry had told him that this is one of the deadliest stretches of road on earth. Cars passed chaotically in the fog. There weren't even any double lines for the drivers to ignore. Everyone drove the way they wanted to. Hairpin after horseshoe turn on mostly wet, slippery road made for a nerve-racking descent to the Pacific Coast. James wanted to take control, but it wasn't his place to do so. Jon was the captain of his Jeep. So James attempted to keep his focus on other things, occasionally getting a glimpse into the chasms and of the tropical vegetation that was thickening beside the road.

Bananas, bananas, and more bananas — in this region more were produced than anywhere else on earth. James knew this because, some years back, he had taken a few shipments of the tropical fruit to Mars. The bananas arrived on the red planet with tiny stickers that had the word Ecuador plainly inscribed on each one.

Larry and Jon said they were going to begin some evangelistic tent meetings in Santo Domingo; they were traveling there to discuss their plans for the meetings with the pastor whose church they had pioneered fifteen years before. However, they hadn't anticipated that he would invite them to conduct a street meeting. This Pastor, Gustavo Chavez, was a go-getter. He couldn't keep himself from winning souls. They said he was a jewel in the kingdom of God. When James had met the mature gentleman with thick black hair and bright, inquisitive brown eyes, he wondered why they had called him a "jewel."

Larry, Jon, and the Pastor had already begun the street meeting, and Larry had started preaching to the people walking by. They were on the corner of a busy intersection. To James, it was a lot like the day he had first met the Christian outers, and what they were doing seemed good to him. He still remembered how he had felt when Jack had preached, and he often wondered about the prayer he had repeated. Could God, as a man, really come to someone's heart? It made no sense to him and, furthermore, it was totally outer, but for some inexplicable reason, it seemed good. So he enjoyed participating in the meeting.

Staring at them from across the street was the famous statue of the Colorado, which was "dressed" (really painted) in the radiant, picturesque indigenous costume of the tribe. Jon had explained that you rarely saw a Colorado in town, and that in recent years they had abandoned their native dress and had begun to use the same clothing as everyone else, reserving their colorful native dress to make money from the tourists.

* * *

The Road to Quito

COMPACTED into a small space, Ashley looked out of the bus's window trying to see the surroundings, but from her aisle seat it was difficult. It had been a long trip and there was more to go. Mile after mile of green tropical plantations and bamboo houses standing on stilts above the marshland passed her window in a blur. So it was of some interest to her when the surroundings began to change into what was obviously a city.

As the number and height of the buildings increased, she watched out her window. The bus crept into a plaza where she noted a brightly colored statue of one of the natives. The statue's bizarre hairdo was covered with red clay. It was dressed with something that looked like a miniskirt. It was sufficiently curious that she might have kept staring at it, but an instant after seeing the statue, she saw a profile she thought was familiar. However, without vision enhancement to help her, she wasn't sure. He looked like James!

By the time she decided to go see if the man was James, the bus had gone two blocks. She jumped up and grabbed her bag from the rack above. It was all she possessed. The kind people of Manta had given her every bit of it, except her sea-worn uniform.

Only a few hours earlier she had boarded the bus in Manta. Getting off was risky. What if it hadn't been James? She would barely have sufficient money to buy another bus ticket to continue her trip to Quito. But she felt compelled; it had to be him – even if she couldn't think of any good reason why James would be there, dressed like an outer. She made her way to the door and impatiently asked the driver to stop and let her out. The next stop was another block away.

She jumped off to the sidewalk — three yards. She nearly entered a *bio* — a bioelectromechanical powered run. (A *bio* was the most efficient kind of electromechanical running activity, and could be carried on safely for a distance of up to 45 miles — just over an hour — without a rest.) But she realized that her standing long jump had drawn substantial attention, so she wouldn't make any more enhanced movements.

It had to be the longest walk of her life. It was hard to be patient, and she hoped that if she had seen James, he wouldn't be gone. Her brisk walk was catching peoples' attention, she could tell. By the time she was within one block, she could hear the familiar sound of *los hermanos,* and had heard enough to know they were preaching. She had heard them many times in Manta. James, or whoever had been around the corner, wouldn't be visible until she arrived. There weren't many blond men six feet six inches tall in Ecuador, and she felt certain it had to be Captain Smith.

Her pace accelerated, and she was getting plenty of attention. Reaching the corner of the street, and the edge of a building that had been blocking her view, she bolted around and stopped on a dime.

He was only about six meters away, she estimated, but with everything that was going on — the cacophony from traffic and the loud sound of the speakers — he didn't notice her. He had been looking away. She looked at him in disbelief. She knew it was James, and where moments before she had been eager to reach him, now she wasn't sure. Why is he with *los hermanos?* He was just standing there. She stepped back, around the corner, to give herself time to think.

She asked herself why he was there? But she found no answer. Is he on some kind of special assignment? But why *los hermanos?* Maybe he isn't part of them. Maybe he's looking for something, and they just happen to be there. Maybe he was hurt and has amnesia and *los hermanos* took him in like they did me.

Ashley thought — It's just a coincidence. It can't be James. My vision enhancement isn't working, so my eyes were fooled. But she couldn't resist the temptation, and was debating whether she would look again.

JAMES TURNED his head and saw a woman's back disappear around the corner. She reminded him of someone he knew. But she was dressed differently, and her hair was different — loose maybe — he wasn't sure. Could it have been Ashley? In his mind, however, he couldn't get rid of the image of that perfectly shaped blond girl ducking around the corner. But this is impossible — it couldn't be her. He decided to go look. Then he thought — Don't be stupid. You know it can't be her.

Then suddenly her face popped back around the corner of the building and he saw smooth blond locks curling around her feminine features. He recognized her as she disappeared from his view.

He took quick steps to follow her. Then he moved faster, and covered the distance in an instant. Looking around the corner, he saw her walking away hurriedly, down the sidewalk. He hesitated as he wondered why she was there, and why she was walking away from him.

By the time he decided to pursue her, she was thirty meters away. He started walking quickly, determined that even if he had to do a full *bio*, he wouldn't lose her. But even as he did, watching her graceful movements, the dress flowing behind her, golden hair bouncing back, he couldn't believe what he was seeing. You're going to make a scene, and people will talk about what happened, and then TerraNova will hear, and come after you. But James couldn't calm himself. He had to reach her and find out why she was there.

ASHLEY HURRIED ALONG, afraid to look back. If he's there, what will I do? — she asked herself. He is my captain. I can't just run away. He's probably got some good reason to be here. And she finally decided — I can't keep running. I'll get into trouble. I have to present myself. So she stopped, and turned slowly.

He had cut the distance between them in half, and continued moving towards her quickly. Their eyes locked. He came to a stop, staring at her. She felt intimidated. It's James — she fully realized. She had wanted to see him so badly, but now, she wished she hadn't. She was apprehensive as the captain neared. She still didn't know what to think. Her heart began to race, and she was tempted to turn and run, but it would be useless; he would catch her — she knew.

SLOWLY, he moved towards her. It's Ashley — James knew it. There wasn't any question left in his mind. He realized that people on the street were staring at them, but he didn't care. Before his eyes, she stood, and he saw her in a radiant light, as if she was an angel. She stood full posture, shyly holding her pocketbook with both hands in front of her. Her figure was pleasing. Her facial features, though perplexed, were alluring and vulnerable.

His heart jumped. He was near enough to speak. His mind tried to say something, but his mouth was dry, and his throat — choked. He finally persuaded his lips to move, and asked "Ashley?" He was now just a meter from her.

HEARING HIS VOICE, not harsh, but meek and inquisitive, Ashley relaxed her stance and dropped her head a bit to her right, but she didn't say anything. She could feel his eyes looking her over, and she didn't know why, but she liked it. He spoke again, repeating, "Ashley." And then he asked, "Is that you?"

His voice is different. He doesn't sound like he's the captain.

Ashley paused a moment more, and then answered, "Captain — " wanting to say more, but she didn't know what or why. She had many questions, but didn't know where to begin. She waited for him to say something.

HE WISHED she would say something, but he was the "captain," and she had addressed him as such. She was oblivious of his present classification of AWOL, and since she had addressed him as her commanding officer, he realized he should take command, and he should exercise extreme caution. He had no idea why she was there, and possibly he had already committed himself too deeply — just being seen. But he needed to say something, and say it quickly. "Maybe we should find a place where we can talk?" he asked, thinking the question sufficiently neutral.

Ashley nodded her agreement. It was obvious that she was having as much trouble speaking as he was.

JON, when he noticed that James had disappeared around the corner, became curious to see where he had gone. Larry kept preaching as Jon moved away. He looked around the corner just in time to see James moving towards the girl. They seem to know each other — he thought. She doesn't look Ecuadorian. She looks like his sister.

By then Jon had taken a few steps in their direction, but he hesitated, not knowing what was going on, and seeing their distant expressions, he began to think that he probably shouldn't get involved. However, about then, James turned and looked his way momentarily, and having been seen, he decided to keep walking towards the pair.

He watched as they also turned and began walking towards him. Their gait was normal, but they didn't exchange any conversation. They did glance back and forth a few times. Once they were within a few feet, Jon greeted them. Ashley reached out to receive his extended hand and to reply to his introduction, "I'm Ashley Brown," beating James to it.

"Jon, this is an old friend," James said, trying to recuperate after missing the chance to introduce her. "Ashley, Jon Whitten. He's become a good friend in the past few weeks." Then James directed himself to Jon again, "Ashley and I need to talk some. Could we use the Jeep?"

"Sure, James," he answered, and started leading the way back.

It was mysterious. Who was the woman? Where had she come from? But even though it seemed like the woman could be a sign of coming trouble, he couldn't keep a smile from his face. Even if she did mean trouble, she sure looked lovely.

As soon as they were near the vehicle, Jon opened the passenger door and invited Ashley to take the seat. After she sat down, James closed the door and started to walk around to the other side, as Jon accompanied him.

"May I be alone with her?" James asked.

"Sure," Jon replied as he handed him the keys, and then gave a look that demanded an explanation.

"She's my first officer," James replied — realizing too late that he had probably said the wrong thing.

"Did she come from your spaceship?" Jon asked with amazement.

"Let's not talk now," James answered in a hush. Then he whispered, "She might be able to hear us."

After Jon turned away, James reached down to open the door and he looked across at Ashley. "Are you okay?" he asked, as he sat down and looked into her eyes. She really looked fine, but asking her was the best thing he could think of saying, especially seeing her expression, which showed a mix of intimidation and fury.

"Why did you tell him I'm your first officer? Is he Nova Mundi? And why did he ask if I was on your spaceship?" she asked, thinking — If he's with Nova Mundi, he would have called it a DEEP.

I should have known she'd hear us — James considered, feeling himself inept. Her sound processors are probably working better than mine. Now what do I tell her? And then it came to him: the truth.

"He wanted to know who you are, and he's my friend. I've told him everything about TerraNova," but as soon as he said it, he felt as though he had just betrayed himself, and his friends. Yet, there really wasn't any good way to answer. It was one of those questions that didn't have an appropriate answer. Even silence would have been wrong.

"But is he with Nova Mundi?" Ashley demanded.

James hesitated in his reply, since he had been thinking, and said, "No."

His firm reply made her realize that his delay had nothing to do with any lack of decision. That was her captain speaking — calculating and decisive.

James looked steadily into her blue eyes that were passionate with unspoken anger. He didn't know what more to say, and thought — Will she jump out the door and run? She'll inform. And they'll get me — dead — and murder my friends too. But try as he might, he couldn't think of anything else to say. And if she ran, would he dive after her? He couldn't let her go back, not now.

It could have been hours, but it had been seconds. He had no idea what she was thinking, but there was something in his heart — something that had always been there, and had never left him: desire. There weren't any surveillance cameras, nor were there any conditioners to shock away at misbehavior, and it was what he had always wanted, and even though her eyes were hot, he slowly moved his hand towards hers. Almost involuntarily, though driven by his freed will, his body turned towards Ashley.

Then his hand gently touched the back of hers.

INITIALLY, Ashley didn't move. She thought — What's he doing? But she knew, and she wanted it too. She had never forgotten the closet.

James's fingers, and then his full hand, touched hers. She liked it

— even craved it — and responded by clasping his hand softly, turning towards him; after all, there weren't any *inflictors.* They embraced.

It was awkward and hot. The steering wheel was in the way and the bucket seats separated them by ten inches. But they embraced, and soon she felt tears coming from her eyes.

For Ashley, though she didn't fully realize it, her tears came from the depression that often follows an exhilarating moment, and from the memory of James's infliction: something she had felt herself, many times, though it hadn't been hers. Her tears were also for one other reason: She felt safe in his powerful arms. She had been so near death, cursing TerraNova, and the Skotoi too — abandoned and left to the sharks — her life's security gone. Finally, in this moment, she was near someone who made her feel safe. For a moment she didn't have to be invested — she could be weak and vulnerable. The moment she had heard James's meek voice, she knew it. He wasn't the same; he had changed.

However, as much as she liked being with him, distant from TerraNova, in his arms, she wasn't sure she had changed at all, and that caused her eyes to moisten even more.

"Remember, I told you I'd see you back on Earth," James said, as they slowly pulled back from each other.

"I almost didn't get off the bus. My eyes said it was you, but my mind said it couldn't be," Ashley explained.

"Where were you coming from?"

"Manta. Some good people, who found me, took me there after fishing me out of the Pacific. I was as good as dead, but my bioprocessor entered survival mode, and kept me alive a few minutes until they rescued me, or I'd be dead."

"What happened? Why didn't they come get you?"

"I don't know, but the trucks never came, at least not the ones that were supposed to. After three days, my transceiver's confirmation light went off, and I was lost at sea. Then there was a bad storm. When the Ecuadorians rescued me, I was in a dead man's float, and the RSB wasn't anywhere to be seen. I had treaded water and used my jumpsuit as a life preserver for almost two days, until I couldn't stay awake any longer."

"Oh, Ashley!" James exclaimed. "I'm glad you're alive. You said good people helped you?"

Ashley felt a lump in her throat. Why did he have to ask? — she questioned herself. She bit her lower lip.

He questioned, "Were they Christians?"

She looked up, startled, "How did you know?" She wasn't asking; she was demanding — feeling as if she was a child caught in mischievousness.

"That's okay. Don't get excited," he said in a consoling voice.

"What's going on here? These are *hermanos?*"

"They're my friends, and they've helped me; and yes, they are Christians."

"Did they pick you up in the Pacific?"

James chuckled, "No."

This perplexed her — Why did he chuckle? So she demanded, "Explain, please!"

"When I returned to Earth, it was terrible. I plowed down the side of a snowcap, right through a glacier, and rolled into a boulder. I should be dead."

Ashley's expression changed, "Were you hurt?"

"Everything in my body hurt. I was unconscious for three days."

She knew he should have died — if he was telling the truth, and she knew he was. "Why didn't they pick you up?"

"The transceiver didn't survive the fall. It didn't work. But my PLOT worked; can you believe that?"

She didn't answer his question, but asked her own, "How did you end up here? There aren't any snowcapped mountains."

"That's a long story," James answered quickly, as if he didn't need to say more.

Ashley, however, wanted to know much more, and was beginning to question, when she realized why James had shortened his answer. One of his "friends," if they really were friends, was coming.

"Hello, I'm Larry Williams," he said, introducing himself and speaking to her from James's window.

"Ashley Brown," she responded.

James stepped out, and let Larry in — where he could shake her hand.

"You and James know each other?"

"We do," she answered curtly.

It took a moment to finish stowing the equipment and to organize. Ashley had to get down from the seat. James ended up in the back, sitting partially on the wheel well. The Ecuadorian man, whom they introduced to her as Pastor Chavez, sat in the front seat. He looked a lot like the man named "Pastor" who was at the outer church in Manta, and she wondered if he was closely related to the pastor she met in Manta. Ashley found herself sandwiched between James and Jon.

It seemed that they had managed to get back in the vehicle just in time. Initially it was only several large drops of rain that hit the roof and windshield, sounding like golf balls. Then, within seconds, they were in a full-fledged tropical rainstorm.

Looking at James's friends, she asked herself — Why did he tell them anything? Doesn't he know TerraNova will kill them?

She looked up at James as they bounced over the crater-sized potholes. Jon was driving and conversing with Larry, and they both spoke in Spanish to the man they called Pastor, which Ashley had learned wasn't a name, but a title. As she looked up at him, he looked down briefly, and their eyes caught — he was different. With their windows closed because of the rain, the heat became more and more concentrated inside the cabin, which added to the tension.

The outers spoke entirely in Spanish. They were commenting on how wonderful the meeting had been, and souls that had been saved, which was a subject that Ashley still didn't fully understand, even though it seemed to have been very important to María and Pepe, and they had spoken to her along similar lines on several occasions, but it had seemed too outer for her to take very seriously, except for the fact that the outer God had apparently saved her, something she couldn't completely reconcile, so she tended to ignore it. As they began discussing arrangements for their coming evangelistic meetings, she began to wonder if James had succumbed to their "evangelistic" efforts, and if he had become a *hermano*, or a brother, or whatever it was they called themselves.

Having passed through several blocks of potholes, with this thought in mind, that James might have become a brother, Ashley began a private conversation with him in French, attacking him directly, and demanding, "Are you one of them now, a brother?"

He flatly answered, "NO! Why would you think I'm a brother?"

She pursued, "Really, then why were you in a meeting with them?" However, her question made her feel awkward, and she shifted in her confined space. She knew she had been with the Christians in meetings. So why was she bothering James? But she couldn't stop herself. She continued grilling him.

THAT'S DISGUSTING — James thought. Why would she think I'm a "brother"? Maybe she should call me an outer. But a brother? Why? Twisting his watchband, he answered, "NO! Why would you think I'm a brother?"

James felt a pang of guilt as he denied being a brother, for after all, he had prayed that prayer with Jack, and he had been reading his Bible, and he knew that the outer God had saved him from death, even if he didn't want to believe it, and he liked the outer religion more all the time. The idea of a God who was concerned with the individual hadn't been easy for him to shake. Frankly, he liked it. Yeah, he could see himself as a brother, but that wasn't her business!

Then she asked, "Why else would you be in a meeting with the brothers? You must be one!"

He assured her there wasn't any problem, trying to calm things after the bad start, but she wasn't convinced. They batted it back and forth, and it became intense, to the point of nearly making the other conversation stop, even if they didn't understand French.

At one point he said, "And so what? What if I'm a brother? What's it to you?"

Her response was similar to the acceleration of a DEEP when scrambled — she went hyperdimensional. He defended, trying to turn on active camouflage, and hid behind circumstances. The Jeep continued climbing in and out of craters, and with the heat, the cabin atmosphere indicated that supercooling had failed and that the Unit could explode at any time.

ARRIVING AT Pastor Chavez's church, the good pastor had trouble breaking up James and Ashley long enough for him to say good-bye, an important protocol in the local culture.

Jon, seeing the ferocity between James and his "friend," decided to take the front seat that the pastor had vacated, since it sounded like a boxing match in the back seat. Fortunately, regardless of the tone of the discussion, James and Ashley weren't throwing punches at each other, at least not yet — he considered.

The fact that they were speaking French obliged Larry and Jon to sit in frustration without understanding what the strangers were discussing. Whatever it was, they didn't appear to be close to resolving it.

Jon shared with Larry everything he knew, "James said she was his first officer."

* * *

Novus Ordo

STANDING BEFORE WELLER, Nancy Jones felt just a little proud. Really, she felt very proud, but it wouldn't do to show it.

"Well, Chief," Weller spoke, showing admiration in his voice, "it looks like you've got an answer."

"Yes, sir," she replied. "It wasn't easy, but we should be able to do our scans from space now. We'll have to sacrifice some speed and accuracy, though.

"Yes, Jones. True. But with your modification to the meson collector, we'll be able to scan from one thousand kilometers. If we find the general area, we can go down for a closer look and get the exact coordinates later. I promised you a reward. What would you like?"

"I would like a command, sir."

"A DEEP?" he answered, noticeably irritated.

"Yes, sir," she replied firmly.

"Well, Jones ... that's quite a petition."

"Yes, sir," she answered, "but if it so pleases the Cosmokrator, I feel confident that I would be the best commander in the fleet. I was a direct understudy of the late Captain Smith. I have intimate knowledge of his book, *DEEP Warfare Tactics*. I also have experience. And my abilities have been tested under the most demanding circumstances."

SHE'S RIGHT — Weller realized. She probably would make a good commander, but she's too good of an engineer. She must be crazy. She's not from the right lot. But he knew he would need to be careful about the way he dealt with her. She was too valuable to dishearten. So he continued, "True, Jones. You are all that you say you are, but the Committee must approve such a decision."

"I understand, sir," she answered.

Weller looked at her with admiration, but he hoped to find some way to convince her that Engineering was her true calling. He thought — being the best chief in the fleet isn't a bad position. She's tops. And there's more to her than a good head. She definitely has everything. He closely considered the aspect of her perfect Aryan body, but he knew he shouldn't. He would have to disable her bioprocessor, or she wouldn't be as exciting as a mannequin, and disconnecting her would make her useless. She'd never want to have it connected again.

* * *

New York City

IRVING STONEFELL looked at the report. He wished that Janice Allenburg was recovering at a quicker pace, but at least the doctors were hopeful. She might be ready for a visit in a few weeks, they indicated.

He hadn't told Arlien yet. No need to discourage his old friend, at least not until it was necessary, but Stonefell was more convinced than ever that Janice would be the right person for the job of Inspector of Industrial Operations. Her list of seventy-eight points had proven fundamental in revamping the entire Siberian operation. The doctors were telling him that she probably wouldn't be ready for work for at least eighteen months, and maybe not for two years, and that even then, she might not be as prepared psychologically as she had been before the accident.

But Stonefell rested in his memory of Janice. He knew that she wouldn't be defeated. She was a fighter and would claw her way back to the top. He knew it. She had served Arlien well; she would serve him in the same way.

Chapter 33

The Jonah Factor

IT DOES NOT take much strength to do things, but it requires great strength to decide on what to do.

— Elbert Hubbard

That same day — The road between Santo Domingo and Quito

DESPITE HER initial "attack" on James, as it were, having been abandoned by the almighty Committee of TerraNova, and having suffered a near-death encounter, and then experiencing life with outers, Ashley was prepared for much of what James was telling her. He was telling her that he had opted to be an outer, not necessarily a Christian, but he was even thinking about Christianity, and it wasn't as bad as what he had been taught by TerraNova.

She hadn't told him, but she had been thinking similarly, except that she knew she couldn't keep herself from going back to TerraNova.

Even if she wanted to be an outer, she knew she couldn't stop herself from doing what her conditioning demanded. She would find Nova Mundi in Quito, no matter what. This saddened her, knowing that it would likely mean the extermination of James and his friends. How she wanted to hold him! And she thought — Maybe if he touches me some more, if he holds me a little longer, it will change me. Then I won't have to go back, and we can live happily ever after, like some outer's fairy tale.

She could see that James was free. After her resolute rejection of his invitation to stay with him, she began to reevaluate. Maybe she could give it a try — being an outer and all.

It was strange, though, that even María, who hadn't wanted her to leave Manta, had encouraged her to travel to Quito that very day. Ashley recognized that María was quite "spiritual" (whatever that meant she wasn't sure, but it seemed to apply to María) and it seemed that she must have known something special would happen that particular day. Ashley, however, really didn't want to leave María's, but she had to! Conditioning called her back to TerraNova, and her field trip was over. But now what? If she had left Manta one day earlier, or one day later, she wouldn't have seen James. It made her wonder if the outer God wasn't somehow in control of her meeting him, since María had been adamant about her traveling that day. And then she thought, as happy as she was to be with James — It would've have been better if we had never seen each other.

As she continued to ponder, her thoughts became more contradictory. One minute she would be planning to live with James, as if she was an outer, and the next she would be thinking how she would contact Nova Mundi once she reached Quito. One minute she was imagining the freedom of never feeling another infliction, and the next she was dreading the infliction her delayed return would surely bring.

After their initial argument, and after Pastor had gotten out of the Jeep, she and James had sat in silence. She wondered what James was thinking. And it occurred to her that she should be careful. *If he really wants to be an outer, he won't let me go back. He knows I'll turn him in. He would probably kill me before he would let me go back.*

DURING THE SILENCE, James thought to himself. And he had a chance to look over his first officer — she was really attractive. With its lovely floral decoration, her dress was the picture of simplicity, but he couldn't remember that he'd ever seen her quite so beautiful. Her hair was different — she had arranged it in some way — and he had no idea how to describe it, but he liked it. As he looked at her, it became very important to him to dissuade her from returning to Nova Mundi. Not just because he was afraid they might kill him if she did, and his outer friends too, but because he really wanted her to be free. He liked being near to her. Worse, he all too well understood that if she was determined to go back, it would come down to a kill-or-be-killed situation. Killing wouldn't have been a problem for the old James Smith, but he just didn't feel that he could do it, not now. He was different, even if he wasn't sure what different meant. He simply knew that killing Ashley — even if not doing so would mean his own death — wasn't an option. So he had to get her to stay with him; he had no choice.

The silence had been long, and he couldn't find any words, so he gently took her hand. She didn't seem to mind.

ASHLEY FELT HERSELF enjoying his touch. She heard herself questioning — *Why did they inflict us for touching? What's wrong with it? I like it.*

It had gotten dark quickly, as it does on the equator, and only the road noise and the grind of the motor climbing the snaking mountain road could be heard for the next several minutes.

She wanted to stay with him. It was the only thing that made any sense. It would save lives and save her from infliction — but she knew she would go back anyway. Whether in spite of herself, or despite herself, she didn't know, but she would go back to Alpha Force. At least —

she decided — I'll enjoy being with James now. They'll be mad at me when I get back; they'll kill me by infliction — I know that — and yet, I'll still go back. Why? Because I'm invested? Or is it simply because I have to do what they want, even if I don't like it? But James has decided to be an outer. Why can't I do the same?

For a moment she allowed herself to entertain the idea that she could be an outer. But then she thought of something else, and asked, reserving her tone for the back seat and James only, "Why don't you come back to Novus Ordo with me? We can go back together."

He answered, "I can't go back. They'll kill me. And they'll kill my outer friends too. Besides, I don't want to. I like being free."

"Oh, it's that easy?" she asked, feeling betrayed by James, and showing it with her expression. She saw James reacting to her answer, as he delayed, and as he seemed to squirm in his seat.

He answered with a stutter, "No ... It's not. It's not easy at all. And freedom is hard. But it would be easier if you were with me, Ashley. And I think you would enjoy it. Why go back now? You know they'll inflict you."

Ashley wanted to accept James's offer — she really did. After a pause, trying to find it within herself to say yes, she answered, "Let's talk about something else. This subject is giving me a headache. Let's not think about inflictions now."

A moonbeam lit his face as he offered, "Maybe my friends will have a place where you can stay tonight." And then James asked, "Larry, do you think we could find a place for Ashley to spend the night?"

"I'd be honored to have her as our guest," Jon offered, knowing their guest room was available.

Ashley didn't feel comfortable about accepting, but she knew that even to turn herself back to TerraNova she would have to wait until the next day. In a small country like Ecuador, Nova Mundi's office would only be open during office hours, and it was already too late.

James tried to encourage her to accept Jon's offer and said, "It's the same place where I stayed when I came to Quito; you'll enjoy it."

Ashley vaguely wondered why James didn't invite her to stay with him, and why he was arranging for her to be with the outers, but she didn't pursue the thought, still thinking of him as her commanding officer. As to the outer's invitation itself, she realized that she didn't have any other option, and moved her head approvingly, and replied, "Okay. I'll stay. Thank you." Having resolved the issue of staying, she asked James, "How did you get to Quito?"

"As I told you, it was incredible," he answered, and continued explaining about the crash and then said, "When I woke up, I looked at my watch and realized it was three days later."

It was incredible — she considered. How could he have lived through such a crash? — it wasn't possible, even with bioenhancements. Did the outer God save him like He saved me? — she asked herself, even as she felt the greatest temptation to dismiss it all as nothing more than great luck, or the tale of a man who had obviously hit his head. Besides, she remembered, he had been acting strangely just before leaving the DEEP. "So, how did you get down the mountain?" she asked.

"My ankle was injured during reentry. While I was being tossed around inside the RSB, I felt like everything in my body was broken. The boulder I smashed against was twice as big as my RSB. I should've died. I know what I'm saying sounds crazy, but it's the truth.

"When I woke up, everything in my body hurt. I guess that the melted snow from my hot RSB was enough to trigger its automatic collapse. How my head ended up sticking out of the zipper hole, I couldn't say, but I'd have suffocated, otherwise."

Ashley looked at James in the moonlight that was now breaking through the cloud cover they had been climbing through. With warmth from the car's heater reaching her, she felt a little better, but she still felt cool. It was amazing how they had been in the tropics one minute, and now they were in chilling mountain air. The windows even fogged over. A third of a moon sliver dashed in and out of the clouds, and mountaintops sporadically obstructed the dark night's view.

Ashley started feeling colder. Her thin cotton dress didn't offer much warmth, so she found herself nudging closer to James.

Questions and answers continued, and eventually Ashley began to accept that James's experience had been as unbelievable as hers. There were no good explanations for either his story or hers. Even if he had hit his head and was making it up — she reasoned — then she had to ask herself what had happened in the week between the crash and his arrival in Quito? He obviously didn't land in the Pacific, and the only river big enough to have helped him was a hundred miles to the east. It was easier to believe his story than to believe anything else. If he had hit a river, then he would have had to make his way through the jungle, up over the Andes, and into Quito — alive — in just one week. This, of course, would have been astonishing. So it didn't matter what the truth might be; in any event, it would have taken something as incredible as the intervention of the outers' God to have saved him. And the same could be said in her case too.

After James finished his story, he asked her, "So what happened in the Pacific?"

"My splashdown was perfect. Everything worked like I was in a training simulator, even easier. The RSB floated to the surface and the electroseal opened. In a few minutes it converted into a lifeboat and then the wait began. I waited and waited until the transceiver died on the third day."

"You mean the trucks never came?"

Ashley began to laugh, and James joined her.

"The truck that finally came was an Ecuadorian fishing boat," she explained. "But only after I'd weathered two days of storm and spent two more days treading water. I fought sleep the whole time. They found me facedown, in a dead man's float. They treated me like a queen, and gave me everything I've got, and even made several dresses for me. They bought me other things and gave me money for the trip to Quito."

"Who were they?" Larry asked.

Ashley paused; she was having trouble trying to say the word, "Christians."

Without much warning, after they crested a rise, Quito appeared below them. It was like a sea, stretching out to the horizon with over twenty miles of lights filling the valley towards the north. Once they were above the clouds, Ashley noticed the Big Dipper, but where the North Star should have been, there sat Quito.

Now in the final approach, James began, "Ashley, It seems like a higher power made it so we could meet today. And maybe a higher power kept us from dying. I don't think it was a Skotos. So maybe it's the outer God?" She didn't respond. He looked into her eyes, city lights flashing across her pleasant features. Then he added, "We've got so much to talk about."

"Are you saying good-bye?" she inquired.

"No, just good night. I'll be anxious to talk more tomorrow. It's going to be late by the time you're settled in. The Whittens are great people; they'll take care of you."

"Where will you be?" Ashley asked, nearly adding, "Why can't I go with you?"

"I live close, and you can call me if you need to. Jon and Judy have my number. I'd come over, but I'll just be in the way. Everyone's tired, and will want to get in bed."

They left James off at his apartment, just minutes from the Whittens. Ashley nearly felt that she just couldn't leave him. She didn't want to trust herself to these outers. Not that she feared any harm from them. No. Not at all! Really, she just didn't want to leave James. However, she felt unable to complain, or to even ask to stay with James. And then, just when she thought she would say something to him, as he got out, she silenced herself and began reasoning — I'm going back to TerraNova. It'll be better if he doesn't know. He might try to stop me. But I can escape from the outers easily.

LATER, having gotten under his covers, between the sheets, James said a weak prayer, not really convinced it would do any good. He said in a silent voice, "Outer God, if You're really real, and You really saved me and Ashley, and You've caused us to meet today, then please, Lord, Yahweh, ASMI — or whatever Your name is — keep Ashley from going back to TerraNova. I've heard the outers, when they pray, and they always say, 'in the name of Jesus.' I don't know why, except they say He's supposed to be the only mediator between You and people, and that He said we should pray that way, so Lord, I'm asking You, in the name of Jesus, just like an outer would. And Lord, help me understand what it means to believe in You. Thanks."

James didn't know why, but he felt peace after he prayed. It was especially strange, however, since he felt that trouble was brewing. Then he remembered Jonah, and asked himself — Why Jonah again? After a moment's thought it came to him that Ashley would spend time in the whale's belly, and he remembered the tract and the story about Jonah once more. He couldn't say where the thought came from, but he knew it was true.

Realizing that he had seen a portion about Jonah in the Bible that Jack gave him, he took it from the dresser and sat on the side of his bed as he opened it to the table of contents. He found the page where Jonah was, and flipped through its pages to the spot. He began reading. It took him about twenty minutes to get through the story. He tried to put aside his intellectual concerns about the validity of the story and to ignore the fact that no whale known to live in the sea could do what Jonah's was supposed to have done. He decided that if the outer God was so great, then He could have made a whale just for Jonah, even as the text he was reading seemed to indicate. Putting aside his questions concerning the physical nature of the fish, James began to see that Jonah's time in the belly had caused him to do what God wanted. He asked himself — Is that the reason why the outer God put me in the "whale's belly"? Am I now doing what God wants? Will Ashley do what He wants?

James's conclusion brought him a measure of comfort, since both he and Jonah had made it through their particular "belly" experiences alive. If such an encounter awaited Ashley, then she would also make it through her own Jonah experience — alive. Maybe it should be called "the Jonah factor" — he thought, and he chuckled to himself.

Not long afterwards he rolled over and slept soundly.

About the Author

Kepler Nigh served for 23 years as a missionary in Ecuador where he lived with his wife Blanca and their three children. His travels have taken him throughout Latin America, including extensive visits in the Amazon region and in the Andes, where he often lived with the resident people. He is the author of *Manual de estudios proféticos*, which was published in both Spanish and Portuguese by Editorial Vida (Life Publishers). In it Daniel and Revelation are studied extensively, and the volume was used in his classes at Quito Bible Institute and at Cristo al Mundo (Christ to the World), coming from the fruit of over 15 years of investigation.

Since returning to the USA, Kepler has taught classes in Information Technology at Hagerstown Business College, now known as Kaplan College, and more recently he has worked as an adjunct instructor at Blue Ridge Community and Technical College. He presently works managing all IT and computer networking for Cedar Ridge Ministries, and lives with his family in Hagerstown, Maryland.

The epic continues:

Before the Apocalypse

Book Two

Haven Quest

Information about publication dates and more may be found at:

www.beforetheapocalypse.com

Printed in the United States
201172BV00002B/1-57/P